imago

BOOK ONE

tales from the west

L.T. Suzuki

Book Cover, graphic design and layout:
Scott White
Shinobi Creative Services
email: shinobicreativeservices@shaw.ca

Printed in Victoria, Canada

National Library of Canada Cataloguing in Publication

Suzuki, L. T. (Lorna T.), 1960-
 Imago / L.T. Suzuki.
Contents: bk. 1. Tales from the west.
ISBN 1-55369-656-5 (bk. 1)
 I. Title. II. Title: Tales from the west.
PS8587 U98 I43 2002   C813'.6   C2002-902763-2
PR9199.4.S92I43 2002

TRAFFORD

This book was published *on-demand* in cooperation with Trafford Publishing.
On-demand publishing is a unique process and service of making a book available for retail sale to the public taking advantage of on-demand manufacturing and Internet marketing.
On-demand publishing includes promotions, retail sales, manufacturing, order fulfilment, accounting and collecting royalties on behalf of the author.

Suite 6E, 2333 Government St., Victoria, B.C. V8T 4P4, CANADA
Phone   250-383-6864   Toll-free   1-888-232-4444 (Canada & US)
Fax   250-383-6804   E-mail   sales@trafford.com
Web site   www.trafford.com   TRAFFORD PUBLISHING IS A DIVISION OF TRAFFORD HOLDINGS LTD.
Trafford Catalogue #02-0469   www.trafford.com/robots/02-0469.html

10   9   8   7   6   5   4

Imagine...

There is a secret place that exists; unknown to most, forgotten by many, and lives on only for the few who believe.

Though you cannot look to a map to find this magical realm, it is still very real. In this world, lost on a plane that hangs in the twilight where one enters a dream as sleep takes over the mind and body, Imago lives on.

Here, as in all places where man dwells, the eternal struggle between good and evil plays out. In this land, there are places fair and foul, heroes that are larger than life and villains that one hopes exist only in our nightmares.

In this mystical world, life is an extraordinary adventure where revenge and redemption, betrayal and salvation, and love; lost and found, are woven together to create this rich tapestry of life.

Where is this kingdom you ask? To find Imago all you must do is close your eyes, and believe...

*This book is dedicated to my muse
and inspiration, Nia Kioko and to Scott,
for his unwavering support and assistance.
Without his advice and attention to detail,
this book would not have been possible...
With much love and gratitude.*

*To Phillip Legare, Shihan
for sharing in the wisdom and
teachings in the Japanese warrior art
of Bujinkan Budo Taijutsu.
Students are only as inspired
as their teachers...
Thank you for the inspiration.*

Contents

Prologue

In another world, in another time, there is an ancient realm where mortal man shares the world with Wizards, Sorcerers, Elves, and yes, even dragons.

In this enchanted place, the people of this fair land existed in relative peace for one thousand years, but of late, a growing darkness had spread across the country. Like the curling edges of a dying leaf, the cold fingers of death itself gripped its talons around the hearts of all those living in Imago.

An uneasy fear crept into the souls of all. Whisperings of an unseen evil, long laid to rest, had re-awakened.

Prophets of old warned of this second coming when the Dark Lord, Beyilzon would rise again to reclaim what he had lost. It was said that Beyilzon was once the chosen one of the Maker of All. He was favored above all others.

When man was created, Beyilzon was consumed by jealousy and hate for he felt that his attention and his love were cast aside to make way for the mortals.

In the end, Beyilzon fell from grace and lived an earthly existence with those he despised the most. He dealt with his rage and grief by inflicting the ones the Maker of All held so dear, to a life of great torment.

In the years that ensued, many lives were lost in battles and skirmishes against Beyilzon and his followers, men who had succumbed to greed, lust and power, all fueled by his promise of greatness and eternal life.

At the very pinnacle of this war, when all seemed lost, one light shone that redeemed this mystical realm. Through the actions of a single man, Beyilzon was driven deep into the underworld, never to be seen again.

Now, as the spring solstice of the one-thousandth year approached, the Watchers cast their eyes to the stars dotting the evening sky.

Placed onto this world to observe the doings of man and his kin, the Watchers do not sit in judgment, nor do they have the power to alter the course of destiny. Believed by some that the Elves were descended from the likes of the Watchers, they actually evolved long before the Elves, and man, came to being.

Elora, recording life as it was. Enra, watching as life unfolds, while Eliya, Watcher of the Future foresaw the shadows of what is yet to be. Also referred to as the Three Sisters by both the Elves and mankind, the Watchers transcend age; through the eons they have remained untouched by the hands of time.

From their lofty temple on Mount Isa, nestled between the highest peaks of the Cathedral Mountains, the Three Sisters quietly studied the stars that shone brightly, like tiny jewels set against a black velvet canvas.

Instructed by the Maker of All to reveal to the prophets of old, the return of Beyilzon, the Watchers could see the alignment of the constellations that were to herald this time of great change.

Eliya passed her hand slowly over her crystal orb. "On the first night of the full moon when Earth aligns with Mars and Venus, man shall face his darkest hour and his greatest challenge. When the moon glows red and the sun grows cold, it shall mark the beginning of great calamities for mankind, his kin, and all that is good in the world. Life hangs in the balance: The time draws near."

Elora and Enra took their place next to their sister. They gazed into the orb to observe what fate Eliya predicted for the citizens of Imago.

They watched in silence as evil visions of a land enveloped in growing darkness unfolded before them: Villages left in ashes and ruin; the innocent being hunted and slaughtered like animals; soldiers of the Alliance charging into battle against those of Beyilzon's Dark Army.

In the midst of all this carnage, a company of friends struggled against their own fears and sorrow as they fought to keep hope alive. As Eliya observed, she shared these words with her sisters:

One pure of heart,
One weak of will,
So your lives shall be entwined.
One strong in faith,
One brave to fault,
Your strengths shall be combined.
Look not to the face,
For truth not be told,
Look to the heart, those loyal and bold.
The innocent shall not kill,

Though many shall die.
Life hangs in balance, voices will cry.
The time draws near,
Day turns to night,
Steady your soul & be ready to fight.
In the midst of carnage,
Of lives lost and found,
Deliver this light and you shall gain new ground.

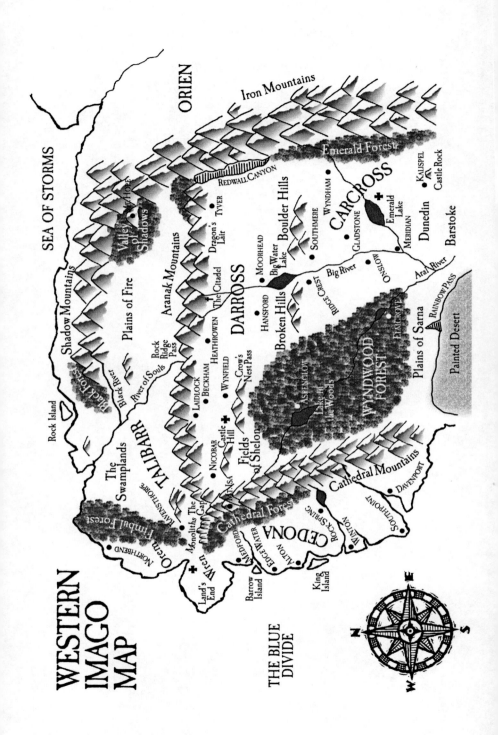

CHAPTER 1

THE CALL TO ARMS

As the warm morning sun shone brightly against the towering, snow-capped spires of the Cathedral Mountain Range, a small figure could be seen silhouetted against the cold, gray granite of the castle's high wall. Leaning far out over the battlement, an outstretched hand was struggling, straining as if to touch the white peaks of the distant mountains.

"Young man! Do you wish to meet your Maker before your time?" A stern voice called out as a powerful hand reached over, pulling the boy back onto the walkway.

"No, my lord. I mean to save a life," the boy answered. "See… A bird lies injured on the ledge."

The man moved closer to the boy's side. He peered out over the edge, and there indeed rested a falcon. The young bird's beak was agape; it was panting heavily. Its right wing hung limply by its side.

"You risk your life for that of a bird?" he asked, reprimanding the boy. "It is a foolhardy risk you take!"

"With all due respect, my lord, it is not my place to judge whether my life is of more value than that of the bird's," responded the boy, in a small voice. "I do know it is in need of help and I do not have the heart to deny it aid, when it is the one thing I know I can offer."

"So be it! Your heart is much too large for your body, my young friend. Fetch a servant to aid you. Call upon Lindras to heal the falcon. Then report to the king's great hall when you are done." The man promptly turned away, disappearing down a gloomy corridor.

In the still of his small, dim-lit room, the young servant watched with great interest and concern as a tall, lean figure draped in a great, dusky blue-gray robe toiled. His long fingers and hands were lined with many wrinkles - worn and deeply tanned against his cascading whiskers. Near the end of his flowing, silver beard, a band of gold held his whiskers neatly together. His ears, pointed like that of an Elf, were aged and tattered like a piece of parchment paper from an ancient book.

With its eyes shielded by a strip of cloth, the falcon remained calm in its enforced darkness as the Wizard set its wing in place. "Ewen, fetch water and some fowl from the cook. I am sure this falcon shall be in need of both when her ordeal is done," said Lindras, motioning the young servant away with a wave of his hand as he secured the makeshift bandage with the other.

The boy, nodding his head in understanding, slipped out the door.

Outside the king's great hall, a dark figure, in deep contemplation, quietly paced the shadows of a wide corridor. His fingers ran through his dark brown hair, sweeping it away from his brows to reveal gentle, brown eyes. In its depth, one could see they disclosed a soul burdened with a kind of sadness that only he knew and understood. Although his eyes seemed to belong to a man of advanced years - one who had experienced much in his lifetime, his clean-shaven face gave him the appearance that he was much younger than his true age.

A flowing, black cloak shrouded this man from his shoulders to the ankles of his dark, leather boots. He was dressed in shades of deep blue, dark gray and white. His long cloak was held in place by a brooch adorned with a dark blue stone that was engraved with tiny stars and embossed with a white cross. The true colors of his clothes were only revealed when he crossed through the shafts of sunlight streaming through the windows. He wore the colors of the House of Whycliffe, the royal family that had reigned over Carcross since these lands were first settled by his people.

The prince awaited the arrival of his father, King Bromwell. Word was received of late that a party of kings and knights from the surrounding countries to the north and west were converging in Carcross with an urgent request to meet with the king.

He quickly pushed open the heavy, wooden door at the entrance of the great hall upon hearing the approach of rushed footsteps. A young servant held the door open as King Bromwell stepped through, followed by a knight.

As the king took his place at the head of the vast table, Prince Markus bowed, and then greeted his father with kiss on each cheek. He then proceeded to his chair that was situated to the King's right side. Across from him to the king's left, Sir Darius Calsair, the protector of the House of Whycliffe, loyal knight and servant to King Bromwell took his place at the table.

Leaning over to his left, Prince Markus whispered to the servant now standing behind, and to the right, of the king's large, stately chair. "Ewen, how is the bird?"

The boy's eyes remained fixed straight ahead. Standing at attention, he whispered his reply, "I believe she will be fine, my lord. Thank you for asking."

The prince smiled inwardly, it pleased him to know that the boy's efforts to save the bird would not be in vain. He then turned his attention back to his father.

"So, what news have you heard from afar, my king? Surely it cannot be good. The Alliance has not gathered in such a manner since the last Great War."

The king drew a weary, deep breath. His eyes slowly closed. "Markus, I did not believe that I would live to see this day come to pass. The prophets of old warned of this event, now the stars are set in motion heralding the beginning of a calamity like none other."

As King Bromwell spoke, the sound of approaching footsteps echoed heavily in the corridor as a party moved swiftly towards the great hall. As they entered the room, all rose up from their chairs.

A page announced their arrival as the men entered the room, taking their place at the table: "King Sebastian, of the House of Northcott, Lord of Darross; King Augustyn, of the House of Calaware, Lord of Cedona; King Kal-lel, of the House of Wingfield, Lord of Wyndwood."

Next to each king sat the captain of their great armies: Faria Targott, protector of the House of Northcott; Lando Bayliss, protector of the House of Calaware; and Arerys Wingfield, son of King Kal-lel.

"Lord Bromwell, we bear bad tidings. The day we all dread is close at hand. Beyilzon's armies gather in the Shadow Mountains, they are advancing south from Talibarr." King Kal-lel warned.

"Are these not just rumors?" Prince Markus inquired.

"I am afraid they are not," answered King Sebastian, "Beckham, Wynfield and Laidlock are already under siege. My people have scattered, seeking refuge in the Aranak Mountains or they flee to the south."

Speaking on behalf of his king, Faria Targott added, "Up until now, the attacks have been sporadic. At first, they seemed random, but it would appear that the armies are seeking someone as they move westward."

"Or perhaps, something," suggested Bromwell.

"We speak the truth," insisted Kal-lel. "It is as the prophets foretold; Beyilzon is already at work, though he has yet to make his presence known."

"Why does this concern you, Lord Kal-lel?" Bromwell asked, staring into the Elf's cold, blue eyes, as if searching for an answer. "I thought it no longer mattered to you, or your kind, what happens to the race of man."

Arerys leapt up from his chair to defend his father. "King Bromwell, my father means no ill-will and though we do not wish to be involved in the affairs of man, the coming tides of change shall wash over us all, if we are not careful!" warned the younger Elf.

Kal-lel placed a hand on Arerys's shoulder, upon which his son grew silent, reclaiming his place at the great table.

"Lord Bromwell, I have stood by your people for what you would deem an eternity. I have fought side by side with your ancestors to rid Imago of the Dark Lord," declared Kal-lel, with great indignation. "I wish not to embroil myself, nor my people, in the follies of man for it is in the blackness of man's heart that Beyilzon lives on. Unfortunately, this problem is one that we must all bear together or be destroyed, one by one."

"I beg your forgiveness, Lord Kal-lel. You are quite right. You have been there from the beginning. None of us should question your motives or integrity. If we wish to defeat Beyilzon again, then we must stand united once more, mankind and Elves. This Alliance must remain true!" proclaimed Bromwell as he placed a closed fist over his heart.

Upon his words, all rose to their feet. With their right fist over their heart, both men and Elves declared, "For the Alliance!"

"Lord Kal-lel, you are the only one amongst us who faced the wrath of Beyilzon almost one thousand years ago. How do we defeat one that is not of flesh and blood?" Augustyn asked.

"Yes, how do we fight against such evil?" asked Sebastian, pondering this dilemma. "I do not believe we possess the power or the weapons to defeat such an unearthly adversary!"

Soon, all those in attendance at King Bromwell's table were talking at once. Kings, princes, and captains, one speaking louder than the other to be heard. As voices rose and fists slammed against the table to punctuate their angry words, a sudden burst of air swirled through the great room, enveloping all inside with a great chill.

"Be silent! How can any of you be understood when you cannot even be heard!" boomed a resonating voice emanating from the darkened corridor.

A tall, shadowy figure loomed at the doorway. Lindras bowed as he entered, lowering the great hood covering his head with one hand, the other hand leading the way with his worn wooden staff. His long silvery beard and balding head crowned by a thinning circle of flowing, silver hair made his blue-gray eyes blaze against his lined and weathered face.

"Lord Kal-lel, you know there is only one answer: The Stone of Salvation. It is the key that locked Beyilzon into his own darkness," said the Wizard. "It shall be his undoing again."

"The Stone of Salvation? That is merely a myth, and if it were real, we do not know where it is now!" snapped Augustyn.

Sebastian leapt from his seat and with great indignation, began to denounce the old Wizard: "This is an outrage! Are you all fools? Do you entrust your lives and the lives of your people to the words of a Sorcerer?"

In the storm of all this controversy, Ewen had remained silent and steadfast throughout. He finally retorted, "You are wrong sire. Master Lindras is not a Sorcerer! He is a Wiz—" His sentence was cut short as Lindras raised his hand for silence.

"The boy is quite right you know. I do not deal in mischief and black magic as Sorcerers do. As an advisor and trusted friend to King Bromwell, I regret to say that the only hope lies with this Stone. It must be returned to Mount Hope and it must be done so quickly!" said Lindras, holding forth his staff for all to see.

The crystal orb that was embedded into the top of Lindras's staff glowed softly. Inside, a curtain of mist melted away, allowing a shadowy image to be made clear: The Three Sisters could be seen in their temple. One was looking skyward; one was looking out to the east while Eliya, the Watcher of the Future, was gazing into the crystal orb set before her.

"The Watchers? What do the Three Sisters have to do with the Stone?" asked Augustyn, his tone of voice rising in anger.

"They are the guardians of the Stone of Salvation," answered Lindras.

"Do you know this for a fact?" countered Sebastian.

"He does," replied Kal-lel, staring back at the king, his blue eyes devoid of emotion, "for it was Lindras who bore witness when King Brannon and I delivered the Stone of Salvation to the Watchers after Beyilzon was defeated one thousand years ago."

Like the wind escaping from the billowing sails of a tall ship, Sebastian slumped back into his chair. A moment of silence passed as all reflected on this news.

"I believe King Kal-lel's words to be true. And Lindras, though he be a conjurer of magic, he does not conjure up lies," Prince Markus stated. "The coming of this calamity was foretold by the prophets. It is recorded in our family annals, but we chose to turn a blind eye because we did not wish for these events to come true. Well, the time is now at hand; we cannot stop it from happening."

"Time will not stand still, however we may still be able to alter the course of our destiny," added Lindras.

Bromwell stood up from his chair. Both his hands rested heavily on the table like a weary knight having just returned from battle. "The Wizard is right. We cannot turn back the hands of time; our only salvation is in the Stone. There is only one who can bear this burden, the direct heir of King Brannon of Carcross: That would be I."

Markus slowly rose to his feet. "Father, you cannot do this! It is a perilous quest that shall be fraught with many dangers. Carcross, the people of Imago, they will need your leadership and guidance during the dark days that lie ahead. Tend to your armies; protect the people and this fair land. I request this mission. In your name and honor, I shall see it done, even if I shall die trying."

Bromwell's brows furrowed into a frown as he stood before Markus. Placing his hands on his son's shoulders, he whispered, "Brave Markus, you know not what you ask for."

In desperation, Markus dropped down on his left knee before his father. Taking Bromwell's right hand into both of his, Markus pleaded, "Father, I beg of you; let me go in your place. I am younger and faster. I have learned from your wisdom. Grant me this quest and I shall not let you down. The people need their King and I swear, I will do right by you."

With these words, Bromwell stood upright as though a great weight had been lifted from his shoulders. Clasping his son's hand, he raised Markus onto his feet. "You are my one and only son, Markus. It is with great trepidation that I grant you this request." He searched his son's face for a sign that he would change his mind, but when their eyes met, Bromwell knew. Markus could not be swayed.

"So be it!" announced Bromwell. "I shall assemble our armies in preparation for battle. For you Markus, this mission cannot be undertaken alone, you will need your own army to reclaim the Stone and return it to Mount Hope."

"Forgive me, my king, but it is ill advised to enter Talibarr with an army of any size," warned Lindras. "I am certain that Beyilzon has spies stationed everywhere. Such a presence shall only serve to forewarn him."

"Lindras is right. There may be strength in numbers, but this shall only alert Beyilzon to ready his forces to thwart our attempts to return the Stone to Mount Hope," agreed Kal-lel. "It is crucial this quest be done in secret."

Bromwell turned to his guests seated at the great table. "Who amongst you is brave of heart and great in might? Who will answer this call to arms? Who shall join Prince Markus of Carcross on this quest?"

Without hesitation, Darius Calsair immediately arose from his chair. "I will be honored to aid you in this mission, Prince Markus. I shall follow you to the end. You shall have my shield and my sword!"

"I too, shall see this evil put to an end!" said Arerys Wingfield, standing proudly to his feet.

Lando Bayliss rose from his chair. "I shall serve on behalf of King Augustyn and the people of Cedona."

"And I, for my king and the people of Darross!" said Faria Targott.

"Ah, this is all well and good, and I applaud your unity," nodded Lindras in approval, "but there is one thing that you forget. The Stone of Salvation can only be handled by one pure of heart, whose hands have not been washed in the blood of others. He must be one who is willing to give his life for another, when all others may deem that life unworthy. Is there any one of you in this great hall that can make such a claim?"

"Lindras is right," sighed Kal-lel, with great disappointment. "Though our intentions may be honorable, I know that each of us have bloodied our hands in battle. I, for one, have claimed more lives than all of you combined."

Bromwell slumped back into his chair. "What to do, Lindras?" lamented the king. "What to do? Is there not one who has the strength, or heart, to take on this quest? Is there not one who has not soiled his hands with the blood of others?"

The great room was filled with profound silence as each reflected on their own past and the blood they had spilled in the name of king and country. But in this silence, Lindras, his eyes closed and his mind deep in thought, reached out to Markus' heart. *There is one.*

Prince Markus looked up at Lindras, hearing his unspoken words. "There is one…" he repeated, but barely in a whisper.

Lindras, his eyes now open, met the prince's stare. Lindras bowed his head in acknowledgement. Markus studied the faces of all who shared the table, searching the eyes and hearts of those in his presence.

From beside him, a small voice declared: "I shall go with you, my lord. I shall carry the Stone for you."

Markus turned to see his servant and squire, Ewen Vatel, earnestly staring at him. "I am your humble servant and I am indebted to you," continued the boy. "When no one else was there to care for me after my father died, it was you who had shown me kindness and mercy. Please, allow me to repay my debt."

The silence was broken by a sudden burst of laughter as the men looked on at the young servant. Kal-lel, Arerys and Lindras continued to listen in silence.

Markus was momentarily stunned by young Ewen's offer. He looked him in his face and kindly smiled, "You are your father's son, Ewen. He was a loyal knight and a trusted friend, dedicating his life to my father's service. You owe me nothing. You are an innocent, do not let your heart be caught up in the affairs of hardened men."

The laughter was cut short; abruptly stifled by the resonating *'crack'* of Lindras's staff striking the floor in anger. "Prince Markus, do you not see? He is the one! His hands are not soiled. His heart is pure and it is his innocence that shall be his armor to shield him against the evils that has touched us all."

Markus looked aghast at Lindras. "I cannot ask him to do this, Wizard!"

"You did not ask. It is he, who willingly makes this sacrifice."

Markus was appalled. Staring into the boy's innocent, brown eyes, he said, "Ewen, you are not bound to this duty. This is not a wise choice, change your mind while you still can."

Lindras responded, "My lord, for some the choice is easy and the path is clear; for others the choice is already made for them."

Dropping to his knees before Prince Markus, Ewen pleaded, "My lord, I will go with you. I fear no evil as long as you are by my side and we have Lindras' staff to guide us!"

"I believe his mind is made up, Prince Markus" said the venerable old Wizard.

"I dare say," sighed Kal-lel, "I do not believe we have a choice in this matter."

With the new Order in place and the Alliance restored and affirmed, King Bromwell requested his staff to prepare the horses and supplies for the journey ahead. Beds were made ready for the guests, as darkness had fallen upon the land with unsettling swiftness.

In the soft glow of a lantern, Ewen watched in amazement as Lindras hand-fed the falcon that now sat perched in the corner of his room. The bird eagerly took the food that was offered, swallowing the meat whole or holding it in her talons as her sharp, hooked beak tore more manageable strips of flesh for her to swallow.

"What spell did you cast upon this bird to make her so tame, Lindras?" asked Ewen, as he moved slowly towards the Wizard and falcon.

The old Wizard smiled at the boy's question. "Ah, it is no magic, my boy. This bird already has a master." He pointed to the narrow strips of leather that were fastened onto the falcon's feet. "See. And look at this, there are initials: NT."

"Will she mend?" asked Ewen with great concern as he studied the letters branded onto the leather strip.

"She shall be fitter than you or I in no time! Her wing received only minor damage, but she was extremely hungry and thirsty as though she had been on a long journey with no time to rest, let alone eat or drink," answered the Wizard. "The staff shall care for her in our absence. She will be released once she is well enough to take flight."

"This is a beautiful bird befitting of royalty," stated Ewen. "Did the nobility arriving today speak of a lost bird?"

"No, she may be the bird of a hunter from a field afar," replied the Wizard as he stroked the falcon's dark feathers. "But enough about the bird, young sir! Tomorrow, we leave the safety of Carcross for perils unknown. Are you not afraid?"

Ewen packed what little possessions he held dear into his bag. "I know no harm shall come to me with both you and Prince Markus by my side. I do not have any reason to fear."

The Wizard, peering from beneath his great hood to search into Ewen's naive, brown eyes, nodded. "You are braver than most, my lad, for even I fear this journey."

As the cool bite of the last winter night lost its teeth to the warmth of the coming spring sun, the men of the Alliance had converged in the great hall once again. All were well into their breakfast when Ewen, having drifted in and out of a troubled sleep throughout the night, woke with a start.

Ewen readied himself with haste, then raced down to the king's hall. With the greatest care, he attempted to discreetly take his place as servant behind King Bromwell's chair.

"What is the meaning of this? Why do you stand here?" bellowed Bromwell.

"I am sorry, your highness. I beg your forgiveness," apologized Ewen in a small voice. "I slept not well last night and now, I am late to serve you."

Bromwell laughed. "My lad that is not what I mean. You are now part of the Order. You must take your place at this table immediately!"

"Surely you jest, my king. I am merely your humble servant," Ewen meekly replied, still standing at his usual place – his head bowed.

"No, Master Vatel, from this day forward, you are the servant of mankind. Take your place next to Sir Darius, do not argue with me," said Bromwell, motioning Ewen to the empty chair at the table.

The room fell silent. All eyes watched as Ewen Vatel, the king's servant and Prince Markus' squire, timidly crept to the empty chair next to Darius. The knight pushed the heavy chair back to allow the boy to be seated.

As Ewen took his place, a sense of importance befell him; he never dreamed in his entire life that he, a commoner, would be sitting amongst such noble kings and brave knights. His eyes were wide open in awe, staring across the vast table at the faces of the great men and Elves gazing back at him. His feet barely reached the floor as he sat back in his chair.

"It is better to eat now and stare later, Ewen. There is much to be done before we leave," said Prince Markus as he motioned for a servant to fetch Ewen some breakfast. "This may be the last decent meal you shall receive in a very long time. Enjoy it now."

Ewen took great care not to wolf his food down. He made careful note of those whom he shared the table with, and their good manners.

Bromwell pushed aside his untouched food. "We must devise a route that shall ensure the Order arrives at the temple on Mount Isa with the greatest expedience."

"The most direct route is obviously the fastest and shortest however, these roads shall be carefully watched by Beyilzon's spies," reminded Kal-lel.

"What would you suggest?" Sebastian asked.

After careful consideration, Kal-lel answered his question. "Arerys and I shall guide the Order into the safety of Wyndwood, it shall be a three-day journey if we leave this morning. From Aspenglow, I shall set them on a course that will take them to Mount Isa in the Cathedral Mountains. From the Temple of the Watchers, Lindras shall continue on eastward to Mount Hope. As we discussed last night, they shall move in secret. The fewer who know of their route, the safer it be for all."

"I agree," nodded Prince Markus. "King Kal-lel and Prince Arerys know the unmarked trails and paths throughout Imago better than anyone else. Lindras knows the way too, as he is one of the few who has ever made the journey to Mount Hope."

The members of the Alliance all nodded in agreement. The first leg of the journey was about to begin.

As the Order made ready for their departure from King Bromwell's castle in the heart of Carcross, the bright, golden sun moved steadily above the jagged, snow-capped peaks of the Iron Mountains as it traveled to the west.

Markus bid farewell to the staff of Whycliffe Castle as Bromwell wished King Kal-lel, Prince Arerys, and the knights, now in his son's service, a safe journey and a speedy return.

"Stay safe my son. Keep the boy close to your side and keep both eyes on him throughout this quest. These are dangerous times; you must take extra care," warned Bromwell as he embraced his son. "Do not waver from the task at hand."

Bromwell then turned to Lindras. "My old friend, I pray you have the strength to make this journey again. Guide them with good wisdom and judgment."

Lindras bowed low to the King, before mounting his magnificent gray stallion.

Lowering himself down onto his left knee, Bromwell rested a hand on Ewen's shoulder. Looking into his eyes, the King said, "Young Vatel, your father was once a mighty knight and dear friend. I know in your young heart you bear the same will and strength that he once bore. Though many dangers might lie in wait, fear not; be brave for you shall travel with some of Imago's finest warriors. Rest assured, they shall keep you safe."

Ewen lowered his head. "Sire, I feel that I am no longer a boy, but not yet a man. I am a commoner to boot, not even suitable to bear my father's title in your service," sighed Ewen with great humility. "I do not know how I shall fend off such evil, but I shall do my best."

The king raised Ewen's chin so their eyes could meet. Bromwell smiled upon his face and responded: "That is what King Brannon said before he set out to reclaim Imago from the Dark Lord."

CHAPTER 2

THE ELVES OF WYNDWOOD

The seven riders headed due west, traveling swiftly through the gentle, rolling farmlands and lush, green pastures of Dunedin County. As the Order entered Barstoke, they continued on westward through the barley fields that still lay fallow throughout the land.

They took great care to avoid the heavily traveled routes and the network of trails feeding into these roads. Kal-lel and Arerys showed the way followed by the prince, Lindras, Ewen, and Darius, while Faria and Lando took up the rear.

Avoiding all bridges, they followed the Aral River to a point where it was shallow enough for all to cross safely. Although the water was not deep, it ran cold and swift. The steeds ridden by Lindras, Arerys, and Kal-lel quickly and confidently trotted through the fast running water. The other horses stomped and nervously paced along the river's edge before following the Elves' horses through the churning, white water to the other side.

"Let the horses drink and rest for a moment," said Kal-lel as he dismounted from his gray, dappled stallion.

Arerys whispered words to his steed in his people's tongue; he instructed RainDance to stay near as he headed up the riverbank.

The Elf moved swiftly. Light on his feet, he leapt up the embankment from rock to stump to fallen tree. As he reached the trees growing in a thick stand along the top of the bank, Arerys, dressed in his people's typical sylvan colors of earth tones and deep moss green, disappeared against the backdrop of the forest.

Except for the breeze catching his long, wheat-colored hair, Arerys remained motionless as he stared with his far-seeing eyes. Shielding them with his hand against the sun flickering through the canopy of the trees, they penetrated deep into the deciduous forest searching for any sign of hidden danger. Arerys now strained to hear: What his eyes failed to see, his ears would surely hear.

There was nothing unusual that his senses could detect. The only sounds he did hear were nothing more than the movements made by the creatures of the forest: wrens and thrushes calling and flying from tree to tree and the rhythmic cud-chewing of a doe hidden with her fawn in a distant thicket.

A red squirrel scurried up the trunk of an oak tree, but it did not sound its usual alarm call; chattering in protest of any stranger that may wander into his territory. Instead, the squirrel stared intently at the Elf as it sat amongst the newly unfurling leaf buds of a tree, still laid bare by winter's cold touch. Arerys turned, heading back down to the river to join the others.

"We should move now while all is quiet," said Arerys, leaping onto RainDance's bare back. With the reins held slack in his slender hands, Arerys leaned towards his horse's twitching ears, urging her up the bank. The others followed behind him.

"Why do we go so far out of our way to reach Wyndwood, my lord?" asked Ewen as his horse trotted up next to Markus' steed.

"Beyilzon has many eyes; all roads well traveled shall be watched. This is a longer route, but it shall assure us of a safe passage," replied Markus, his dark brown hair blowing across his face as his steed picked up its pace.

Ewen turned to Markus again. "My father once told me of Wyndwood. I have never actually met an Elf until yesterday, you know? Is it true that they are all fair and tall like King Kal-lel?" asked Ewen. "My father told me that Elves are magic and they can talk to animals. I have also heard that they live in trees and eat only greens. Do you know if it is true that —"

The prince raised his hand to dissuade the boy from continuing with his barrage. "You ask too many questions, Ewen!" stated Markus with a smile.

Suddenly, RainDance dropped from her lead position as Arerys turned his horse about. He reined his mount in, sidling up next to Ewen's mare.

"Young sir, if being one with the land makes us magic, then I suppose we are. Yes, we are all fair of complexion and hair, and no, we do not eat meat. And that may account for why we live so long, and man does not," said Arerys, rather succinctly as he leaned over to the prince's squire.

"You shall learn more about the Elves of Wyndwood in due time." Arerys clucked his tongue against the roof of his mouth and his horse responded by galloping off to join the others in the lead.

"Oh my! Elves have good ears!" Ewen whispered in surprise.

"Yes, and we have good eyesight too!" Arerys shouted back from his place next to Kal-lel at the front of the procession.

Markus and the others laughed at Ewen's stunned expression.

"Let us move on men! We still have far to go!" said Lindras, coaxing their horses on to keep up with the Elves.

As they left Carcross behind them, the lands west of the Aral River became drier: the vegetation sparse and course. Except for the towering succulents that thrive in this arid climate, there were no trees to speak of.

"We shall spend the night here," said Kal-lel as he dismounted from his steed.

Under the shadow of the tall thorn bushes, a small fire crackled and blazed. The night air embraced them in its chilly breath under a cloudless, early spring sky.

Ewen gathered whatever dried plant material he could find; mostly the skeletal remains of the thorn bushes' twigs and branches.

He returned to the others with an armful of fuel for the fire. He sat quietly next to Markus as the Prince and the others discussed the next day's journey, the timing of their travel to reach Mount Isa and the perils that may lie ahead as their trek brings them closer to the Plains of Fire and Mount Hope.

Ewen stifled a great yawn as the conversation carried on late into the night. Fighting a losing battle, his eyelids slowly drooped and finally closed as he slumped against Markus' shoulder as sleep took over his mind and body.

The boy slept soundly and in the morning when he woke, he could not recall how he managed to find himself lying near a cold fire pit with his blanket wrapped securely around him.

The others were already awake before the first signs of the approaching morning. After all had eaten a quick meal, Kal-lel ordered them to mount their horses and make haste before the sun hampered their progress across the dry, arid lands awaiting them to the west.

As the noon hour approached, the riders found themselves staring out at the sands of the Painted Desert. The dry, stifling air shimmered and danced over the bland landscape as the sun continued to climb and the heat increased in intensity.

"We shall follow the edge of the desert until we reach Rainbow Pass, then we shall journey into the canyon lands," said Kal-lel, coaxing his stallion on.

"When shall we rest and eat?" asked Ewen.

"Only after we have reached the Pass," answered Arerys. "We shall rest then."

It was late in the afternoon when they finally navigated around the edge of the Painted Desert. Before them lay Rainbow Pass.

"Everyone dismount," ordered Kal-lel. "You must lead your horse down through this pass to the floor of the canyon. It is unsafe to attempt to ride down these narrow trails."

Kal-lel took his horse by the reins and proceeded to lead his stallion down the path that narrowed and tapered dangerously in many places. Arerys followed, as did Lindras. The men dismounted too, following in close procession: Markus, Ewen, Darius, Lando and Faria.

As they cautiously made their way down, many parts of the path seem to crumble underfoot. The horses would hesitate, tossing their heads in anxiety, but their fears were quelled as Arerys and Kal-lel spoke in Elvish, using a gentle tone to calm their frayed nerves. As their steeds settled and resumed their journey, the other horses too, seemed to calm down and follow without hesitation.

The warm sun was almost directly over the southern range of the Cathedral Mountains when Ewen looked up to admire the changing sky. It was transforming into a rich hue of lavender as the sun edged closer to the mountains. Its golden rays illuminated the high clouds that seemed to be snagged on the peaks, casting them in a fiery glow.

Ewen's eyes squinted into the bright, yellow orb as it touched the top of the mountain, spreading its ray of light like a thin sheet of gold against a deepening blue sky. As he turned his gaze back to the Painted Desert to follow the last traces of the sun's dying light, his eyes beheld a wondrous sight. To his amazement and delight, the desert was shifting from the pale beige color that seemed to cause the landscape to blur and blend under the heat of the midday sun, into quivering, iridescent shades of gold, mauve and even pale blue as the changing angle of the sun's light reflected off the grains of sands.

"Look, Sir Darius! Look at the desert! It is alive with color!" said Ewen excitedly, pointing across to the vibrant backdrop.

Darius looked over his shoulder to admire the warm glow of the breathtaking landscape. "Indeed, after all it is not called the Painted Desert for no reason," smiled the knight, gazing upon the shimmering colors dancing across the arid, barren desert.

Ewen turned forward to resume his downward journey. The gap that lay between he and the prince was now made wider by his brief interlude when he had stopped to admire the view. Picking up his pace to close this gap, Ewen pulled on his horse's reins.

In an instant, the edge of the path gave way. Standing too close, Ewen's weight caused the shifting sands and loose rocks to break away.

Darius gasped in disbelief as the sound of falling rocks caught his attention first, followed by Ewen's abrupt disappearance from his line of sight.

"Help me! Help! Please!" shouted Ewen as he dangled dangerously into the gaping mouth of the canyon, both hands still firmly gripping the horse's reins. His mare was backed against the wall of the sheer cliff with her head bowed low, straining against the weight of Ewen's body.

Lindras, and the others who led the way, stopped immediately. "We cannot turn around, nor pass our horses to help!" the Wizard cried out.

Markus attempted to squeeze between his stallion and the wall of the cliff. There was no room to maneuver. "Do not move Ewen. Try to get a foothold!" called out Markus, struggling to pass his steed.

"Do not risk your life needlessly, Prince Markus. I have the situation in hand!" called Darius as he grabbed the coil of rope that hung from his saddle. He took a running a start, vaulting onto the back of Ewen's horse. Dash whinnied in protest. Her back seemed to sway under his weight, but she stood fast. Darius quickly looped one end of the rope around the saddle, the other around his own waist before he cautiously lowered himself down to Ewen.

"Do not let go until we are on solid ground!" ordered Darius.

"I do not intend to let go, sir, but I fear these reins are coming away from the halter!" shouted Ewen, his eyes dark with fear as he slipped down a little farther.

The little mare continued to strain under the weight of the boy hanging from her head, and now, she bore the additional weight of the large knight hanging from her body.

Darius, with his feet braced against the unstable cliff, held onto the tether with one hand as the other worked to wrap the end of the rope around Ewen's waist.

"Do as I do; lean out and use your feet to walk up as Dash moves backwards," instructed Darius as he held Ewen against his body.

With his one free hand, he motioned the chestnut mare to back up; Dash moved slowly, carefully placing hoof behind hoof until Darius and Ewen were raised up, standing before her.

"Ah, thank you, Dash!" said Ewen gratefully, throwing his trembling arms around the horse's sweating neck and mane. "Thank you, Sir Darius! I am indebted to you! How shall I ever repay you?"

Darius wiped the sweat from his brows with his forearm as he recoiled his rope. "You can be more careful for a start!" he answered briskly.

"Is everyone safe?" called out Lindras.

"Yes, Wizard, we are still in one piece; the Order remains intact!" Darius answered as he carefully made his way back to his horse.

"I recommend we all focus on the task at hand. Keep your eyes on the path ahead and remain close to the cliff wall. We must descend before darkness falls!" Kal-lel ordered, motioning them to move downward.

The first star appeared high in the sky as the sun finally slipped behind the Cathedral Mountains, withdrawing the last of its waning light from the darkening skyline.

The riders reached the bottom of the pass without any further incident or mishap. Weary and thirsty, they set up camp in the shadows of the gap between the deep canyon walls.

The horses took a long drink from a small, still pool, and then the animals turned their attention to food. Grazing upon the coarse grasses growing along the water's edge, they nodded and snorted with approval.

Faria and Lando began the task of gathering wood for a fire. When they both returned, Faria had gathered some dried grasses into a loose heap, igniting it as tinder beneath the stack of kindling.

"The wood is so dry, there should be no smoke to draw unwanted attention," said Faria as he glanced up between the walls of the pass that sheltered them, towards the sky as it assumed an ever-darkening hue.

"We should save what food we have for the long journey ahead. Arerys, is there game bird or rabbit in this area?" asked Markus.

Arerys nodded. "Follow me," said the Elf as he readied his bow. He drew an arrow from his quiver. With great stealth, he moved towards the low shrubs growing by the far edge of the pool. "Over there," Arerys said, motioning with the point of his arrow.

"I see nothing in this growing darkness," Markus whispered.

Just then, three grouse burst forth from the shrubs, flying straight out and high over their heads. Arerys whispered some Elvish words, perhaps a prayer, as he lined up his sight. He released an arrow that pierced two birds in a single stroke. Arerys quickly drew a second arrow from his quiver, releasing it to strike down the third grouse from the air.

He and Markus retrieved the birds. Arerys, having reclaimed his arrows, quickly wiped them clean of blood before placing them back into his quiver.

From his place near the fire, Ewen saw Markus and Arerys silhouetted against the twilight sky. He stared in amazement when the Elf released the arrows in such rapid succession, each hitting its mark with perfect accuracy.

Against the amber glow of the small campfire, the men dined well on grouse, bread and wine. Kal-lel, Arerys and Lindras sat upwind to avoid the scent of the roasting birds, partaking in the wine and bread, but politely refusing the meat.

"We are still a day's ride from the forests of Wyndwood," said Kal-lel, "We shall enter through Elmgrove by day's end if we leave at first light, and then we shall travel north to Aspenglow."

Arerys added, "It shall be an easy ride for our people know of our coming. The borders of Wyndwood are secured. They shall ensure a safe passage."

"Lord Kal-lel, when we reach Aspenglow we must take further measures to safeguard the Order. What have you in the way of attire that shall allow the prince and the knights in his service to pass through the country unnoticed?" asked Lindras.

"We shall adorn them in Elven cloaks and vests of Elven chain mail. From this point forward, Prince Markus, you shall shed your crown and title," added Kal-lel. "None shall address you by your true name, lest we care to reveal your identity. We must set aside all pretenses and airs, for word of the coming of the prince shall only serve to alert Beyilzon."

"That is wise," agreed Markus. "It is best to take these precautions."

"Faria, Darius and Lando, you too must do away with the colors of your house," said Kal-lel, striking the breastplate of Lando's armor with his fist. "You must all shed your skins of iron for it is far too apparent that you serve a king. Plus, unencumbered you shall travel farther and faster."

As Lindras and the others conversed, Ewen sat next to Arerys, watching him as he stoked the orange flames of the fire. He studied the Elf's face as the glow of the fire's light softened, almost blurred his facial features. The dancing light and shadows cast by the flames appeared to accentuate the points of his Elven ears. Arerys' eyes seemed to sparkle like two brilliant sapphires in the dim light as they reflected every spark of the crackling flames.

"Arerys, you look younger than the Prince, yet I know that your people are long lived. Exactly how old are you?" inquired Ewen.

"Much older than you, my young friend. I was born in the spring of the two hundredth and sixty seventh year of the Second Age of Peace," replied the Elf.

After doing some quick calculations in his head, Ewen summarized: "That would make you seven hundred and thirty three years old!"

"That is quite right. I believe the mortal equivalent would put me at about thirty-five years of age, but when you live for an eternity, what is the point of keeping count?" responded Arerys with a smile.

After a moment of silence, Ewen changed the subject. "Arerys, you are a great archer. I have never witnessed the likes of you in my life! Are all your peoples as good as you?" asked the boy, with great interest.

Arerys placed another piece of wood onto the fire and sat back next to the prince's squire. He smiled at his young companion. "I am flattered, but that is a strange question. Is it not akin to me assuming that all mortal men have mastered the sword, or all are loquacious, having the same gift of gab as you do?"

"I suppose you are right," answered Ewen as he contemplated Arerys' question.

Arerys confided to him; "I learned archery from my father. He is the greatest marksman in our fair land. He has taught me well, but as good as

I may be, my abilities still pale in comparison."

"What I would give to be able to set one arrow on an even course to meet its mark!" sighed Ewen.

"If we should prevail and return to our home safe and sound, I shall be most honored to share with you some of the finer points of archery," promised Arerys.

"Why, thank you, kind Elf!" responded Ewen, with genuine appreciation.

Arerys rose from his place in front of the fire, throwing his bow and quiver over his shoulder. "Father, I shall take the first watch down by the mouth of the canyon. From that vantage point, none shall go unseen or unheard."

Kal-lel nodded to his son in approval before continuing with his discussion with Lindras and the others.

"I shall share this first watch with you, Arerys," said Markus, as he adjusted his sword to his side. The two took their leave, melting into the darkness as they disappeared from the glow of the firelight.

Arerys was light on his feet as he silently moved through the darkness. Markus followed closely behind, guided by the Elf's dark figure outlined against the horizon. Coming to a large boulder near the mouth of the pass, Arerys leapt up, landing lightly onto the flat, smooth surface of the weathered boulder. Markus clambered up, taking his place next to Arerys. For a moment, Elf and man did not speak.

Eventually, Markus broke the silence. "We are fortunate that the weather is clear tonight."

"Indeed, my lord" agreed Arerys, his eyes scanning the heavens above. "Look at that star," said the Elf, pointing to the planet, Mars. "It seems to grow brighter with each passing night as that other star nears."

"Let us hope the stars do not join as one any time soon. There is still much to be done and we still have far to travel," said Markus, his eyes still struggling to adjust to the darkness.

Markus laid down on the flat surface of the boulder so he may look skyward into the star-studded heavens.

Arerys stood, like a lone sentry, in the night as he leaned against his bow. He looked down at the prince stretching out against his cold, hard bed.

"Prince Markus, there is no need for you to be here," said Arerys.

"You are in need of sleep; the days ahead will prove to be long and arduous. I suggest you get rest, while rest can be afforded to you."

"Arerys, of all my friends, I have known you the longest… although in your lifetime, it is a mere trifle. I wish for you to address me as Markus; I am your friend first, not your lord or prince. Besides, you too, are a prince, yet you rarely disclose or use your true title. You have always been Arerys, while you have always addressed me as Prince Markus. Why?"

The Elf thought upon his words. "The race of Elves is not meant for this world; it is changing too quickly. It shall only be a matter of time before the last of my people leave for the Twilight. My title is a mere formality."

"Nonetheless, you are like a brother to me. To you, I am not a prince, I am merely Markus. Besides, I shall not bear this title again until our lands are safe once more."

"Of course, Markus," nodded the Elf in understanding, "but as I said before, you need not be here. Go rest with the others by the warmth of the fire; the air is still chilled by winter's cold breath."

Markus propped himself up onto his elbows. He looked up at Arerys. "It is a tempting offer you make, for I am weary, but what of you? I rarely recall ever seeing you asleep. Are you not in need of rest yourself?"

Arerys smiled down at him. "For now, I am quite fine. Two or three hours are all I require."

"Well, Arerys, I shall stay here with you for as long as my eyes will allow it. I shall have Darius or another replace me when I am ready for sleep."

"As you wish."

Three hours had elapsed when Darius came forth to replace Markus on the watch. Arerys was alert as ever.

At three o'clock, Lando and Faria took over sentry duty as Darius returned to catch more sleep, while Arerys settled for his first bit of rest.

As Darius settled down once more, his movements woke Ewen from his slumber. He was unaware that Arerys had quietly stepped over him to lie down near the dying embers of the fire. It was not until Ewen felt a gentle '*whoosh*' of air that he became aware of Arerys' presence.

The Elf had thrown his cloak around his body as he lay down on the cool sand. He was on his back, his eyes closed as sleep fell upon him instantly, but as Arerys' body slept, his mind and ears seemed to stay attuned to the world around him.

Ewen laid his head back down on his bag to catch a bit more sleep before the sun reappeared in the morning.

Kal-lel, Arerys and Lindras were awake long before the men were able to shake off their drowsiness. Ewen stretched and yawned as he rose from his slumber.

"I shall prepare breakfast, Prince Markus," said Ewen through a yawn.

"Ewen, remember, you must not address me as such," reminded Markus.

"My apologies, Markus. It shall take some getting use to," acknowledged Ewen as he dusted off the ash from the cold fire that had drifted and settled onto him as he slept.

The members of the Order ate in silence as the sun's rays stretched over the Iron Mountain Range to brighten the dark sky before the sun even peeked over the summit.

Ewen helped to saddle all of the horses with the exception of RainDance, WindWalker, and Tempest. The Wizard, Kal-lel and Arerys had no need for saddles and there even seemed to be no real need for bit and bridle either; their horses knowing exactly where their riders wanted to go with just the shifting of their body weight on the horse's bare back and a few whisperings of Elvish words.

The prince's black stallion, Arrow, snorted and stomped impatiently as Markus raised himself into his saddle.

Seeing that the prince was ready to move on, Ewen scrambled into the saddle on his chestnut mare's back. All were ready to begin the next leg of their journey.

Again, Kal-lel, Arerys, and Lindras led the way through the floor of the canyon, their horses galloping at top speed. The Elves' keen eyes were constantly searching the steep walls for any signs of danger. Stopping only once during the mid-afternoon to allow the horses to rest and drink while the men ate a small meal, the party was soon on the move again.

With Rainbow Pass well behind them, the canyon walls became less steep as they ascended the course of an ancient, dried riverbed. As the land leveled out, the horses picked their way around the rocks and boulders that had long since washed down this course. Kal-lel guided the riders out of the riverbed onto the west bank, steering them up a small knoll where they came to a stop.

"Over there," said Arerys, pointing with his finger. "There ahead lies the forest of Wyndwood."

The men looked across the vast plain, their eyes strained to see the dark form lining the horizon: the trees marking the edge of the forests of Kal-lel's domain, the Kingdom of the Elves.

As the men of the Order galloped through the rolling, treeless Plains of Sarna, Arerys' heart felt light as he neared his homeland. Riding through the vast, rippling sea of grass, they finally reached the forest's edge, Kal-lel escorted them through the invisible trails weaving between the tall stands of poplar and birch trees.

Ewen gazed up at the sunlight dancing between the small, green leaves that trembled in the gentle spring breeze. He drank in the earthy, warm air and he could feel that the forest was alive and teeming with life.

As darkness settled, Elmgrove was still one league away. Kal-lel and the Wizard led the way; the night was exceptionally dark and the tall trees cast such deep shadows, it was difficult to see very far in front of them. Arerys took up the rear to ensure that the party did not get separated.

"By night, this forest is very gloomy and dark, Arerys," said Ewen, squinting his eyes to focus on the riders in front of his own horse. "I do not know how you can see in such blackness!"

Arerys smiled at the boy as he responded, "You need not always trust your eyes to make your way, young master. Where your eyes may fail you, your sense of hearing and even smell can be your guide."

"That is all very well and good if you are an Elf, I suppose," laughed Ewen. "I do not put that kind of trust in my others senses. My ears tend to hear only what they want to hear. Even my nose has led me to food, where none was to be had!"

Arerys looked at his young friend and laughed. He then gazed up into the night sky and for a brief moment, closed his eyes and under his breath, whispered some words in the language of his people.

Slowly, one by one, tiny beacons of golden light flickered on. They slowly floated down from the tree canopy, swirling and congregating around the riders.

"Fireflies!" Ewen gasped in delight. "Arerys, you truly are magic! Can you teach me how to do this?"

Arerys grinned with amusement that the boy was so amazed by such a small feat. He thought upon his request, reflecting on the fact that the Elvish dialect was a dying language of a diminishing race – now only kept alive by the Elders and royalty, to be used in celebrations and incantations. "I am sorry, Ewen. Though I can teach you to speak Elvish, I am afraid that any incantations that we use are never to be heard, nor repeated, by a mortal."

"But why?" asked Ewen, in obvious disappointment.

"It is too easy for man to take the gifts our race has been blessed with to use it to their own devices," replied Arerys, his smile quickly fading. "Throughout history, mankind has repeatedly demonstrated this weakness. It would appear that the race of man is easily swayed - corrupted by their need for power. This is something we cannot risk."

"I would only do good if I was blessed with the powers bestowed upon your people."

"I am sure you would, Ewen," nodded Arerys in agreement. "However, my people are bound by this promise to keep mankind safe, even if it is from himself."

With their way now illuminated by the soft, steady glow created by the fireflies called upon by the Elf, the group made their way through the nighttime forest. Kal-lel raised his hand for all to stop. He cocked his head; his ears listening for a sign that would tell him which direction to travel.

"This way!" he said, urging WindWalker on. In the distance, the inviting sounds of a waterfall beckoned him to Elmgrove.

The water shimmered and glowed, coming alive in the light cast down by a thin crescent moon and the multitude of stars from above. The cold, clear water gently danced over moss-covered rocks, collecting and swirling in little pools before cascading over a large, flat sheet of granite. Here, the water came spilling down in a transparent sheet to form a thin, white veil before splashing into a deep pool and overflowing into a creek.

The horses moved between the tall ferns to drink from the creek before settling for a night of grazing and sleep.

Arerys headed to a nearby meadow with his bow in hand, in search of rabbit or fowl for the men to dine on while Lando and Darius gathered firewood to last them well into the night.

Faria prepared a campfire in an old, abandoned fire pit surrounded by stones that now lay in disarray. He carefully rearranged the stones to contain the sparks that crackled and snapped from the burning wood.

In the glow of the fire, the forest had taken on an unsettling ambiance. It did not look, nor feel, like the same forest they had traveled through by day.

Arerys returned soon after; his hunt successful. He had with him two rabbits and a grouse. Ewen dressed and cleaned the fowl and rabbits before roasting them over the fire.

As dinner was shared around the campfire, Ewen looked at the tall, ancient trees surrounding them. They seemed alive and yet, they did not move nor speak. Everywhere he looked, he could see ancient relics and reminders of a civilization that was no more. He turned to the Wizard.

"I feel as though we are being watched," he whispered as he searched for clues in the shadows of the forest.

"Ah, it is better to be wary in these woods, my lad," said Lindras as he passed some wine and dried fruit to the others. "They do not call Elmgrove the Haunted Forest of Wyndwood for no reason."

"Fear not, Ewen," assured Kal-lel, "The people of Elmgrove departed long ago."

"Who were these people?" inquired Ewen.

"They were Elves, much like us," answered Kal-lel.

"Hmm? What do you mean by 'much like us'?" asked Ewen, wishing to learn more.

"According to the elders, they were a race of Elves that were somewhat different from us," said Arerys. "They had dark brown hair and many had dark, brown eyes."

"Are you saying they were more akin to some of us mortals?" asked Ewen. "I have brown hair and brown eyes."

"No, they were definitely Elves," replied Arerys.

"But, is it not similar to me saying that I am different from Faria because he has ginger-colored hair and hazel eyes, while I do not?"

Arerys thought for a moment, then replied: "No, it is deeper than that, Ewen. They were just different. They chose to worship differently than we fair Elves did. They too, honored the Maker of All, but they also worshipped other spirits they believed to be working in partnership with the *One*."

Lindras and the others settled near the fire, leaning in closer to listen to Arerys' account of the mysterious *dark* Elves. Although the men all knew of these Elves, none in their company, with the exception of Lindras and Kal-lel, were personally acquainted with them.

"And that is wrong?" asked Ewen.

"Well, there is only one who is responsible for creating all life," Arerys stated tersely.

"Have you ever seen one of their 'spirits'?" Ewen continued with his questioning.

"No, of course not," replied Arerys with a frown.

"Have you ever seen the Maker of All?"

"No," answered Arerys. "The old adage of 'seeing is believing' cannot always be applied where religion is concerned; sometimes, believing is to see."

"Then, how do you know these spirits do not exist when you have never seen the Maker of All yourself and yet, you believe him to exist?" argued Ewen, still attempting to understand.

The others chuckled at the boy's persistence. They watched Arerys tactfully counter his barrage of questions, while still trying to maintain some sense of patience and decorum.

"Because he has been the *One* since the beginning of time. It is what we know to be true," answered Arerys, his patience beginning to wear thin.

"But if the Maker of All is real to you because you believe then, does it not stand to reason that it is possible that these 'spirits' are real to the 'dark' Elves because they too, believe?"

Arerys released a weary sigh. He became silent, unsure how to answer this question.

"He has you there, my friend!" laughed Darius as he finished his meal.

"Enough talk about the dark Elves. They have long departed from the forest of Wyndwood," responded Kal-lel.

"But what happened to them? Where did they go? Did they choose to enter the Twilight?" asked the boy, still full of curiosity.

"Before the Second Age of Peace, they chose to dwell here in

Elmgrove, the southern forest of Wyndwood; away from Aspenglow, apart from my people," explained Kal-lel. "During the last Great War against Beyilzon, Dahlon Treeborn, the Lord of Elmgrove and his people fought side by side with mine, along with King Brannon and the soldiers of the Alliance. Together, Beyilzon's forces were brought down in defeat and the Dark Lord was vanquished. When the war was done and peace returned to the lands, Dahlon and his people chose to seek a new home and a new beginning elsewhere."

"But where did they go?"

"They headed east, disappearing somewhere far over the Iron Mountains," answered Kal-lel.

"Were their numbers many?"

"No, they were fewer than the fair Elves and many of Dahlon's people were slaughtered in the last Great War," replied Kal-lel, growing weary of the boy's questions.

"Perhaps they all left for the Twilight?"

"Perhaps," sighed Kal-lel. "Master Vatel, the hour grows late. I believe it is time for sleep. I recommend you do get some for we shall be on the move at first light."

Ewen rolled his eyes as he reluctantly laid down, resting his head upon his bag, his blanket carelessly flung about him.

Arerys reached over Ewen to grab his bow and quiver as he prepared for sentry duty.

"Arerys, have you ever met these 'dark' Elves?" asked Ewen in a hushed voice to avoid a reprimand from Kal-lel or Markus.

"No, my friend. They left Wyndwood before my time," whispered Arerys.

Arerys and Lando left for the first watch while Ewen, still brimming with unanswered questions, settled for a night of sleep.

As the sun crept up into the morning sky, the group readied for the final leg of their journey to Aspenglow. It would be a good day's steady ride northward along the Aral River to King Kal-lel's home in the northern forest of Wyndwood.

With Kal-lel in the lead, the Order left this ancient forest and the ghosts of those who still lingered in the shadows of the trees. Ewen was not sorry to be leaving, for even though this forest was beautiful, even inviting by day; at night it seemed to be a mere shell of its former self. This forest felt haunted; its heart, dark and lonely.

The farther north the group ventured, the larger the aspen, poplar and birch trees seemed to grow. Their small leaves that trembled in the slightest breeze, looked darker green against the trees' papery, white bark. It was then that Ewen realized why the Elves had a preference for horses that were a dappled gray: The broken sunlight dancing through the forest canopy against the backdrop of the whitish-gray tree trunks made the horses one with the forest!

As the horses trotted at an unhurried clip, Ewen marveled at the lush greenery surrounding them. The forest was alive with songbirds heralding their arrival. Even the great willow trees lining the trails seemed to bow down in royal salute as King Kal-lel rode by.

"We shall ride straight through without stopping," announced Kal-lel. "If we forego an afternoon meal now, we shall be well rewarded when we reach Aspenglow. A bountiful feast shall await us there."

Ewen was disappointed by the decision to skip lunch; his stomach was already rumbling in protest. "Maybe we should hurry on," he suggested. With those words spoken, WindWalker broke into a full gallop; the other horses racing close behind.

From a distance, the group could make out Aspenglow against the impending darkness. Lights flickered on like tiny, stationary fireflies illuminating the walkways and the homes of Kal-lel's domain. They were like gently glowing beacons guiding them homeward.

As the horses galloped into Aspenglow, Kal-lel's people were there to greet them. Young squires quickly gathered the horses to water and feed before housing them overnight in the king's stable. Many of the young Elf maidens were also present to welcome home their wayfaring prince, shyly smiling at him in a bid to catch his attention as he walked by.

"Arerys! Father!" a voice called out excitedly from an overhead boardwalk. "You are here at last!" An Elf, not unlike Arerys, dashed down to greet them, embracing both in an exuberant hug.

"Artel, it is good to be home!" said Arerys with a broad smile reserved for loved ones.

Kal-lel introduced the members of the Order to his son and to the members of his household. The Elves were polite and gracious as they welcomed the men into Kal-lel's home.

Inside, a sumptuous banquet was awaiting their arrival. Around a great table, they dined and drank fine wine while Arerys recounted the tale of their misadventure at Rainbow Pass to his brother.

Ewen was surprised at how similar the two Elves appeared; Arerys was slightly taller and appeared to be six or seven 'mortal years' older than Artel. Both had their father's deep blue eyes and both brothers sported long, straight, golden hair, but Arerys was a shade darker.

While Ewen was studying Arerys and Artel, trying to determine how many decades or centuries separated them; Faria, Darius and Lando were busy admiring the women of Wyndwood. The Elf maidens quietly went about their business of serving food and wine. They were tall and willowy with flowing blonde hair, gentle blue eyes and demure smiles.

As the men watched, the women moved with grace. Their lightness of being was almost like a drug to their souls, lulling them into a state of stupor much like the warm haze that takes over the mind and body after too much wine.

"King Kal-lel, the Elf maidens are truly of exquisite beauty," Lando stated with much admiration. Faria nodded in agreement.

"Yes, I believe the women-folk of Wyndwood are the fairest in all of Imago!" declared Darius, with a sparkle in his eyes.

"Yes, and this is where they shall remain," responded Kal-lel curtly. "Besides, Arerys has yet to accept one of these lovely maidens as his wife, but he shall, when the time is right I imagine," sighed Kal-lel, as though he was becoming impatient with Arerys' indecision.

Arerys continued his conversation with his brother and Markus, but his father's words did not go unnoticed. It was not a matter he was willing to discuss, let alone rush into or take lightly, especially when such a commitment may well indeed last an eternity.

With appetites well sated, the Order relaxed in their chairs that were now pushed back from the table.

"Lindras, I wish to meet with you to discuss plans for tomorrow," said Kal-lel as he rose from the great table. "I shall bid you all a good night as I shall retire directly to my chambers when we are done. I shall excuse myself now."

Before he and Lindras departed, the members of the Order all rose to their feet as they nodded in acknowledgement, thanking Kal-lel for his warm and gracious hospitality.

Arerys and his brother led the men down to a large and beautiful courtyard surrounded by carefully tended gardens. There, an inviting fire blazed in a hearth situated in the center of a large gazebo. Ewen admired the beautiful woodwork all around them. Everywhere ornate homes, walkways and gazebos adorned with elaborate and intricate detailing and beautifully carved statues gave the courtyard a surreal, magical feel.

Ewen was amazed at the craftsmanship. "Arerys, this is absolutely beautiful. These carvings are truly a work of art," he marveled as his fingers touched the delicate woodwork.

"We Elves have a history that is older than the oldest trees in Imago. We are the hewers of wood, we can see and understand the beauty hidden within the grain of every type of tree," responded Arerys, with great pride.

As they settled about the fire, the men lit their pipes and the conversation returned to the Elf maidens.

"What fair and delicate creatures live in Aspenglow," sighed Lando.

"Indeed! I do believe one of them actually fancies me," boasted Darius as lit his pipe, gently blowing a slow rising spiral of gray smoke into the night sky.

"Yes, Darius, you keep dreaming your dreams," laughed Markus as he lay back to watch the stars shining through a clearing in the tree canopy. The others chuckled in agreement with Markus.

"What of you, Arerys?" asked Faria, recalling Kal-lel's comment. "Surely, there must be one fair maiden here that appeals to your senses."

Arerys did not offer a response.

"My brother is not easy to please, Faria," Artel answered in an exasperated tone. "What he seeks in a woman does not exist."

"But the women of Wyndwood are all fair and beautiful. What more can you ask for?" asked Faria, genuinely perplexed by Artel's statement.

"Beauty is not everything," answered Arerys, staring coldly into Faria's hazel eyes. "Even the most *beautiful* woman becomes ugly if her nature is to be petty and wanting."

"What my brother desires is a woman who is intelligent and brave; one that can hold her own in battle, if need be!" said Artel with a laugh as he rolled his eyes in ridicule. "Yes, a woman who apparently is willing to leave the security of Wyndwood for places far and away to share in his adventures!"

"Ha! Surely you jest, Artel!" laughed Faria. "Such a woman only exists in dreams, and if she were to appear in your dreams, it would quickly become a nightmare!"

"Maybe, Faria, you are only secure with beauty because a woman who is any more than what she appears to be, may be more than you or your ego can handle," Arerys stated tersely.

"Well, my friend, each to his own I suppose, but if this is what you desire in a woman, then it is a good thing that you are an Elf. You may indeed need to live for an eternity before you find your warrior maiden," responded Faria with a smile.

"I suggest we stop harassing Arerys. He is entitled to his choices just as we all are," interrupted Markus. "Besides, dawn shall soon be upon us, we should all get some rest while we can."

As they settled for the night, it was the first time since they departed from Carcross had the entire Order slept without the need of a sentry. It would also be the last time they would have a peaceful night's sleep in a long while.

Their fast was broken by a simple, but filling meal served by the Elf maidens. As the men awaited Lindras and Kal-lel, Darius, Faria, and Lando were attempting to make small talk with some of the women.

Arerys watched in mild amusement as the three men were met with shy giggles and bashful glances. He could not deny these women were indeed beautiful and delicate flowers, but taken out of their element they would surely fade and wilt. Somehow, they lacked substance.

Overhead, Lindras and Kal-lel appeared. An entourage followed them as they made their way down from the high walkways.

"Knights of the Order, shed your armor," commanded Kal-lel. He turned to present each with a glittering, fine-meshed vest of chain mail that shone like polished silver. "Wear it under your clothing to conceal the nature of its power. This mail is light, but it shall protect you as well as your suit of iron."

Kal-lel turned to Markus and Ewen. He held forth a vest of mail to both. "I had these crafted for the two of you. This quest is doomed to fail if either one of you fall to the wayside. You will need every bit of luck and help to survive this journey."

"Arerys, you are no exception. I would like to see my eldest son return safely to Wyndwood," said Kal-lel as he passed onto him his own armor of chain mail that he had donned during the last Great War.

"I am honored, father," said Arerys, as he bowed before him.

As the men of the Order donned their new armor, they were surprised at its lightness and the ease with which the mail adapted to their bodies. Ewen felt particularly proud of his new Elven wear, perhaps his father felt this way the first time he put on his armor.

"This is truly amazing! I wish my own armor was as easy to wear," marveled Lando.

"And this can really serve to protect us?" asked Faria with great skepticism as he ran his open hands against the fine-woven mesh.

"Yes," answered Kal-lel. "It can stand up to the blow of a sword or halberd, but be careful not to be pierced by the tip of a sword or arrow, it is the only thing that will force the links to separate."

Unbeknownst to Faria, Darius suddenly swung his sword horizontally, striking his companion directly across his chest with a hard 'swack'! The impact knocked Faria clear off his feet, backwards, hard onto the ground.

Faria lay there, momentarily stunned by this unexpected assault. He gasped, struggling to recapture the breath that was knocked out of him as he went down.

Darius' large frame loomed over his prostrate body. "Does that answer your question, Faria?" He smiled down at his friend. "I myself think it will serve us most adequately."

Everyone laughed as Darius helped him onto his feet. Faria's vest of mail did not even show a single mark where he was struck by Darius's sword.

Somehow, Markus and Lindras were not surprised by this knight's antics. They simply shook their heads as they smiled.

Kal-lel then presented to each man an Elven sword of exquisite beauty and craftsmanship. Markus, Lando and Darius bowed graciously to Kal-lel as they accepted this gift. They were in awe at its lightness and its ease of comfort when gripped in their hands. It was certainly lighter than any sword made by mortal man! Kal-lel presented a sword to Faria.

Faria politely declined. "Thank you, my lord, but I wish to keep my own sword. We have done battle together many times; it has never failed me."

"Very well," said Kal-lel with a nod. "I understand."

"I shall be pleased to accept such a wondrous gift, sire!" said Ewen, eyes wide with anticipation.

"I am sorry, Ewen, but you shall bear no arms, not on this quest," apologized Kal-lel. "It is a risk we cannot take."

Ewen cast his sad, brown eyes down; his disappointment clearly visible for all to see.

"My boy, why would you care to burden yourself with the weight of a sword?" asked Darius as he exaggerated the heft of the weapon hanging from his left hip. "You have five at the ready, plus the staff of this venerable old Wizard to protect you."

"I wish to be a man," Ewen replied wistfully.

"Ewen, a sword does not make a man. A man must master this weapon otherwise he is merely a boy with a dangerous toy," advised Markus. "Besides, your day shall come, but for now, do not rush to grow up so quickly or you shall only long for your days of youth sooner."

The Elf maidens presented each member of the Order with a cloak much like the one worn by Arerys. Ash gray in color, it would provide them with camouflage against a backdrop of rocks or forest, as well as warmth against the still cool, evening air.

Two jade green pins, each carefully crafted into the shape of an aspen leaf and held together by a short length of silver chain, secured the cloak about their shoulders.

As they donned their Elven attire, Ewen and the knights felt as though the cloaks had a life of their own. It fell lightly over their shoulders, providing a warmth unlike any provided by their own conventional trappings. The material seemed to breathe, allowing them to feel comfortable, no matter what the surrounding temperature; they were neither too hot, nor too cool.

No longer clad in their heavy, traditional suits of armor, the knights of the Alliance momentarily stared at each other.

"Now there is a semblance of order to this Order," smiled Lindras proudly.

As the men mounted their waiting steeds, Kal-lel inspected them. "You shall bear no identification other than the brooch bearing the insignia of the house you serve to protect. Keep it concealed. If you should fall in battle, none shall know your identify or mission, but your own brothers-in-arms."

All nodded in understanding.

"If all should go as planned, we shall meet again, after the first night of the full moon on the Plains of Fire. We shall unite for one last time to do battle against the Dark Lord," explained Kal-lel. "Until this day arrives, I shall muster the armies of Carcross, Cedona and Darross. We shall combine forces to end the skirmishes that seem to break out like wildfire throughout Darross before it spreads southward beyond the shadows of the Aranak Mountains. When the time is right, we shall deploy our armies as one. This shall create enough of a concern for Beyilzon's soldiers that their attention should be diverted, long enough for the Order to enter the Valley of Shadows to reach Mount Hope."

As the morning sun continued its ascent into the pale blue sky, it shone brightly on the emerald-green waters of the Lake in the Woods. The sunlight danced, sparkling like diamonds carried on the small ripples created by a gentle breeze.

Arerys gazed across the serene lake. He sighed. There was sadness about him as he closed his eyes, as though he was creating a mental image in his head of his beloved home.

"We shall be off now, King Kal-lel," announced Markus as he and Kal-lel clasped wrists in a final farewell.

"Lindras shall lead the way to the Cathedral Mountains and onward to Mount Isa and the Temple of the Watchers. The Three Sisters know to expect you."

As they turned to follow the trail winding westward around the Lake of the Woods, Arerys glanced back at his brother and father. He had a strong feeling of foreboding that he may never return. RainDance picked up her pace to catch up to the other riders. As Aspenglow disappeared into the forest, Arerys heard a gentle whisper in his ears: "I love you, my son. Return to us safely."

Arerys did not turn around for a second look, he merely whispered, "I love you too, father."

CHAPTER 3

THE ROAD TO MOUNT ISA

"It shall be a full day's ride to the Cathedral Mountains and at least another day and a half to travel the steep trails leading to the Temple of the Watchers," said Lindras as the Order finally reached the tree-lined border of Wyndwood.

In front of them lay the open and sparsely treed Fields of Shelon. Beyond, looming before them on the horizon stood the slate blue, snow-capped peaks of the Cathedral Mountain Range. Mount Isa was safely nestled between the pinnacles of two of the highest peaks in this range.

"From this point forward, we must use extreme caution on this trek. We are no longer in the safety of Kal-lel's kingdom so none of his pow-ers can protect us now," said Markus as he leapt down from Arrow's broad back. "We shall wait until nightfall before we cross the Fields of Shelon. If we ride all night, we shall arrive at the Cathedral Mountains as the day breaks."

Freshly stocked by Kal-lel's people with drink, dried fruits and other staples, there was no need to prepare a fire. After their meal, the men enjoyed a smoke from their pipes, stretching out to relax under the shade of a large, sprawling chestnut tree.

"It would be wise to sleep now," advised Lindras. Chewing on the mouthpiece of his pipe, he deliberated on which route they were to take once they reach Mount Isa.

Arerys took the first watch, while the others tried to sleep in the light of the midday sun. Sleep was elusive. Between drowsing for only short periods of time, none of the men found any comfort or reprieve in their dreams, if dreams were to be had.

As dusk approached, Arerys rested for an hour until the last rays of light cast by the sun had dissolved into the deep blue of the evening sky. Refreshed from his brief sleep, he found quick sustenance after only sev-eral bites of the thin, crisp Elven bread and some water as the others read-ied their horses for the long ride across the Fields of Shelon.

By the meager light shed by the night sky, the Order rode their horses hard over the rolling hills and vales, and across the meadows. They allowed the animals the opportunity to rest only when they came across islands of trees scattered across this stretch of land. The trees provided some degree of cover for the riders as they stretched their weary legs, while their horses drank from a nearby stream.

When the horses were adequately rested and their thirst quenched, from under the cover of the trees, Arerys would softly call. RainDance, hearing his Elvish whisperings, would snort and toss her head in response. She trotted over to the Elf as the other horses came along trailing behind her. Tempest took up the rear to keep the stragglers from grazing or wandering off in another direction.

"It is only another two leagues or so to Mount Isa," said Lindras as he pointed to its peak. "We must move with haste if we wish to still arrive under the cover of darkness."

Lindras urged Tempest on. The great, gray stallion broke into a full gallop. The other horses followed Tempest as he thundered across the open fields, through streams and over hills, setting a straight course to Mount Isa.

As he charged down one hill, through a wide creek, and then up its tall embankment, Tempest suddenly encountered a large tree that had toppled over. It lay hidden to the eyes, until just passing beyond the crest of this wall of earth. The stallion snorted in consternation at the large barrier that lay dead ahead, but his steps did not falter as he raced towards the remains of the fallen tree. Tempest effortlessly leapt over the wooden barrier.

The tree appeared too quickly for the other horses to veer around, so they too, were forced to follow Tempest, leaping over the obstacle.

Ewen knew he had no choice but to follow the others. At the speed they were traveling, it would be impossible to have Dash stop, or even slow down, without crashing headlong into this deadly barrier. He hoped that although his mare was at least two-hands shorter than the other horses, her smaller rider might compensate for her lack of size.

Ewen urged Dash on, to pick up enough speed to carry her over the tree. The chestnut mare raced forward and with a mighty leap, she easily cleared the barrier. Ewen temporarily held his breath and closed his eyes as his horse attempted to clear the fallen tree. He released an audible sigh of relief as Dash landed on the other side.

As the mare's weight came down onto the ground, her right front leg abruptly buckled. The mare violently pitched forward. As she went down, her rider was sent flying forward, over her head.

Ewen was momentarily airborne. When he eventually came back down to earth, his only comfort came from the tall grasses cushioning him against the cruel bite of the hard earth.

His heart raced as he struggled to regain the breath that was knocked out of him. Dazed by the impact, he slowly sat up. Suddenly, from the corner of his eye, he saw Dash come tumbling down, head over tail.

Without even thinking, Ewen instantly rolled out of her way. She came crashing down, coming to an abrupt stop just short of where he had been lying seconds earlier.

All the riders came to an immediate halt, wheeling their mounts about to come to the boy's aid. Markus was the first to reach him. "Ewen, are you hurt!"

Ewen did not speak; still in a daze, he was trembling badly from his near miss.

"Are you hurt, boy?" Lindras asked him as he quickly ran his hands over Ewen's body to check for signs of any broken bones.

Ewen gazed up at the Wizard and just shook his head.

When asked if he could stand, Ewen nodded, struggling to his feet with Markus' aid.

"My little friend, luck is with you. The mare would have come down squarely upon your head, had you not moved when you did!" stated Darius.

"This is not luck, Darius, this was divine intervention. Something or someone is watching over the boy!" commented Lando.

"Let us hope this is so, Lando, for it shall take more than luck for us to see this quest to an end," said Faria, helping Markus to steady Ewen back onto his feet.

"Unfortunately, Dash is not so lucky," said Arerys, gently stroking the mare's sweat-stained withers.

The Elf collected her reins, coaxing her onto her feet. Dash struggled to stand and when she did, she favored her right front leg. Arerys passed the reins onto Lindras as he proceeded to check on the extent of the mare's injury. He knelt down before her and with both hands; he ran them quickly, but gently along the length of her leg. His hands eventually came back to rest on her knee. The Elf closed his eyes, whispering in the language of his people as his hands wrapped around Dash's injured knee.

The mare was just as shaken by her tumble as Ewen was by his impromptu flight from her saddle. She trembled as Arerys took her by the reins, encouraging her to take a few steps. Dash complied, slowly limping as she shifted her weight onto her other legs. She continued to favor her right knee, her hoof cautiously touching the ground as she moved.

"Tell me she did not break her leg, Arerys," cried Ewen as he gently rubbed her velvety muzzle.

"No Ewen, she is not broken," assured the Elf. "She is lame and will be so for some time."

"Oh no!"

"She will be fine, but she is unsuitable to bear a rider or to endure the unforgiving trek up Mount Isa."

"It is best to rid her of her saddle and halter. Set her free," recommended Lindras.

"But, she will surely die by herself," cried Ewen, watching Arerys uncinch the saddle.

"No, she will be quite fine. I shall set her on a course back to Wyndwood. It shall be a trip she can now take at her leisure," said Arerys, as he stripped her of her halter. "When she reaches the forest again, my people shall lead her back to Aspenglow. She will be in good hands, Ewen. They shall provide her with proper care."

Ewen was relieved that Dash would recover, but now his thoughts turned to other matters. "Now what shall become of me? I have no horse of my own."

"You shall ride with me, my young friend," said Arerys as he extended a hand to Ewen.

He hoisted the boy onto RainDance's back. Ewen held onto Arerys as they rode, the ride seemed much rougher on bareback than in a saddle, but Ewen appreciated that it was still better than having to walk the distance.

"Daylight shall soon be upon us; we must move now," said Lindras as he urged Tempest on. The horses and riders continued on their course to Mount Isa, but as Ewen glanced back, his heart sank. He watched as Dash slowly hobbled back in the direction of Wyndwood, her pace now faltering; hampered by her lameness. For a moment, Ewen wished he were heading back in that direction with her.

In spite of their misfortune crossing the Fields of Shelon, the Order still made good time as day was yet to break when they arrived at the foot of Mount Isa.

"We shall eat and rest until darkness falls on the land again," said Markus as he removed Arrow's saddle, releasing him to graze with the other horses. Beneath the shadows of the trees fringing the base of the mountain, the men tried to sleep while always two kept watch.

Sleep was not as elusive this time; the long ride through the night had worn them out. Even Arerys slept for almost three hours, but even when sleep was found, it was often interrupted as they tossed and turned in restlessness.

When the night returned, blanketing the land in darkness, the horses were made ready. Under the pale light of the stars and a waning crescent moon, the Order proceeded up the steep trail that would eventually lead them to the Temple of the Watchers. As the loose substrate and the steep sections of the trail made it difficult for the horses to maintain a secure footing, everybody dismounted, hiking up the treacherous terrain.

The hours wore on slowly, as did the distance they traveled. For every few steps forward, they seemed to slide back one. The ground seemed to crumble and dissolve under their feet. Even for the horses, the upward journey on this precipitous terrain was a struggle.

Eventually, the Order came to a fork in the trail. "Which path do we take Lindras," asked Markus.

Lindras took a moment to contemplate the choices. "To the right, the way is easier to travel, but it is longer and leaves us no protection against prying eyes that may alert Beyilzon's men to our whereabouts. To the left, the road is more direct, but it is treacherous. Its only redeeming feature is that it shall offer us areas of cover. Either path we choose to take, we shall not reach the summit before daybreak."

"Then, left it is, Wizard," said Markus, confident that this was their better option.

Ewen looked ahead to the unforgiving path looming before them. It was at least another four hours before sunrise - another four, tedious hours to travel. His sluggish muscles ached with each step; he wondered how many more could he endure.

As daylight approached, Lindras and the others reached a large, relatively flat area of the trail. Protected on one side by a steep rock wall, the other side by a huge rocky outcrop that sheltered them from above; the Order stopped to rest. Arerys and Lindras took the first watch at either end of the outcropping sheets of rock. The others collapsed into a deep sleep, not even waiting to eat or drink first, exhausted by the difficult journey that was now slowed even further by the thinning air.

Ewen crumpled to the ground in exhaustion. He drew his Elven cloak tightly about him. Although it provided his body with adequate warmth, the thin, cold air stung his lungs with each breath he drew. The cold seemed to penetrate his body from the inside out. He shivered as sleep finally caught up with him.

It was late into the afternoon when Ewen woke from his slumber. The men had already eaten and were now biding their time, waiting until blackness enveloped the mountain.

Ewen yawned and stretched. His body ached terribly after sleeping on the cold, hard ground. When he joined the others, he slowly came to the realization that as darkness descended upon them, they would have to resume this torturous ascent to the temple.

The horses were becoming impatient. They quenched their thirst from the fresh, cold water that flowed and seemed to even burst forth from the high rocks as it cascaded down as small rivulets and waterfalls. What sparse grasses and browse there were, was already consumed.

After Ewen finished eating, he busied himself by replenishing everyone's water flask.

As the last fingers of light withdrew from the darkening horizon, the Order prepared for the last leg of their trip to reach the summit.

Half staggering, half walking, the men trudged along the narrow trail. Ewen and the men all suffered from the effects of the thin air. Their heads pounded, muscles ached and their lungs felt as if they were ready to burst with each breath they fought to gulp down.

Arerys and Lindras did not suffer from the same ill effects of oxygen deprivation at this high altitude. They stopped frequently to allow the others to rest and catch their breath. The altitude and the rough terrain did not particularly bother the Elf; often, he would dash ahead to scout out the trail, then return to inform the others of what lay ahead.

Though Markus had no desire to possess the eternal life bestowed upon the race of Elves, the thought of having Arerys' stamina certainly would have helped them all on this arduous and painful trek.

As the men stood up to resume their ascent, Arerys came silently bounding down the trail. "Markus, something is wrong! I can sense it in the air!" he said in a hushed voice.

"Do you know what it is?" asked Markus.

"I cannot place it, but danger is near. There is something evil in the wind," whispered Arerys.

As Markus motioned for all to cease talking, he turned to Arerys. "Do you think there are others onto our trail?"

"I cannot be sure, but I definitely have a feeling something evil is near to us," warned the Elf.

"It may be possible that either Beyilzon's men are using the other route as we speak to reach the temple first, or they may already be descending the mountain with the Stone of Salvation in their hands," said the Wizard.

"Either way, Lindras, we cannot turn back now. We must reach the temple to find out," said Markus, drawing his sword from its scabbard. "Have your weapons ready, men."

The Order continued their arduous trek, one hand on the horse's reins, the other on their swords. Markus peered up at the summit. It was now visible; not very far from reach. He tapped Ewen upon his shoulder as he pointed to the soft glow of light illuminating from the temple above. The boy was greatly relieved to see the end was almost at hand.

As the group neared the summit, the chilled mountain air that was carried on a stiff breeze was no more. The air was calm and still, it actually felt warm against their exposed skin.

Lindras released a heavy sigh of relief as he announced for all to hear: "Behold! The Temple of the Watchers!"

As he hastened his steps towards the temple, the others ran to catch up. Suddenly, a wall of flames erupted from the ground to encircle the temple. Lindras was thrown back from the explosive force of the flames. Their horses reared and snorted in fear, pulling at their reins to escape from the wall of fire growing before them.

A disembodied voice declared: "Even the pure of heart shall not pass beyond these gates without the three keys to the temple."

The heat of the flame was very intense; there was no way to get around, beneath or over the wall of fire.

"Lindras, how are we to pass? Why did you not tell us about this obstacle?" asked Markus, helping Lindras back onto his feet.

"Markus, do you recall what you had dined on a week ago?" responded the disgruntled Wizard.

"No, of course not," answered Markus, perplexed by his line of questioning.

"Well, it has been almost one thousand years since I had last set foot in the temple. I am an old Wizard with a memory that may falter from time to time," grumbled Lindras as he struggled to recall the details of this barrier of fire. He sat upon a large rock, playing with the silver whiskers of his long moustache as he deliberated on the barrier that now stalled their progress.

As the Wizard sat in deep contemplation, the others quietly gathered and waited. Ewen squinted through the fire; he could just barely make out the three figures within the stone temple.

"It would be a terrible shame to have come all this way, and not be able to pass through this wall of fire. I shall hold out for hope that Lindras shall find a way," said Ewen as he sat down next to Markus.

Lindras slowly raised his head. His blue-gray eyes sparkled as they peered out from beneath the great hood as he turned to look at the boy. "What did you just say?"

"I had said it was a pity to have come this great distance; I just hoped that—" The Wizard cut Ewen's sentence short.

"That is it, my boy!" said Lindras with great excitement. "Hope! That is the key to gain entry: Reverence for the past; duty to the present; hope for the future!"

"What keys though, Lindras? We have no keys!" stated Markus, confused by the Wizard's revelation.

"One thousand years ago, when the Stone of Salvation was first delivered to the Three Sisters, we were posed with this same puzzle. I was the key to the past. Arerys' father, Kal-lel, was the key to the present, for it was he who united the Alliance and struggled day after day to preserve Imago. It was King Brannon who carried the hope for the future," said Lindras.

"Kal-lel is not here! King Brannon died shortly after Imago entered the Second Age of Peace!" responded Markus, still troubled by Lindras' answer.

"No, it is not who they were, but what they represented. Think Markus! All eyes have turned to you. Your duty is to keep the Order united; to carry the burden of weight each day to take us one step closer to Mount Hope," said Lindras, excitement rising in his voice.

"So, if you represent the past, and I represent the present, then who is it that holds the key to the future?" asked the Prince.

Slowly, the men of the Order all turned to Ewen. The boy felt like shrinking into the blackness of the night as hopeful eyes cast their gaze in his direction.

"You are our last hope for the future, Ewen, our destiny is in your young hands," said Lindras as he laid a reassuring hand on the boy's small shoulder.

The significance of his role in this quest was now all too apparent. In the beginning, Ewen thought he was being the good and loyal servant to Prince Markus; that he was merely the bearer of the Stone embarking on some great adventure with the men he most respected and admired. He now realized he also carried the Stone that could tip the scales either way for Beyilzon, or the citizens of Imago.

Ewen's head began to spin. The future of all the good people of Imago, both Elf and man, rested squarely upon his shoulders. He was overwhelmed by the responsibility that came with this knowledge. His body trembled as he began to weep in fear.

"Ewen, do not despair! Though the weight of this burden is great, we are here to help you. We shall lessen your load," said Markus.

As overwhelmed as he was, Ewen drew a long, slow breath, attempting to compose himself. He realized and understood that he had a duty and loyalty to Prince Markus. His father never failed to honor the House of Whycliffe; neither will he. He knew now that he was honor bound to Markus and the Order. There was no turning back. There was no going home.

Together, all three rose to their feet to face the flames that danced and licked high into the ebony sky.

"Have you taken leave of your senses, Markus! This is madness, the mission shall fail before it has barely begun!" cried Faria in anguish, obstructing their path.

Markus gazed into Faria's fearful eyes and tried to reassure him. "Faria, have faith. That is all I can ask of you - just have some faith." He stepped around him as the trio walked on.

Lando, Darius, Arerys and Faria stood back against the ink black sky as Markus, Ewen and Lindras stood before the wall of fire.

"Do not be frightened, Ewen; just believe," whispered Lindras, staring through the flames.

Ewen placed his trust and his hands into theirs. He closed his eyes, held his breath and the three stepped into the inferno. They felt no heat, no searing of skin nor flesh, not even a singed strand of hair as they passed through.

Ewen was in absolute awe! He turned back to see Arerys and the others on the other side of the wall of fire; they were embracing in joy and relief. He smiled back at them. As he turned his eyes forward, the image of the temple and the three figures that were like a blurred mirage through the flames were now clearly visible.

The Three Sisters beckoned the travelers to come forward and enter the temple. Ewen was quite taken by their loveliness. The Watchers were of exquisite beauty. All were tall and slender in stature. All three had long, flaming red hair, deep green eyes and skin as pale and smooth as alabaster. Their flowing, white gowns seemed to sparkle, as if sprinkled by fairy dust.

"Welcome, Lindras, the time has finally come that we would meet again," said Eliya with a bow.

Lindras drew back his hood as he bowed in respect.

Eliya walked over to Ewen and knelt before him, his hands clasped into hers. "So little one, hope for the future lies with you."

She led him into the temple. "I am Eliya, Watcher of the Future," she said as she turned to introduce her siblings. "This is my sister, Elora, Watcher of the Past and this is Enra, Watcher of the Present. Welcome to Mount Isa."

Elora and Enra nodded in greeting to Markus and Ewen.

"You have come for the Stone of Salvation, Prince Markus," said Eliya as she removed the black cloth that concealed the blood-red stone that rested on a large, granite pedestal.

"Yes," answered Markus.

"You chose the bearer of the Stone wisely," she continued.

Ewen smiled inwardly upon hearing this encouraging bit of news.

"Take heed my words of warning, Prince Markus. None other than the innocent who is pure of heart shall safely handle this Stone. Ewen is the only one who shall remain untouched by its powers. Do you understand?" asked Eliya, her eyebrows rose as she searched into his soul through his dark eyes.

"I do," Markus answered as he nodded his head in acknowledgment.

"Ewen, you must place this Stone back into the key that locks Beyilzon into the underworld before the total eclipse of the sun," instructed Elora, the Watcher of the Past.

"But how will I know--"

"When the time comes, Ewen, you will remember what to do," said Elora, interrupting the boy's question.

"I will remember?"

"Yes, Ewen. You will remember."

Her statement baffled him.

The Sisters led Lindras, Markus and Ewen to the three seats they usually occupy. Situated at a large, triangular stone table with a circular impression in the center, the three guests took their places in the chairs. Each sister held out a crystal orb before them.

Elora, Watcher of the Past spoke first. "Although you shall all look upon the same orb, what you shall bear witness to are moments in your own life that have shaped the person you are now. If you are wise, you shall use this time to learn from past mistakes and to draw strength from these moments that have touched your lives."

The Watcher of the Past then placed her orb into the impression on the table. The mist that swirled inside the crystal dissolved to reveal a different story from each of their pasts that flashed before them.

For Lindras, hundreds of images appeared before his eyes representing the thousands of years he has existed. He watched as he parted ways with the Wizards of the North, South and East. He observed as his first meeting and friendship with Kal-lel unfolded. He recalled the encounter with the great Dragon of the Shadow Mountains, the defeat of Beyilzon at the last Great War, and of his frequent and often-solitary wanderings after Imago entered the Second Age of Peace.

The last image to be revealed to him was the arrival of Beyilzon's men at the Temple of the Watchers earlier in the day. Lindras observed with great interest as the soldiers of the Dark Army departed eastward, down Mount Isa, after their failed attempt to enter the gates of fire.

For Markus, his past was marked with passages filled with both happiness and much sorrow. Images of his mother's life and untimely death, his strong bond with his father, his privileged life in Carcross, and his desire to follow in the king's footsteps to be a fair and just ruler played out before him. Scenes of his past adventures traveling the land with Arerys and Darius, and finally, the heartbreaking scenes of the death of his wife and son during childbirth repeated itself in the orb set before him. Silent tears rolled down his face as the images of his departed wife, Elana faded away. Five years had passed since he last looked upon her fragile beauty. He felt as though the loss of his long-time love was now as fresh as the first day of her passing.

For Ewen, his images were fewer but longer. He smiled as he watched with wide-eyed fascination as images of he and his father at play flashed before him. His smile quickly faded as he relived his own grief when he learned of his father's violent and untimely death while assisting the soldiers of Darross to drive back an invasion by the Dark Army; of Prince Markus bringing him into his service so he may live in his care at Whycliffe Castle; his decision to assist the Order, but the last image confused and frightened him the most.

Staring deep into the orb, he saw himself in what appeared to be another time and another place. He was violently cast down to the ground as the sky about him grew dark. A deep and resonating voice repeatedly mocked him.

"Will you die for him?" shouted the voice. "Will you die for him?"

These haunting words echoed in his ears. Ewen looked on in both fear and bewilderment as he watched himself lying on the ground cowering, too scared to move.

This frightening image dissolved to black. Greatly disturbed by these dark scenes that played out before him, he looked up to Elora.

She closed her eyes and spoke to his heart. *Do not be frightened by your past Ewen; learn from it instead.*

His confusion was evident. *How can this be? I do not recall this happening in my life.*

"In time, you shall understand. You will remember," said Elora as she stepped forward to claim her crystal.

Enra held forth her crystal orb. "What you shall see now is the present as it unfolds. Because your lives are now entwined, what you shall
bear witness to, shall be shared."

Markus and Ewen were surprised for what was revealed was not so
much images, but rather what was felt and thought by those around them.
On the other side of the wall of fire sat the men of the Order. Now within this orb, their hearts were laid bare for Lindras, Markus and Ewen to
see.

It saddened Markus to discover that his lifelong friend, Arerys
Wingfield, loyal and true to those in the Order was contemplating a different existence. His desire was to leave this earthly realm to make a journey to the Twilight; if he were to survive the perils of this quest. He no
longer felt fulfilled; his long existence left him feeling empty. He resolved
that this would be the last adventure he would share with Markus in
Imago.

The image of Arerys faded, to be replaced with that of the protector
of Carcross: the charming and high-spirited Darius Calsair. Without a
doubt, he was a true knight, through and through. Loyal, brave and willing to lay his life down for King Bromwell and his country without hesitation and yet, none were surprised to find that his thoughts strayed to the
beautiful Elf maidens of Wyndwood.

The image dissolved again to reveal another: Lando Bayliss, the protector of the House of Calaware. A man of great faith, honesty and integrity; Lando was deep in prayer. His thoughts were with Lindras, Markus
and Ewen, praying for their success in securing the Stone of Salvation. He
hoped for the powers that be, to come to their aid; to bring a swift and
successful end to the quest so he may return home to his beloved Cedona.

The crystal orb faded to black, only to reveal another image, this time
of Faria Targott. It became quickly obvious to all present that doubt and
worry overshadowed Faria's troubled heart and plagued his worried mind.

*How can we entrust a boy to do a man's job? We are doomed to fail.
There must be another way.* He wrung his hands in woe, pondering the
likelihood of whether the quest would end with a happy outcome.

Lindras and Markus were equally troubled by the revelation of Faria's
dark thoughts,

Enra cautioned, "Trust your feelings. Do not be deceived by the one
who may feel compelled to take whatever actions he believes shall justi-

fy the ends. He is driven by his own doubts and fears."

As they continued to look on, they watched as Beyilzon's soldiers congregated in growing numbers in the Shadow Mountains. The soldiers and knights of Darross, with the assistance of those in the Alliance, had always succeeded in destroying small incursions as the Dark Army periodically breached the Aranak Mountains. The enemy was always driven back into Talibarr. Now, they witnessed the random acts of violence the Dark Army dispensed as they roamed the land and even now, soldiers anticipating the Order's arrival at the temple, were waiting in ambush to claim the coveted Stone of Salvation.

These troubling images swirled like a whirlpool into an abyss of darkness. Enra collected her orb, stepping aside for Eliya.

The Watcher of the Future placed her orb into the table's impression. In the stark blackness of the crystal, images came to surface that were terrifyingly real. Before their eyes, one scene quickly dissolved into the next: villages in ruin; a darkened castle devoid of life; the alignment of the stars, and the red moon that is to herald the release of Beyilzon from the underworld.

The trio looked on as horrible scenes of Elves and men, slaughtered in an all out war on the Plains of Fire played out before them. In the midst of these terrifying images rode forth four dark harbingers of evil on great, black steeds. They were carried on a wake of death and destruction as they scoured the countryside in pursuit of the Order. These images began to darken as the eclipse of the sun plunged all of Imago into blackness.

Lindras and Markus were greatly disturbed and moved by these powerful images. Ewen could not hide the fear in his eyes. The muscles of his neck tightened as he involuntarily swallowed the lump caught in his dry throat.

Markus drew a deep breath as he searched Eliya's lucid, green eyes for answers. "Do we have any hope?"

She smiled at him and answered in a gentle voice. "Prince Markus, from the beginning of time, both mankind and Elves have been blessed with what you call *hope*. There is always hope. When all else fails, it is hope that allows you to continue on. It is when you lose hope that all will be lost and the quest is doomed to fail."

"But how best to defeat Beyilzon and his men?"

"It shall take all of your strength and your unwavering belief that it can be done. It will also require Ewen's compassion and unselfish courage to help you see this quest to its end," answered Eliya.

"Surely you can advise me on strategy as you know the outcome?" asked Markus, again looking for more decisive answers.

"Man's future is not predestined by myself or even by the Maker of All. Ultimately, you shall steer the course of the future, whether it shall lead to success or ruin. I cannot advise you on the course of action to pursue, but I will tell you this: In your darkest hour a most unlikely ally shall come to your aid. Though your men may resist the help, do not be deceived by appearances, for even the smallest ember can still burn and ignite intoa massive inferno."

"It is good to know we may have an ally in all of this," smiled Lindras.

"Yes, it is Wizard, but will the Order recognize this when the time comes?"

"But what about me? How can I help Prince Markus fight such a formidable enemy?" lamented Ewen. "I am merely a boy, I am not even skilled in the ways of the warrior. How can I be of any good to Prince Markus and the Order?"

"Oh, little one, do not despair. It is not the power of your strength that Prince Markus shall call upon. It shall be the strength of your heart that shall see you through," said Eliya. Her hand gently raised Ewen's chin so she may look into his eyes to allay his fears.

Eliya looked at Lindras and decided to share this with him: "As you leave the Valley of Shadows, the Order may encounter a menace like no other. He is a manifestation of your own powers, Wizard. Do not call upon the Keeper of the Gate unless you can control him. He will confront all who dare to trespass onto Mount Hope. You stand to jeopardize the quest if your powers cannot contain him. Remember Lindras, this is one adversary that cannot be brought down by the hands of man."

Lindras nodded as he stroked his long beard. He carefully contemplated this bit of information disclosed by the Watcher.

Eliya then turned to Markus and warned him: "Beware of Beyilzon's agents. Four of his dark emissaries scour the land in search of the Stone of Salvation. Neither dead nor alive, they are caught in a shadow world created by Beyilzon; they are forced to do his bidding. Battle them if you must, but only a fatal pierce through the heart shall release them from the

Dark Lord's hold."

Markus shook his head in despair as the warnings and foreshadowing images that played out in the orb filled his mind with great turmoil and worry. He knew the difficulties and perils that lay ahead for the Order were going to be great, but were they insurmountable?

"Tell me, my lady, are these the shadows of things that shall come to pass?"

"The future is not engraved in stone. Even a single grain of sand may tip the scales to set into motion a great many changes. The shadows you see are merely the shadows of what shall be, if you fail to defeat Beyilzon," stated Eliya.

"Then we have no choice," said Markus, with determined resolve as he rose from the table. "We shall defeat the Dark Lord."

The Three Sisters nodded in approval to Markus. Eliya turned to the pedestal, taking the brilliant gem into her right hand. Kneeling before Ewen, she presented him with the Stone of Salvation.

Ewen studied the many facets of this oval, blood-red jewel that fit so neatly into the palm of his hand. *How can such a small thing wield so much power?* Ewen wondered as he held the Stone up for Lindras and Markus to admire.

Reading his thoughts, Eliya's answer touched Ewen's heart. *You shall soon learn that you cannot measure power by size alone, Ewen. Just as there are people much larger than you, who do not possess your inner strength and will, there are also those who may be small in stature, but have the power to control great armies. What they may lack in size, they make up for in skill and knowledge. Do not be fooled by what you see, instead, search the heart for what your eyes will not reveal to you.*

Eliya carefully placed the Stone into a black velvet pouch with a long, golden drawstring. Pulling the pouch closed, she hung it about Ewen's neck.

"We shall watch over you, little one," she said, gently planting a kiss upon his forehead.

With those words, the wall of fire vanished as suddenly as it had appeared. Markus, Lindras and Ewen were now free to continue their journey. They bowed to the Three Sisters before turning to regroup with the other members of the Order.

As Ewen turned to wave a final farewell to the Sisters, Eliya, Enra and Elora were already seated at their table. Elora recording the events that had just transpired, Enra gazing into her crystal orb to observe what treacheries Beyilzon's men were now scheming, while Eliya watched the night sky for celestial signs that would herald the release of Beyilzon from his prison.

CHAPTER 4

EAST OF LAND'S END

"We cannot return the way we have come. Even now Beyilzon's men await in ambush," advised Lindras to the men of the Order, as he contemplated their next move. "The soldiers have doubled back, passing us on the other trail."

"Your senses serve you well, Arerys. You were correct when you said something evil was near," added Markus. "It was revealed to us by the Watchers that Beyilzon's men did indeed reach the temple before we did, but they failed to secure the Stone. They are aware of our quest now and mean to steal away with the Stone of Salvation for their own evil doings."

Lindras thought for a moment. "Markus, Enra revealed that Beyilzon's men returned by way they came. They believe we too shall return in the same manner. Because the two paths do not cross and the mountain is impossible to traverse, they shall be awaiting to ambush us where the paths converge."

"Yes, they will either ambush us at this junction or at the base of the mountain," agreed Markus.

"It stands to reason they believe we shall head eastward, directly across through Darross and the Aranak Mountains to reach Mount Hope," said Arerys.

"Well, shall we allow Beyilzon's *welcoming* party to wait a while longer?" asked Lindras, with a look of mischief. "It shall take them half a day to reach the junction, and another half day to reach the base of Mount Isa."

"You are not suggesting that we eventually engage in battle with them?" asked Faria, with growing concern. "We do not even know their numbers. We may be overwhelmed!"

"If the fates conspire and luck is with us, they shall head directly to the base of the mountain to await our arrival," said the Wizard. "Now, if we head westward through Cedona, we can travel onward through the mountain gap between the Cathedral and Aranak Mountain Range. By the time Beyilzon's men realize that we have taken a detour using the western passage, we shall be a good two to three days in the lead!"

"So be it!" announced Markus. "Mount your horses, gentlemen! Let us make haste."

The western slopes of the Cathedral Mountains were more forgiving, its jagged edges worn down by a millennium of westerly winds and driving, winter rains. These gentler slopes gave way to trails that easily traversed the face of the mountain.

Vegetation was sparse at the higher elevations, but where life precariously hung to areas where soil managed to collect in between cracks in the rocks and boulders, tiny, heather-like alpine flowers with compact stems and leaves were beginning to bloom. Even where snow still lay, tiny magenta blossoms bravely pushed through the insulating blanket of white to take in the weak morning sun.

Pine trees, stunted and twisted from the constant exposure to the cruel winter winds, grew sparsely on this face of the mountain. For Ewen, it was a most reassuring sign that even under the most adverse conditions, life was still able to take hold.

The descent from Mount Isa took less than eight hours. For most part, the journey from the Temple of the Watchers was completed on horseback. It was approaching noon when the Order reached the forests hugging the base of the mountain.

"We shall wait until nightfall before we move on," said Markus as he dismounted from his steed.

As the horses rested and grazed, the men of the Order shared a meal as they listened to Lindras and Ewen tell of their meeting with the Watchers. They listened intently; obviously fascinated by the beauty and power bestowed upon the Three Sisters. As Ewen proceeded to tell the men about Enra's revelations of the present, Markus suddenly interrupted him. Grabbing Ewen by his arm, he abruptly led him away from the group.

"Ewen, there are some things better left unsaid," whispered Markus. "The Order must remain strong. If you divulge the fact that Faria may somehow falter, it may lead to the collapse of the entire Order. The difficulties that lie ahead for us shall be great; we cannot function if there is turmoil within. Do you understand?"

Ewen meekly nodded his head. Markus released his hold on the boy's arm. He turned to join the others, leaving Markus alone to ponder this dilemma.

Lindras stood next to the prince. Between contemplative puffs on his long pipe, he asked, "You are starting to have doubts about Faria, are you not?"

Markus nodded his head in response, watching Faria from where he stood.

"Remember, Markus, we are all here because we each have a role to play," warned the Wizard. "Do not let your thoughts be plagued by what Faria may, or may not, do. Whatever action he takes, there shall be a reason for it."

As the afternoon sun rose high into the sky, Arerys and Lindras took first watch. The men were all exhausted after their long night's journey into day. Sleep came quickly and soundly for most, but for Markus, he was deeply disturbed by Faria's thoughts. In his dream, he watched as a desperate man resorted to desperate measures, turning on Ewen and the other members of the Order.

Ewen too, was haunted by his own dream that quickly fell into a nightmare. He watched as soldiers from the Dark Army threw him to the ground. All around him, the sky grew black as he cowered on the ground. A deep, resonating voice asked, "Will you die for him?"

Ewen looked on as he watched himself scramble to his feet to run, only to be knocked down to the ground once more.

Again the voice asked, "Will you die for him?"

Looking on in horror, he saw tears staining his dirty face as he cowered, shaking his head in response.

Suddenly, soldiers converged around him. He watched helplessly as they made off with him into the darkness. Terrified, Ewen bolted up from his sleep. Sweat poured from his brows, his body trembled in fear.

Arerys came to his side, "What is wrong, Ewen? Did you have a bad dream?"

"I am scared, Arerys. I am frightened of what may happen," whispered Ewen.

"We are all scared," said Arerys as he laid Ewen back down. "Close your eyes and dream of home, Ewen. Dream that we are going home," said the Elf in a calming voice as he passed his hand lightly over Ewen's face.

Ewen's eyes closed and he soon fell back into a deep, quiet sleep, undisturbed by any further nightmares.

Daylight passed quickly; too quickly as the men struggled to rouse themselves to their feet. Even Arerys struggled with little more than two hours rest.

After a quick meal, the Order was ready to head westward. They were now forced to round the monolithic structures that made the Cathedral Mountains impassable at this point to access the Gap into Darross.

They were now in Lando's territory: Cedona. As the landscape rushed past them in the darkness, Lando escorted them through the forest and into a valley. They were taking the less traveled route to guide them around the great monoliths that loomed like silent, stone giants.

These massive structures were once believed to be the colossal beings that built the mountain systems throughout Imago.

Legend tells of how, long before man and even the Elves came to being in this country, these giants fought to control the lands. The Shadow Mountains to the far north, the Iron Mountains to the east, the Aranak Mountains that separated the regions now known as Talibarr and Darross, and the Cathedral Mountains to the west, rose from the depth of the earth because of these great beings.

These giants forcibly rammed massive sheets of earth, rocks and boulders against each other to give rise to these great landforms. Used to define their territories, the mountain ranges stood as visible barriers. Still dissatisfied with the division of land, their rivalries and disputes ensued, erupting into numerous devastating earthquakes that rocked Imago.

In disappointment and anger, the Maker of All reclaimed the lands he have given to them, and as punishment, condemned the giants to a life frozen as inanimate stone monoliths. They were made to endure the ravages of time and the elements; forced to watch while others stepped into their place to occupy the lands they had fought over in vain.

As the Order emerged from the northern border of the Cathedral Forest, before them was the County of Wren. Its lush pastures and fertile farmlands sprawled all the way to Land's End. Perched on the highest ground on this outcrop of land jutting into the sea, was King Augustyn's castle. All could see the white spires of his great watchtowers, banners flying high and proud in the morning sky as the sun peeked over the Cathedral Mountains to herald a new day on this magnificent, seaside kingdom.

"There, in the distance, Ewen; that is Land's End. That is my home," said Lando as he pointed towards the great white castle that seemed to shining like a pearl against the backdrop of an indigo blue sea. "It is a pity you shall not see King Augustyn's great castle during this trip. Perhaps another time though. For now, we shall spend the day here and proceed again at nightfall."

As they dismounted and prepared for another long wait, Arerys heard something far off in the distance approaching from the east. He strained to discern the exact direction and identity of the sound. He motioned the others for quiet as he listened.

"Someone approaches," he said, straining now to see the movement through the forest. "Over there!" he pointed, "There are four dark riders on black steeds. They are moving fast in our direction!"

"Lando! To the castle now!" ordered Markus, leaping back into his saddle.

"Who are they?" asked Arerys, concerned by the urgency in Markus' voice.

"They are the dark emissaries, sent forth by Beyilzon to search us out. We must leave now!"

Lando led the charge through the fields and farmlands. As he rode, he sounded his horn. After a long minute, within the walls of the castle, came the resonating sound of distant horns, trumpeting in answer to his call. Help was imminent.

As the horses raced onward, Markus glanced back. The four dark horsemen were closing the gap quickly, their swords drawn and held high as they rode. They emitted an ear-piercing shriek as Lando sounded his horn again.

"Markus! Take the boy!" shouted Arerys.

RainDance's strides brought her next to Arrow. As the two horses galloped in time, Markus reached across for Ewen, hoisting the frightened boy onto his dark steed. Arerys wheeled his horse about to face the fast approaching figures cloaked in black.

RainDance reared up on her hind legs. Without hesitation, she fear-

lessly charged straight towards them. As they approached within Arerys'
striking distance, the Elf dropped his reins, drew his bow and launched an
arrow. The arrow traveled on a straight course, striking one of the horsemen, piercing him through the heart.

The impact caused this dark harbinger of evil to tumble backwards
off his horse. Falling to the ground with a loud shriek, his body abruptly
disintegrated into a swirling heap of black ashes.

The three remaining riders continued straight on towards the Elf,
undaunted and unmoved by their fallen comrade.

Arerys picked up his reins, directing his gray steed to veer around in
a large circle. She galloped past the dark horsemen in a large arc that
brought them about to face their adversaries once again.

This time, RainDance stopped and stood her ground. Arerys quickly
strung the nocks of two arrows onto his bow, prepared to dispatch two
horsemen simultaneously. He leveled his bow horizontally, lining up his
sight at the incoming dark forms.

The dark horsemen came to an abrupt halt. They reeled their horses
about, and in a full gallop, retreating eastward.

Arerys turned to see what would cause this sudden withdrawal. Far
ahead, the members of the Order were charging towards the castle.
Heading in their direction, a swarm of armor-clad men riding on horseback, poured forth from the gates of the castle in answer to Lando's call.
It was a sight to behold. Arerys smiled, turning RainDance to join the
others.

Within the safety of the castle walls, the Order met with King
Augustyn. In a great room, ensconced in rich paintings and beautifully
woven tapestries, the king and his advisors received their unexpected
guests. Lando entered the room first, as the others followed behind him.
He dropped to his left knee, bowing before his king.

"The day begins with much excitement, Lando," said Augustyn,
motioning for his knight to rise before him. "What ill tide was lapping at
your heels this morn?"

"They were the agents of Beyilzon, my lord. They know of our mission."

"So you have the Stone then?" asked Augustyn, rising from his
throne.

"Yes, my liege," Lando answered. He turned to Ewen, motioning the boy to approach.

Ewen came to the knight's side, pulling the small black pouch out from under his shirt. He held it out for Augustyn to see.

"My eyes wish to behold the beauty of this precious Stone," said Augustyn to the boy.

Ewen glanced over at Markus, unsure of what to do. Markus nodded in approval. Approaching the throne, he carefully removed the Stone from within its pouch. Placing it in the palm of his hand, the boy held it forth for the king to see.

"It is beautiful! I wish to take a closer look," he said as he reached out to touch the dazzling, red gem.

"No, you may not!" said Ewen. He quickly withdrew his hand, but was too late. Augustyn's fingers barely touched the Stone, yet he let out a painful wail.

The surrounding air was filled with the acrid smell of seared flesh, a wisp of white smoke escaped from Augustyn's fingertips at the intensity of the burn.

"That cursed thing!" he swore, dousing his fingers into a bowl of water that was rushed to his side.

"I am sorry, sire, but none shall handle this Stone but I," apologized Ewen as he quickly concealed the gem back into its pouch for safekeeping.

"That thing is not meant to be around man," muttered Augustyn, nursing his wounded fingers. "Evil follows; the sooner it is out of Cedona, the better."

Markus stepped forward to King Augustyn's throne. "Sire, I ask that we may seek sanctuary within your castle walls. It was not my intention to lead the Dark Army to your doors but undoubtedly, Beyilzon's spies shall be watching for our departure so we are better to wait until night fall."

"Of course, Prince Markus," answered Augustyn. "I have my suspicions the dark horsemen have gone to muster Beyilzon's army to mount an attack on Land's End. Whether you stay for the day or for the night, it makes no difference. They shall come when they come."

"If they are intent on claiming the Stone of Salvation, then I have no doubt they shall follow us to the ends of the earth to do so," assumed

Lindras, bowing to the king as he approached Augustyn's throne.

"Well, Lando, you command my armies; what plan of attack would you recommend in the event the dark hordes appear at our gates?" asked Augustyn, still favoring his injured fingers.

"I am confident Beyilzon's army will arrive. It shall only be a question of how many and when. Are all your soldiers within Cedona, my king?

"I have sent two battalions to aid King Sebastian in Darross, I do not have a full contingent as we speak."

"Very well, we shall make do."

Lando turned his attention to a massive table in the middle of the room that was buried beneath numerous maps. Quickly, he glanced at the various scrolls of parchment until he found what he was looking for. Waving for all to join him at the table, he laid the map out flat.

"First, we shall send out scouts with birds. We shall station them here, here and over here," said Lando, pointing to several strategic locations on the eastern outskirts of the County of Wren and into the Cathedral Forest. "They shall warn us of the Dark Army's approach."

Augustyn turned away from the table to instruct one of the battalion leaders to make it so. With a hasty bow, the leader exited the room to prepare scouts, horses and falcons for this mission, to depart the castle immediately.

"As soon as we receive word, we shall deploy one battalion to lie in wait here, at Orem," continued Lando. He pointed at a spot just northeast of Land's End. "When the army's advance becomes visible from our watchtowers, we shall send forth seven riders dressed in gray to ride directly to Orem."

"Imposters?" asked Ewen, intrigued by Lando's strategy.

"Decoys," answered Lando. "As soon as our decoys have been dispatched and the Dark Army moves to intercept them, we shall deploy the second battalion. Between pursuing the decoys, and being pursued by our men, it will not be difficult to funnel them into the steep pass that leads into the County of Orem."

"So you plan to trap and ambush Beyilzon's men?" asked Faria.

"They will not even know what hit them," assured Lando.

"And what of us? How do we leave without being noticed?" asked Darius.

"We shall take the underground tunnel beneath the castle. It leads directly outside the castle walls onto the shores of Land's End. If we are forced to leave by day, we must do so when the Dark Army is almost upon the castle walls. When the decoys are on the move, then we too, shall depart. We shall follow the beach northward, and then take these trails cut into the cliff walls along here," said Lando as he traced the route with his finger.

"We shall emerge just beyond Orem, and then we shall cut a path straight through to the Gap," he continued, his finger now traveling east of Land's End.

Lando turned to Markus. "I ask to have time to meet with my men to prepare them for battle, Markus. We shall leave tomorrow at nightfall, if not sooner, if you will permit this."

"Very well," answered Markus, glancing over at Ewen. "One night in a safe haven can only do us some good."

As King Augustyn's guests were escorted to their quarters for some much needed rest, Lando met with the battalion leaders to review his strategy. This is the part of the battle he enjoyed the most, planning the strategy to secure the upper hand in order to win. Lando would have to rely on his men to be ready to move, executing this plan with precision, even in his absence. Although, he felt strongly compelled to stay and lead them into battle, he knew it was not possible; not this time. Nevertheless, Lando had great faith in his army; after all he did train them.

After the Order had regrouped for an evening meal, Lando showed Ewen up to one of the castle's great watchtowers. From this vantage point, they could see far to the east towards the Cathedral Mountains and westward to the horizon where the sky touched the deep blue sea.

Ewen marveled at the view. "Lando, I have never dreamed I would see the lands of Cedona, let alone this huge body of water!"

They watched the sun slowly sink into the sleepy, blue sea, turning the horizon into a dazzling color of crimson against the mauve evening sky. Lando turned to the boy as he cupped a hand to his ear. "Listen, Ewen. You can hear the sun sizzle as it touches the water!"

Ewen watched him for a moment. Lando's dark wavy hair was blowing in the evening breeze; a broad smile emerged from behind his dark beard that was peppered with gray whiskers.

Cupping his hand to his ear, Ewen strained to hear this sound.

"Lando, I hear nothing!" said Ewen after a while, disappointment in his voice.

Lando laughed. His large, calloused hand playfully tossed Ewen's mop of curly brown hair. He turned to the boy and confessed: "Ewen, this is the fairest land in all of Imago. I am truly blessed to serve on this Order for it is my duty to protect this beautiful country I hold so dear to my heart. I have all the faith in the world that we shall succeed."

Ewen admired Lando's determination and his unwavering faith that this deed was far from impossible. Looking east towards the dark silhouette of the Cathedral Mountain Range, he realized just how far from home he had traveled. At that moment, Ewen took instant comfort in knowing he was indeed, in the company of some of Imago's finest warriors.

As the sky became as dark as the sea, there was still no word from the sentries posted along the outskirts of Wren. The Order decided to rest as much as they could, but they would be dressed, their provisions and horses readied so they may leave immediately, if need be.

With soldiers stationed high along the battlement, the perimeter of the castle was secured. Within these walls, the members of the Order slept soundly in the safety of the great white castle. The night passed without incident and in the morning, the Order gathered to break fast in the company of King Augustyn.

For Ewen, it was wonderful luxury to have slept in the comfort of a soft bed. Now, to enjoy a meal at a table seated upon a chair rather than on a cold, hard rock; this indeed was a treat!

"Men, we shall leave by nightfall," announced Markus. "Whether the Dark Army arrives tomorrow or in a week's time, we cannot wait. Time is of the essence. We have much farther to go now."

The men were all in agreement. All there was left to do was to wait until darkness embraced the land. Just as they rose from the table, the trumpeting of a horn echoed from one of the towers. Soon after, a squire ran to the side of King Augustyn, whispering into his ear. The King nodded in understanding.

"We have received word; a falcon has returned with a message," announced the king. "Beyilzon's soldiers are on the move; they are heading to Land's End."

"Sound the alarm!" ordered Lando to the squire, "I shall meet with the battalion leaders now; we shall move swiftly!"

Guards stationed in the watchtower were now on high alert. The Order glanced out from the balcony overlooking the center courtyard, below they saw row upon row of soldiers in gleaming armor. They stood at attention in the morning sun, patiently awaiting Lando's instructions.

As Lando gave his final orders, the first battalion armed with spears and bows marched out, heading straight for the pass leading into the County of Orem.

The second battalion waited for their orders to move. As they waited, seven soldiers disguised in gray cloaks, riding horses of roughly the same size and color of those ridden by the Order were readied. They waited at the main gate of the castle for their instructions to move out.

Almost two hours had passed since the first horn sounded from the watchtower. The enemy was now within sight.

As he stood high atop the castle battlement, watching the Dark Army surge forward, Lando motioned for the gates to be opened. He ordered the decoys to move out with the greatest possible speed. On his mark, the seven riders exited from the gate, their horses galloping northward, carrying them away from the castle.

Lando continued to observe. Beyilzon's men were indeed after the Order. He watched as the entire army quickly shifted direction to pursue the decoys. He patiently waited and watched as the army advanced northward, completely bypassing the castle in full pursuit of the seven horsemen. Waiting until he was certain that the entire Army was moving towards the pass, Lando motioned for the gates to be opened as the second battalion converged behind them.

They shall be in for a surprise, Lando thought, smiling inwardly as he raced down the stairs to the courtyard.

King Augustyn wished the men of the Order good luck and a safe journey. Before turning away to prepare to join his soldiers in battle, he said to Lando: "I have already dispatched three of my most trusted men on the speediest mounts to send word to Wyndwood and on to Carcross to alert King Kal-lel and King Bromwell of your progress. They shall be informed that the mission is still alive. There is still hope."

He and Lando grasped each other's wrist in a final farewell. "Lando, you are wise in the ways of war, I know you shall deliver them safely to Mount Hope."

Lando bowed in understanding. "Stay safe, sire, Cedona needs her

King."

"Let us move," shouted Lando as he mounted his steed, waving the others on to follow.

The men's horses all galloped after Lando's stallion, through a great vault in the ground. The massive stone slab that was usually kept it sealed was already rolled to one side on a series of logs. Lando's steed, already familiar with this passage, galloped confidently through the descending walkway as he guided the others out. With the logs squealing in protest under the weight of the great stone, the tunnel jarred with a loud, resonating *'boom'* as the vault was resealed. The large passageway quickly grew dark as the soldiers left to defend the castle secured the stone slab back into place.

Arerys' eyes quickly adjusted to the dim-lit tunnel. Daylight shone brightly just a short distance away; they could hear the sound of the sea lapping against the cliff.

As they exited out of the tunnel that had been carved into the land, they were met with the cold, salty splash of a wave. The tide had not yet fully receded. The horses stood knee-deep in the foaming, churning sea water.

Lando urged his steed on, hugging the steep walls towering above them as he led the others northward around the tall, white cliffs of Land's End, to those skirting Orem.

The quickly retreating tide exposed a white, hard-packed sandy beach that made the run for the horses very easy and fast. The breaking of the waves crashing onto the shore made it impossible for all, even Arerys, to hear the sounds of war. Lando's men were now fully engaged in a battle on the land above.

As the seven horsemen left the safety of the castle, they set a straight course to the pass that would lead them directly into the County of Orem. Their horses galloped at top speed through the fields all the while, knowing that surging behind them, like a horrible black swarm was the Dark Army, some on horses, but most on foot. The soldiers on horseback quickly passed the infantry, racing towards the narrow pass in eager pursuit.

The gray-clad decoys swiftly galloped into the pass and were quickly swallowed up in the chasm. Following the only road descending into this narrow gap, they rode hard, charging straight through into a large field that opened into the County. As they turned their horses about in the field to face the oncoming evil, all seven riders armed their bows and waited.

The dark soldiers on horseback followed the seven decoys through the pass. As they emerged onto the open field, they were met with an immediate and deadly hail of swift-flying arrows. Directly behind them, the foot soldiers were streaming into the pass with Lando's men pressing in from behind. They sealed the soldiers of the Dark Army into the gap so they had nowhere to escape.

There was a moment of eerie silence. A terrible sense of foreboding filled the soldiers that were packed into the pass. As they gazed up to survey their surroundings, Lando's men suddenly appeared from the many caves and ledges lining the steep walls. The soldiers of the Dark Army were met with an immediate hail of arrows and spears cascading down upon them like a shower of death.

The remaining soldiers that had not yet made it into the pass turned to escape the fate that met their comrades. As they fled in panic, the swords and halberds of Lando's second battalion overwhelmed them.

Just as Lando had predicted to the king, the battle would be short-lived. The soldiers of Cedona would experience a minimum of injuries and/or casualties.

From atop a hill overlooking the land, the three dark horsemen watched the slaughter of Beyilzon's army. They shrieked in disgust as they turned their horses eastward.

CHAPTER 5

THE FALL OF DARROSS

Lando escorted the Order from the white sea cliffs to the high grounds, just north of the County of Orem. His pleasure was unmistakable as he smiled at the others when he heard the distant trumpeting of the familiar horns at Land's End, announcing the defeat of the Dark Army.

For Lando, the sweet taste of victory was short-lived, his thoughts quickly returned to the quest. Now, the Order must journey from the extreme west of Imago to its farthest corner in the east, bordered by the Iron Mountains.

"We must find shelter until nightfall, Lando," said Markus. "It is much too dangerous to move by day, especially since Beyilzon's agents know we have the Stone. They are aware of our general proximity now."

"Yes, Lando," agreed Lindras. "Nightfall is at least another seven hours away. Let us use this time to rest and think of our next course of action."

"Very well," replied Lando as he steered his stallion into the dark forests of Fimbul. "Under the cover of darkness, we shall travel southward, and then east through Ravensthorpe. Until then, we shall pass the hours in the forest."

Thick with great spruces and towering fir trees, this ancient, coniferous forest was indeed dark. Even by the light of day, these tall trees cast deep shadows that seemed to shroud the ground and everything around them in a permanent, unnatural darkness.

As they rode, Arerys constantly surveyed their surroundings and listened for sounds that may alert him to impending danger.

Lando dismounted by a small clearing to allow his horse to drink from the stream. He glanced about, deciding that this would be a suitable place to bide their time until nightfall.

As Ewen organized their food and replenished the water flasks, he looked up at the remains of a large fir tree that had been leveled by a bolt of lightening. Balanced on what was left of this large moss and lichen-covered stump was the Elf. Ewen observed Arerys, bow always at the ready as he kept watch over them.

Ewen carried the flasks back to the others who were just finishing their meals. Lindras was discussing their next possible route and it was becoming obvious to the boy there was growing discord amongst the men of the Order.

"There are two possible options," said the Wizard. "We can travel directly eastward and enter Darross via the Gap, where the Aranak and the Cathedral Mountain Ranges converge, or we may head north, then eastward along the Aranaks straight through Talibarr."

"If we bypass the Gap and cut through Talibarr, we shall make better time," recommended Markus.

"But if we travel through Darross, King Sebastian shall guarantee us safe passage, especially now since his soldiers have combined forces with King Augustyn's men," suggested Faria.

"Then we might as well march on to Mount Hope with a full army!" argued Lando. "Beyilzon will divert all his men for a confrontation to bring this quest to a quick end!"

"If we travel through enemy land, we shall court certain disaster," countered Faria. "We shall be right under their noses! Why not just offer the Stone to Beyilzon on a platter, if that be the case?"

"But if Beyilzon's men have already been deployed from Talibarr and they march through Darross as you had claimed before Faria, does it not stand to reason there shall be fewer eyes searching for us in Talibarr than in Darross?" replied Darius.

"Faria, sometimes the best way to go undetected is to be brazen and indeed, pass right under the enemies' noses, as you put it. Sometimes an object held directly in front of one's face is so close, the eyes do not even focus on it. It is an illusion, the mind playing a trick on the eyes. I believe it is safe to assume their eyes shall be cast far ahead, watching for what may skulk by in the distance," said Lindras.

"Seven on horseback, traveling through enemy country, can hardly pass as an illusion, Wizard," snapped Faria.

"Faria, Lindras may be onto something. Beyilzon's men shall be occupied in battles throughout Darross; there will be a greater number of soldiers in Darross than in Talibarr. Would you not all agree the normal course of action is to flee from the enemy when one is outnumbered, than to run directly towards the danger?" asked Markus, as he considered their options.

"I think we can at least agree that Beyilzon's agents shall be scouring the countryside of Darross. They probably perceive us as cowards; not willing to undertake such a dangerous risk by detouring through Beyilzon's former stronghold," added Lando.

"You demonstrate a reckless regard for our lives and safety. This is suicide!" Faria stated, frustration and anger rising in his voice. "If we are able to travel through Darross, at least we may be able to seek sanctuary at King Sebastian's castle. We can replace our horses for some fresh steeds for the remainder of the journey."

As Ewen listened to the men, his heart began to sink. He could see the anger flash in their eyes and felt the harshness of their voices as each stated their case. Reaching under his shirt, he pulled out the pouch containing the Stone, staring at it for a moment.

Finally, Ewen stood up before the men of the Order. "How do you expect me to carry the burden of delivering this Stone when you cannot even agree on how to get me there?" He held the black velvet pouch before his companions, his hand trembling in anxiety.

Arerys, hearing their argument from his post, leapt down and ran to Ewen's side. "The boy is quite right, we are bound by duty. We have sworn to be united on this quest. We must remain so if we wish to see this done. Already Beyilzon's dark thoughts have clouded your minds and your souls. Do you not see this is exactly what he strives for? He works to divide and conquer the Order even from the underworld."

The men grew silent upon Arerys' words. They knew he was right. The men sat back in regret as they watched the mounting fear grow in Ewen's dark, troubled eyes.

"Arerys is right. We must remain strong. We must stand united as one," said Markus as he rose to his feet. He walked towards Ewen, taking the pouch from his extended hand. He placed it back around the boy's neck.

"I am truly sorry, Ewen. This is a terrible burden we must all share, but I swear, I shall stand by you," said Markus. "I shall see you delivered to Mount Hope with the Stone, no matter the cost, even if it be by my own life."

Markus embraced the boy. He could feel his heart pounding; Ewen was genuinely frightened. This was definitely not the great adventure he had thought it would be, instead it was now a mission that was a matter of life or death. *The lives of many shall now depend on the actions of few.*

"Fear not Ewen, we shall discuss this no further. When we reach the Gap, we shall decide on our course of direction after we assess the gravity of the situation in Darross," promised Lindras, as he offered a comforting pat on the boy's small shoulder. "We shall let fate guide us."

Lando and Darius took over sentry duty, allowing Arerys an opportunity to eat and rest for a while. As the Elf lay down to sleep, he looked over to Ewen who sat on the ground against a moss-covered stump, his right hand resting on his chest over the Stone. It saddened Arerys' heart to no end to see Ewen struggling with the monumental weight of his responsibility.

"Ewen, try to get some rest while you can. Darkness shall fall sooner than you think."

Ewen's sad, brown eyes peered up at the Elf. "I wish I could Arerys, but now I am even too afraid to sleep lest my dreams catch up with me; to torment me all the more."

Night fell rapidly on the forest of Fimbul and the depth of the blackness was unsettling for all, even for Arerys and Lindras.

Lando guided them through the forest and they soon emerged from the stands of great coniferous trees to look down upon a valley. Below, the soft glow from the lanterns of the cottages in the village seemed to beckon them.

"There lies the village of Ravensthorpe. Beyond to the east is the Gap that shall lead to Darross, or the pass that shall take us into Talibarr," said Lando, pointing to the distant silhouette of the Aranak and Cathedral Mountains against the ever-darkening horizon.

The Order deliberately skirted the village. Other than the few dogs that would bark their protest of their presence as they trespassed through the farmlands, the group passed through Ravensthorpe unnoticed.

Riding on RainDance with Arerys, Ewen looked back upon the village as it slowly shrank into the darkness. He thought about all the people safe in the warmth of their beds. He wondered if they had even the slightest inkling of the dark figures riding past their village on this perilous journey that would eventually touch all of their lives. *Probably not, and better for them*, thought Ewen as they rode on into the night.

They passed the northern face of the great stone monoliths that originally blocked their path when they had traveled down from Mount Isa. In the darkness, the stone giants loomed ominously, as if waiting to be awoken from a deep sleep. Before them, the Gap now lay only a fraction of a league away. Markus ordered all to dismount and settle for the day, even though there was at least another hour of darkness before the sun rose.

"Whether we make the run through the Gap into Darross, or we take the pass leading into Talibarr, we must do so under complete darkness. I am confident Beyilzon's soldiers or his emissaries shall be waiting; watching for our arrival," stated Markus as he led Arrow into a thick stand of oak trees.

The daylight hours passed slowly, in between meals and sleep, the men spoke little. Each struggling with their own thoughts of the challenges ahead.

When the land was cloaked in darkness once more, the Order mounted their steeds, moving eastward towards the Gap.

When they reached their destination, Arerys, always on alert, transferred Ewen onto Markus' horse so he may venture ahead to see what may await them beyond the rocks and boulders obscuring their view.

Markus ordered the men to remain close to the walls of stone that surrounded the entrance to the Gap.

"If I do not return within the half hour, be prepared to take flight," warned Arerys, taking his bow into one hand and the reins into his other. He clucked his tongue against the roof of his mouth. RainDance turned away, boldly trotting off into the darkness.

Arerys listened for any unusual sounds. His eyes studied the dark forms of the rocks and shrubs around him. A eerie hush blanketed the landscape; all was strangely quiet.

As he rounded the bend, before him was Darross. As far as Arerys' far-seeing eyes could see lay the bloodied and mangled bodies of soldiers. They were men belonging to both the Dark Army and the soldiers of Darross and Cedona. They were strewn about like broken, dismembered dolls -scattered and thrown to the wayside by careless children.

The village of Nicobar was reduced to ashes and ruin; smoke was still slowly rising into the night sky from the smoldering embers of what remained of the cottages and shops. In the distance, King Sebastian's castle lay dark and dismal.

Arerys stared in disbelief at the carnage his eyes were forced to witness. Turning RainDance about, with a heavy heart, the Elf headed back through the pass.

With the sound of an approaching horse, the men mounted their steeds and waited, swords at the ready. Lando and Darius armed their bows in anticipation.

"It is I, Arerys," announced the Elf, coming into view.

The men thankfully sheathed their swords and lowered their bows.

"Arerys, what did you see? Is it safe to enter Darross?" asked Faria hopefully.

Arerys did not answer. He only shook his head.

"What do you mean?"

"We cannot go through Darross, Faria. It is much too dangerous. The devastation is too great. We must now travel through Talibarr. We have no choice in this matter!"

"No, that cannot be!" cried Faria in shock. The knight angrily sank his heels into his steed's flanks. The horse reared, and then bolted, charging through the Gap into the country he swore to protect.

"No! Faria, come back!" shouted Markus as he rode after him. "Do not be a fool!"

Arerys instructed the others to stay as he turned to pursue them.

"Faria, there is nothing you can do. We are too late," shouted Arerys as RainDance galloped hard to catch up.

At the mouth of the Gap, Markus and Arerys caught up to Faria. An expression of shock was etched across his face. He was unable to comprehend the magnitude of the devastation that lay before him.

Nicobar, his childhood home, was but a memory. On the horizon, King Sebastian's castle was dark. The banners that once flew high and proud over the castle walls were now conspicuously absent. Everywhere, there lay body after body.

Faria leapt from his saddle. He raced madly from one corpse to another, searching the faces of the fallen knights that once served King Sebastian. As he came to a body that lay near the banner bearing the emblem of a dragon, the insignia of the House of Northcott, Faria finally fell to his knees. Many arrows pierced the knight's body that lay before him. Arerys and Markus came to Faria's side.

Carefully, he removed the helmet; gently cradling the dead man in his arms. Faria began to weep.

"Who is this fallen knight that you grieve for?" asked Arerys, as he knelt by Faria.

He gazed up at Markus and the Elf. Through his tears he cried, "Here lays the protector of the House of Northcott, trusted servant and loyal knight to King Sebastian." He laid the young knight down. Slowly rising to his feet, in a solemn whisper, Faria answered, "Here rests the body of Davenrow Targott, my brother."

Markus and Arerys were taken aback by the news; both felt the tragic blow dealt to Faria, but nowhere near as severely as he.

Faria stormed back to his horse. He threw his leg over the saddle and with sword drawn; he raced away from Arerys and Markus, charging straight towards the darkened castle that seemed to mock him from the distance.

Seething in both rage and grief, Faria raised his sword high, bellowing at the top of his lungs: "I shall avenge you, my brother! Your death shall not be in vain!" Faria's angry call echoed off the surrounding hills and mountains for all to hear.

Suddenly, lights began to flicker on along the battlements of the distant castle. Markus and Arerys leapt onto their horses, racing after the grief-stricken knight.

"Faria, stop! Do not let it end this way!" shouted Markus.

Faria raced on into the blackness, on to the castle to confront the foes responsible for the devastation of Darross and the untimely death of his younger brother.

Markus caught up to Faria's horse. He struggled to grapple control of his reins. Each time, Faria kicked him away and sped off. Arerys quickly closed the distance on RainDance, but even he was unable to reason with the knight. Finally, in desperation Arerys leapt off of RainDance, knocking Faria off his steed.

Both man and Elf tumbled to the ground. Faria fell hard onto his side while Arerys went over his right shoulder, rolling forward, almost effortlessly landing back onto his feet. He dashed over to Faria's side. "I am sorry Faria, though your grief is great and the wound still fresh, you cannot storm the castle," said Arerys, expressing his regret and fear. "You do not know what lies in wait there! It may well be swarming with Beyilzon's men."

Faria struggled onto his feet. As he wiped the tears from his eyes, he picked up his sword and sheathed it in its scabbard. He stood for a moment; staring coldly at the castle that was now aglow with many blazing torches.

Markus returned with their horses. "Come, Faria. I assure you, this is not over."

As they retreated back in the direction of the Gap, Arerys turned to face the castle one last time. His eyes strained to make out the dark figures darting along the high walls of King Sebastian's great castle. They were much too far, and the night sky much too black to distinguish their identity with any certainty. The only thing he knew for sure was that whoever they were, they were now on the move.

Faria returned to the body of his fallen brother. He knelt before Davenrow, and, with a heavy sigh, he proceeded to undertake the grisly task of removing the arrows that riddled his brother's body.

Before Arerys or Markus could say anything, Faria emphatically stated: "You cannot ask me to leave my brother to be scavenged upon by ravens or to be further desecrated by those who were responsible for this."

Arerys and Markus understood. They helped Faria carefully lift his brother's body onto his horse's saddle. Faria reclaimed Davenrow's sword and shield from where they lay upon the ground as he turned to walk his horse back to the Gap. Arerys rode on ahead to gather the others and to deliver the sad news.

As Markus turned to follow behind Faria, the fluttering of the banner bearing the insignia of the House of Northcott caught his eyes. No doubt Faria's brother carried it high and proud as he marched into battle. Markus picked up the staff and carefully rolled the banner up, taking it with him as he left.

When Faria arrived at the mouth of the Gap; his comrades greeted him. Their sorrow seen in their eyes as they helped Faria drape his brother's body in the colors of the House of Northcott.

"My brother belongs in Darross. We shall bury his body beneath these stones. Here, he shall remain for an eternity to watch over the land and people he loved so." Faria kissed his brother upon his forehead, and then lovingly lay Davenrow's shield upon his chest and his sword by his right hand.

After the last stones were carefully placed over Davenrow's body, the men of the Order prepared to leave the Gap. Darross was no longer an option.

Following the others, Faria turned for the last time to look upon Davenrow's grave. "I swear upon my life, my brother; Darross shall be a free land - its people shall rise up once again."

Lindras directed Tempest northward to the pass that would lead to the dreaded land of Talibarr. The rest galloped in time to keep pace with the great, gray steed. As they emerged from the pass, they all came to a stop.

For a moment, the Order looked upon the vast, desolate landscape stretching out before them. To the north were the Shadow Mountains; to the east, the Plains of Fire where the last Great War was fought and won by man. Beyond this battlefield was the Valley of Shadows. Standing in the darkness cast by the Shadow Mountains and the Iron Mountains to the east; where these two mountain ranges converge, Mount Hope, their final destination, awaited.

"Well my friends, it would seem that fate has indeed made the choice for us. Onward through Talibarr," said Lindras. "Let us make haste before the sun rises."

As the first light of morning began to dissolve the blackness of night, the travelers remained close to the base of the Aranak Mountains. They deliberately concealed themselves in its shadows. From the forested slope, the group slept and ate, speaking in low voices and taking turns to act as the lookout. As usual, Arerys took the first watch; Markus joined him.

Ewen's eyes gazed to the north. It seemed so odd that such a forbidden place that was only spoken of in whispers, seemed in most part, not that different than some of the places in Carcross. He turned to Lindras. "Wizard, this land looks as fertile and as habitable as some of the places back home, and yet for one thousand years it lies empty. Why?"

Lindras drew a long, thoughtful breath on his pipe. His fingers subconsciously fondled the band of gold on his beard as he peered across at the land in question. "Talibarr has a terrible history, my boy. The Plains of Fire has played host to many horrific battles since the beginning of time. This is where the fate of mankind and Elves has been decided by the edge of a sword and the blood of many."

"But we have had many years of peace, and yet this land is devoid of life," continued Ewen, between bites of food.

"Oh, life does exist in Talibarr, but it is the dark and corrupt souls of those in Beyilzon's service that frequent the forbidden places of the Shadow Mountains," responded Lindras. "It is said that on the nights of the full moon, when the skies are clear, one can see the ghosts of those who died in battle, rise with the mist. They are trapped in this terrible twilight to do battle, again and again, for an eternity."

Ewen shuddered at the thought of ghosts, especially those that may wield weapons of swords or halberds.

"Enough talk of ghosts," said Lindras. "It is time for you to get some sleep."

Ewen agreed wholeheartedly, wrapping his cloak around his small frame and resting his head on his small bag of possessions.

Lindras stood up and after a long stretch; his weary bones carried him over to where Arerys and Markus stood guard.

Lando and Darius finished their meal while a demoralized Faria brooded in his dark thoughts.

Faria addressed the men in a hushed voice: "Look at us in this forsaken place. Darross has fallen; we are pursued and outnumbered. Time is running out for us."

"Faria, you know we could not enter through Darross. You saw the devastation," responded Darius.

"If my men cannot defeat Beyilzon's army to protect the homes and people of Darross, then we are all doomed," snapped Faria in disgust and anger.

Lando leaned over, looking Faria in his eyes. "I know your loss is great and you mourn for your brother, but do not tell me that you have lost your faith, too," sighed Lando. "There is still hope, we are almost half way there."

"Hope? You speak of hope where there is none," said Faria, his eyes burning with anger. "I know of one thing that may work in our favor…"

"What do you speak of?" asked Lando, suspicion mounting in his voice.

"Think on this: If we can turn Beyilzon's own men against him; if we can convince them that we have something far more powerful than Beyilzon himself, we may be able to turn the tide against evil," whispered Faria. His gaze turned to the sleeping boy; the Stone clenched tightly in his hand.

"I do not understand. What you are suggesting here, Faria?" inquired Darius.

"Listen. If we prove to Beyilzon's hordes we have the power to defeat the Dark Lord, do you not think that those spineless souls would switch allegiance, rather than to go down in defeat with Beyilzon?" reasoned Faria.

"You have truly lost your mind, Faria. Come to your senses, man. Do you understand what you are even saying?" asked Lando.

"We have a chance to save the good people of Imago, plus, we can also offer salvation to all those fools who have sided with the Dark Lord," suggested Faria.

"You are asking us to betray Markus and Ewen," said Lando, struggling to control his angry tone as he grabbed Faria by his collar, lifting him onto his feet.

"It is not betrayal," answered Faria, as he motioned Lando to lower his voice. "We stand a chance to do a greater good. We have a chance to turn Beyilzon's own men against him. Right now, they do not know the potential power we wield. If they knew, surely they would turn their backs on the Dark Lord."

"This is madness, Faria," said Darius in disgust. "I shall pass this off as the ramblings of a man speaking out of sorrow and rage."

"Do not speak these words again," growled Lando, releasing his grip on Faria. "So help me, if you should utter these words once more, then I shall personally deliver you to the Dark Army, and I shall not look back when they turn on you."

With those words said, Lando grabbed his sword. He and Darius left the dejected Faria so they may relieve Arerys and Markus of sentry duty.

Slumping back to the ground, Faria's eyes turned to the sleeping form of the boy, who now held the key to mankind's fate. He watched as Ewen twitched nervously in the midst of his reoccurring nightmare.

The dream was becoming more vivid. Each time, the dark soldiers threw Ewen to the ground. They jeered and mocked him as that same sinister voice interrogated him, repeatedly asking him: "Will you die for him?"

Ewen watched himself in the nightmare as he tried to run, only to be thrown down again. He cowered on the ground as he shook his head in fear as the voice asked the same question. The world suddenly went black.

Ewen bolted up from his sleep. Drenched in sweat and visibly trembling in fear, his eyes darted around as he fought to recognize where he was. Not far lay Faria, asleep; coming down the slope to join him was Lindras, Markus and Arerys.

Arerys, upon hearing Ewen cry out in his sleep, dashed down towards the boy. "Did you have a bad dream again?" asked the Elf as he hugged his trembling body to offer him some comfort.

"I do not understand it, Arerys. Why am I haunted by the same dream?" whispered Ewen, wiping away the beads of perspiration from his face with the sleeves of his shirt. "It is as though I am being forced to witness an event that has yet to happen."

"Perhaps you are being made to recall something that has happened in the past, but you choose not to remember?" suggested Arerys.

"How can that be? I have never left Carcross in my life. I have never encountered a soldier from the Dark Army. The torment seems so real and yet, I know I have never experienced this type of torment or agony in my life."

Arerys helped Ewen settle back down. He passed his hand lightly over his face, and as Ewen's eyes closed, the Elf whispered: "Sleep Ewen. Dream you are safe in your own bed. You are safe in Carcross."

Ewen quickly lapsed into a deep, restful sleep by the time Markus and Lindras joined Arerys.

"He is plagued by bad dreams yet again?" asked Markus.

The Elf nodded his head. "And they are not dreams, Markus; it is one dream that haunts him so."

"Well, I have a feeling, given time, Ewen shall unravel the mystery of this nightmare himself," concluded Lindras.

As the others slept, Lando and Darius stood watch as dusk settled down upon the land.

"Darius, I fear that Faria is deeply troubled," whispered Lando as he scanned the ever-darkening landscape.

"Let us hope it was his grief speaking," said Darius with concern. "He is weary and he is still very much wounded by the loss of his brother, his country, and possibly his king, too."

"We shall have to watch him closely," whispered Lando. "There is no telling what actions a desperate soul may take."

CHAPTER 6

THE LAST WARRIOR

Seven hours into their trek, the Order covered much ground as they traveled through the dark, forbidden land of Talibarr. Thin, wispy clouds occasionally filtered out what little light was cast down by the many stars on this moonless night.

Lindras and Arerys escorted the others eastward. They took great care to always remain hidden within the shadows of the Aranak Mountain Range and the forests growing along its base up to its lower slopes.

Arerys constantly monitored the night sounds, scanning for any movement. The quiet was unnatural; very unsettling.

"Listen, Markus," whispered Arerys, turning his head about, straining to hear.

"I hear nothing."

"That is what concerns me. I hear no owl, nor the chorus of frogs. Not even the sounds of crickets."

"This is most unusual indeed, Arerys," agreed Lindras.

"We must use utmost caution as we tread through this cursed land," said Markus, peering through an opening in the tree canopy, into the dark, starry sky.

Arerys raised his hands for all to stop. He motioned for silence as he dismounted from RainDance. "Something lies ahead, I can smell the smells of a campfire, but there are no sounds," whispered Arerys. "Remain here and I shall venture ahead to see what await us."

"I shall go with you, Arerys," suggested Markus.

"No, stay here with the others. I shall not be long," said the Elf as he darted silently into the deep shadows.

"I do not like this, Markus," whispered Faria.

"Yes, it is as though something evil watches us from afar," added Lando.

"You feel it too?" asked Darius.

"Hush, enough talk," ordered Markus, attempting to quell Ewen's growing fear. "We should be listening for Arerys' approach."

All waited patiently for the Elf's return, listening for any unusual sounds or movements that may alert them to his presence, or that of impending danger.

"Someone approaches," said Markus, in a hushed tone as he drew his sword.

As the tall, dark figure approached with both hands raised to show he meant them no harm, it became clear it was Arerys.

"So tell us, what lies ahead?" asked Markus.

"It is most unusual," stated the Elf, obviously baffled by what he had just witnessed. "I came upon the camp, and as I neared, I counted at least two dozen of Beyilzon's men."

"I take it, they did not see you?"

"They were all dead," answered Arerys, his brows furrowed with obvious worry.

"So, could it be that Sebastian or Augustyn's soldiers have breached the Aranaks and pursued the Dark Army back into Talibarr?" asked Faria, hopefully.

"Unless your men are into using the black arts, I would hardly think so."

"What do you mean?" asked Markus, greatly puzzled by Arerys' statement.

"It quickly became apparent there was something peculiar; I realized they were slumped over each other and lay scattered on the ground. At first, I believed them to be intoxicated, merely sleeping off the effects of too much drink, but as I approached the camp, I grabbed one soldier by his throat as he lay against a tree. He did not make a sound, nor did he fight back. He was quite dead."

"Death by sword? Knife perhaps?" asked Markus, intrigued by the Elf's account.

"No, that is just it. I checked them all, and none were marred by sword, arrow, nor knife," said Arerys. "It was as if they all died in their sleep. There is no sign of a struggle, no footprints that would indicate they were ambushed. Nothing."

"Well, it would appear something evil got to them before we could," said Lando.

"Or perhaps, something got them before they could get to us," suggested the Wizard with a troubled sigh.

"Whatever the case, they met their demise within the last hour or two. The campfire still smolders."

"We must get out of this area as soon as possible, Lindras," instructed Markus. "Whatever it was that did away with those soldiers may also be searching us out."

With a nod, Lindras leapt onto Tempest's back and escorted the group through the darkness; around the camp, its dead soldiers and beyond. They rode through the night until the stars began to disappear in the waning night sky.

As dawn broke, the Wizard escorted the men into a narrow valley resting between the bosom of Aranak's two larger peaks. The stands of ancient trees sheltered them from any prying eyes that may be searching for them from the higher vantage points of the range.

"We shall rest in this valley until dusk," said Lindras as he dismounted. The others left their horses to graze and drink from a nearby stream that ran through a clearing.

As the men settled for a meal, and to seize the opportunity to sleep, Arerys grabbed his bow and quiver to take the first watch. The Elf's keen ears then picked up a distant sound coming from the west.

"Something follows us," said Arerys, straining to see the invisible menace. "I can sense its presence although I cannot see it."

"Is it Beyilzon's henchmen?" asked Markus, his hand poised on his sword.

"I do not know what, or who it is, but I have noticed this presence last night when we came across the dead soldiers and again, when we entered this valley," replied the Elf. "This feeling has been growing stronger with each passing minute."

"Yes, I too share this feeling, Arerys. It is very strange indeed," agreed the Wizard.

Suddenly, the Elf stood up very tall and straight, his body stiffened in anticipation. "Something evil comes our way! Brace yourself men, be ready to fight!" Arerys was already reaching for an arrow from his quiver.

For a moment, all stood motionless. It was deathly quiet, and then a low rumbling sound stirred the earth. As the sound intensified, it became clear that it was the sound of many footsteps pounding the ground in synchrony.

"It is Beyilzon's soldiers, and there are many of them!" announced Arerys as he raised his bow to draw back the arrow.

"From which direction do they come, Elf?" asked Faria.

"They are everywhere! We are surrounded!"

At least twenty-four dark soldiers emerged from the forest, coming from every direction, encircling the Order. With nowhere to run, they braced themselves for the certainty of battle. Arerys was already taking aim and launching his arrows while Darius and Lando where still in the midst of arming their bows.

In a bid to protect Ewen, Lindras grabbed the quaking boy by his shoulders, throwing him to the ground into the middle of their circle.

Faria and Markus faced the oncoming army, swords unsheathed and ready for battle. Lindras took up his staff in both hands.

With a great roar, they collided headlong into their attackers. The dark soldiers pressed on, striking with halberd, sword, and mace.

At such a close range, Arerys was able to dispatch two soldiers with a single arrow. It pierced the first soldier straight through his throat, causing him to stumble back with the impact. The arrow continued on, traveling through to strike the next soldier coming up from behind - plunging deep into his torso, killing him instantly. As he pulled his last arrow from his quiver, a soldier raced towards him with his halberd raised. The giant axe came down with a vengeance, but Arerys lithely angled out the way. With no time to arm his bow, the Elf rammed the arrow, deep through the soldier's temple as he spun around to avoid the blade of the halberd. In one swift, flowing movement, he yanked it out and strung the now bloodied arrow onto his bow, letting it fly into another oncoming soldier.

His supply of arrows now depleted, Arerys drew his sword and joined the fray, ducking once to avoid a wild swing from Lindras' staff as the Wizard pummeled and bashed his adversaries.

Ewen was cowering in the midst of this battle. He was too frightened to run, let alone move, if there were somewhere he could retreat to. He remained motionless - huddled close to the ground.

Darius laughed aloud, swinging his sword in large sweeping circles, slicing through any body within striking distance, while bashing others with his shield.

"I am glad one of us is enjoying this!" shouted Lando, his sword locked against that of a soldier's.

Darius spun around, striking Lando's opponent across his chest, knocking the soldier hard to the ground. He smiled at Lando, winking as if it was all in a day's work. He headed off in search of his next opponent.

As he turned, a soldier charged towards him, the tip of his halberd pointed directly at his chest. Darius steeled his nerves as he boldly ran headlong to meet his foe. As the soldier neared striking distance, Darius raised his sword and lifted his shield in preparation to deflect the blow of the halberd. Instead, the soldier suddenly dropped dead, crashing down before him.

Darius was momentarily stunned, perplexed by this strange death as neither arrow, nor sword penetrated the soldier's body. There was no time to lose though. He leapt over the fallen body; another soldier was ready to engage him in battle.

Markus was in the midst of extracting his sword from a freshly fallen soldier when the staff end of a halberd crashed down upon him from behind. He stumbled forward and rolled onto his back, almost dropping his sword in the process.

The soldier moved in swiftly, the halberd raised again for a second strike. Markus lunged forward, landing just to the soldier's right side. Locking his left ankle against the soldier's right ankle, Markus swung his right leg about, striking the soldier just behind his knee; causing him to fall, face first to the ground. Markus wheeled around over top of the fallen soldier, and, with both hands on his sword, plunged it straight through the soldier's back until he felt earth through the tip of his deadly blade.

As he struggled to release his sword from the dying soldier's convulsing body, a shield came crashing over his right shoulder, knocking him squarely onto his back. Without a sword, Markus prepared to dodge the next strike, but as the soldier raised his sword to deliver the killing blow, he suddenly lurched backwards, clutching his throat. His eyes were opened wide in surprise as he staggered towards Markus, almost collapsing on top of him. The soldier fell dead.

Markus scrambled to his feet. Recovering his sword, he ran to Lindras' aid, but even as he prepared to engage in combat again, he could not help but wonder about the soldier's mysterious demise.

The sound of steel crashing against steel, and screams of agony as metal met flesh, filled the air. Bodies littered the blood-soaked clearing.

Both sides were now more evenly matched.

All of the sudden, from the depth of the shadows in the surrounding forest emerged a menacing specter: a dark horseman clad in a flowing black robe. He came riding forth upon a large, fearsome black steed. It was one of Beyilzon's dark emissaries; his horse careened around the soldiers and the men of the Order, leaping over dead bodies, straight through the middle of the battle. His sights were set on Ewen.

Upon seeing his approach, Ewen scrambled to his feet to run, but a powerful hand caught up with him. Seized by the scruff of his neck and unceremoniously hoisted onto the saddle, in a blink of an eye, the dark horseman made off with him.

"Help! Markus! Lindras!" shouted the boy as he struggled to no avail against the large, black figure. The horse reared up and sped out of the clearing and into the forest.

In the midst of the battle, Markus and Lando, who were fighting side by side, both looked to each other. Without saying a word, they thrust their swords deep into their respective foes, each planted a foot on a soldier's breastplate, kicking him over to extract their swords.

As their horses had been spooked, fleeing when the altercation began, Markus and Lando were forced to pursue the dark horseman by foot.

Sweat poured from their brows as they ran with all their might, but the dark emissary was quickly putting great distance between them. Lando and Markus were gasping for air; their chests heaving as each painful breath filled their bursting lungs. They had to go on.

Arerys dropped his last foe before dashing to edge of the clearing. Plucking his spent arrows from the fallen bodies as he went, he flicked off the blood before thrusting them into his quiver. He gave a sharp whistle and listened for a moment. The Elf turned, bounding into a stand of trees and there, coming to meet him, was RainDance. He leapt onto her back and rode hard, following in the direction of Lando and Markus.

The dark horseman stopped momentarily with his precious cargo. The black gauntlet he wore pressed painfully into the boy's flesh as his hand clasped firmly over Ewen's mouth to stifle his cries. His head darted from side to side with the uncanny movement of a wild animal, listening for any sound that may alert him to the approach of a rescue party. The forest grew quiet, only the wind rustling through the tree canopy could be heard. As the horseman turned his steed to head down the hill, a figure clad in a dark gray cloak suddenly dropped from the overhanging branch of an oak tree onto the horseman, knocking both him and Ewen from the black steed.

Ewen met the ground, rolling away to avoid being trampled by the angry hoofs. He watched in fear as the dark horseman rose up to his feet. He towered menacingly above the hooded figure that had knocked him off his mount.

As a brilliant glint of steel flashed before Ewen's eyes, a voice demanded, "Let the boy go!"

With a laugh, the dark horseman drew his sword, lunging at the figure that leapt as agile as a cat, out of harm's way. Again, the horseman raised his sword high over his head to bring it down with all his might. His tiny adversary quickly angled out of the way, diving to the ground and rolling straight towards him, rising up before his dark, looming body.

With one swift upward stroke, the dark horseman was slashed from his left hip, diagonally to his right shoulder. The horseman let out a horrific scream as an inner vapor escaped from his wound, only to seal itself up again. The dark horseman once again drew his sword high over his head. He swung the blade downward. It was met with a deafening crash against his assailant's shimmering blade. Braced against each other, sword against sword, will against will, the horseman bore down with all his weight upon his diminutive opponent.

As the small, hooded figure appeared to buckle under the horseman's might, the figure took an unexpected step back. Using the counterweight of the dark horseman's own weapon against him, it caused the tip of his little assailant's sword to spring up and strike the dark horseman in the neck, almost decapitating him. As before, dark vapors gushed from the horseman's injury and as quickly as it had been slit open, the wound mysteriously healed.

Urging RainDance on, Arerys thundered past Markus and Lando, following the sound of the commotion ahead. As he approached the crest of the hill, he dropped his reins. With RainDance at full gallop, Arerys loaded his bow, releasing an arrow. Just as the mysterious figure moved in once again, in an attempt to finish off the dark horseman, Arerys' arrow whizzed by, striking Beyilzon's agent straight through his heart. With a ghastly shriek, he was instantly reduced to ashes.

Arerys leapt down from his steed. Drawing another arrow, he aimed it directly at the hooded figure.

"No! Arerys, do not shoot him!" shouted Ewen as he ran to the Elf. The figure turned to flee as Arerys took aim.

"Arerys, no!" Ewen insisted, as he tried to wrestle his bow away. "He saved my life!"

The Elf reluctantly lowered his bow as Lando and Markus finally caught up to his side. Both were breathing hard, Lando clutching his side in pain as he tried to catch his breath.

"Ewen, are you hurt?" asked a winded Markus, gasping as he wiped the sweat from his brows.

"No Markus, a stranger saved my life!" Feeling under his shirt, he drew out the velvet pouch. The Stone is safe! He raised the pouch for all to see.

Markus was relieved, motioning Ewen to put it away as he struggled to breathe.

Lando approached the pile of ashes being blown about by a brisk breeze. Using the toe of his boot to sift through the black ashes, he checked to see if what was all that was left of Beyilzon's emissary. Finding Arerys' arrow partially hidden amongst the ashes, he picked it up, passing it to the Elf.

"Do you know who it was that came to your aid, Ewen?" asked Arerys, as he slung his bow over his shoulder.

"I did not see his face, I only know that he was very brave and daring. And dangerous with the sword!" Then he added: "He was small though, even shorter than I!" He showed the men how his mysterious rescuer stood about two or three inches shorter than his own five and a half foot frame.

"Well, whoever he was, he is gone now," said Arerys as he gathered RainDance's bridle. "I do not hear, nor see, any trace of him."

As the four turned back to join the others; Ewen on horseback, Arerys, Markus, and Lando walking, a small shadow peered out from beneath the gnarled, exposed root of an old fallen tree, watching as the men departed.

When they returned to the scene of the battle, Lindras was seated upon a tree stump, leaning heavily against his staff. His eyes were closed as he rested. Faria was absent, he had wandered into the forest in search of the other horses that fled at the beginning of the battle.

Darius had busied himself by retrieving what arrows he could. The arrows used by Arerys' people lacked the cruel, barbed tip, so they were easy to extract. He went from body to body, wiping the arrows clean of blood on the trampled grasses. As he went about this grim business, he came across the body of the soldier that mysteriously collapsed before him. There was no sword wound and no arrow pierced his body.

That is curious, thought Darius as he rolled the body over to examine the other side. To his amazement, what killed the soldier was found in his neck: a single, needle-like blade. He plucked this weapon from the soldier and began to scour the other bodies that had fallen without the mark of sword or arrow.

Each of these bodies had the same small, unassuming weapon lodged in either the neck or in the eye. These too, Darius collected. As he stood up from his task, he saw Ewen dismount from RainDance, while the others gathered around the resting Wizard. At the same time, Faria emerged from the forest with Tempest and the other horses.

Darius was relieved to see that all had returned safely. He greeted his comrades with a broad smile, handing back to Arerys his spent arrows. "Look... what do you make of this?" asked Darius, as he extended his hand towards Markus and the Elf. He held out a fistful of the odd-looking darts.

All looked upon his open hand with the same curiosity.

"It must involve some kind of black magic for such a small weapon to dispense such a quick death," declared Faria, regarding the strange darts with a suspicious frown.

Avoiding the needle-sharp tip, Lindras carefully picked one up by its less offensive end to examine it. He held it to his nose to take a whiff. He then passed it to Arerys. He too sniffed the dart. The Elf's head recoiled in disgust at the vile smell. "This is no black magic; these darts are poisoned."

Markus examined them too, but failed to detect the scent that Lindras and Arerys found so offensive. "Have you ever seen the likes of these, Wizard?" asked Markus.

Lindras thought for a moment. "Indeed I have; far to the east on the other side of the Iron Mountains."

Markus recalled tales his grandfather shared of the people who lived in the distant country called Orien. There, dwelled a race of raven-haired people who lived as part of the land, much like the Elves, but they were mortals. "How can that be?" thought Markus out loud.

"Do you think the owner of this strange weaponry is the same one who came to Ewen's rescue?" asked Lando.

"I have a feeling it may be one and the same," answered Markus, as he turned to mount his steed.

Too exhausted by the events of the morning to venture any further, the Order made camp on a rise. It was a good distance away from the clearing where the early morning blood-bath had taken place. From this elevated location, it was easier for all to watch for approaching danger as well as to keep a watchful eye on their horses as they grazed and rested into the night.

Dinner was eaten without the comfort of a campfire. None wished to attract the attention of any other soldiers that may be watching from the distant slopes.

Arerys stood apart from the rest of the men. He felt that same uneasy feeling he had felt earlier that day. He scanned the ever-darkening horizon. He could not see *it*. He could not hear *it*, yet somewhere in the darkness, *it* was out there: waiting and watching.

As night fell, the darkness brought with it a heaviness to the air. The land was curtained in a steady fall of gray rain. The Order had to make up for lost time due to their slowed pace as the darkness, hampered by this driving rain, made visibility difficult through the uneven terrain.

They trudged on through the morning until the precipitation finally let up in the early afternoon. All was quiet, yet Arerys still felt ill at ease as they traveled, as though something, or someone, was watching their every move.

They dismounted and stopped briefly to eat. As the horses grazed, the men fed on cured venison and dried fruit. Arerys and Lindras nibbled on the crisp, thin wafers of Elven bread; it satisfied their hunger after only a few bites. Arerys took another drink of water, then passed it on to the Wizard.

"Something is very wrong here, Lindras. I can feel it in my heart and it gnaws at the back of my brain. I shall scout out the area," said the Elf, his troubled eyes piercing through the stand of trees that sheltered them.

"I shall come with you, my friend," said Darius, rising to his feet.

Together, the two climbed to the top of a ridge. As they reached the crest, Arerys suddenly grabbed Darius' arm. He pulled him quickly to the ground, motioning for him to be quiet.

"What is it?" asked Darius, in a whisper.

"In the valley, there is a great congregation of men, and they are *not* from Darross," whispered Arerys.

Darius inched up closer to the edge of the ridge to peer down. Indeed, Beyilzon's men were there, some eight hundred strong.

"Well, I suppose this route is no good to us now," said Darius, rather smugly as he eyed the Dark Army below.

"This would be one battle we cannot win. At least, not today," responded Arerys. "We must go back to warn the others."

As both turned to head back down the ridge, they were startled by a loud, explosive noise coming from the direction of their camp. Darius and Arerys glanced down into the valley. The Dark Army had heard the explosion too. For an instant, Beyilzon's men below all froze in their tracks. They slowly turned in the direction of the noise, then like an angry swarm of wasps agitated from their hive; the army was on the move, a sea of black surging in their direction.

Back where the Order had been resting, young Ewen had taken it upon himself to handle Lindras' staff. Unbeknownst to the Wizard, the boy had muttered some words he had heard Lindras use in an incantation. Waving the staff in the air, Ewen copied Lindras' actions as he drove the end of the magical staff into the ground.

With this incantation, a blue bolt of lightened exploded from the darkening sky to strike the staff. Ewen was sent flying to the ground.

"What were you thinking? You foolish boy!" shouted Lindras in anger.

"I am sorry, Lindras. I was careless!"

"More foolhardy, than careless I would say!" snapped the Wizard, snatching the fallen staff from the ground. As he righted himself, he pulled Ewen onto his feet. It was then, he saw Arerys and Darius at a full run, charging down the ridge.

"The soldiers are coming! Make haste, we must move now!" shouted Darius.

"Beyilzon's soldiers?" asked Markus

Lindras passed his hand over the staff's crystal, holding it before Markus and Faria to gaze into.

"Beyilzon's men! More than we can handle! Quickly! We must leave!" shouted Darius.

Arerys gave a sharp whistle. RainDance turned, galloping in his direction. The other horses were following close behind her. Everybody climbed onto their mounts, racing away with Lindras in the lead.

"Do you know where to go?" asked Markus as Arrow pulled up to the Wizard's great steed.

"No, but anywhere is safer than here!" said Lindras, urging Tempest on.

He led the horses eastward out of the valley as they charged downward into a gully. Soon, high, smooth limestone walls engulfed the Order.

"This does not bode well, Wizard!" said Markus, his eyes darted about.

They rode through the gully only to reach a dead end. The horses wheeled around, rearing as the men peered up at the sheer walls surrounding them. With no caves, or even many trees to offer sufficient cover, the Order was in great peril. The walls seemed to echo as the distant army advanced on foot.

"We cannot turn back now, Markus. We shall never get past them!" cried out Arerys, listening to the sound of the approaching soldiers.

"Well, I shall at least slow them down!" said the Wizard. He leapt down from his steed, turning to the rocky walls at the mouth of the deep gully. He raised his staff on high, where upon, blue bolts of lightening exploded from the crystal. The surge of energy struck the high walls of limestone, causing an avalanche of rocks, boulders, and other debris to come crashing down to seal off the mouth of the gully.

Markus dismounted. "Now we are trapped Lindras! I do not think this was a wise move!"

"I have bought us more time!" responded the Wizard.

"More time for what? We are trapped! We have no escape!" cried Faria as he leapt from his saddle.

"There must be a way," whispered Markus, surveying the inhospitable surroundings. "Everybody! Check the walls for caves or tunnels - anywhere that we may be able to climb out!"

The group scattered, scanning the high walls. The army was drawing ever closer.

Suddenly, a small figure dropped down from a large elm tree, landing lightly in the midst of the trapped party. "If you want to live, follow me!" said the voice that was shrouded in the hood of a dark gray cloak.

"It is you!" announced Ewen. "You are the man who saved me from the dark horseman!" He moved closer to the mysterious figure.

Faria laid hold of Ewen's shoulder to stop his advance. He glared at the stranger. "Who are you?"

"That is not important right now. Do you wish to live, or do you wish to die? If you choose life, then follow me!"

Faria abruptly lunged, grabbing the unknown figure by his throat. "Reveal yourself or you shall meet the wrath of my sword!"

Before Faria could draw his weapon, the stranger grabbed onto the knight by the lapels of his vest. In one smooth, flowing move, he dropped to the ground, using one foot on Faria's hip to launch him into the air. He landed on his back with a heavy 'thud' as the figure, not releasing his grip, used Faria's own momentum to roll over his body, landing squarely on top of his chest. The cloaked figure pinned Faria's arms to the ground with his knees, and with both hands free, threw back his cloak to draw out a sword. With its glistening blade barely touching Faria's throat, the voice growled, "That was uncalled for."

Racing to the aid of their comrade, all gathered around Faria. Bow and swords were drawn and pointed at the ready, all directed at the stranger that had Faria firmly held down to the ground.

"Do not hurt him, sir. Faria means no harm!" cried Ewen as he pushed his way through the circle of weapons. He ran up to Faria. Dropping to his knees, Ewen pleaded for the knight's life.

"Unhanded him or I shall let my arrow fly!" ordered Arerys, taking another step closer.

The figure slowly placed the sword onto the ground, cautiously rising up; hands opened and held high.

Faria scrambled to his feet, holding his hand to his neck, checking for signs of blood.

"Who are you?" Markus asked, stepping forward, sword still drawn.

Slowly, the hands moved to the hood, drawing it back. Everyone stared in disbelief. The shadow of the hood gave way to reveal a woman's face. She raised her eyes to meet those who had encircled her. Her diminutive stature made them wonder how this could be the same person who, only a moment ago, had a much larger man immobilized – firmly pinned to the ground.

Her hair was such a deep shade of brown, it was almost black. It was long, straight and drawn away from her face into a braid that extended to the middle of her back. Her large, almond-shaped eyes were deep brown and flashed with a hint of anger at the men who now held her at bay. Drawn to the sparkle of silver adorning her right ear, Arerys noticed how they were small, delicate - and pointed almost like that of an Elf!

How can it be? Arerys thought, studying her tiny frame. This woman was clad in dark, leather boots that rose to her knees. A richly embroidered, deep rust colored vest was worn over a dark, charcoal colored silk garment with a laced bodice, the length of which wrapped around her hips like a skirt. Indeed, there was absolutely no doubt this was a woman.

Around her waist, she wore a leather belt from which the scabbard of her long sword hung from her left hip. A short sword was worn at her front, while a dark leather pouch hung across from her left shoulder, coming to rest on her right hip.

"It is a girl!" gasped Ewen, genuinely surprised by this discovery.

Lindras gently cuffed him on his ear. "Of course she is!"

"We wish you no harm," said Markus, motioning the others to put away their weapons.

"Nor I to you," said the female. "Time is at hand, the army is almost upon us. I ask you once more, do you wish to live?"

"Do you know of a way out?" asked Markus, sheathing his sword.

"No. I shall make a way out though. Follow me. Take only what you need. You must leave your horses." She led them to the far wall of the gully as she too, sheathed her sword.

"Markus, have you taken leave of your senses! We cannot climb these rock walls, there is not a single foothold to even reach that ledge!" said Faria, pointing up to the smooth, high, limestone face.

"I did not say we were going to climb this wall," she answered calmly. "We shall use a ladder."

The men all looked at each other; confusion quite telling on their faces. She quickly studied the men. Grabbing the largest of them, she led Darius to the rock wall. "Stand like so, brace yourself against this rock," said the female as she demonstrated.

Darius looked puzzled, but he asked no questions. He did as she instructed. With his knees bent, his arms held out and his hands braced against the wall, the small female nimbly climbed up onto his shoulder, using his knees and arms much like the rungs on a ladder.

She climbed down with the agility of a feline, landing lightly on her feet again. She turned to Faria. "You are next my friend!"

The Elf, being the tallest and the lightest of the lot, was asked by the female to climb up onto Faria's shoulders. Grabbing a long, thin, silken coil of rope from her pouch, she climbed up over Darius, Faria and the Elf.

"Now stand upright. Stand tall men!" she shouted.

To those watching from the ground in amazement, this human ladder now reached much higher than they had imagined possible. The female pulled herself over the top of the ledge, disappearing for a brief moment.

"Markus, she better hurry. I cannot bear this weight for much longer!" grunted Darius, sweat beading on his forehead like a dam ready to burst.

A rope was lowered down just as the female reappeared. "Elf, take the rope, I shall help you up."

Arerys took the rope into his hands, quickly hoisting himself up onto the ledge. The female grabbed him by his belt, pulling him up as he swung his legs over.

When they looked over the ledge, Faria was already on his way up, while Darius was securing the rope around the boy's waist.

"Stand aside, I shall pull him up," Faria said, taking the rope into his callused hands.

"Then you better do so quickly, the army is at the gate!" warned the female.

As Ewen was pulled to safety, Lindras worked with Markus to remove saddles and halters. The Wizard then turned to his gray stallion. He whispered instructions to Tempest, who whinnied and tossed his head in response.

One by one, they were pulled to the safety of the high ledge. Hugging the rock wall overlooking the gully, the female led them around the tall face of limestone to the other side. The rope made fast and easy work of the climb down and soon, the Order was racing deep into the forest. They disappeared into the valley below.

They were long gone when Beyilzon's army, thinking they would still be trapped, broke through the Wizard's stone barricade. As the army prepared to push through to storm the gully, Tempest reared up and, with the other horses at full gallop, they stampeded towards the soldiers, knocking them to the ground. The gray stallion sped away with his small herd. They were setting a course back to Wyndwood.

The Order asked no questions; they followed the swift-moving figure as she ducked in and out of the shadows of the trees. She escorted them to the edge of a fast flowing creek swollen from the day's earlier rainfall.

"Everyone into the water," she instructed them. "Head up stream. Do not get out of this creek until I catch up to you!"

As they waded knee-deep into the chilly water, the woman waded across to the other side of the creek. She proceeded to lay down numerous tracks where weeds and grasses grew tall. She then leaned hard against a large rock, sending it tumbling downhill along the bank of the creek. It cut a swathe through the tall grasses and shrubs, leaving an easy to follow trail. The rock traveled quite some distance downhill before coming to a crashing halt against some boulders; as if it had always been a part of this rocky escarpment.

Markus and Arerys looked back to see the female busily back tracking on her own prints.

"Look Arerys, she is creating a diversion!" stated Markus, splashing against the rushing waters.

"Let us hope it works," said Arerys, with an air of skepticism.

As the others sloshed and splashed their way up, the female silently moved through the creek. Each step was deliberate; dipping her toes in first, then setting her foot down on the rocky creek bed before lifting her next step up high, slipping her foot into the water without a splash. She quickly and silently caught up to Markus, who had taken up the rear. She startled him with her silent approach when she instructed the men to follow her out of the creek, onto the stony, rock-strewn embankment.

"Keep your feet on the rocks, avoid treading on the sand. Let us not give those soldiers any reason to believe we were here," she said.

Lightly, she sprang from rock to rock, up and over the embankment, coming to rest on a fallen tree. Turning to the men, she ordered: "Stay on this log. Walk in single file and when you reach the end, follow in my footsteps. Do you understand? Place your feet exactly where I have tread."

"It would be much faster if we just ran than play this silly game," protested Faria.

The female was unmoved by his comment.

"Faria, it makes sense. I understand what she is trying to do," said Lando. "If the soldiers split up to head in different directions, they may eventually come across our prints here and those she left behind downstream. They will pursue the more obvious tracks of many that she created, than follow what they may perceive to be the single track of one man."

Markus nodded in agreement. Without hesitation, he waved them into formation. Falling into a single line, they followed behind the woman; across the fallen tree and into a meadow of grasses and early spring wild flowers.

Because of her small stature, she deliberately took large, bounding steps to accommodate the men's larger stride as she moved through the grass. Each of them took great care to step into the small impressions left by her feet. They followed her in this manner until she reached a large rock quarry.

There was no sand or grass to bear their prints here. She waved at them, urging the men to follow her up and over a wall of slate. Ewen followed close behind. She offered her hand to help him over the top. Faria breached the top next and the woman leaned over offering to assist him. He looked at her for a moment, and then bluntly declined, "I am fine."

"I was not asking about your condition, sir. I was merely offering you assistance." She slowly withdrew her hand.

Arerys felt along the top edge, testing his hold in case the slips of shale came loose. The woman extended her hand to help him. The Elf considered the small hand that presented itself to him, and then he looked up at her face.

"I assure you, I rarely bite," she said with all seriousness. Then a small smile appeared on her lips.

Arerys reached up. They grabbed a hold of each other's wrist as she pulled him over the top.

Arerys and Faria assisted the others, but when all had reached safety, they turned to see the female was already on her way moving westward.

Markus ran after her. "Wait! Where do you go in such haste?"

Confident that Markus was not associated with Beyilzon and his Dark Army, she stopped in her tracks. "I am on my way to the west, to a place called Wyndwood."

"Wyndwood? What business have you there?" asked Markus, perplexed by her statement.

"I have been sent forth by my father's people to seek out Kal-lel Wingfield, the King of Wyndwood."

Arerys, upon hearing his father's name spoke of from a distance quickly approached Markus and the female. "I am from Wyndwood," declared Arerys. "What do you want with my people?"

The woman's eyes took in the Elf's tall form; at slightly over six feet tall, he towered a good nine inches above her. She studied his blue eyes, his long wheat-colored hair, and the long, thin braid that hung behind each pointed ear. She had no doubt he was one of the 'fair' citizens of Wyndwood.

"My business is with the King of Wyndwood. It is none of your concern."

"If it is a concern for my father, then it shall be my concern too," stated Arerys.

The woman eyes widened in stunned surprised. She dropped to her left knee, immediately lowering her head. "Oh, my goodness! I am sorry, my lord. I did not know!"

"Do not bow before me, rise up," ordered Arerys, extending his hand to her. "Who are you?" he asked, his eyes flashed as they scrutinized her dark features.

"I have come from afar," she answered, as she rose to her feet, "from the other side of the Iron Mountains. I am Nayla, daughter of Dahlon, Lord of the House of Treeborn."

For a moment, Arerys was taken aback by this news. The fair Elf pondered this introduction: *The daughter of the one who once ruled over Elmgrove? I thought his people were no more.*

"The daughter of Dahlon Treeborn!" exclaimed the Wizard as he drew back the hood of his great cloak to reveal his face fully; his silvery white beard and blue-gray eyes. "Nayla, it is I, Lindras Weatherstone, the Wizard of the West! My! Little one, you have grown! Why, you have your mother's beauty and fire, and your father's will and determination! How could I have not known it was you?"

"Lindras, never had I dreamed that our paths would cross again!" said Nayla, hugging him. Her tiny frame disappeared amidst the Wizard's towering body and flowing robe as they embraced.

"You know her, Wizard?" asked Arerys in quiet surprise.

"Most certainly, I do!" said Lindras, his happiness he did not conceal.

"You are a *dark* Elf?" asked Ewen with fascination as he studied her face.

"Well, I am certainly not *fair*, am I?" she answered, as she gazed over to Arerys.

The evening fire played host to another wanderer on this night. Nayla led the group to a safe bluff. Here, she raised three of the men's shields upright, planting them into the ground so they were turned outwards.

With this barrier in place, she arranged a small pile of wood, dried grasses, and leaves. She asked Faria to ignite the fire, only after the light of day had waned sufficiently. At least this way, the heavy, gray smoke from the wood, still damp from the day's rain, would dissolve into the darkness of the night sky.

The fire threw off much welcomed heat for those still chilled by the walk through the creek. The shields created an effective windbreak and a heat reflector. It also functioned as a visual barrier, so the flames licking up into the air, and the light it cast, could not be seen beyond the cover of the shields and the surrounding trees. Beyilzon's men would not easily be able to detect their fire from the distance.

Much of the evening meal was eaten in silence. All were in deep contemplation as they studied the stranger sitting in their midst. Aside from Lindras, it was difficult for the rest of them to believe that this diminutive female was the one and the same who had, only the day before, came to their aid by wreaking such havoc on Beyilzon's men. Now, it would appear this unexpected ally had come to their aid once again, helping them to escape certain death in the gully.

Lindras ended the long silence by introducing the members of the Order. "You have already met Arerys and Markus, let me introduce you to Lando Bayliss from Cedona."

Lando and Nayla both nodded to each other in acknowledgement of their introduction.

"This gentleman whom you so soundly trounced upon earlier today is Faria Targott of Darross," smiled Lindras, pointing in his direction.

Nayla smiled and nodded to Faria. He chose to ignore her.

"And this is—" before Lindras could finish his sentence, Darius rose up onto his feet, approaching Lady Treeborn.

"And I am Darius Calsair of Carcross, at your service, my lady," said the tall, dark knight, with a disarming smile. He knelt down upon his left knee, taking her right hand into his to gently planting a kiss upon it.

"Well, it is a pleasure to meet your acquaintance, kind sir."

"Let me assure you, the pleasure is mine."

Ewen stood up, boldly cutting in between Darius and Nayla. "And I am Ewen Vatel, squire to Markus." He snatched Nayla's hand from Darius, looking into her dark brown eyes and smiling a broad smile, he too, planted a kiss upon the back of her hand.

"Well, Master Vatel, I am pleased to meet you," smiled Nayla. It had been such a long time since she had engaged in conversation with anybody, she reveled in this interaction.

"So Nayla, tell us. What is your business with Arerys' father, King Kal-lel?" asked the Wizard.

"As you know, after the Dark Lord's defeat, my father and his people journeyed eastward in search of a new home and a new beginning that would allow them some hope of peace and acceptance," she began while gazing at Arerys. "They came across a race of mortals that held very similar beliefs as they did. Together, we have lived in peace for almost one thousand years."

"Although the people of Orien never knew of the Elves, they still accepted my father's people. These mortals are brave and skilled in the art of war. They have helped us to hone our skills and develop our senses to new heights, but because our combined numbers are few, we have been overwhelmed by a great calamity," said the little warrior.

"Go on. What calamity?" asked the Wizard.

"Lindras, my people are besieged. The Dark Lord's armies have extended their deadly hold on lands far beyond the Iron Mountains. I have been selected by my father and sent forth by the elders as a messenger to find King Kal-lel. It is said he may hold hope for our future."

All eyes turned to Markus and Ewen.

Nayla made an impassioned plea on bended knees before the Prince of Wyndwood. "My lord, I beg of you, please do not stop me from reaching your father. I must speak to him before it is too late. If he still has the wisdom and compassion that I have been told, he will come to our aid. Please help me to get word to him."

Arerys gazed into her dark, troubled eyes. Her despair was all too real. The Elf stood up and turned away from her. Standing just beyond the warm glow of the fire, he looked pensive, his hand rubbing his chin as he deliberated on her words.

Markus stood up to approach Arerys. "My friend, I believe her. It stands to reason that Beyilzon's men would go beyond their former boundaries to hunt down Dahlon and his kind, just as he would seek to destroy your people," said Markus in a hushed tone.

"I have my doubts, Markus," whispered Arerys. He watched Nayla sitting by the fire with the others.

"Do you doubt what she is saying, or do you doubt her? Think carefully before you answer for there is a big difference, Arerys."

"She is different!" retorted the Elf.

Lindras, catching the tone of the conversation, cautioned the Elf. "What you feel and hear about her kind is something that should be left in the past. I myself know her father, and he is not unlike your own father, Arerys. Dahlon is wise and has great compassion for others. It was his bid to bring peace to both sides that he chose to leave Wyndwood. Do not look harshly upon her because she differs from you. If you wish to keep it in proper perspective, it would serve you well to understand that you both share a common adversary."

"Lindras is right, Arerys. Do not let appearances cloud your judgment. Whether she is a dark Elf, or not, this is not the issue. Just as we all assumed she was a man because she wields a sword better than most men do, we were all fooled by our perception until she revealed her true identify to us," advised Markus. "I have a feeling Arerys, that if I drew blood from the both of you, the blood would run the same color. Besides, do you think she was not aware of what you were when she first came to our aid? I suggest you hear her out. We owe her at least that consideration, after all she has done for us."

Without another word, the Elf turned, reclaiming his place with the Order. He turned to the female warrior: "Address me as Arerys… I shall hear you out."

Markus sat next to his friend, laying a hand on his shoulder as an unspoken 'thank you'.

"Then you shall call me Nayla," she said. A spark of hope flickered in her eyes.

"Surely, you did not venture forth on your own?" asked Markus.

"No, I am the last surviving warrior. There were three of us sent forth by the elders," sighed Nayla, "My comrades have fallen, even before we could reach the Iron Mountains. Beyilzon's soldiers are everywhere, and they are many."

"You have been on your own? You crossed the great mountains by yourself?" Faria asked, in an incredulous tone.

Nayla's eyes burned as she glared at Faria. "Yes, I did," she flatly answered.

"Ha! How can a maiden, especially one such as yourself, survive such a journey?" grunted Faria, looking her up and down with some disdain.

"Of all people… You who had a small taste of my blade. Need I remind you of our first encounter?" she asked with raised eyebrows.

The others met her comment with a burst of laughter. Faria squirmed with discomfort.

"Although I am a woman, let me assure you, I am quite skilled in many things, sir," Nayla responded with great confidence.

At that moment, Darius was reminded of something. He reached into his pack and drew out a small package that was wrapped in a small strip of material, bound together with a short length of string. "I believe these are yours, my good lady!" said Darius, handing her the package.

Nayla took the package from his hand, carefully unwrapping it. "My darts! Thank you, Darius. These were the last of my supply. How fortuitous!" she said as she bowed in appreciation. She carefully wrapped them up and stowed them into a special pocket in her vest.

"Those darts you hold; they are poisoned are they not?" asked the Wizard.

"Most definitely! In fact, it is a highly potent poison," said Nayla. She pulled out a small vial of the lethal powder she carried in her worn, leather pouch.

"That would explain the sudden demise of those soldiers from such a small wound," nodded Markus in understanding.

"Are you also responsible for the soldiers we have found dead at their campsite; their bodies unmarred by weapons?" asked Lando.

"Yes. I had entered their camp at night to poison their water supply. Sometimes it is better to take a more subtle approach when you are forced to be an army of one, against an army of many."

Ewen was most impressed by her cunning and bravery.

"So Nayla, was it you I sensed following us?" asked Arerys.

"Yes. In fact, I felt your presence long before you tried to kill me along with the dark rider. I was most curious about your business in Talibarr for there are more reasons to flee from this place, than to venture into this region."

"Tell me, Nayla. Why did your father spare only three warriors for such a perilous mission?" asked the Wizard.

"Oh Lindras, it was not his choice to do so. With Beyilzon's armies mounting numerous attacks throughout our land, many of our people fled to the fortress city of Nagana. All who were fit to do battle remained to secure the gates and walls of the fortress; to maintain our last stronghold," explained Nayla, her mind and body growing weary just thinking of this burden she had been left to bear. "The elders advised Dahlon to send only three, for if even a small army was to be deployed for this mission, not only would we draw attention to ourselves, but the chances of holding the fortress until help arrived would be severely compromised. If the mission failed, at least we have some chance of saving Nagana."

"Not to question your abilities, my lady, but why you? Why a woman?" asked Darius.

"Once I shed my weapons, I am no longer a threat; men tend to view me as a harmless little flower. I can slip by unnoticed, or at the very least, men tend to drop their guard. This alone makes me more dangerous than most men. Where my companions may be barred from entrance to some areas, by virtue of the fact that I am a woman, I can slip through. It is like inviting the fox into the hen house at times," Nayla mused.

"I for one would have never guessed that you were a warrior had I not seen with mine own eyes what you are capable of!" admitted Darius.

Nayla blushed at his kind words. "My comrades have not been so lucky. I have survived thus far, rather unscathed, but I still have far to go."

"My lady, how did you hope to find my father in time?" asked Arerys, with genuine concern. "At this rate, even if you had reached Wyndwood, I have grave doubts my father and all those in the Alliance would ever make the journey in time to aid your people."

"I had come so far, I had to try. In my last bid to get word to King Kal-lel, I sent forth my falcon to deliver a note, in hopes that my call for help would be answered. Alas, it has been many days now; Tori has not sought me out. I am afraid she has perished." Her voice was soft, almost a whisper.

Ewen, Markus and Lindras looked at each other simultaneously, realizing that the mystery of the falcon had been solved.

"My lady, I believe your bird is quite safe!" said Ewen.

"What do you speak of, boy?"

"You are NT, on the falcon's tethers. I had found your injured bird on the ledge of our castle. Lindras had healed her wing, we left her in the care of the household staff when we departed."

"Then you received my message?"

"I am sorry, Nayla. There was no message; only the bird," answered Lindras.

"So, she is safe in Wyndwood?" asked Nayla, her voice still full of renewed hope.

"I am afraid not. She had strayed far off course, coming to my father's castle in Carcross," said Markus.

Nayla was puzzled, her head tilted as she considered his words. "Your father's castle?"

"Yes, King Bromwell."

Nayla's eyes widened in surprise. She abruptly knelt and bowed low before him. "Prince Markus, please forgive my impudence, I was not aware of your identity."

"Nayla, until this quest we have embarked on is done, I am merely Markus," he said, offering his hand to the little figure that knelt before him.

"It is of the utmost importance our true identity remains hidden until we see this to an end," said Lindras. "Do you understand, Nayla? In time, the true nature of our mission shall be revealed to you."

"Yes, Wizard," nodded Nayla. "This is most curious though: my bird should arrive to Markus; and that I would even chance to cross paths with you and your comrades. It is almost unfathomable."

"Ah, it was our destiny that we would find each other," smiled Lindras.

"Well, I have found my destiny and it calls me to sleep," yawned Darius. "I am ready to fall asleep where I stand!"

"I shall take the first watch, Markus," said Arerys as he slung his bow over his shoulder.

"I wish to join you, if you will allow it," requested Nayla, adjusting the scabbard of her sword to her belt.

Arerys considered her for a moment, surprised that she would offer to take the watch with him. "As you wish."

As they turned away from the fire, Faria laughed. "Yes, keep an eye on this one, Arerys. Be careful that you are not beguiled by her feminine charms. She may try to poison us in our sleep too!"

Nayla leaned close to Faria and whispered into his ear, "It is ill advised to plant any ideas in my head, good sir."

The large man was startled by her response, his hazel eyes burned as he glared back at her. She smiled coolly at him before turning to follow Arerys.

Markus watched as Nayla and Arerys vanished together into the darkness. He turned to Lindras. "Wizard, do you think she is the unlikely ally the Three Sisters spoke of?"

"Well, Eliya did warn us that whoever this ally was to be, his or her help would not be well received by all," reminded Lindras. "I can hardly say we have been gracious to her thus far."

"Do you think it is a wise idea, Lindras? Arerys and Nayla? Would that not be akin to throwing a cat and a dog into a pit together?" asked Markus as he laid his head down to rest.

"Markus, given time and the right conditions, even a cat and dog can learn to live together in relative peace and harmony," answered Lindras, his eyes sparkled beneath the shadow of his great hood as they followed the thin, gray wisp of smoke that escaped his lips. "Besides, I do think Arerys is in need of some education, and I do believe there is none better to provide it than the daughter of Dahlon Treeborn."

CHAPTER 7

STRIKING A BALANCE

They stood alone in the darkness, keeping watch atop of the bluff; overlooking where the men of the Order now slept. Arerys silently studied the constellations. As the thin cloud cover drifted away, he could see two of the brightest stars in the heavens, shining down upon them. The thought crossed the Elf's mind of the irony that these two beautiful, sparkling lights bejeweling the evening sky were also the harbingers of the dark days that lay ahead for the citizens of Imago, both to the east and west of the Iron Mountains.

Mars and Venus continued on its alignment with earth. Each night they drew ever closer, becoming ever brighter.

"You look to the stars, my lord," said Nayla. "Do you seek a sign that may change the course of mankind's destiny?"

He shook his head in response. "The signs are not good."

"Arerys, though you do not know me, I assure you, I am no fool."

The Elf did not respond to her comment.

Nayla continued to speak. "My father was once part of the Alliance, as was your father, and the kings of Cedona, Carcross and Darross. This is no coincidence you have gathered men from these very same places, as you head eastward through Talibarr. Markus already disclosed that you are on a quest. Though you may feel I am not privy to such information, please know this: if it is to crush the Dark Lord's armies, then let me be an ally in your cause."

Arerys looked down at her. "You assume too much, Lady Treeborn."

Nayla's dark eyes flashed at the Elf as she responded coldly, "This is not by chance that you are in the heart of Beyilzon's territory." She turned to walk some distance away, and then she faced in his direction again.

"I know what you do, Arerys," whispered Nayla. "I may only have half the Elven blood coursing through my veins than you do, but I assure you, I can still see and hear, almost as well as you."

Arerys, startled by her words, looked at her and answered softly, "If you truly can hear me, then tell me by what name you go by in your mother's tongue?"

"My mother called me 'Takaro', in the common speech it means *Noble Child*," whispered Nayla, turning away indignantly to join the others who slept around the fire.

It was now obvious this woman may well indeed know more than any of them had anticipated. "Do not leave, Nayla. I did not mean to offend you. The night is long; it would be a pleasant change to speak to someone new."

Nayla slowly turned about. She considered Arerys' words for a lingering moment. *Apology accepted*, thought the little warrior, walking back to join the Elf. She sat beneath an aging oak tree that looked sickly and gnarled. Resting with her back against its twisted, moss-covered trunk, she scanned the dark forest that lay beyond the bluff.

She sat with her knees drawn up to her chest, her small arms wrapping around them. The Elf looked down upon her. She was a tiny figure, almost child-like once her weapons were concealed beneath her cloak. Arerys joined her beneath the tree. For a long while, both said nothing.

Finally, Nayla spoke: "This is the first time in many days that I have spoken to anyone."

"It must have been a very long and difficult journey to endure alone."

"Yes." Her answer was barely audible.

After another long silence, Arerys asked, "Nayla, tell me about your mother's people. Tell me about the people of Orien."

"The Taijins are mortals that have a long history, as I understand, even longer than the people inhabiting this western portion of Imago," replied Nayla. "They are a proud, honorable and tolerant people, with a great reverence for life."

"I overheard Lindras say to you that you are your mother's daughter. Did he mean that your mother was a skilled warrior?"

Nayla giggled with almost the innocence of a young child at Arerys' question. "No! My mother did not wield a sword as I do, but she did wield a sharp tongue and great wisdom. Lindras was probably referring to the fact that he believes we both go out of our way to look for trouble. My mother was regarded as an upstart and a vexation to men, because of her efforts to make a woman's life more rounded than just that of maid and servant."

"She left her home to make a life of her own although she was ordered to stay put until the man her parents had arranged for her marry, claimed her," Nayla continued. "She just wanted so much more for me, than life had afforded her. She actually defied her own family to marry one who was not even of her own race!"

"And what of your father, Nayla? Forgive my ignorance, but I know little about Lord Dahlon Treeborn. It is a subject that is not easy to broach with my own father, or the elders of Wyndwood."

"Dahlon has grown bitter with life. Although his people did settle amongst the mortals of Orien, it was not home - it was not Wyndwood," said Nayla wistfully. "The new land he sought for his people never lived up to his promise. Many chose to enter the Twilight, than to linger any longer in this realm."

"Nayla, you speak about your mother's kind and your father's kind as though they are two separate entities from your own. Are you not a product of both?"

"I am both, but neither. I suppose I am cursed, or blessed, depending upon your point of view, with greater life than that of a mortal, but I shall never enter the Twilight, nor shall I have an eternity to walk this earth for as long as you do. Alas, I appear different from my mother's people and I am even darker than the 'dark' Elves that your fair kind despise so."

Arerys looked at her, not knowing what words he could offer to ease her apparent sorrow. "That was long ago, Nayla. My father's people—"

She raised her hand, not wishing to hear any more. "You are right, that was long ago." After a moment of awkward silence, Nayla changed the subject. "Do you have a family, Arerys? Other than your father and mother?"

"My mother chose to enter the Twilight to be with her family. She tired of the turmoil of her earthly existence, departing when she felt my brother and I were at an age that any mischief we found ourselves in, we could get out of on our own."

"Ah, you do have a brother!" smiled Nayla. "Tell me about him."

"His name is Artel. I have been told we are quite the opposites. He is a true sylvan Elf, he prefers to stay in Wyndwood; I prefer to see the world. He is content to limit his knowledge to what the elders teach him; I strive to see if there is more."

"Is he younger than you?"

"Yes. He was born five hundred and forty years ago. In mortal terms, I suppose he is the equivalent to being almost twenty-seven years of age," answered Arerys. "And what of you?"

"I was born two hundred and ninety years ago, so I suppose, given that I age twice as fast as an Elf, I understand that I am about twenty-eight or twenty-nine in mortal years," responded Nayla, after much thought.

"I was actually inquiring about your family," smiled Arerys. "I would never ask a lady about her age."

Nayla laughed with embarrassment at the misunderstanding. She smiled inwardly when she realized how long it had been since she last had anything to laugh about.

"You are very fortunate, Arerys. I have no siblings to speak of, I am an only child. My mother died when I was young and to Dahlon's regret, his desire for one son to carry on the Treeborn name and legacy shall go unfulfilled."

It was then Arerys noticed how Nayla always addressed Lord Dahlon Treeborn as 'Dahlon' - never father. "Is that why you chose to be a warrior? To prove your worth to your father?"

"It is rather strange how all this came about. Dahlon and I, we have had a very turbulent and violent history from the time I was a child. My desire to learn the ways of the warrior was initially instigated by my desire to protect myself from his hands," said Nayla, reflecting on her past.

"That is terrible, Nayla!" said Arerys, staring at the little figure sitting next to him.

"Show me no pity, Arerys. We are all shaped by events of our past. It is how we choose to deal with them that make the difference. I am a stronger person for all that I have endured. In fact, like my mother, I view all the barriers I have encountered in my life as merely challenges. Where my father sought to control me - to stifle my standing in life, my mother expected me to pursue my dreams. Where my father did not encourage me to strive for greatness because more people may know if I had failed in the process, my mother always believed the greatest failure in life is never to have tried at all."

"So you do this in defiance to your father?" asked Arerys, wishing to understand her better.

"At first, yes. As I matured I came to realize that my mother, even in her death, has had greater influence over me," answered Nayla. "My mother taught me about honor, loyalty, and duty. She is the one who taught me to protect those weaker than I, because it is the right thing to do. She is the one who made me understand – to find the courage and strength needed to die for a brother-in-arms, because you are honor bound to do so. After all, in the end, one's honor is all that is left to define one's true character. Though I shall never please my father, if I remain true to myself, then that is the right thing to do to honor my mother, and myself."

"Is that why you requested this mission? You wanted to prove to him that you are as capable as any of his other warriors?"

"No. In fact, I never asked, nor did I volunteer for this onerous task."

"Then, why you? Why were you sent? I myself would never endanger my own child on such a deadly quest."

Nayla hesitated momentarily before answering his question. "In Dahlon's eyes, I am expendable... Suicide missions such as this are deliberately assigned to me. It would be an honorable method for him to wash his hands of me. Ironically, where the elders trust my abilities, Dahlon trusts that one day, I may fail. So far, I have proven him wrong. Like some insidious disease, I return each time."

"You are his flesh and blood, Nayla. How can you withstand such treatment?"

Nayla's brown eyes peered up at Arerys. "In my life, it is all I have ever known."

"How can you not be angry?" asked Arerys, unable to comprehend Dahlon's cruelty to a member of his own family. He looked at her face silhouetted against the night sky.

"He is my father, Arerys," shrugged Nayla. "Life has dealt him some terrible blows; Dahlon has lost many things that were rightfully his. His rage is vented upon me as I am a reminder of his hopes and dreams that had been dashed. I hold no bitterness towards him. He chose to wallow in despair and self-pity, rather than help himself. I chose to rise above my situation, for he made me realize that I did not want to become like him; full of self-pity and regret."

"He does not sound like the same person Lindras knows," noted Arerys.

"No doubt," agreed Nayla. "The elders know him as a wise and compassionate soul, for he is discreet in his dealings with me. He is careful to present only that *noble* side of his personality to the public. I however, had to deal with his darkness and his misery. I fear he is a mere shadow of his former self."

"If I may be so bold to ask, has Dahlon offered you the eternal life of an Elf?" asked Arerys. "I know he has the same power as my father to do so."

"He has never offered, nor would I accept it from him, if he had."

"But, why not, Nayla? Of all people, you seem to relish and value life more than most mortals I know," asked Arerys, his eyes searching hers for answers.

"Whether I shall perish in battle, or die of old age, long before my father should even chose to enter the Twilight, I would rather live a finite lifetime and hold my head high. I prefer to live my life as I choose than to be condemned to an eternity, scraping by on other people's pity and expectations," declared Nayla. "Every offer comes with a price. This is one I refuse to pay; I wish to owe him nothing."

Both sat enveloped by the stillness of the night. Arerys thinking upon Nayla's words as she studied his Elven features and golden hair that seemed to capture and reflect the faint light emitted by the stars. She had never seen one so fair in all her life, with the exception of Lindras, who she had last seen as a child just before her mother's death.

"Tell me, Nayla," inquired Arerys; "why do you divulge such intimate details of your life to me so freely? I am a stranger to you. Besides, it cannot be easy to admit to be the victim of such ill fortune."

"Make no mistake, Arerys, I am no victim. I prefer to think of myself as a survivor of unfortunate circumstances." After a brief pause, she continued, "I chose to tell you such intimate details of my life because, in case you are not already aware, I am attempting to solicit your help. I have no secrets to withhold from you. I have nothing to hide."

Arerys did not respond. He searched her dark eyes for other possible mysteries that seem to surround this stranger.

"My lord, if you truly are the son of Kal-lel Wingfield, then I believe it is fair to assume that you cannot be bribed nor seduced. Am I correct?"

"You are correct."

"Then, how else am I to earn your trust?"

Nayla rose as she heard the approach of two sets of footsteps; it was

Faria and Markus - arriving to relieve them of sentry duty.

"Ah, Arerys still lives!" mocked Faria, in a sarcastic tone.

"Faria, it is not wise to make an enemy where there is none to be had; it is a terrible waste of energy. My presence will not bother you after tomorrow, I shall be on my way," advised Nayla, turning away from the knight. She silently disappeared into the darkness.

Markus turned on Faria. "What is the matter with you? Why are you so threatened by her presence?"

"You should ask that of Arerys. She should be no more trusted than the *dark* Elves that were vanquished from Wyndwood by his father," growled Faria, leaning against the oak tree as he lit his pipe.

Arerys said nothing; he shook his head in silent disapproval of Faria's conduct as he turned to follow Nayla back to camp.

When he arrived, the others were still deep in sleep, Lindras sitting upright near the dying flames, snoring quite loudly. Nayla lay curled up under her cloak at the base of a tree away from the others, a lone figure, even amongst the members of the Order.

The day began gray and overcast, extending night's dark grip late into the morning. The men were still asleep when Darius and Lando returned from sentry duty.

Arerys awoke alert, as though he was never asleep. He glanced around to see the others stirring from their slumber. He looked over to where he had last seen Nayla sleeping. She was gone.

"Lindras… Nayla has departed," said Arerys, waking the Wizard.

Lindras' eyes snapped open. "We must find her, Arerys. She is critical to our quest!"

Arerys snatched up his bow and quiver. He quickly checked for signs that indicated the direction Nayla was traveling in. He sprinted after her at top speed. She was moving westward.

The Elf leapt over a stream and continued to run, following her nearly invisible trail. As he entered a clearing surrounded by many large trees with full crowns of leaves, Arerys came to an abrupt stop. There was no sign of Nayla – it was as though she had vanished. He looked closely at the ground, scrutinizing it for telltale signs of her movements. There was nothing.

His eyes pierced through the dense forest beyond the clearing, but there was no sign to indicate her presence or the direction she had taken. He listened for the sounds of her footsteps, her breathing, even her heartbeat. Nothing. All he could hear was the sound of his own heart pounding anxiously in his chest.

Arerys listened one last time. He glanced about to survey the forest before returning to the others. As he turned to head back, a single leaf wafted down from the tree he stood beneath. It slowly fluttered through the air, gently floating on an invisible breeze.

His eyes turned upwards, retracing the movement of the leaf from high above. Much to his surprise, there sat Nayla, perched high up on a branch, hidden in the shadows of the great tree.

"Most people tend to look ahead, they rarely look above," marveled Nayla. "Are you seeking someone?"

"Yes. I have come to fetch you."

"Upon whose request?"

"Lindras. The Wizard urgently requests your presence," answered Arerys, approaching the tree's heavily branched trunk.

Without another word, Nayla nimbly made her way down. As she reached the last branch, Arerys extended both his hands to assist her. She took his hands into hers as he lifted her down to the ground. Nayla turned and proceeded to sprint back in the direction they had both come from. Arerys followed behind, staying close to ensure she was indeed heading back to the Wizard.

As they entered camp, Lindras and Ewen ran up to greet them. "You are as impetuous as your mother, Nayla!" scolded the Wizard; his concern for her placed him in a cantankerous mood. "It is dangerous for you to be alone out there!"

"No more so than it is for your men," answered Nayla. "I only came back because you are a friend, Lindras. What do you need from me?"

"I believe we can help each other, Nayla. It is obvious we share a common enemy. Here is a chance that we, together can smite him and be rid of the Dark Lord for good."

"Interesting… so you are on a quest of sorts," said Nayla. She sat down next to Markus. Ewen, obviously pleased that she had returned, brought her some food. She smiled her thanks to him.

"As we speak, armies from Carcross, Cedona, Darross and Wyndwood prepare for war," admitted Lindras. "I will tell you this now;

none shall come to the aid of your people in Orien, there is none to spare. The soldiers of the Alliance march towards the Plains of Fire in preparation for battle at the next full moon. If they do not defeat Beyilzon there, your people are doomed to fall anyway."

Nayla's heart sank upon receiving this news. She said nothing.

"Your skills are better put to use assisting us," insisted Lindras.

"And you are familiar with this region, you know it better than any of us, perhaps even better than Lindras now," added Markus. "Plus, there is no denying your skills, I am sure there is much you can teach us."

Nayla thought upon Markus' words for a moment. "If I do this, tell me one thing," Nayla requested of Lindras, "does your quest take you to Mount Hope?"

Markus and Lindras looked at each other, then the Wizard nodded his head.

"Say no more," responded Nayla. "I am now in your service."

"Very well," said Lindras. "We shall stay here until nightfall and move on with the darkness. We shall bide our time and rest now while we can, or it shall make for an extremely long journey tomorrow."

After they ate, Lando resumed his watch with Markus as the others waited around the cold campfire. Lindras was burdened by his thoughts as he reflected upon the images the Three Sisters revealed to him. Arerys sat quietly next to the Wizard, in deep concentration as he carved a small piece of white oak into an exquisite, delicate figurine of a winged fairy. Ewen wiled the time away, watching Faria and Darius test their abilities with knife throwing against an old tree stump.

Nayla sat alone beneath the tree she had slept under the night before. Her legs were crossed, her back straight, the fingers of both hands entwined together as her eyes closed. For a moment, Ewen thought she was asleep.

He quietly approached her for a better look. In front of Nayla, lay her sword, still sheathed, blade edge facing towards her with the handle deliberately positioned to her right hand in case she was forced to make a fast draw.

Ewen examined the beautifully engraved, black, wooden scabbard that her sword was sheathed in. He knelt down before her for a closer look, reaching out to pick up her sword. Suddenly, Nayla's hand darted out, seizing him by his wrist.

Ewen was startled by her swiftness and gasped when he realized her eyes were still closed. "My lady, how did you know?"

Nayla's eyes slowly opened as she released her grip on his wrist; she snatched up her weapon from the ground. "You must never touch my sword, Ewen. Do you understand?"

"I am sorry, but how did you know I was going to touch it? Your eyes were closed."

"The sword and I are one. You touch my sword, you touch my soul. I felt your intention."

"I do not understand," said Ewen, unable to comprehend the meaning of her words.

"I do not expect you to understand, Ewen. Just respect my wishes."

She stood up to pluck a large, green leaf from the tree. She tossed it high into the air; the leaf slowly spun and fluttered down to the earth. Nayla quickly drew her single-edged sword so the blade was held upright. As the leaf slowly drifted down, it lightly kissed the blade. Nayla did not move a muscle, the sword remaining perfectly still as the leaf sliced neatly in half as it continued to float to the ground, now in two pieces.

Ewen was stunned; he had never seen a sword with a blade of such razor-sharpness before. Even his father's fearsome weapon now paled in comparison.

"You must never touch my sword, Ewen. It is not to be handled lightly or treated as a toy," warned Nayla, using a stern voice.

"That is incredible, my lady," said Ewen, still in awe.

Nayla's sternness quickly dissolved. She smiled at him as she knelt down to pick up a handful of dried leaves that had accumulated at the base of the tree. She asked Ewen to stand clear. With one swift movement, Nayla tossed the leaves high over her head. With sweeping, circular movements, she sliced into the leaves as they floated through the air. They fell in many pieces, like brown confetti showering down upon them.

Ewen eyes were wide with excitement. "Arerys! Did you see that?"

Arerys and the men did indeed see Nayla's display; the flash of polished steel was difficult not to notice. They approached for a better look at her handiwork and were amazed at the straight edges made on the leaves. There was not one that had a shredded or torn edge. Where her blade touched the leaf, the cuts were clean and precise.

"May I have permission to examine your sword, my lady?" asked

Darius.

Nayla sheathed her sword into the ornately crafted scabbard as she considered Darius' request.

"Very well, but do not draw it and allow the blade to touch the scabbard, it shall cut clean through," she warned him.

She presented the sword to him, holding it out so it was balanced in her open hands, held at thirds. The blade edge was turned to her while the handle was held out to her left so Darius may take it into his right hand.

Darius carefully grasped Nayla's sword. He was startled by its weight, or rather, the lack of. Even shielded within its scabbard, it was still half the weight of the Elven sword he now carried. He cautiously withdrew it from its scabbard, the razor-sharp blade flashing like polished silver, even in the dull light of the gray morning.

"This is incredible! It is as light as a feather!" marveled Darius.

"It may be extremely sharp, Darius, but do not be fooled. That does not mean it has the strength to cut through limb or armor," said Faria as he defiantly thrust the blade of his knife into the tree's trunk.

Nayla took the sword from Darius. Without taking her eyes off of Faria, she spun the sword in her right hand and, with a sweeping upward cut, she struck Faria's knife. It fell to the ground, the blade embedding itself into the soil.

Faria knelt to retrieve his weapon. "Now what does that prove, my lady?" he grunted, unimpressed by her display.

Nayla did not answer; she merely offered him a small smile.

Yanking his knife from the ground, he was rendered speechless.

"What is it, Faria?" asked Arerys.

Faria held forth the knife for all to see: the blade was cleanly cut in half. The remainder of the knife was still embedded in the tree trunk!

As Nayla moved to sheath her sword, she held out the portion just before the hand guard.

"See these five score marks?" she asked, her finger gingerly touching the flat edge of the blade. "This sword was forged by the mortals of Orien. They mark the quality of the blade by these scores. Each score represents the number of bodies the blade may pass through in a single stroke."

"You can cut down five men in a single stroke?" asked Ewen in astonishment.

"No. Three bodies perhaps, as I lack the strength, but a man such as

Darius can do so quite easily with such a weapon."

"If you inspect the blade, you shall see that it is absolutely flawless, even after cutting through Faria's knife, it will not leave a knick on the surface," added Nayla.

"This is incredible!" stated Arerys. "Surely, this must be a combination of Elven magic and precious metals to create such a fantastic weapon."

"No, Arerys," answered Nayla. "The mortals use iron, but it is in the way the metal is forged. Each blade is folded and pounded one thousand times, no less, during the shaping of the blade."

"Well, it is still truly a marvel," said Arerys.

Nayla passed her sword to Arerys for his inspection. He nodded in thanks, slowly withdrawing the sword from its scabbard. There was no doubt it was much lighter than even the Elven sword, so sought after by the mortals of Imago. Arerys also noted her sword had only a single edge, whereas typical Elven swords were doubled-edged.

"This is truly a fearsome weapon," admitted Arerys, handling Nayla's sword with great respect. "It feels as though it is one with my hand."

"As it should be; after all, the sword is merely an extension of your body. It should be handled as such," said Nayla.

Arerys nodded in agreement, carefully sheathing the sword before handing it back to Nayla.

"So you have mastered the sword?" inquired the Elf.

"I am proficient with the sword - I know few who have truly mastered it," answered Nayla. "Besides, I have spent much of my life training in many other weapons. It is important to be skilled in all manners of war if one is to survive in this world."

"You know of other weapons?" asked Ewen, with growing fascination.

"I am trained to use many weapons, young master; most that you probably have little or no knowledge of."

"Arerys is a great marksman, Nayla," said Ewen. "Are you an archer too?

"My stature makes it difficult for me to handle the long bow efficiently, and admittedly, I would be dead several times over if I had to rely on my strength to load a crossbow. So, in answer to your question, the bow is not my weapon of choice but yes, I can use one. I assure you though, I am not as proficient as your friend."

"Care to demonstrate for us?" asked Faria with raised eyebrows and a challenging smile.

"Not really."

"Come now, be a sport, Nayla!" goaded Darius, with a mischievous grin.

"Arerys, you go ahead first," said Faria. "Show Nayla what you can do."

Arerys was reluctant at first, but taking his bow in his hand, he selected a tall fir tree that was devoid of branches on its lower trunk. From sixty feet away, he rapidly fired off several arrows. Each arrow struck the tree trunk, one above the other, each perfectly spaced exactly three inches apart.

"You are showing off, my lord!" insisted Nayla, accepting the challenge as he passed his bow to her.

"As I lack your keen eyesight, may I be permitted to take a few paces forward?" asked Nayla.

"Of course," responded Arerys.

Taking a single arrow from Arerys' quiver, Nayla stepped forward about five paces, standing balanced on a flat rock. Held vertically, the Elf's bow was as tall as she, but now slightly elevated, she was able to draw the bow unhampered by the ground. Nayla took aim, drawing a deep breath, she released the arrow as she exhaled.

The arrow flew straight and true, striking its mark. To everyone's surprise, the middle arrow Arerys had placed with great precision, suddenly exploded, shattering into many small, sharp splinters of wood!

Nayla tossed the bow back to Arerys. Reaching into her vest pocket with her left hand, she withdrew four of her darts. Almost completely concealed in the palm of her right hand, Nayla threw the darts, one after another, her hand a blur.

Ewen could not believe his eyes. He ran ahead to examine her handiwork. Just as Markus and Lando returned to camp; Ewen waved for them to join the others. "Come! You must look at this!"

Markus and Lando approached them. Even Lindras, who was taking all of this in from the campfire, stood up to see.

As they neared the tree, it not only became apparent that Nayla had shattered Arerys' arrow, she also delivered four darts around the very same fractured projectile, all neatly grouped in a circle around the arrowhead that was embedded into the tree.

Darius laughed. "So, little one, I believe you are now the one who is showing off."

Nayla just gave him a small smile as she went to retrieve her darts.

"Well, I think there is none here who can dispute it is better that you are on our side, than on the side of the enemy, Nayla," laughed Lindras, as he admired her marksmanship.

Ewen ran up to her side as she carefully concealed her darts back into her vest pocket.

"My lady, can you teach me some of what you know?" asked Ewen earnestly.

Before Nayla could respond, Markus interjected; "Ewen, the time is not right. You know you cannot wield a weapon."

Ewen, like any boy his age, was just excited and inspired by what he had just witnessed. His shoulders slumped in disappointment at Markus' words.

"I just thought that if I could at least protect myself, it would give you less cause to worry over me," sighed Ewen.

Nayla turned to the boy. "Ewen, you need not bear arms in order to protect yourself. Your body is a weapon, if you know how to use it."

Ewen looked at her with bewildered eyes.

"I am also knowledgeable in unarmed combat," continued Nayla. "One cannot always rely on a weapon to be close at hand at all times. You can still learn to fight off an adversary, even if he is armed to the teeth."

"Whoa now! You are going to convince us that you, a woman, can fight a man, one-on-one, without a weapon?" asked Faria. "This is ludicrous!"

Nayla's arms unfolded as she slowly turned to face him. A small smile crept across her face as she said in a calm voice, devoid of any emotion: "Punch me, Faria."

"What?"

"Go ahead. *Try* to punch me."

"I am not going to fight with a woman!"

"I insist. Indulge me."

"You are crazy!" growled Faria, turning away from her.

Suddenly, Nayla's left hand seized Faria's right shoulder, spinning him about to face her. Her right hand, already chambered, flew straight out from her hip. Clenched into a rock-hard fist, it struck the large man in his midriff. He crumpled to his knees as she knocked the wind out of him.

Arerys was surprised, for he observed that when Nayla delivered the debilitating blow, her arm was not fully extended. Instead of relying on the strength of her arm to deliver the punch, Nayla had placed her entire body weight behind her fist, sinking with the strike to give the full impact of the explosive hit.

The men were stunned by Nayla's swift assault. Markus struggled to help the winded Faria onto his feet.

"What are you doing, Nayla? This was uncalled for," he scolded her.

"It occurred to me that Faria might be a gentleman… he would probably never hit a woman. I am giving him good reason to."

"Young lady, I do believe you have proven your point! Leave the man alone," insisted Lindras. His efforts to avert a further confrontation went unheeded by both Faria and Nayla.

"I am fine, Wizard!" said Faria, struggling to his feet. Pushing Markus aside, he squared off against the little warrior.

"Oh, goodness…" grumbled Lindras, as he turned away, no longer wishing to witness anymore. "You were warned."

A disheveled Faria swung out with his right fist, Nayla deftly angled out of the way. Again, Faria swung at her face, this time with his left. Nayla merely pivoted, his fist just skimming past her. After several more attempts to strike Nayla, beads of perspiration were beginning to form on Faria's forehead and his breathing was becoming more labored. Nayla, on the other hand, showed little sign of exertion. In mounting frustration, Faria blindly attempted to back-fist her face, but once more, she effortlessly ducked below his arm. In final desperation, Faria turned to lunge at Nayla, his fist coming straight for her.

Suddenly, Nayla leapt backwards, and then dropped from his sight. She dove to the ground into a tight ball as she rolled directly towards Faria. She came to an abrupt halt on her back, landing directly in front of him, between his legs. Her hands caught hold of his ankles as she brought both her legs up, slamming them against his upper thighs to send him crashing backwards.

Faria lay on his back, completely vulnerable. Nayla raised her right leg up high to drive her heel downward onto his groin. The men all grimaced as though they too, were about to share in Faria's experience - to be assaulted by a phantom pain. Their knees instinctively locked together and their hands dropped to their nether regions as Nayla's heel came down with great force.

Faria gasped, his eyes clenched shut as his hands desperately tried to intercept Nayla's strike. Just as her foot was about hit its mark with painful accuracy, all the men averted their eyes, not wishing to see anymore. Instead, Nayla stopped - just short of making contact with Faria's manhood.

She quickly rolled back onto her feet, and then leaned in close over Faria, who lay on the ground breathing hard. She helped him onto his feet and as she did so, she asked: "So tell me, do you still believe it was a mistake, or sheer luck, that the first time we met, I had you pinned to the ground?"

"You caught me off guard," protested Faria, still struggling to recover his breath and composure.

"Faria, do not be a fool," said Markus, trying to dismiss his remark.

"You do not get it, do you?" asked Nayla, grabbing Faria by his shoulders.

Placing her right foot on his left hip, she sank to the ground, hoisting him up, and over her body. Faria again, landed on his back with a heavy *'thud'*. Nayla, having not released her grip on his body, used his momentum to roll directly over the large man to land squarely upon his chest. Once more, she used her knees to pin his arms to the ground.

"I suppose I caught you off guard yet again, using the same move, at that!"

Markus shook his head in disapproval. He looked down upon his hapless companion. "Unfortunately, Faria, this time you are deserving of this fate."

He was just relieved that Nayla did not exact the potential injury she was fully capable of dispensing. This time, the other men did not sympathize with Faria either. They laughed as Darius came to his aid, plucking Nayla off of him.

"Teach me that, Nayla. Show me how to fight like that!" cried Ewen.

"How did you do that, little one?" asked Darius as he helped brush the dust and embarrassment off of Faria.

"It is easy," insisted Nayla. She instructed Darius to grab her by her shoulders, or the lapels of her vest. In an instant, Darius was airborne. He fell hard onto his back with Nayla immobilizing him in the same manner. This time, it was Faria who was laughing.

As Nayla stood up, she offered her right hand to help Darius onto his feet. As he took her hand, she could feel a subtle shift in his arm tension, as if to pull her down.

Nayla used her left thumb to strike a pressure point on his triceps, just above his elbow. His arm was now locked out. She used his straightened arm against her shin as a fulcrum. Wrenching his locked arm against her leg, Darius was catapulted from his back, face first, onto his stomach. Pinning his right arm behind his back, Nayla smiled at the boy. "Lesson number one, Ewen, always turn him on his side or stomach so he cannot retaliate."

As the men took turns on sentry duty, Markus encouraged Nayla to show them more. Most men in western Imago were trained to fight with a weapon, whether it is a sword, spear or a halberd. Their training was very limited when it came to unarmed combat.

Nayla was pleased to share some of her knowledge. It soon became apparent to all size was not a determining factor in her ability to immobilize even someone as large as Darius. It was timing, precision, and movement; not strength that allowed this diminutive warrior to take them down each time.

As Lindras conducted watch with Faria, Ewen worked with Markus, while Lando paired off with Darius, leaving Arerys with no one to work with, until Nayla approached him.

At first, Arerys felt awkward grappling with a woman, and a tiny one at that, but it quickly changed after Nayla sent the Elf flying onto his back as she rolled over him upon his chest, pinning him to the ground.

He looked up at her to see she was actually looking quite pleased with herself.

She stood up, helping Arerys to his feet. He suddenly dropped and sent Nayla flying overhead. This time, he landed on top of her, pinning her down.

She smiled up at him and generously responded, "You are a good student."

"Well, you are a good teacher," replied Arerys.

As they gazed at each other, Arerys' long, blonde hair cascaded down around her face. For a lingering moment, it seemed to form a sheer, golden curtain that blocked out all the noise and commotion of the others struggling around them. Arerys looked into her eyes; he could see the spark in them that no doubt fed the fire in her soul.

For an instant, he felt himself being drawn into her deep brown eyes, as if he were being lulled into a trance. Suddenly, he leapt to his feet; raising Nayla onto hers. He apologized before abruptly turning away. Grabbing his bow and quiver, he set off to find Faria and Lindras.

Nayla watched him disappear before turning her attention back to the others.

"I think we should all get some rest before darkness falls," suggested Nayla, looking up to the dimming sky.

"Oh, Nayla! I am just getting started," sighed Ewen in obvious disappointment. "Please show us more."

"Ewen, there is much more to life than learning how to fight. If I were to teach you more, then you must promise not to limit yourself to the warrior arts. You cannot expect your entire life to revolve around fighting and weapons. You must learn to appreciate the other things in life."

"Like what?"

"Ewen, some of the greatest warriors in Orien are also great poets, writers and artists."

"Nayla is right, young man," interjected Lando. "Look at Arerys' people; they are great warriors, but they are also great craftsmen, capable of turning an ordinary piece of wood into a beautiful piece of art. And even I dabble in the written words."

"But Nayla, we all know the sword is mightier than mere words," said Ewen. "If I learn the way of the sword, I shall wield the power to make great changes."

"Ewen, change is not always affected by the blade of a sword, even your own people appreciate that sometimes the written word is indeed mightier than the sword," advised Nayla. "In Orien, we believe in the saying 'pen and sword in accord'."

Ewen looked at her, it was obvious her statement puzzled him.

Nayla just smiled. "In other words, to be a great warrior, one must strike a balance. Learn the warrior arts, but do not neglect the beauty of the other arts that surround you. Knowledge in the ways of the world is a powerful weapon, Ewen. Combined with the warrior arts, you shall be better prepared to address all the circumstances that life may present to you."

"So you are a writer too?" asked Ewen.

"No, I prefer to express myself through other means. However, when I say to achieve a balance for example, I am a healer as well as a warrior. After all, if you are trained to hurt others, then it is just as important to learn how to heal."

He looked at her, intrigued as much by her words, as her actions.

Nayla turned to gather her cloak and to find a few minutes of solitude. As she walked away, she said to the boy, "Balance. It is all about finding a balance… one cannot exist without the other, Ewen."

CHAPTER 8

THROUGH THE RIVER OF SOULS

Darkness fell rapidly upon them as the land was already blanketed in a gray shroud of low hanging clouds.

"Well, Nayla, what course did you travel to get you thus far without being captured by Beyilzon's soldiers?" asked Lindras.

"There is a large encampment; his men congregate near the southern edge of the Valley of Shadows. They were at least five hundred strong. Now undoubtedly, there may be even greater numbers," said Nayla as she gazed eastward across the Plains of Fire. "We may take this course, but it would be at great risk, or you may take the route I chose. It is longer, but there is a greater chance that we shall arrive at Mount Hope alive."

"What shall it be, Markus?" asked the Wizard.

Markus' eyes scanned at the sprawling, inhospitable landscape before him, contemplating his options. "We shall follow Nayla."

Nayla nodded in acknowledgment of his decision as she turned to lead the way. She moved swiftly and silently through the cover of night, as naturally as if it were daytime, with Arerys and Darius close to her side, Ewen and Lindras in the middle, while Markus, Faria and Lando took up the flank.

Almost six hours had passed since Nayla began her fast paced trek eastward. For the men, she set a comfortable pace, even though for her, she was basically at a steady run. Ewen was astounded by her stamina, for though he was slightly taller than her, he was tiring quickly. They rested only long enough to eat and drink before she was on her feet again, guiding them through the darkness.

About two hours into their trek, Markus noticed that they were on a steady ascent. "Nayla, are you sure you know the way?" he asked. "Exactly which way do you plan to take us?"

"It is much too dangerous to pass through the Plains of Fire because of Beyilzon's army, so I am taking you through the Aranaks, back into Darross. Around the eastern point of these mountains, there is a canyon;

its pass cuts through where the Aranaks and Iron Mountains meet. It shall add about three days to the trek, but we shall reach our destination alive, if all goes as planned," assured Nayla.

"Of course!" said Faria. "Rock Ridge Pass into Darross and onward, through the Redwall Canyons"

"You know this way?" asked Markus.

"Yes, Nayla is taking us to a mountain passage. If we travel at this pace, we should arrive by morning." Faria was excited by the prospects of returning to Darross. "It is a low mountain pass that is sheltered between two of the smaller peaks of the Aranaks. Because of its situation, it should not be covered by snow, even this early in the spring. It should be an easy trek back into my country."

In his excitement, Faria raced ahead with Nayla as they continued on the gently ascending slope.

"Nayla, when you came by this way, was Darross under siege?" inquired Faria.

"That was almost one week ago, Faria," answered Nayla, continuing on her relentless pace. "The towns and villages in the eastern half of Darross were not yet under attack, but as I climbed higher into the pass, I could see in the far distance – smoke was rising from several areas. I can only assume it was villages being razed and set fire upon by the Dark Army."

"So the citizens have not all fled?"

"I moved through Darross only by night so I would not be seen. What I can tell though, is many of the able-bodied men have moved on to do battle, leaving behind women, children, the infirmed and the elderly."

"There is still hope then," whispered Faria.

"There is always hope, my friend."

The gray light of the approaching morning leached out the last of the darkness from the sky. As the tired group trudged on, they finally came to a stop when the entrance to the Rock Ridge Pass became visible to Arerys in the distance. "Let us set up camp here," said Markus.

Without another word, Ewen collapsed in utter exhaustion to the hard ground. The others too slowly slumped down, much in need of rest.

Lindras turned to the Elf, "Arerys, I will need you to travel on ahead to see if the pass is guarded."

Arerys nodded as he allowed himself a quick sip of water from his flask.

"I shall accompany you," said Nayla.

"No, Nayla. Stay here," ordered Markus. "I shall go with Arerys. I shall need your keen ears to listen for us in case trouble lies ahead. You shall warn the others, if need be."

"As you wish," nodded Nayla, settling next to an already drowsing Ewen.

Arerys and Markus moved on swiftly and silently to scout ahead. The others who remained behind took the opportunity to eat and drink, while Ewen slept.

As Faria ate, he glanced over at Nayla. "So tell me, sword maiden, are you prepared to take up arms to help us slay the Dark Lord?"

"Why do you question me so, Faria? Do you still doubt me?"

"Fighting hand to hand is quite different than engaging in battle with many soldiers in the field, my lady, that is all."

"I assure you, I have survived more battles in my time than you have in your entire, miniscule life," replied Nayla. Inside, her nerves were beginning to bristle at his arrogance. "I have walked this earth for almost three hundred years, so I have won and lost far more than I care to remember, or care to admit."

"Ha, so you are an old war horse!" laughed Darius.

Nayla smiled at him. "I have been called worse in my time."

"So you have fought as a soldier?" questioned Faria.

"As a soldier," she replied coolly, staring Faria into his eyes, "and as the captain of my own battalion."

Faria glared at her in disbelief. Lando and Darius gazed upon her with raised eyebrows.

"So little one, you are full of surprises!" smiled Darius.

"You command your own army?" asked Lando, in awe. "How many men?"

"When their number was at its greatest, I have led an army of five hundred men into battle," stated Nayla proudly. "The men of my battalion are skilled and fierce warriors, comprised of both Elves and mortals. They are the most decorated and honored battalion in all of Orien."

"So you don armor as the rest of us then?" asked Faria.

"No, in fact I choose to wear little more than Elven chain mail over what I wear now. I do not wish to be encumbered by heavy sheets of metal."

"So you enter battle like a real warrior, yet you refuse to don the armor of a real man?" asked Faria.

"Why should I dress like a man just because I wield a sword?" asked Nayla, with a frown. "I am a woman who happens to be a warrior, not a woman who pretends or wishes to be a man."

"She does have a good point, Faria," said Darius, winking at Nayla. "You cannot deny, she is a woman."

"Besides," she continued, "my style of combat reflects the teachings of the Taijin warriors of Orien. I cannot move as I need to if I am weighed down by heavy weapons and armor."

"Well, you certainly have my respect, Captain Treeborn," said Lando with a bow.

The Wizard sat back with his pipe as he listened to their conversation. "Believe me, Lando, Dahlon Treeborn and the elders would not commission her to command an army if she were not capable," said Lindras between contemplative puffs on his pipe. "Do not be deceived by Nayla's size, or the fact that she is a woman, for not all battles are won by sheer numbers and strength. Strategy has much to do with how wars are won."

As the men relaxed after their meal, they lit up their pipes just as Arerys and Markus returned from their brief expedition.

"So, what did you see?" inquired the Wizard.

"The pass is now indeed guarded, but it would appear to be secured by only a small party of perhaps a dozen or so men," answered Markus. "They were in the process of changing the guards for sentry duty."

"It is nothing that we cannot handle," said Arerys as he sat next to Nayla.

"There is also the matter of a river to cross," added Markus. "It is not wide, but it is fast flowing and deep."

"That would be the River of Souls," said Faria. "I know of a foot bridge we can use. It is very old, but it should still be passable."

"Yes, it was there when I last crossed, however, the recent heavy rains may have washed away what was left of it," Nayla added, recalling the less than stable structure.

"I suppose we shall find out soon enough," responded Markus, sitting himself down next to the Wizard.

"Well, eat and rest now. I shall take the first watch," volunteered Darius. As he rose, he turned to Nayla. "Care to join me, Captain Treeborn?" he asked, extending his hand to her as he smiled.

Nayla took hold of his hand as he pulled her onto her feet. "Come along then, little one!"

Together, they headed up the slope to watch over the camp.

"Captain Treeborn?" repeated a puzzled Arerys as he looked at Lando and the others for an explanation.

"It is a long story, my friend," said Lindras. "You best speak to Nayla about it."

As the sun attempted to burn through the low hanging clouds, the gray skyline lightened marginally. From their post, Darius and Nayla could see far out across the Plains of Fire. The hours passed quickly as Darius shared tales of his adventures of daring-do. Nayla shared stories of her life amongst the *dark* Elves and the mysterious people of Orien.

By noon, Markus and Arerys arrived to relieve them of sentry duty. They watched as Darius and Nayla headed back to camp. It was then, that Markus noticed a strange look come over Arerys' face as he watched Darius place a friendly arm around Nayla's slight shoulders as they walked away. It was an expression Markus had never seen before on the Elf's face.

He smiled at him, giving his friend a good-natured nudge with his elbow as he asked, "You are not jealous are you, Arerys?"

"Darius has a mistress in every village from Cedona to Carcross." A look of distaste clouded his blue eyes. "I do not wish to see him treat Nayla as another conquest, or as a mere trinket. That is all."

"Well, I am confident she can handle Darius, if need be," said Markus, his eyes studying the gray horizon.

By late afternoon the heavy, low skies dissolved into a cold, starless night, devoid of any celestial lights to guide the Order through the darkness.

Up ahead, the sounds of rushing, turbulent waters grew louder. "There should be a crossing just below this rise; where the slope levels out," said Faria as he led them down.

When they reached the edge of the River of Souls, the water churned and seemed to boil in some areas. In others, it appeared deceptively calm where the water gathered in deep pools before spilling over.

"There!" pointed Arerys. "I can see the bridge up ahead."

As they approached the footbridge, to their disappointment, all that was left of the decrepit structure was the handrail. The two logs that formed the crossing, lay for most part, submerged under almost one foot of water. They stood there for a moment, wondering how to proceed.

"This is still the safest place to cross," insisted Faria. "I shall go first."

Faria moved along the length of the submerged logs as he held tightly onto the handrail. He warned the others where the log was especially slippery with algae, or where the currents seemed unusually strong. One by one, the others ventured across, trailing behind Faria: Markus followed by Darius, Ewen, Lindras and Lando. They proceeded cautiously along the remnants of the bridge as they waded through the river, knee-deep in its chilling embrace.

Arerys grabbed the handrail, pulling himself up so he was balanced on top. He glanced down at Nayla. "Do you think you can cross from here?"

"Like a cat!" answered Nayla confidently, taking Arerys' hand. He lifted her up to join him on the narrow, unsteady strip of wood. With poise and confidence, Arerys moved along the narrow beam as though he was walking on the ground. He stepped lightly as he skimmed along the handrail. Nayla, with her arms extended out to her side for balance, her knees slightly bent to lower her center of gravity, moved with a greater degree of caution as she made her way behind the Elf.

"Lindras, why do they call this the River of Souls?" asked Ewen, fighting to maintain his footing on the slimy, algae-covered log.

"Because this river courses through the Plains of Fire where many people have lost their lives," answered the Wizard as he concentrated on his grip and footing. "At one point, the river was so thick with the bodies of fallen soldiers, you could actually walk across its surface where the bodies washed down. It was a terrible sight."

Ewen shuddered. The faster he moved, the faster he would be out of this terrible place, he thought. Ahead, Faria and Markus waited on the bank of the river, he and the others were over half way to the other side when suddenly, in his haste, Ewen lost his footing. Lighter than the men, the fast flowing currents claimed him; his hands were wrenched away from the handrail.

Darius turned to see Ewen's frightened face blanch as the force of the current pulled him in. He leaned back to reach for Ewen, but the boy abruptly disappeared under the cold, rushing waters.

Ewen bobbed up on the other side of the bridge, but before he could scream for help, the currents pulled him under again. The river swallowed him up with a hunger that raged. He churned and tumbled through the darkness, crashing against rocks and other objects that lay submerged in its depth.

Ewen groped in the murky water for something to hold onto to prevent him being washed away. He frantically sought out anything that would allow him to pull himself to the surface. His hands came across what he thought was a tree branch. Grabbing hold to hoist himself up, the object instantly gave way: it snapped loose, floating towards him. To Ewen's horror, it was the skeletal remains of a soldier; it had been decomposing in the water for quite some time.

Ewen released a silent scream that bubbled up to the surface. He finally burst through the turbulent waters, coughing and gasping for air, just in time to see Markus and the others frantically running down along the river's edge.

Arerys quickly removed his pack and the weapons he bore, throwing them onto the riverbank. He leapt from the bridge, diving in after Ewen as Nayla dashed along the handrail, leaping down on the other side to catch up with the others.

The fast flowing current pulled Ewen under its turbulent surface again. His lungs felt as though they were ready to explode as he struggled to break through for a breath of air. Suddenly, he felt a powerful hand grab him by his collar, forcing him upwards; it was Arerys.

"Grab the rope!" shouted Markus as he tossed one end to the Elf.

Holding Ewen up with one hand, Arerys quickly looped the rope around the boy's waist, instructing him to hang on tightly as the others started to pull him to shore. Just as the line lost its slack, the Elf abruptly disappeared beneath the cold, dark waters into a deep, swirling pool.

"Where is Arerys?" asked Darius, searching the waters as he helped the others pull Ewen out by his tether.

"There!" shouted Lindras, pointing to where Arerys broke through to the surface, gasping for air. "He is heading to the logjam just ahead."

"Lindras, stay with Ewen," ordered Markus, as he followed Nayla. She was moving swiftly, leaping from rock to rock, rope ready in her hand. She sprinted as fast as she could as she watched Arerys surface once more, only to be pulled beneath again.

Nayla plunged into the deep pool to search for him. Darkness. Nothingness. There was no sign of the Elf. She surfaced for air before diving below again. Finally, she spotted a writhing shape… It was Arerys! He was firmly wedged, almost to his waist, between a large boulder and some partially submerged logs. The water gathering into this deep pool was being siphoned through this opening like a swirling funnel of a whirlpool. She could see Arerys struggling to free himself, but the force of the out flowing water was too great. His movements began to slow as air escaped from his lungs. The watery tomb prepared itself for another victim.

Nayla resurfaced, inhaling several deep breaths before plunging beneath the water again. Arerys was no longer struggling, as if saving his energy for a new beginning. As she looked to his face, his eyes were closed. Nayla took hold of Arerys' face and placing her mouth over his, she blew a steady stream of air into his lungs. Arerys eyes slowly opened to see Nayla. She swam behind him, pulling at him from around his shoulders, but to no avail. The rushing waters had a deadly hold on his body.

Nayla looked into Arerys' face, motioning that she was going up. The Elf nodded in understanding.

She resurfaced, gasping for air. "Arerys is trapped!" she shouted. "Find a reed or any plant with a hollow stem!"

Nayla filled her lungs with fresh air before diving under again. Arerys was struggling once more to free himself when Nayla reached him. She tapped him on his chest. Arerys looked at her, not understanding. Again, she tapped him on his chest, and then she motioned to her mouth against his. He understood, quickly expelling the spent air from his lungs. Nayla drew his face to hers, placing her mouth over his, she quickly replenished his air supply. Again, she motioned that she was going up.

"He is going to drown if we do not get him out now," shouted Faria. "The water is rising!"

"I am breathing for him," said Nayla, between gasps of air. "Did anyone find a reed?"

"No," answered Markus. "Nothing of the sort grows along here, Nayla."

"Quickly, Markus! I shall need you to hold Arerys up!" shouted Nayla as she took another deep breath.

Markus dove into the chilly water after her. As he reached Arerys, she was transferring air into his lungs. She motioned Markus to rise up with her.

As they broke the surface, Nayla instructed him. "Markus, I need you to hold Arerys up. Support him so he is as close to the surface as you can hold him."

After several deep breaths, Nayla disappeared under the water once more. She tapped Arerys on his chest at which he expelled the spent air from his bursting lungs. Nayla placed her mouth over his, delivering another lifesaving breath-full of air. She searched his face to see if he was still okay. Arerys nodded, calmed by her presence, he motioned her to go up. Nayla nodded her head in understanding before breaching the surface.

"Markus, take hold of Arerys now." Nayla raised both her hands out of the water. Taking the sword into her right hand, her left hand quickly turned the scabbard upside-down. Using her sword, she took a quick swipe at the tip of her scabbard; the bottom was cleanly sheared off. Tossing her weapon to the bank of the river, Nayla sealed the top of the scabbard with her thumb, trapping air inside the hollow. She plunged back into the dark, swirling waters to Arerys, who now lay propped up against Markus' body.

She tapped Arerys, motioning him to place the end of the scabbard in his mouth while holding the other end up to the surface. The Elf immediately understood her. He placed the tip of the scabbard into his mouth as Nayla held the other end up high so it rose above the surface of the water. As Nayla removed her thumb from the top of the scabbard, she felt a sudden rush of cool air enter the tube. To her relief, Arerys was now breathing on his own.

"Darius, throw me your rope," she ordered as she tied the end of her line around Markus. She tossed the other end to those waiting on the river's edge.

Catching the rope that Darius tossed to her, Nayla plunged under the water. She quickly secured the rope around Arerys' chest, just under his arms. As she looked into his face, she motioned that he would soon be surfacing. She placed her hands on his shoulders, giving them a gentle squeeze to reassure him.

Nayla resurfaced with the rope in her hand, throwing it to Darius. As she waded to shore, she instructed them to pull both Markus and Arerys out together as the current would be exceptionally strong once the Elf is dislodged.

At the count of three, Darius and Lindras pulled upon Markus' tether while Faria, Lando, and Nayla fought to pull Arerys in. Struggling with the combination of their dead weight against the rushing current, both man and Elf were eventually hauled to the surface. Markus struggled to his feet with Arerys still in his arms. Together, they clambered onto the dry bank.

Both collapsed onto the ground, shivering from the frigid waters. Nayla picked up her sword and as she reached the two men, unable to speak, Arerys gratefully handed her back her scabbard. He noticed her hands were shivering and her lips were blue from the cold.

"Well, this is much more excitement than any of us had bargained for tonight," stated Lindras. "I suggest we find a safe place to build a fire and let these people find some warmth."

Faria led them up to a rocky outcrop that sheltered them from the pass, and from the prying eyes on the Plains below. Those who were not shivering from the cold, busied themselves with gathering firewood.

Even with the roaring flames, the cold cut right through to their bones. Ewen's teeth were chattering quite loudly as he dried out by the fire. He wrapped his arms around his chest to warm his frigid hands under his armpits when panic rose in his heart. *The pouch! Where is it?* He clutched his chest where the Stone was usually nestled. He breathed a great sigh of relief when he realized the pouch containing the precious gem was still around his neck. The water current did not sweep it away after all; instead, it was carried around, falling to his back.

The wet cloaks were hung about the fire to dry and to act as a windbreak. Faria offered Markus his cloak, as did Lando to Ewen. Darius removed his cloak, turning to Nayla, "Here little one, there is room for the both of you, if you care to share my cloak with Arerys."

"Thank you, Darius," said Nayla as she moved to sit down next to the Elf. "Do you mind, Arerys?"

"Please do," said Arerys, blowing warmed air into his frigid hands.

Darius gently placed his great cloak around them both. It seemed to trap the warm air inside; they began to immediately thaw from the cold.

"I suppose this is as good a time as any to eat and rest," decided Lindras, with a sigh. "We shall make up for lost time tomorrow."

As they huddled next to each other, Arerys felt Nayla's small body still shivering against him. He moved closer to her so she could rest against his body. He felt badly as she obviously felt the bite of the icy water more than he did. He slowly placed one arm around her shoulders as he turned his head to look Nayla into her eyes.

"What you did tonight was foolhardy... and brave. Thank you," said Arerys. "I am indebted to you."

"There is no need for thanks, Arerys. I know you would have done the same for any of us."

That night, Lando, Faria and Darius took turns keeping watch as the others slept or tried to warm up. Arerys removed their now-dry cloaks from about the campfire. As Nayla slept, he gently drew her cloak around her small body, whispering "good night" as he settled down to rest not far from her.

Under the darkness of an overcast morning sky, Markus retrieved Darius from sentry duty. When they returned, he woke the others in preparation for their journey through Rock Ridge Pass.

"We shall wait until the changing of the guards," said Markus as he ate. "That way, at least twelve hours shall elapse before the Dark Army returns to replace their soldiers. This should give us an adequate lead before they even suspect something has gone terribly wrong."

After all had eaten, Nayla and Faria led the way to the mouth of the pass that lay just beyond the raging waters of the River of Souls. The Order remained concealed behind the large boulders and rocky outcrops as a fresh contingent of soldiers replaced the dozen that had spent the night guarding the entrance through the mountains leading back to Darross.

As they waited for the evening shift to disappear far down the slope, Nayla began to put her plan into action.

"Be ready to fight, men," said Nayla. With those words, she removed her cloak and the short sword she wore at her front, passing them both over to Ewen for safekeeping. She loosened her braid allowing her long, dark hair to cascade around her shoulders. She then smoothed out her skirt, removing her long sword from her belt. She slung it over her back so the butt of the handle was just barely noticeable over her right shoulder. The men were momentarily stunned by her transformation.

"What do you think you are doing, Nayla?" asked Markus, demanding an explanation.

Nayla smiled coyly at Markus. With great exaggeration, she flirtatiously batted her long, dark eyelashes at him. "The spider is about to entice some flies into her web," she said as she turned away, heading up the path towards the soldiers that were standing guard.

As she came within sight, the men who were not already on their feet, leapt up with sword in hand. A voice called out: "Who goes there?"

Nayla said nothing in response. She approached slowly with hands raised to show she was unarmed. She gingerly sauntered up to them, her hips swaying in a provocative, feminine manner. She was smiling demurely at the men as she neared.

"Why, it is only a woman," said one soldier as he sheathed his sword.

"So what are you doing here?" asked another, enticed by her sultry smile.

Nayla still said nothing. With her right index finger, she gestured for the men to follow her as she started slowly walking backwards, still smiling invitingly at them.

Against his better judgment, their leader motioned for the others to remain on guard as he foolishly proceeded to follow Nayla off the path. As she enticed the soldier onward, he followed her around a large boulder. It was not the surprise he anticipated; the soldier was shocked - there before him stood the men of the Order. Before he could draw his sword or call for help, Lindras cracked him over his head with his staff.

"Well, that was easy!" said the Wizard as the soldier tumbled to the ground.

"I shall return," she said, skipping up the path once more.

When she came into view again, Nayla called out to the soldiers. "Come quickly! Your comrade is in need of help!" All eleven soldiers came running in her direction; Nayla led them around the rocky outcrop.

Just as they became aware that she had led them into an ambush, Nayla turned to face them. Drawing her sword with her right hand from behind her back, she passed her blade over her head, sweeping it in a large circular motion from the left, diagonally to her right, neatly slicing through the armor and flesh of the two closest soldiers.

Instantly, all were engaged in battle as Lindras and Ewen hugged the rocky wall, creeping unnoticed onto the trail leading to the pass. Darius quickly finished off his opponent, turning on the two soldiers that had set upon Lando.

Raising his shield to deflect their strikes, Faria exchanged blows against the two swords that had turned upon him. Nayla silently approached the soldiers from behind. With one swift, broad stroke of her sword, she dispatched both soldiers. Faria nodded in thanks before joining Arerys, to aid him in his skirmish.

With a quick twist of her wrist, she flicked the blood off her sword, turning her attention to Markus who was pitted against two other soldiers.

As Markus dodged the blows of the incoming swords, he found himself forced up against a rock wall. While one soldier flailed upon him with his sword, Markus raised his shield to deflect each blow as he countered the attack of a second soldier with his own weapon. Suddenly, the first soldier turned on Markus, slamming the edge of his shield hard into his body. The shield struck him across his right arm and shoulder with such intense force, the impact caused Markus to cry out in pain, his sword tumbling from his grip.

Nayla acted quickly. Dive-rolling over fallen soldiers, she rose up onto one knee behind the prince's assailant as he raised his sword to strike down Markus with deadly intent. Slashing horizontally from right to left, she cut through the muscles and tendons at the back of the soldier's knees. The soldier screamed in pain. His own weight now the enemy, his knees buckled causing him to fall backwards. He promptly met with Nayla's sword as she impaled him through his chest.

Nayla struggled to remove her sword, but the sucking wound that penetrated deep into his right lung had a firm grasp on her blade, as the soldier fought for his last dying breath. As she continued to wrestle with her sword, the second soldier turned his attention away from the injured Markus, onto her. He swung his sword, slashing downwards from his right to left, aiming to separate her head from her shoulders. Nayla ducked to her left. Her timing slightly off; the tip of the blade just caught her high across her right cheek.

The soldier raised his sword over his head, coming down with great speed. Nayla did not back away. She proceeded to roll straight towards him, rising to her feet. She lunged straight up against his body, jamming his arms so he was unable to complete his strike.

Grabbing him by his right hand, Nayla squeezed it in both of hers. The excruciating pain she inflicted on his hand as it bit into the hard edges of the sword's handle caused his wrist bones to grind, collapse, and fold. Suddenly, she twisted his wrist sharply with a loud *'crack'*; his own sword was now turned against the left side of his throat. As the soldier fell onto his back, Nayla took his own sword, driving it through his jugular, sending him on his way.

The din of sword striking against sword and armor gave way to an eerie silence. Nayla glanced around to see soldiers lying motionless and strewn about the bloodied ground. To her relief, all who were left standing were of the Order.

Nayla felt the warm trickle of blood running down from her cheek. She touched the gaping wound with her fingertips, wincing at the biting pain. It would become a permanent reminder of her battle that day. *Well, I suppose it could be worse,* she thought.

Darius came to her side, helping her to her feet. He held her chin in his hand as he looked upon her bloody face. "Nayla, you are hurt."

Nayla pulled away from his hand. "No, he is hurt," she said, turning to Markus as he leaned heavily against the rock wall, his right arm hanging limp as his left hand braced his right shoulder.

He dashed over to Markus' side. "I fear his arm is broken!" stated Darius, helping him stand upright.

Nayla stood over the body of the dead soldier that still laid claim to her sword. She used both her hands to dislodge her weapon, pulling it straight out of his torso. It was a much easier task since the soldier had stopped breathing. She headed to Markus' side.

"I believe I can help to ease your pain, but it must wait for the moment. We must leave this place immediately," said Nayla. With a quick twist of her wrist, she wrung the blood from her sword before sheathing it into the scabbard.

Markus nodded in agreement. He grimaced in obvious discomfort as he bent to pick up his sword.

"We must somehow cover our tracks," said Nayla.

"What do you suggest?" snapped a weary Faria. "Shall we simply bury all these bodies?" His voice was oozing with sarcasm.

"That is actually an excellent idea, Faria!" responded Nayla.

Faria rolled his eyes in disbelief at her words.

"Arerys, I need Lindras," she said.

Without uttering a word, Arerys sprinted up the trail to retrieve the Wizard as the others helped Nayla drag the bodies into a heap against the rock wall.

Lindras appeared from around the corner. With a frown, he stared down upon Nayla's bloodied face. "You beckoned, Nayla?"

"Lindras Weatherstone, you must work your magic," said Nayla. "Bring down those rocks to conceal these bodies. Do so quickly."

"Ah, you cannot rush magic," said Lindras, motioning all to stand aside if they wish to behold his awesome powers. The Wizard raised his staff on high above his head as he closed his eyes to call upon the energy of the earth. He brought his staff down sharply, striking the ground before him.

All were expecting a great, earth-moving spectacle, but to everybody's surprise and amazement, a single rock fell from a high ledge. A trail of loose soil and a small cloud of dust followed it.

After a moment of stunned silence, Darius and Ewen attempted to stifle their laughter.

"Well, that was most impressive, Wizard!" said Lando, one eyebrow raised as he nodded his approval. "Quite an earth-moving experience, if I should say so myself!"

Lindras, flustered by his results, flung his hood from his head as he re-evaluated his spell.

"Just give me a moment," muttered the Wizard. "I am getting old."

Lindras closed his eyes in concentration, drawing on his powers. Again, whispering an ancient incantation, he brought his staff down with a resounding 'crack'!

The earth around them began to tremble as the rocks along the ledge above came crashing and tumbling down in a great cloud of dust. With the dead soldiers sufficiently concealed beneath the fallen rubble, Lindras nodded in approval of his handiwork.

"Now, the others will think they have deserted their post. No one shall be the wiser," said Nayla as she took Lindras by his arm, pulling him away as he sheepishly admired his latest accomplishment.

The Order moved swiftly up through the mountain pass. They crested the summit of Rock Ridge Pass as the sun's dull glow could be seen high in the sky as it filtered through the building cloud-cover. As they began their descent along the meandering passage, they came upon an area sheltered by massive sheets of granite that protruded like giant, jagged teeth.

"We shall rest for a while," said Lindras to the others as he glanced over at Markus.

Markus continued to clench his injured shoulder. Each step he took sent excruciating shockwaves shooting through his body. The pain traveled into his right shoulder, migrating down the length of his throbbing arm.

The prince slumped to the ground, his pain obvious for all to see. Arerys and Darius tried to ease his discomfort. The Elf helped him to remove his cloak as Darius went to fetch his flask of water. Arerys carefully assisted Markus with the removal of his vest and his protective layer of mail that lay over his shirt, as Darius returned with Ewen and some water. The Elf examined Markus' bruised and swollen shoulder.

"Is it broken, Arerys?" asked Darius.

"I believe it is dislocated," answered the Elf. "I can ease your pain Markus, however I do not know how to fix this. If I attempt to heal you in this condition, your arm shall remain in this state. You shall have no pain, but you shall be limited in the movement of your arm." Arerys gently pressed the bone protruding from the top of his shoulder. Markus flinched at the Elf's touch.

"Let Nayla help him. She is a healer, she can fix Markus," insisted Ewen, turning to fetch her.

He returned with the warrior maiden, leading her by his hand. She knelt down before Markus. Using her fingertips, she applied gentle, but steady pressure along his shoulder and arm to assess the nature of his injury. As she did so, Markus glanced up at Nayla's face. He noticed for the first time that she too, was injured. Her right cheek was caked with drying blood.

"Nayla, are you hurting?" asked Markus, wincing at her touch.

"Not as much as you shall be." She turned to Arerys and instructed him to hold Markus steady. Taking a small stick, she asked Markus to bite down on it.

"What is she doing to him?" asked Faria.

"I believe she is attempting to reset his arm back into his shoulder," answered Lindras, watching with fascination as Nayla tended to the injured prince.

As she placed Markus' right arm level with his shoulder, she braced her right foot under his arm, her left foot against the base of his neck. She took hold of his wrist with both her hands. "Are you ready, Markus?"

He nodded in response.

"Take a deep breath, try to relax," instructed Nayla. "Do not try to resist when I begin to pull."

Markus, his face beading with sweat, anticipated the worst. He drew in a long, slow breath.

She glanced over at Arerys. He nodded that he too, was ready as he held Markus firmly to the ground.

Nayla gazed down at the prince. As she gave his arm a steady pull, Markus bit down hard, his eyes looked wild with agony, begging her to stop. He then squeezed them shut to block out the excruciating pain she dealt him.

"I am sorry, Markus," apologized Nayla. With those words said, she suddenly gave his arm a sharp, hard yank.

'Aarrrgh!' Markus managed a stifled cry through his clenched teeth. With the popping and grinding sound of his arm moving back into the shoulder socket, everything began to swim before his eyes in a darkening blur. In an instant, all went black.

Darius caught Ewen as his knees buckled. He fainted at the crunching sound of bone against bone.

Arerys laid Markus down upon his cloak as Nayla fashioned a sling for his arm, securing the cloak in place with his brooch. She then instructed Lando to soak a cloth in the icy spring water that bubbled up from the rocks just beyond their shelter. Her forceful manipulation of Markus' arm will cause more swelling and bruising to his already injured shoulder; the cold compress shall help to reduce the extent of the inflammation.

With Markus taken care of, now resting next to Ewen, both in a forced state of unconsciousness, the others used the time to wait, eat and rest.

Nayla walked to the spring where she knelt before a small pool of water. She examined her reflection on the water's smooth surface. The cut was thickly encrusted with dried blood, but the wound itself was visibly open. Nayla splashed water onto her face. She gasped as the cold water stung the wound. She cursed herself for not moving sooner to avoid the blade.

Darius came to her side to look upon her face. "It is really not that bad, Nayla," he tried to assure her. "It is merely a minor flaw on your beauty."

"Hmm, a flaw nevertheless," replied Nayla as she examined the open wound.

Arerys knelt down next to Nayla as he gazed upon her reflection in the pool. "I believe the healer is in need of some healing herself," said the Elf, looking to Darius to give him a moment alone with Nayla.

Nayla asked to borrow Arerys' knife. She leaned closer to her reflection, as she carefully traced the edge of the wound with the tip of the blade. Blood began to flow fresh from her wound again. She quickly rinsed away the crimson droplets. The warrior maiden then attempted to staunch the flow a blood with a piece of cloth, pressing the two edges of the cut together.

"Let me help you, Nayla," said Arerys, tilting her chin up so he could better examine her wound. Removing her hand from her face, Arerys gently placed the middle finger of his left hand along the length of the cut. Nayla's eyes closed at the touch of his hand upon her burning cheek.

Arerys closed his eyes, whispering an incantation used by his people to heal as his finger touched her wound. His hand felt cool against her hot face; the wound no longer had the same stinging bite. After a few minutes, Arerys was done. He looked down upon her face that was framed by her long, dark hair that hung loose about her shoulders. Nayla's eyes were still closed; she looked serene, as though she was dreaming about another place or time, bereft of the savagery of war.

As he removed his hand from her face, Nayla's eyes fluttered open.

"It is looking much better now, Nayla. You may have a small scar, but it is healing nicely," said Arerys, examining her face. He knew that had she been a full-blooded Elf, a wound of this nature would have disappeared under his touch. It was the best he could do for her.

Nayla leaned over the pool. Arerys was right. Where once there was an open wound, his touch sealed the edges together. There was now only a thin, red line.

"Thank you, Arerys," said Nayla, her fingertip tracing the line of the wound. It still felt cool from his touch. He helped her to her feet.

"So you finally wake, Markus," said Darius when he noticed the prince struggling to sit up.

"How long have I been out?" he asked as he touched his aching shoulder.

"Maybe an hour," answered Lando.

"Nayla did you in," quipped Darius. "I believe she enjoys inflicting cruel and unusual punishment on you."

Nayla knelt next to Markus. "How do you feel?"

"Very sore and stiff, but I feel I can move my arm again, thank you," said Markus, demonstrating by rotating his arm in his shoulder.

"Sit up for a moment," requested Nayla as she removed the sling. She raised her hands just above her head, and then sharply clapped them together. Closing her eyes, she briskly rubbed the palms of her hands against each other. The friction generated ample heat, enough that when she placed her palms over Markus' shoulder, he almost jumped upon contact. Nayla's hands felt as though they would burn right through him. Her touch gradually eased the pain and the stiffness.

"What are you doing?" asked Arerys, with great interest.

"The heat will increase the circulation of blood to this area. It shall help his injury to heal faster, plus the warmth shall relieve the stiffness," answered Nayla. "In fact, Arerys, you should be doing this. It shall be far more effective with your powers."

After explaining how one's fingertips and palms are the portals for receiving and transferring energy, Nayla quickly instructed Arerys, showing him what to do. She asked the Elf to envision the energy that he was generating in the palms of his hands as a white light.

When Arerys placed his hands on Markus' shoulder, he felt instant relief from his pain. Very soon, there was sufficient relief from his agony that Markus was able to dress himself. Nayla refashioned his sling to alleviate some of the pressure from his shoulder.

Markus turned to Nayla, thanking her again. "I must say, fortune smiled down upon us when she sent us in your direction, my lady."

Nayla smiled back in response, her fingers deftly braiding her hair back into place. "Let us hope that good fortune continues to look favourably upon us," said Nayla, drawing her cloak around her shoulders.

Soon the Order was traversing down the slope of Rock Ridge Pass, back into Darross. Faria assessed that they should be on the flats of Heathrowen in less than three hours, just before nightfall.

They continued with their descent, when a small shadow silently glided over them. Arerys glanced skyward to see the small shape of a falcon silhouetted against the heavy, gray clouds. Its pointed, sickle-shaped wings were held open wide so it may glide on the warm, rising thermals.

Nayla gazed up to see what Arerys was watching so intently. Her eyes widened in delight and surprise. "Tori!" she called. "It is my falcon!" She held her arm up high as a signal for the circling bird to land as she whistled at the little raptor.

The falcon circled several times, each time descending lower, as if she was making certain that it was indeed her master who beckoned. Finally, the falcon swooped down at a frightening speed. She landed lightly upon Nayla's outstretched hand.

Lindras and Ewen approached them slowly, so as not to frighten the little bird. They were both pleased to see that the falcon was fully healed and apparently, looking well fed too.

"I must get a note back to Nagana," stated Nayla.

"We have no parchment, Nayla," said Lindras.

"Parchment will not hold up for this trip, especially if the rains should come," replied Nayla, looking about for another option.

Arerys quickly studied the different species of trees that grew in the area; he spotted a bitter cherry tree up ahead. With his knife, he carefully peeled off a thin, flat square of bark.

He returned to Nayla. "Will this do?" he asked, handing her the wooden parchment.

Nayla passed her bird onto Lindras as she asked Arerys for his knife. Leaning against a boulder, Nayla etched a message onto the smooth bark: *Send army to Plains of Fire by the next full moon. – Capt. Treeborn.*

"Markus, I shall send this message to my people," said Nayla, holding it up for his approval. "My army shall come to my assistance, if they are able to do so."

She turned away from Arerys and Markus to attach the rolled message onto the strip of leather that hung from around her falcon's leg.

"Captain Treeborn?" Arerys asked of Markus, with a puzzled look upon his face.

"Her army?" asked a bewildered Markus.

"Do you two never listen when the lady speaks?" asked Darius in his usual, jovial manner. Slapping the two of them on their shoulders, he answered, "She is the captain of one of the largest, most decorated battalions in Orien!"

Arerys and Markus were both dumbfounded as they looked at Darius.

"Well, that certainly explains a lot," said Markus to Arerys as they watched her stroke the feathers on the bird's back

Nayla gently placed a kiss on Tori's head before releasing the falcon aloft to be caught on the rising thermals. They all watched as Tori sped away, winging eastward towards the Iron Mountain, home towards Orien.

Suddenly, Nayla gasped in horror: From out of the darkening sky, an eagle soared through the cloud-cover in pursuit of the little falcon. They watched as Tori, in desperation, folded her wings against her body. The falcon spiraled downward at breakneck speed, moving as swiftly as one of Arerys' deadly arrows, in a bid to elude the eagle's fearsome talons.

A hush fell over the group as they watched the falcon dive behind a tall mountain, disappearing from their view.

Nayla shook her head in sadness as her eyes followed the eagle as it too, disappeared along with her bird.

"Do not despair, Nayla. Tori may be smaller than the eagle, but she is much faster," said Lindras, trying to offer some hope. "She will escape – she will be fine."

Under overcast skies, darkness embraced the countryside early - the sun settled without ever fully showing its face. Its disappearance seemed to herald a change in the weather as the dark clouds, heavy with moisture, finally opened up. A torrent of rain began to fall steadily from the heavens.

Before them, the lights of Heathrowen flickered invitingly. As they stood looking at the village, all appeared quiet. Faria led the way.

As they neared the settlement, the cold rain would not relent. Soon, all were soaked through to their skin, with the exception of Nayla, who was still relatively dry. The outer shell of her cloak was treated with beeswax and a special oil preparation. The rain merely beaded, rolling off of her cloak, like water off of a duck's back.

Nayla peered from beneath her hood. Ewen was a pathetic sight; drenched and shivering. "Markus, can we not take a reprieve from this foul weather," she asked, her eyes turning to the boy.

"Markus, there is an inn not from here, just on the outskirts of the village," suggested Faria. "We can be discreet. And it shall allow me a chance to find out the status of Darross and the war against the Dark Army."

"Very well," said Markus, "but we must use extreme caution. We do not know what sordid characters may frequent this place."

The chill of the spring rain penetrated their flesh, gnawing straight through to their bones; even Arerys admittedly felt the cold. The prospect of a dry place to while away the hours was very appealing to all. Plus, the opportunity to partake in some ale was especially appealing to their palates.

"We shall only stay until the rains let up, people. And remember; do not use names and please maintain a low profile," cautioned Lindras. "Nayla, Arerys; it is best to conceal yourself, keep the hood of your cloak about you. Elves are few and far between in these parts. We do not want to draw unwanted attention to ourselves."

With all taking heed of Lindras' warning, they entered through the door of the inn. All the patrons, whatever their level of inebriation, stopped their drinking and conversation momentarily when the strangers stepped into the smoky, dim-lit room. They quickly resumed to their business as Markus led the group to a secluded table in the corner of the crowded establishment.

As they settled around the table, a barmaid came by to take their order. Markus requested some red wine for Arerys, Lindras and Nayla and a pint of ale for the rest of them.

The young woman nodded, smiling at her dripping wet customers. She promised she would be back momentarily with their drinks.

Faria left the table to speak to the man tending the bar for news of the war raging through western Darross as the others waited for their drinks.

Though the damp, warm air of the inn was stifling due to the thick haze of pipe smoke, it was still more bearable than the cold, wet, spring air outside. With a pleasant smile, the barmaid returned to their table to serve their refreshments. After depositing their drinks, she quickly moved on to other waiting patrons.

"It has been far too long," sighed Darius, hugging his pewter mug in both hands as he gazed longingly at his ale.

Lando took a deep drink. "Ah! What sweet nectar!"

Ewen sampled his ale. Wishing to be one of the men, he pretended to savor his drink with as much gusto as Lando did. Between sips of his wine, Arerys laughed to see Ewen's contorted face as he swallowed the dark liquid. He was trying hard to acquire a taste for the wicked brew.

All enjoyed their reprieve from the elements, as well as the simple luxury of a good drink seated at a table. Markus ordered another round from the barmaid, who promptly returned with a loaded tray. She politely smiled at her guests as she removed the empty drinking vessels. The young lady was maneuvering around the room full of tables with her full tray when she was waved over to another table.

While the men talked, from beneath her lowered hood, Nayla's dark eyes scanned the room, studying the faces of those seated at the surrounding tables. From the corner of her eye, she noticed the young barmaid having words with an obviously intoxicated man. As she turned to pick her tray up from the table, the man abruptly seized her by her wrist. He stood up, forcing the barmaid down onto a long bench where upon he climbed over her small body. He proceeded to kiss her as she struggled to get away. A round of ignorant laughter erupted from the men seated at the nearby tables.

Nayla's blood boiled. Before any of her companions became aware of her movements, she was already crossing the room. She silently walked up behind the drunkard, grabbing him by the hair on the back of his head. She leaned into his ear and hissed, "What do you think you are doing?" Then Nayla promptly yanked him off the barmaid; the frightened woman quickly rolled off the bench and onto the floor, scrambling to her feet - panic in her eyes.

The man rose up, staring down at the diminutive figure before him. He laughed aloud as he rubbed the back of his head, and then he abruptly swung his fist directly at the face of his assailant.

Nayla ducked under his arm only to reappeared behind him. Startled by this sudden move, the man turned, aiming a wild punch for her face. Nayla's head snapped back to avoid the incoming blow, but in doing so, her hood fell back from her head, revealing her face.

The room was filled with gasps of disbelief from those sitting at nearby tables. Markus and the others turned, only now realizing that Nayla was no longer in their company.

The man stared in shock. How dare a woman accost him in front of his friends! Then a lurid smile crept across his face. All of the sudden, he lunged at Nayla, knocking her back along the length of the bench. As he straddled her body, he leaned in close to her face. She could feel and smell his rancid breath as he snarled with malicious triumph, "You are in need of a lesson!"

"No! You are!" declared Nayla as she snapped her right knee up, slamming the man hard in his back. The man was pitched forward, displacing his weight that held Nayla down. With her hips now free, she kicked both of her legs out, rocking forward to land back upon her feet.

The man was catapulted to the floor with Nayla crouched over his prostrate body, like a small tigress that had pounced upon its prey – ready for the kill. The fingers and thumb of her left hand wrapped around his windpipe as if she were going to separate it from his throat as she began to squeeze. As the man gagged and struggled for his breath, Nayla reached across for her sword with her right hand. Ramming the butt of the handle hard into his chest, she knocked what little breath he had left, painfully out of him.

"You chose the wrong girl to do this to," Nayla growled, "either get up and fight, or run right now!"

All those sitting at the surrounding tables leapt up, moving away with their precious ale in hand to make room for an anticipated brawl.

Suddenly, Nayla's companions rushed her. "So, little one! You must go seeking trouble!" reprimanded Darius as he scooped her up in his arms, throwing her over his shoulder. He charged out through the doorway with the others following close behind.

As the man struggled to regain his breath and his wounded pride, Lindras slapped him on his shoulder. The Wizard apologized with a laugh. "Sorry, she is having a very bad month!" Then he too, disappeared into the night.

In the dimmest corner of the room sat a solitary figure, concealed deep in the shadows. He watched with great interest when he realized the obnoxious drunk that had accosted the barmaid, was confronted by a diminutive female - one that was obviously trained in combat.

"So she is the 'little one' they have been speaking of," he muttered to himself under his breath as he swigged down the last of his ale. The man threw his money down on the table before slipping away into the blackness of the night.

In the cool evening air, Nayla struggled against the knight's grasp. "This is most unbecoming! Unhand me, Darius!"

"When you have come to your senses, woman!" snapped Darius, struggling to maintain his hold on the little wild cat.

"Well, so much for a low profile," muttered the Wizard. "You are your mother's daughter, Nayla! You must learn to control your fiery nature!"

In her anger, Nayla abruptly slapped Darius sharply on the small of his back. The sting delivered by the palms of her hands caused the knight to yell out, instantly releasing his grip about her body. Nayla quickly grabbed hold of his belt. With a sharp tug, she flipped over his shoulder, landing back onto her feet behind him.

The men laughed as Darius stood before them in stunned pain and surprise.

Nayla apologized, "I am sorry, Darius."

The knight immediately leapt out of her way as she stepped towards him. "Do not touch me!" he yelped in protest. His pride was more hurt than his smarting back.

Arerys looked down at Nayla, smiling even as he shook his head in disapproval. The Elf was confronted by mixed emotions. He was angry that Nayla had succeeded in drawing unwanted attention to them and yet, he was touched by her compassion to help a stranger in need. He was also impressed by her tenacity, eluding Darius' grasp, for he was much larger than she.

"I understand your need to come to the aid of a lady in distress, but please, next time have more consideration for your friends. At least wait until we have finished our drinks first," laughed Lando.

"Well, we shall not be coming this way again, any time soon," said Markus, leading the group away into the slow rising mist of the forest. At least for now, the rain had ceased, he thought, as they melted into the darkness.

CHAPTER 9

OF WIZARDS AND OTHER REVELATIONS

Skirting the edge of the village, Faria led the group eastward until they came upon a dense stand of trees. Under the canopy of a massive, ancient oak, with leaves growing so thick the ground below was still relatively dry after the heavy rainfall, the group came to a stop.

Here, the Order rested for several hours after their long trek through Rock Ridge Pass and their little misadventure in the village of Heathrowen. Faria and Lando took the first watch, while Darius and the others rested.

Darius was soon embraced in a quiet slumber. Ewen fell asleep almost immediately after eating; a combination of exhaustion and the ale he had consumed. As he slept, he soon fell into his nightmare. Again, the details were becoming more vivid than the last time, and each time Ewen would cry out, waking with a start – confused and dazed by the realism of his tormented dream.

Arerys was there to calm him, easing him back into a more restful slumber.

"What troubles him so?" asked Nayla of Lindras, as he drew air into his pipe. "He cannot seem to find peace, even when he sleeps."

"He is haunted by a reoccurring nightmare of which he does not understand, nor can he escape," answered the Wizard, releasing a swirling wisp of gray smoke from his lips.

Nayla watched as Ewen lay in his sleep, his right hand clutched to his chest as he twitched uneasily. "Does it have anything to do with what he wears about his neck?" asked Nayla.

Lindras looked at Arerys and Markus for a moment. They both nodded their approval that he may divulge to Nayla the true intent of their quest.

"What I shall disclose to you now, will not be repeated to another soul," instructed Lindras. "I know you can be trusted, Nayla."

Sitting across from the Wizard, she drew closer in her eagerness to learn more.

"Ewen has been given a second chance," said Lindras. "He does not know it yet, but one thousand years ago, he was there when King Brannon took up arms against Beyilzon on Mount Hope."

"As a soldier?" asked Nayla, intrigued by his words.

"No. As he is now, the squire to the man who shall eventually become the king."

After a long, reflective pause, Lindras continued with his story. "I was there, with Kal-lel Wingfield, on Mount Hope when the boy you now know as Ewen Vatel failed to do what was intended of him. Because he failed the *test*, Beyilzon was allowed to rise again."

Markus and Arerys listened intently. They too did not understand why the boy was plagued by this reoccurring nightmare, nor did they fully comprehend Ewen's role in this quest other than to help deliver the Stone of Salvation to Mount Hope.

"When the moment arrived that Beyilzon had grappled control over King Brannon, he turned to the king's squire, asking him, 'Will you die for him?' What Beyilzon was asking the boy was if he was willing to sacrifice himself on behalf of all mankind," explained Lindras. "He wanted to know if man was worthy of salvation. When the boy fled, leaving Brannon at Beyilzon's mercy, he demonstrated that man was indeed selfish and weak. The one person, chosen by the Maker of All, to deliver salvation to mankind only sought to save himself."

"In a last, desperate bid to save Imago, King Brannon sacrificed himself. He was mortally wounded when he was made to handle the Stone of Salvation. It was the only way to unlock the power of his sword, to bring Beyilzon and his Dark Army down in defeat," continued Lindras, reflecting on this very dark moment in history. "Unfortunately, the boy who was to represent hope, salvation and man's unselfish act of love for others, failed to find the courage and compassion in his own heart to spare Brannon's life. Because of this, the Dark Lord continues to exist, his black soul kept alive - nurtured in the hearts of evil men. This is the place that Beyilzon lives on, in the darkest corner of man's heart."

"Are you telling me that we are taking a lamb to his slaughter, Lindras," whispered Markus, appalled by this terrible revelation.

"It is no wonder he fears to dream so," said Arerys. "It is a terrible burden for one so young."

"Arerys, Ewen's soul has carried this burden for almost one thousand years," reminded Lindras. "He has been given a chance for redemption - to allow his soul some peace. He himself begged to the Three Sisters, asking the Maker of All for mercy. He asked for this second chance. He just does not remember that he did so. At least, not in this present lifetime."

"Can we not spare him of this terrible fate, at least warn him?" asked Nayla.

"Events have already been set in motion. We cannot interfere. When the moment of truth comes, Ewen must make this choice of his own free will, Nayla," advised the Wizard. "If he chooses to sacrifice himself to merely free himself of his own guilt - to ease the burden he has carried for so long, he shall only serve to fail mankind again. If he is compelled to sacrifice himself for the cause, he must do so because he truly believes that man is worthy of such a sacrifice. He must truly believe, in his own heart, that mankind is worthy of salvation."

"The Stone of Salvation?" asked Nayla, searching the faces of those who sat before her. "Does he carry the Stone?"

"Yes," answered Markus, feeling great pity for Ewen.

Nayla stared at Markus in silence, her mind cogitating on this bit of information.

"Why is the Stone so important? Can Brannon's sword not be used without it?" asked Nayla.

"From the bowels of the earth, from a secret place never seen by man nor Elf, the Stone of Salvation was extracted and cut. I delivered this Stone to the Watchers, the Three Sisters who dwell in the temple on Mount Isa," explained Lindras. "There, it was blessed by the Watchers. The four great Wizards who were placed on earth to counsel and guide mankind, gathered to empower the Stone in an attempt to circumvent the Dark Lord's efforts to dominate all life in Imago."

"I, Lindras Weatherstone of the West, control the element of the earth. Eldred Firestaff of the East controlled the element of fire," continued Lindras with his history lesson. "Tor Airshorn of the North controlled the element of air, while Tylon Riverdon of the South controls the element of water. Our combined gifts, bestowed upon us by the Maker of All, empowered the Stone to harness the energy of all four elements. When used in combination with King Brannon's sword, the wielder of this weapon has the power to defeat the Dark Lord."

Lindras went on to explain how the sword was forged and blessed by the Elders of Wyndwood for the purpose of this quest. Together, with the Stone of Salvation, not only did this tool serve to do away with the Dark Lord, it worked like a lock and key to trap Beyilzon into his underworld prison. To ensure that it never be abused, only the scion of King Brannon may handle the sword. The same applies to the Stone; it may only be handled by one pure of heart whose hands were free of the blood of others.

"So, Markus cannot handle the Stone, just as Ewen cannot handle the sword?" queried Arerys.

"Yes, that is why King Brannon eventually died. Because his squire fled, dropping the Stone, King Brannon was forced to place the Stone into the sword's handle," said Lindras. "In doing so, he was able to slay Beyilzon's physical form, but without Ewen, Beyilzon's spirit was allowed to live on. The Stone drew upon Brannon's own life-force; he succumbed shortly after we delivered the Stone to the Three Sisters."

"What will happen if Ewen declines again?" asked Markus. "I am afraid he may be so overwhelmed that he may fail, not so much out of selfishness or lack of compassion, but out of pure fear."

"Only time will tell, Markus. If Ewen fails, then you may succeed in locking Beyilzon away, but his banishment shall again be temporary," warned Lindras. "Take this to heart; it is crucial that Ewen is not fore-warned of this matter. It is absolutely vital not one of us breathe a word of this to him. Is it understood?"

Nayla, Arerys, and Markus all swore to honor this promise, although it broke their hearts to do so.

After a long silence, Markus spoke up again. "Lindras, whatever became of the other Wizards?"

"We have existed long before man came to being," answered Lindras. "We were placed here to provide mankind with the wisdom of the ages for the Maker of All, in all his infinite wisdom, created man with a clean slate so to the speak; gifting man with the ability to choose."

"Choose what?" asked Nayla, perplexed by the Wizard's statement.

"Choose everything! Anything!" responded Lindras with a heavy sigh. "The gift of choice: a blessing and a curse."

As Lindras paused to think upon mankind's history, he elected to choose his words carefully.

"The race of Elves and Wizards know that the Maker of All is the

'*One*'; the creator of all life. We know what is right and wrong - what is good and evil. Man, on the other hand, was even given the choice to believe, or not believe, in the Maker of All. That in itself, created many problems: mankind had to learn what was right and wrong, to discern what was good and evil. This freedom of choice is also tempered with the responsibility that comes with taking action. Man, like little children, seem to take great pleasure in testing, teasing and embarking on all manners of bad behavior, just because they do not know better. When they do know better, they do not feel they should be held accountable for their actions. They believe if they repent to the Maker of All, all would be forgiven. So, they continue on their merry way, repeating the same mistakes, always asking for forgiveness."

"So mankind was like a great experiment gone awry?" asked Arerys with fascination.

"For lack of a better analogy, I suppose so," responded the flustered Wizard. "Arerys, your people were placed here as the healers and the guardians of earth. In retrospect, I suppose to heal and guard the earth from some of man's more despicable actions."

"Are we all as bad as you make us out to be?" asked Markus, his brows furrowing with genuine concern.

"Let us say, some of you are more enlightened than others. Yes, some of you have come a long way," said Lindras, giving him an encouraging smile. "The wisdom of the four Wizards was to guide mankind, but after all these years, I am afraid Tor, the Wizard of the North chose to enter the Twilight; disappearing almost one thousand years ago. Apparently, he felt he no longer possessed the wisdom, nor the patience, to guide man much further."

"What became of the others?" asked Markus.

"Tylon Riverdon of the South has exiled himself, high into the peaks of the Cathedral Mountain. He has chosen to distance himself from mankind. Apparently, he is a frequent visitor to the Temple of the Watchers.

"But what about you, Lindras Weatherstone," asked Markus. "Why do you continue to exist amongst mankind when we seem to be a lost cause?"

The Wizard's eyes sparkled from the depth of his great hood. "Because I believe that within the heart of man, there is far more good that exists than evil. I believe man's love and compassion, his humanity, has an incredible capacity to shine through under the most dire and adverse situations," answered Lindras with a reassuring smile. "I still hold great hope for mankind."

"And what of Eldred Firestaff, the Wizard of the East?" asked Arerys. "I understand he disappeared into the Iron Mountains, never to be seen again."

"It is believed that he too, chose to enter the Twilight."

Nayla stared in disbelief at the Wizard. "I am afraid you are wrong, Lindras," said Nayla. "Eldred of the East lives on. He is no longer a Wizard. He has turned to the forbidden arts, wreaking havoc amongst the people of Orien as a Sorcerer."

Lindras sat upright, his back as straight as an arrow as he thought upon this news. "Are you positive, Nayla?

"Oh yes, I am positive," answered Nayla. "I wish it were not so, but it is indeed a fact."

"The last trip I made to see Dahlon Treeborn was also to hunt down Eldred. Just in case he had exiled himself somewhere in eastern Imago - in Orien; I had to find out for myself," said Lindras. "Obviously, he had remained cleverly hidden during my sojourn."

Lindras was deep in thought; he was greatly troubled by this news.

"Something concerns you, Wizard," said Arerys, this silence gnawing at his heart.

"Indeed. This quest is not without its perils, but now our situation is more complicated just knowing that Eldred has resurfaced as a Sorcerer. He may greatly affect the outcome for all."

"How so?" inquired Markus.

Lindras turned to face Markus. "He knows of the power of the Stone. I am sure he knows that we possess it, just as I am sure he knows that we are on our way to Mount Hope," answered Lindras, his eyes growing dark with new concern. "He may want to possess this Stone for his own evil gains. If he is successful, he may become even more powerful and more fearsome than Beyilzon."

"Our situation becomes more dire with each passing day," moaned Markus, clutching his aching head in his hands.

"We must remain ever vigilant of his presence," warned Lindras. "If he has indeed turned to black arts, then let us hope that his own follies may lead to his ruin and eventual demise. It just may not happen as soon as we may all desire."

"Why did Eldred turn to the forbidden arts?" asked Nayla. "The people of Orien never knew he was once a mighty Wizard until his identify was revealed to us by Dahlon Treeborn. He would vanish for long periods of time, only to resurface to vent his wrath. He is a fire hazard; a troublemaker of the worst sort. He works to divide the people of Orien as he conspires with those who inhabit the areas east of the Furai Mountains."

"It was shortly after Imago was immersed in the Second Age of Peace that Eldred became truly disenchanted with man. After all mankind stood to loose, he believed life was still taken for granted by those who continued with their wicked ways, even after the sacrifice made by Brannon," said Lindras, recalling a time long ago from his past. "He failed to see that for every bad soul that exists, there were many more good ones. He felt that the Maker of All should have punished mankind for the squire's shortcomings, for he felt the boy's selfish and cowardly act was representative of all that mankind stood for. In his bitterness and loathing, he took it upon himself to dispense punishment."

Tylon, Tor and I combined forces to capture Eldred, so he may be returned to Mount Isa to stand in judgment, but he fled. Now it is clear where he has been all this time," said the Wizard, taking a long, contemplative puff on his pipe.

The group was silent. They pondered this new revelation and how it may affect the outcome of their quest, but the momentary silence was broken as Ewen stirred in his sleep.

"Whatever became of the king's squire? Did he escape from Mount Hope?" asked Nayla, watching the boy as he slept.

"No," answered Lindras with a heavy heart. "He was hunted down by Beyilzon's men – he was killed. He did die, but not in the manner that was intended. His death was in vain."

CHAPTER 10

OBVIOUS SIGNS

Markus had the Order on the move again. They would journey through the remainder of the night for as long as they could endure, into the next day, in a bid to make up for the time lost at Rock Ridge Pass and in Heathrowen.

As the day wore on, the clouds gave way to blue skies. The warm spring sun cast a golden hue upon the land Faria loved so dearly. The deep green sea of grass that lay before them rippled like waves with the gentle breeze. Early flowering wild cherry trees opened their papery, white petals to the sun. Their fragrant blossoms filled the air with a delicate perfume.

Faria looked to the west, across to the horizon. It was difficult for him to believe his people were in the midst of a war: everything seemed so still and calm. It was apparent that spring would come when it was ready to do so, no matter what mankind was intent on doing.

At least Faria found some comfort in that, during their brief stay at the inn, he was able to speak to the owner of the establishment. He discovered the king's castle was indeed stormed by Beyilzon's men, but King Sebastian and a good number of his soldiers had escaped. They had retreated towards the borders of Carcross as they awaited the arrival of King Bromwell's army to combine forces. For now, Faria's fear that he had lost both his beloved brother and country was no longer compounded by the knowledge that his king had fallen too.

With Arerys and Faria taking the lead, and Nayla trailing with Ewen and the others, they covered many leagues. There was now no need for Arerys to continually backtrack to the others to warn them if it was safe to proceed. Arerys and Nayla were now the eyes and ears for the group.

By day's end, all were relieved that their journey thus far was uneventful. With no sign of Beyilzon's men in this region, the group was a bit more at ease, but always watchful.

One by one, the men collapsed to the ground in exhaustion. Ewen was already braced in a deep, dreamless sleep. Nayla stood up, walking over to the boy, she gently stroked his wavy mop of hair before pulling his cloak high over his shoulders, up to his neck.

"Markus, I shall take the first watch," whispered Nayla as she fastened her long cloak around her small shoulders.

"I shall join you," said Arerys, taking his bow and quiver into his hand.

"Very well," answered Markus, stretching his weary muscles. "We shall be on our way well before the first light of day, so your watch shall not be long. I shall relieve you of duty, shortly."

Nayla and Arerys crept through the low hanging tree boughs to the top of a small hill overlooking the camp and the outlying areas. An old oak tree; twisted and gnarled from years of exposure to the driving winter winds, leaned down. Still very much alive, it seemed to invite them into its large, welcoming branches that stooped low to the ground.

"How beautiful it is!" said Nayla, her hand gently touching the moss-covered trunk.

Arerys gazed up into the branches; tiny stars danced in and out between the leaves that moved with the slightest breeze. He nimbly leapt onto one of the heavy, old, main branches. "Let me help you up, Nayla," said Arerys, extending his hand to her.

She took his hand into hers as he lifted her lightly into the tree, onto the large branch that he was skillfully balanced on.

She thanked him and smiled. He returned her smile, but he quickly turned his face away, as though he did not wish for her to look into his eyes. For a moment, there seemed to be awkwardness about the Elf that Nayla had never noticed before. She smiled nevertheless, sitting with her back erect to the tree's great trunk.

With her legs crossed, Nayla held her hands out in front of her body. The middle finger and thumb of each hand touched and these interlocking rings joined the two hands together. The tips of the other fingers met with that of the opposite hand and, with her fingers woven in this unusual configuration, Nayla's eyes closed.

Arerys watched her with great interest. "Are you going to sleep now?"

"My mind seeks the rest that it cannot find, even when my body sleeps," answered Nayla, peering at him through one open eye. "I am not sleeping, I am mediating. I wish to be one with the sea."

Arerys looked at her with some bewilderment. "I do not understand."

Now, both eyes opened. Nayla looked at the Elf and smiled at him. "Arerys, you claim your people are one with the land, yes?"

Arerys nodded his head in response.

"My people, or more so, my mother's people, are one with the land too, but they embrace all the elements: earth, water, fire, air - even the secrets that lie in the Void beyond what man can see, hear or touch," Nayla said, feeling the powerful energy coursing through the tree. "These are the elements that make the earth whole: a land without water would soon become a parched desert; without fire to scorch it, the earth would not be renewed. There is an energy that is in all things of this earth. It can be harnessed and channeled, if you know how to do so."

Arerys listened intently, absorbing her every word.

Nayla continued her explanation. "It is a feeling that cannot be described by words; it can only be experienced to be truly appreciated. This is the same feeling - the forces of nature's energy - that I call upon to survive in battle. Do you understand, Arerys?"

"I wish to, but it is an unusual concept to grasp," responded the Elf. "I would like to experience this feeling, if it will help me to better understand it."

Nayla briskly rubbed the palms of her hands together. As they warmed, she stopped. Her eyes closed as she concentrated on the energy emanating from her palms. As this energy grew, her hands were slowly pushed apart by an invisible force. Nayla's eyes opened. She held her right hand up towards the Elf.

"With your open hand, touch mine," she instructed.

Arerys slowly raised his left hand to meet hers. To his surprise, as his open palm came to within four inches of hers, an unseen barrier stopped his advance. Like the magnetic charges of the same polarity, he felt his hand repelled, as if a cushion of air kept him from making contact. He was stunned. Although he could not see it – it was still very tangible.

Nayla could see his look of surprise. "If I generate enough of this energy, I can actually heal or do harm without physically touching you."

"But how? How did you do that?"

"You have this energy too, Arerys. It is only a matter of learning how to control it," answered Nayla, weaving her fingers back together.

Arerys studied the configuration of her small, slender fingers, struggling to weave his own fingers in the same fashion.

"Here, sit next to me," said Nayla. "Give me your hands."

Arerys sidled over, closer to Nayla. His body perfectly balanced on the tree's branch, his legs crossed as hers were.

Nayla took both of his hands into hers. She carefully maneuvered his fingers so the middle finger and thumb of each hand were joined, linked together by these rings while the index and other fingers of each hand met with their corresponding fingertips.

He noticed the warmth of her hands lingering on his, long after she was done.

"Now relax. Close your eyes. Take a long, slow breath in through your nose, then exhale quickly through your mouth," said Nayla as she demonstrated the breathing cycle.

Arerys closed his eyes; listening and copying the rhythm of Nayla's breathing pattern.

"Now in your mind, envision yourself by the sea. The waves are lapping upon the shore, shifting the driftwood and seaweed about as the tide moves in and out. Now with a deep breath in, feel the wave receding from the shore; see the driftwood, seaweed, and the grains of sand all moving back with the ebbing tide," whispered Nayla.

Arerys drew in a slow, deep breath through his nose.

"Now as you exhale, feel your breath like the water rushing to the shore. Feel it crashing down upon the beach - even water can wear down the greatest of mountains."

Arerys felt the rising sensation of water coursing through his lungs as he breathed. He felt the mighty force of a huge wave crashing onto the shore, sweeping away all in its path. His soul was carried on this great tide; it was most empowering, but also very overwhelming. His eyes snapped open.

Nayla still sat before him, her face serene, her eyes still closed. For a moment, Arerys watched her in silence. He looked upon Nayla's face; the small silver ring that pierced her tiny earlobe was adorned with a thin thread of silver that was looped through this ring and hung from a small, silver ear cuff that sparkled in the darkness. This fine slip of silver seemed to reflect the light cast from even the faintest stars, far above. Arerys studied the intricate design carved into the ear cuff that Nayla wore high around the edge of her right ear, the tip of which ascended into a very gentle, barely noticeable Elven point.

In the darkness, her deep brown hair looked raven black, so black it seemed to dance with blue highlights. It was neatly plaited into a long braid, a few stray wisps lightly brushed against her cheeks and brows – carried by the soft evening breeze. Arerys found himself trying to control his urge to reach out with his hand to gently touch her face.

Nayla sensed a change in the Elf. Her eyes opened in time to see his head quickly turn away from hers. "Are you alright?"

Again, Arerys had that same awkwardness about him. "Yes, I was just feeling a bit light-headed, that is all."

Nayla placed a hand on Arerys' knee. "I am afraid that it does take some getting use to," she said as she tried to assure the Elf.

Arerys did not respond, he only gazed at Nayla's small hand resting upon his knee.

She looked at his face. Noticing that he was staring down at her hand, she quickly withdrew it. "I am sorry," she said, not wishing to cause him discomfort.

Before Arerys could confide to her that the attention was not unwanted, Markus appeared from underneath the tree. "Arerys! Nayla! Where are you?" he called in a hushed voice.

Arerys smiled at Nayla, looking a bit disappointed and flustered by Markus' untimely arrival. He dropped from the branch, landing quietly onto his feet in front of the prince.

Markus was momentarily startled by the shadow that silently appeared before him. His right hand moved to draw his sword. "It is you, Arerys! You must take greater care, I could have hurt you."

"I am here, Markus," Nayla called softly.

He looked up to see her sitting upon the oak tree's mighty limb. She smiled and waved down at him.

"Arerys, Lindras is in need of your counsel. I shall take the watch while you meet with the old Wizard," said Markus, securing his sword back into its scabbard.

"Yes, of course, Markus," Arerys said with a nod. He looked up towards Nayla and smiled. "We shall finish our conversation another time, my lady." The Elf silently vanished into the darkness.

Nayla nimbly leapt down, landing next to the prince. She removed her long sword, resting it across her lap as she made herself comfortable on the ground. Markus joined her beneath the great tree, both sat with their backs resting against the massive, twisted trunk.

"Listen, Nayla – there is not a sound," sighed Markus, enjoying the peaceful calm of the night.

"To the contrary, Markus. Listen again - I hear the sounds of crickets and the distant call of a nightingale."

"Hmm, indeed you are right," answered Markus, his ears straining to hear the night sounds.

"It is when the night grows silent and these sounds cannot be heard, that I may draw some concern," said Nayla, settling her cloak around her shoulders.

"I am curious, my lady, what were you and Arerys speaking of when I so rudely interrupted?" queried Markus as he lit his pipe, his dark eyes reflecting the flicker of the tiny, yellow flame.

"Oh, it was nothing really. Matters that only concern the likes of myself, and my ways," answered Nayla, in a nonchalant manner.

"Ah, the Elf wishes to learn more about you," nodded Markus as he slowly exhaled from his pipe.

"No, he wishes to learn from me," corrected Nayla, watching as a delicate wisp of aromatic smoke rose from his pipe.

Markus looked at her and simply smiled.

"What is it, my lord?"

"Do you really not know?" He looked at her with dismay. "The signs are obvious."

"What signs? What do you speak of?"

"Arerys, he is quite taken by you!"

"No, Markus. You are mistaken," Nayla laughed, her face flushed with embarrassment.

"What is with you, girl?" asked Markus in amazement. "I realize that you are a skilled a warrior, better than most men, but do not tell me that your senses have been dulled like that of a man's too? Are you really as witless and blind as most men are, when it comes to love?"

Nayla sat up, turning to look at Markus. "No. You are mistaken, my lord." Her annoyance clearly visible on her face. "Arerys' interest in me is purely that of curiosity. Though we share the same Elven blood, I am unlike the women-folk of Wyndwood."

Markus laughed, but not unkindly, at her comment. "That is an under-statement. You are unlike any woman I know, Elven or mortal!"

"That is why he distances himself from me."

"He minds his distance because he loves Darius as a brother," said Markus, his voice becoming serious. "He believes Darius has forged a special bond with you; he dare not be the one to break it."

"Darius? Darius is a great warrior; in fact, he is almost brave to a fault. Where he may charge into battle headlong to preserve the life and honor of others, he also wears the heart of a man with great compassion for those around him," responded Nayla, leaning back against the tree trunk. "His show of chivalry and kindness to me is just in his nature. It is nothing more than that. He has proven himself to be a dear friend to me."

"Nayla, do you not see what is in Arerys' eyes when he looks at you? Do you not feel it in his touch, when he takes you by your hand?"

"He draws away from me whenever our eyes meet," Nayla answered wistfully.

"He does so because he has deep feelings for you that he is afraid shall go unnoticed and unreturned."

"No, he cares not for my brash ways. In fact, I do believe he finds my demeanor somewhat intimidating," sighed Nayla, gazing up to the stars. "It is smart for him to keep his distance."

"No, my lady. I assure you, Arerys is not easily intimidated, not even by the likes of you," replied Markus as he released a gentle gray puff of smoke from his lips. "What he fears the most, is to venture into a realm that is uncertain and uncharted. He is afraid to be in love with one who will not return his affections."

"Love is lost and found all the time, Markus. Arerys is older than I. I am sure he has loved and lost many in his long life. He is none the worse for it."

Markus leaned towards Nayla to look her in her eyes. "What kind of Elf are you, Nayla?" he asked with all seriousness. "Love is not some-thing Elves speak of lightly. Love can make them or ruin them."

"Do I need to remind you that I stand with one foot in the Elven world, the other in man's?" asked Nayla, staring back into Markus' dark, soulful eyes. "What are you speaking of? I do not understand this riddle."

"You really do not know, do you?" He searched Nayla's face for a sign. "Elves like Arerys never take matters of the heart lightly. Though his kind has never known pestilence and sickness, they do feel the suffering of others. They have great compassion and love for those around them, including mortal man. This compassion is their undoing."

"So, his kind is cursed with strong emotions," said Nayla with indifference, shrugging her shoulders.

"Did your father not tell you that there are only two ways an Elf can die?"

"I know they can be cut down in battle."

"There is more, Nayla," said Markus as he continued to explain, obviously startled by her ignorance. "Yes, they can be killed in battle, but unlike mortal man who may cleave to another woman, an Elf who has promised his heart to a true love, can also die of a broken heart, if that love is lost."

Nayla grew silent as she thought upon Markus' words.

He continued, "My lady, I have known Arerys all of my thirty-seven years. Although he has walked this earth for over seven centuries and undeniably, has been in the company of other women, I can vouch for certain that he has never declared his love for another, Elven or mortal."

"I wish to hear no more of this," said Nayla as she quickly rose to her feet.

"Very well, my lady. I do not wish to be involved in matters of the heart, but be assured that my involvement is such, because my love for Arerys is great. I wish for him to find some happiness in his life," responded Markus. "He has been alone for too many years."

"And you believe his happiness lies with me?" asked Nayla with a frown.

"Why do you not ask him yourself, Nayla?"

Nayla stood silently before Markus, his question unanswered.

"If my eyes do not betray me, I catch you looking at Arerys from time to time, in the same manner. If I am wrong, please do this one thing for me: Tell him how you truly feel. If I am wrong in my summation, then find it in your heart to tell him so. I know he holds hope that you may find your way to his arms. If you feel nothing for Arerys, then I beg of you; tell him now. Extinguish his fire before he is consumed by it."

"I shall deal with this matter when the time is right," said Nayla, not wishing to hear anymore.

Markus searched her eyes for some sign of compassion. "Nayla, I am afraid there will never be a right time, if what you say shall only serve to pierce Arerys' heart deeper than his truest arrow," Markus responded tersely. "Just do not wait until he can be mortally wounded by your words and actions."

Nayla quietly turned away from Markus. She slowly proceeded down the hill to the fire of their camp. As she approached, Darius and Lando were gathering their arms for the next watch.

"Little one! You did not leave our Markus strung up in a tree somewhere did you?" laughed Darius as he threw an arm around her shoulders, greeting her with a hug.

Nayla could feel Arerys' eyes on her as she moved away from Darius' friendly embrace. She took care to not wake Faria as she quietly stepped around Ewen's sleeping body. She settled down next to Lindras, who had been discussing with Faria and Arerys, the next possible route to take when morning dawned.

"Are you all right, my dear?" Lindras asked, sounding rather fatherly.

"Yes," she answered, her voice barely a whisper.

Arerys looked at her with concern. "You should get some sleep, Nayla."

Nayla glanced over to Arerys and smiled. "Yes, I think I shall." She lay herself down near the fire, drawing her cloak about her body. Although her back was turned to the Elf, she could still feel the steady gaze of his blue eyes - they stared at her, speaking to her. She lay her head down and closed her eyes, hoping for dreams to take over her mind and possibly give her some reprieve from the inner turmoil she now felt.

Darius and Lando bid Markus a good night as they settled into the final shift of the watch. Their conversation quickly turned to Nayla.

"You are fond of Nayla, are you not?" asked Lando with a knowing smile.

"I do not deny that I am attracted to her," answered Darius as his eyes scanned the dark landscape.

"But you hesitate," said Lando, intrigued by his friend's remark.

"She is a unique woman, unlike any I have ever known," admitted Darius as he lit his pipe. "Obviously, she is a skilled warrior who is brave and honorable on the battlefield, yet she is also kind and compassionate.

It is not a quality you will find often, especially in a seasoned warrior."

"So you are intimidated by her?" asked Lando, with raised eyebrows.

"No, to the contrary. In all honesty, I truly value her friendship. Nayla is not one to be trivialized or treated as an object, to be loved, then cast aside. I know intimacy shall only compromise our relationship. It is one that I wish to honor and keep intact."

"Ah, a woman you respect," said Lando with a smile. "And to think, we laughed at Arerys when he insisted that such a woman does exist."

CHAPTER 11

LOVE; LOST AND FOUND

The darkness of night was slowly dissolved by the light of the morning, even before the sun peered over the Iron Mountains. As the last star withdrew its solitary light from the sky, Darius and Lando returned from their watch.

Arerys and Nayla had both been awake for some time while the others were only stirring from their sleep. They were quietly conversing as Nayla shared her version of Elven bread with Arerys. To his surprise, although it looked heavier than the thin, crisp wafers that he was familiar with, it had the same texture and consistency. It did indeed satisfy one's hunger without leaving one feeling heavy, but it was more flavorful. Arerys attributed its delicate taste to the hint of honey and the bits of dried fruits Nayla had added.

Darius and Lando joined them for some breakfast and conversation. Arerys watched as Darius' face would light up when he saw Nayla. He could not deny it annoyed him somewhat to see the knight from Carcross nudging her with his elbow, or poking her like a young boy who knew of no other way to demonstrate his affection. Arerys also noticed how tolerant Nayla was of his antics; how she would lightheartedly laugh off his good-natured teasing and attention.

Lando excused himself from the group as he gathered the water flasks. To save them time, he was going to replenish everyone's flasks, as Ewen was still busy eating. Arerys joined him at the spring.

Lando went about the business of topping up all the flasks and as Arerys assisted him, Lando could see the Elf was deeply vexed. "What is it, Arerys? I know something troubles you. Speak."

"It is Darius," answered Arerys in a whisper. "I love him like a brother, so it is difficult to address this matter with him."

"What matter?" asked Lando as he continued with his task.

"I am concerned with the manner in which he treats Nayla."

Lando looked back at the others. He observed as Darius threw a friendly arm around Nayla's small shoulders.

Arerys turned to watch as a burst of laughter erupted as Nayla removed his arm from about her, quickly manipulating his wrist so Darius was thrown backwards onto the ground.

"That is what I mean," said Arerys, in disgust. "Does Darius not understand, or appreciate, that not only is Nayla Treeborn the captain of her own army, but she is also the daughter of the one who once ruled over Elmgrove. She deserves to be treated with more respect."

Lando glanced over at Nayla as she released her hold on Darius. "No, Arerys, you are mistaken. Darius respects Nayla more than you may even know," Lando responded, in his friend's defense. "It is just unfortunate for Darius that he cannot express himself better around women. You know he is a man of action, not a man of words."

"You would think that he was a love-sick boy," retorted Arerys in a hushed tone.

Lando looked into the Elf's blue eyes. They turned a deeper shade of blue with his growing irritability. "Yes, he loves her, Arerys, but let me assure you, he has no intention of bedding Nayla, if that is what you are worried about. Besides, why is it any concern of yours?" asked Lando, replacing the cork seal on the last flask.

Arerys did not respond. He continued to watch Nayla from a distance.

Lando considered Arerys for a moment. "No! It is you! You are the one who is in love! She is the warrior maiden your brother spoke of."

"Well, even if she were, it makes no difference. It is obvious that she is quite taken with Darius."

"Arerys, how many women do you know, who are not captivated by the likes of him?" asked Lando. "It would serve you well to speak to Nayla yourself. Do not waste your time speculating about what may, or may not, be. You may walk this earth for an eternity, but remember my friend, you may still only chance upon this opportunity but once."

With those words said, Lando collected the flasks and delivered them back to the others, leaving Arerys alone to ponder his dilemma. The Elf rose to his feet when he saw Markus getting ready to move out.

The sun was high in the sky, having traveled a great distance westward by the time the Order came across a crumbling fortress. This once majestic structure faced southward, overlooking a large field that had long lay fallow. The Order cautiously walked around the derelict ruin, its western walls collapsing from many years of neglect as the surrounding ground was littered with fallen stones and broken fragments of mortar. They gazed across the large field sprawling out in front of the citadel.

Arerys glanced about uneasily. He could not explain it, but he had an unsettling feeling about this place.

"Markus, something does not bode well. I am going up to seek out a better vantage point," said the Elf, pointing to the large hill overshadowing the citadel and field.

"Darius, Nayla, remain here with Ewen and Lindras," ordered Markus. "We shall return shortly." He headed up the hill with Arerys in the lead; Faria and Lando following close behind.

Lindras, Nayla, and Darius waited under the shade of a blossoming apple tree. Delicate, white petals gently floated down upon them like little flakes of snow falling from a cloudless sky.

Ewen watched as Arerys and the others swiftly disappeared up the hill as he rose up to his feet. He began to stroll away from the others, walking along at a leisurely pace. He headed towards the edge of the expansive field that lay before him. When he reached the end of this large, open land, the ground dropped abruptly into a valley that the citadel once stood guard over.

He looked down below, gasping in disbelief and horror: the Dark Army! They had set up camp in the shadow of the citadel. Though Ewen stood there but only for a moment, he was too slow in withdrawing from view. Several soldiers were pointing up excitedly in his direction. He heard one of them barking orders at the others. Ewen knew they were coming for him. He turned, dashing back at top speed to where the others were resting.

"They are coming, Darius!" shouted Ewen as he sprinted across the field.

"Who is coming?" asked Darius, rising to his feet.

"The Dark Army! They are camped out in the valley just beyond the edge of this field!" explained Ewen. "They saw me and now they are coming!"

Nayla leapt to her feet. "I can hear their approach, at least ten of them head our way!"

"Take the boy! Get him to safety now!" ordered Darius as he sounded his horn to call the others back.

Nayla grabbed Ewen by his hand; Lindras quickly followed behind. They raced up the stairs of the abandoned fortress.

"Lindras, barricade and lock the doors! Do not open it until I return. I must go now! Darius cannot fend off this horde on his own!"

She bounded back down the crumbling stairs as she heard Darius sound his horn again. Charging back across the open field where Darius now stood, she could see thirteen soldiers of Beyilzon's army surrounding him. Too far away to aid Darius with her sword, Nayla reached into her vest as she ran. She armed herself with the throwing darts she had recently dipped into her vial of poison.

Darius was already caught up in the heat of the battle. His sword was swinging and hacking at his assailants while his shield deflected their angry blows.

Nayla let out a cry that was neither a scream nor a shout; it rose from deep within her small body, but with such force it caught the soldiers off guard. From a distance, she probably appeared to them as no more than a young girl. Five of the soldiers turned in her direction as she came racing straight for them, her cloak billowing behind her as she ran.

One of the soldiers laughed upon watching her bold approach. "Look at this!" he shouted. "They send a girl to do a man's job!"

Before he could take another step, Nayla aimed a dart directly at him, striking him in the throat. The soldier clutched at his neck, his hand struggling to dislodge the poisoned dart. He suddenly dropped to the ground, devoid of life.

Nayla continued on, straight to Darius. As she ran, she threw a rapid succession of darts. Each hitting its mark in a soldier's neck or eye, causing each man to convulse, then collapse.

As she neared her friend, Nayla drew her sword from its scabbard; the forged steel seemed to come alive, flashing against the sunlight.

Darius' back was forced up against the old apple tree by six of the dark soldiers. As he struck down one soldier, another one was already there to continue the assault.

Nayla ran towards the soldiers who encircled him. Holding her sword close to her body, she dove to the ground and rolled forward, rising up upon her feet directly behind them. As she knelt down, a broad sweep from her sword cut cleanly through the muscles and tendons at the back of the legs of three of the soldiers. They let out a foul cry as their knees buckled beneath their weight, causing the soldiers to crumple backwards. Nayla rose up. Without hesitation, the blade of her sword came arcing downward to slice through their throats in one deliberate, final sweep.

Darius was quickly wearing down, the sweat was pouring from his forehead, forming rivulets down his neck and chest as he stood his ground. Without missing a beat, Nayla was upon the soldier that relentlessly pounded against the knight's shield. Approaching from behind with her sword held high, Nayla's blade swung down, cleanly slicing through the soldier's armor, taking his left arm and continuing straight through to his right leg with one blow.

"Eleven down! Two to go!" shouted Darius in triumph as he winked at her.

As Nayla spun around to kick one of the soldiers down as he charged towards her, she shouted to Darius: "You spoke too soon!"

From the far edge of the large field, at least two-dozen dark soldiers emerged. With swords raised and bows armed, they advanced toward Darius and Nayla.

"We must fight the good fight, my lady! We must hold on. I know Markus and the others are close at hand!" said Darius as the broad side of his blade struck the soldier across his head.

Nayla nodded to Darius before turning to face the rising black tide. From the distance, the soldiers armed with bows, took aim. A hail of arrows showered down upon them. Nayla quickly turned her body sideways to the barrage, thereby narrowing their anticipated target. She raised her sword, turning the flat edge of her blade out. Using swift movements of her wrist, she skillfully deflected the incoming projectiles.

Darius lifted his shield as he continued to battle with the soldier. Some of the arrows penetrated his shield. Suddenly, he let out a terrible cry of pain. A single arrow tore deep into Darius' left thigh.

Nayla turned, and to her horror, he had collapsed to the ground. The dark soldier now towered menacingly over him, sword raised high, the tip pointed down to impale its intended victim.

"No!" Nayla screamed. Her arm was poised to hurl her sword as she ran to Darius' aid. Abruptly, a wounded soldier that lay dying seized her by her ankle. She tumbled to the ground, her sword no longer in her grip.

Nayla desperately kicked away the hand that held her. Scrambling to her feet, she saw that her sword did indeed stay true to its course, penetrating the soldier's armor and driving into his shoulder blade. However, the wound it inflicted did nothing to slow the enraged soldier's assault on Darius. Like a crazed beast driven solely by visceral hate, the adrenaline coursing through his veins seemed to deaden his pain.

With sword in both hands, the soldier rammed it straight through Darius' body with such ferocity it caused the links of his chain mail to give. The impact drove Darius onto his knees and finally, down onto his back. The sword penetrated clean through as the soldier continued to force the blade down to its hilt.

Nayla's eyes were wide in shock, the color drained from her face. She raced to Darius' aid. Wrenching her sword from the soldier's back, she raised it aloft and with one swift blow, separated the soldier's head from his shoulders.

She turned to Darius as he lay struggling to remove the sword that was still embedded deep into his body. It was thrust straight through to the ground, pinning him down. Taking the weapon into both her hands, Nayla carefully pulled the sword straight out, as gently as possible. As she struggled with the cumbersome, crude weapon, her heart sank, for she now knew the true nature of Darius' wound.

"Run, Nayla! Leave me be!" ordered Darius, struggling to sit up.

"I cannot do that." She searched for something to staunch the flow of blood.

Darius grabbed her shoulders, weakly shaking her. "Protect Ewen. It is he and the Stone they seek!"

Nayla heard the fast approaching footsteps of the Dark Army. "He is safe with Lindras and I shall not leave you alone. Not like this!" she answered defiantly.

She took her sword up, whipping it around to flick off the blood that now heavily coated the blade. She calmly sheathed her weapon.

"What are you doing, Nayla? Run!" demanded Darius, desperation mounting in his voice.

His words went unheeded. She was now prepared to take on this entire army alone. Nayla faced the oncoming horde. Her face showed no trace of fear. The thumb and third finger of each hand joined in a ring that locked her two hands together. The remaining fingers of each hand met, pointing to the heavens.

"Give me the power to endure this," Nayla prayed under her breath. With those words, her eyes closed - her breaths became short and fast. Inside her body, it was as though a slow burning ember was being stoked into a mighty flame that crackled and burned with such intensity, her energy was becoming white hot.

Nayla now opened her eyes as she strode defiantly into battle. To place some distance between the Dark Army and the wounded Darius, she advanced towards them with the greatest intention to do them harm. She looked skyward; drawing her sword, she held it horizontally before her. Turning the flat edge of the blade out, she quickly aligned herself with the sun. A brilliant flash of light reflected off her sword, striking the eyes of the soldiers on the front line. Momentarily blinded by the sun's rays, some of the soldiers lowered their weapons to shield their eyes from the sun's dazzling light that seemed to intensify and burn as it bounced off Nayla's blade.

At that moment, Nayla's entire being seemed to explode towards the soldiers. Her eyes were full of fire and rage as she raced towards them. Her sword spun in large, circular movements as she lashed out at her foes. Her fierce blade easily cutting through the soldiers' armor, as if she were merely slicing through a grove of young willow saplings. Nayla moved quickly, angling and dodging the swords that aimed to strike her down. They now swarmed around her; as fast as she could cut them down, they were upon her.

As she turned to challenge the next three approaching soldiers, they reeled forward, then collapsed. They fell dead, one by one! Each bore an arrow in his back or head: Arerys was near. She looked up to see the Dark Army turning away from her as Markus, Faria, Lando and Arerys came storming down from the hill.

Arerys lined up his sight again, rapidly discharging one arrow after another, each taking a deadly toll on the Dark Army. When his arrows were spent, he charged into the fray with his sword at the ready.

Markus and his men fought with such ferocity, the earth seemed to tremble and quake in fear. Their swords crashed through shields, bodies, and limbs as they countered the assault.

Nayla was relieved to see the arrival of her companions, but they were still outnumbered as more soldiers seemed to materialize from nowhere. She sheathed her sword. Tearing off a strip of cloth from the cloak of a fallen soldier, she grabbed a round, smooth stone from the ground. She hastily wrapped it inside the cloth. Raising it over her head, Nayla called out, "This is what you seek! If you want the Stone, come take it from me!"

For a second, all soldiers, who were not fully engaged in battle, turned in Nayla's direction. Suddenly, the captain shouted, "Get her!" Seven soldiers were now in full pursuit.

Nayla turned to run. Unencumbered by heavy armor and weaponry, she moved swiftly to the citadel. Removing the long, thin rope that lay coiled in her leather pouch, she tied the cloth concealing the rock to one end. She charged up to the roof, looking out over the crumbling wall. She tossed the end of the rope, dangling the stone over the edge. Holding the other end, Nayla dove cross the floor, huddling close to the broken wall of the tower as the soldiers reached the rooftop.

"Where did she go?" called out a voice.

"Look a rope. She climbed down over the edge!" said another.

"The Stone! There it is!" announced a soldier as he pointed to the cloth secured to the end of the rope.

At that moment, Nayla gave the rope a mighty tug. It whipped back towards her, but as it did so, it snaked around the ankles of two of the soldiers standing the closest to the edge. She gave it another heave. The rope tightened, knocking the two soldiers off balance. They disappeared, screaming over the side of the wall.

As the rope went slack, Nayla stepped out from her hiding place, yanking the rope once more as she came into view. The cloth bag snapped back into her waiting hand. She proceeded to whip the rope over her head. Each time it circled over her, it accelerated faster and faster. With each revolution, she let out a greater length of rope, until the soldiers where forced against the very edge to avoid being struck.

Suddenly, Nayla lunged forward. The rope made a terrible cracking sound as she whipped it, striking three of the soldiers directly across their faces and about their heads. The soldiers stumbled back, the ferocity of her attack caused them to force two of their own men over the edge to their imminent deaths.

Nayla drew her sword and veered towards the three remaining soldiers. Blinded by the blood running from their wounded forehead, they did not even see, let alone hear, her deadly approach. Two soldiers perished instantly with a cold flash of steel. The last soldier stared in shock and disbelief at his smaller adversary. Obviously a greater danger than he dared to imagine, he dropped his sword in surrender.

"Pick it up!" demanded Nayla. The tip of her sword was raised dangerously close to his face. "Pick it up and fight, or do you choose to die unarmed?"

The soldier stared at Nayla: She was like the calm in the eye of a storm, waiting to unleash the fury of her wrath. The soldier quickly stooped to reclaim his sword, and as he did so, Nayla mocked: "Never take your eyes off your opponent!" With those words, she delivered an upward cut that penetrated the armor, slicing clean through his breastplate as if it were paper. The soldier's eyes glazed over in disbelief. He too, tumbled awkwardly backwards to join the rest of his departed comrades.

Nayla wrung the blood off her sword with a quick snapping action. She ran to the opposite wall overlooking the now, crimson stained field; the end was almost at hand. Markus and Arerys were both taking on one soldier, pummeling him into submission, while Faria and Lando were both preoccupied with their own foes.

Nayla sheathed her sword and took up her silken rope as she headed down the crumbling stairway. Stopping briefly at the locked tower door, she called out: "Ewen! Lindras! It is almost done. Darius has been wounded, but stay here for now. I shall retrieve you when it is safe."

Ewen and the Wizard, both just having witnessed a cascade of bodies falling past the window from the safety of the watchtower, hastened to remove the barricade and unlock the door. They felt the urgency to be near Darius.

Nayla was already racing across the field when Ewen and Lindras reached the bottom of the stairs.

Breathing hard and recovering their bearings, the men of the Order were weary. Other than some cuts and bruises, they were relatively unscathed. Nayla rushed past them, freezing in her path when her eyes came upon Darius' still figure lying in a growing pool of his own blood.

She sank down to her knees by his side, gently lifting his head onto her lap. "I have failed you, Darius. I am truly sorry," whispered Nayla with great sorrow.

Darius slowly opened his eyes. He gazed upon the faces of his friends as they gathered around him. His hand reached up to gently touch Nayla's face as he managed to smile at her.

"Do not be sorry Nayla. You fought with great valor and courage. I am proud to have you on my side, and to be counted as your friend." His breathing became more labored.

Nayla looked up at Lindras, the incipient tears stinging her eyes. "Wizard, work your magic. I beg of you! Save him. Do not let him die!"

Lindras took stock of the faces around him. His eyes grew dark with sadness. "I am sorry. I do not possess the power to make him whole again, Nayla. His time draws near. I cannot help him; I can only offer him comfort."

Darius took Nayla's hand into his, gently planting a kiss upon it. "Do not weep, Nayla. I am a knight. If I am to die, then I prefer to die in the midst of battle, with my dear friends by my side rather than as an old, witless fool in a bed safe and warm."

Markus knelt by his fallen comrade; he knew the end was near. "I shall tell tales of your great courage: Sir Darius Calsair, devoted protector of the House of Whycliffe, loyal knight to King Bromwell, and my dearest friend. You shall live on in the hearts and minds of the fair people of Carcross for an eternity."

"Markus, gather my sword and my shield… I feel a need for them to be close at hand," Darius said, his voice starting to falter.

"Of course, Darius," said Markus as tears welled in his eyes.

Darius cast his gaze up to Nayla and now he understood the true depth of her grief. Her tears fell softly like the white petals of the dying blossoms, gently floating down from the tree under which he lay.

"Do not leave me, Darius," begged Nayla in a whisper.

Arerys knelt close to Nayla's side. Darius looked into the Elf's sad eyes and taking his hand, he gently placed Nayla's hand into his. "Arerys, my friend, take care of Nayla, watch over her. She is more precious than you know."

Arerys clasped Nayla's hand into his, "I do know my brother. I promise I shall watch over her."

Darius drew a deep breath. His eyes slowly closed. His body shuddered as his heart gave its last defiant beat. A calm came over his face. Peace was at hand.

"No…" whispered Nayla mournfully. "This cannot be."

Ewen was stunned. He stood at Darius' feet in silent disbelief. Tears fell in a steady stream down his face as he gazed upon his broken body. Faria and Lando knelt by their fallen comrade, his shield and sword now in their hands. Arerys lifted Nayla to her feet, as Markus embraced Darius one last time, kissing him upon his forehead.

Nayla's hands trembled in both rage and grief. She pulled away from Arerys and she began to run. With sword drawn, she leapt over the fallen bodies strewn across the blood-soaked field in the direction of the Dark Army's camp.

Arerys raced after her. "Nayla, stop! Nayla, where are you going?"

She could not hear Arerys' desperate calls. Her blood pounded in her head as she raced onward, willing to meet with certain death if that was to be her fate. Arerys caught up to her at the edge of the field. Fearing the edge of her blade, he threw both his arms about her small frame in an attempt to pin her arms against her body. Nayla struggled to free herself, but Arerys persisted, holding her close.

"Release me, Arerys! I shall hunt them down myself!" cried Nayla in absolute rage. "I shall avenge Darius!"

"Nayla, we shall fight another day. There is nothing for you to do now," his tone was gentle as he tried to calm her grief and anger.

"I swear, Arerys, I shall find them and I will kill them all! And if I should die trying, then avenging his death shall still make mine own demise sweet."

"Listen to yourself, Nayla! You are blinded by your own rage," said Arerys, forcing her to face him.

Nayla railed against her anger and overwhelming sadness, but as she looked upon his face, she suddenly stopped when she saw the tears spilling from Arerys' own eyes.

Her tears welled, burning as they rolled down her rubicund cheeks. Her arms grew limp by her side; her sword falling from her grip. Nayla slowly sank down to the ground, her body shuddering with great sobs that shook her to her very soul.

Arerys knelt down in front of Nayla. He gently wrapped his arms and cloak around her body, as though he was attempting to shield her from the world. Her hands covered her eyes as she cried, burying her face into Arerys' chest. He held her close and together, they both wept for their friend.

As dusk settled, the Order prepared a pyre for their fallen companion.

Darius was lovingly wrapped in his cloak, his great shield was laid upon his chest, his sword by his right hand. He looked at peace. Sadly, it was a peace that could only be found in these cruel and violent times, through death.

They all lowered their heads in silent prayer. Markus laid a torch to the pyre. The flames grew quickly, lapping up at the darkening sky, its gray smoke rising into the evening air towards the heavens, taking the soul of Darius with it.

Markus was the first to leave. He quietly headed into the safety of the forest. Lando and Faria followed in silence. Ewen sadly stared skyward, his eyes had no tears left to shed. Lindras placed his hands on the boy's shoulders, steering him away to follow the men.

Only Nayla and Arerys still lingered. She was withdrawn; her heart numbed by sorrow. He took her hand and without a word, he slowly led her away from the diminishing pyre.

By the light of a crackling fire, Lando and Faria recounted stories of the day's battle to Lindras and Ewen. The boy sat wide-eyed as he listened, and then he told them of Nayla's deed on the rooftop as soldiers rained down from the sky. And the men all spoke of Darius: his skill with sword and bow, his kindness and good humor, his love and loyalty to the King and the people of Carcross. Oddly, Ewen continued to speak of Darius as though he had temporarily left their company; that he would be returning any time now.

Nayla shook her head in sadness. Ewen was in denial, unable to accept the knight's passing. She did not know the words to explain to Ewen that Darius was gone - forever. She sat in silence as though she was lost, mired deep in her own thoughts. Her knees were drawn up to her chest, her arms wrapped about them. Her cloak was draped carelessly over her body.

Markus approached Nayla and knelt before her. "I have something for you, Nayla," he said softly as he bent closer to peer into her downcast eyes. "It is a small token and though it will not bring our friend back, this is still a small part of the man that he was."

He carefully placed the brooch Darius once proudly wore on his vest into the palm of her open hand.

She quietly studied it, examining the intricate carving of white stars set against a deep blue stone embossed by a white cross: the insignia of the House of Whycliffe. It was the same brooch that Markus wore over his left breast.

He gently closed her fingers around the blue stone. "Darius would want you to have this."

Nayla looked up at him, holding the brooch to her heart. "Thank you, Markus," she said softly. "Darius shall live on in my memory for as long as I have my life."

She rose up onto her feet, turning away from him, the brooch still clutched tightly in her small hand. Nayla slipped away into the darkness of the forest; the moonless night swallowing her up into its shadow.

Not wanting her to be alone in her grief, Markus hurried to his feet to pursue her. As he stood, Arerys laid a hand on his shoulder, stopping him in his tracks.

"The stars yield little light, Markus. I shall find her. Stay with the others."

Before he could respond, Arerys was already following Nayla's almost invisible footprints. When he finally came upon her, she was a lone figure standing by the edge of a calm pool. The water's surface was like glass, as ink black as the night sky above. Nayla stared at the reflection of the stars shining upon its mirror-like surface.

Arerys' approach was silent, but Nayla could sense his presence as he drew near. She did not run, nor did she turn to acknowledge him. She merely stood there as though she were the only one left in the world.

"Nayla, why did you leave in such a manner?" he asked with genuine concern. "We all share in the burden of this quest and the loss of Darius, therefore there is no shame that we should be united in our grief."

"It pains my heart to no end to lose Darius in such a manner," cried Nayla in a soft voice. "Because I faltered, a good man is cut down before his time."

"Nayla, how can you believe it to be your fault? We were greatly outnumbered, it was only by your actions the rest of us are alive now."

Nayla held forth the brooch Markus had given to her for Arerys to see.

"Darius is no longer of this world and his soul, like the stars that shine on his brooch, should burn on for an eternity with the stars in the heavens," she whispered. With those words, she threw the brooch into the pool. A gentle splash broke the smooth surface of the water causing the stars reflecting upon it to ripple and dance in the confusion of the moment.

"I shall miss him, Arerys. He was my brother-in-arms and he was a true friend," she said with a long sigh. "He was the one who first embraced me into the Order when the rest of you turned your backs on me."

"Darius was a wise man, Nayla. He was wiser than the rest of us to see through your armor. Take comfort in knowing that he spoke of you often, and with much fondness. He held you in the highest esteem, and with the greatest respect... I do believe he was in love with you."

"You are mistaken, Arerys. Darius did love me, but he was not *in* love with me. He held me in the same esteem as a loving sister, but one who chose to take up arms beside him. Nothing more."

"Did you love him, Nayla? Is that why you grieve so?"

"I loved him as I would a brother, and now I fear that I am all alone again. Darius is now in a better place and I shall die a little more with each passing day until I am at that place too," sighed Nayla. "I believe I envy him."

"Please understand you are not alone in this," Arerys tried to comfort her as he stepped closer to her side, moving slowly, as though she were a wild bird about to take flight.

Nayla continued to gaze out, her eyes now searching the darkness beyond the pool, into the forest.

"Arerys, you do not understand. I am very much alone in this world," she confided to him. "I am shunned by my mother's kind and denied by my father's. You know the fair Elves despise the likes of my father's kind, though we are of the same blood."

Arerys hung his head in sorrow. "Nayla, that is a part of our history we shamefully regret... but it is history," he admitted with sadness. "It is time that cannot be rewritten, therefore, it is better to look ahead to the future."

"What if we fail, Arerys?" lamented Nayla. "Then there shall be no future to speak of."

"Yes, that is true. But as we speak now, hold this true to your heart my lady, when I look at you, I see not the things that make us different," said Arerys, his sincerity was present in both his voice and in his eyes. "I only see what is in your heart and in your soul, and what I see; I deem to be pure and good. Though you may wield a mighty sword in your hand, your heart betrays you, for you are a gentle and kind soul. That is why you grieve for Darius as you do now. That is why you feel the weight of the world bearing down on you."

Nayla stood before him in silence as she absorbed his words.

"When we enter battle together, I see the fire, and the will, that exists in only the bravest of warriors, though this fire burns within the form of a beautiful and tiny maiden," Arerys said as he smiled down upon her.

For a moment Nayla was silent, her face flushed upon hearing Arerys' kind words.

"This fire that you speak of serves me well in battle," said Nayla as she placed her hand on the scabbard of her sword, "but it is this same fire that burns me after the battle is done."

"How so, my lady?" asked Arerys, bending closer to see what her eyes might reveal to him that her heart would not.

"Men, whether Elf or mortal, do not wish to be in the company of a maiden that can bare arms in the same manner," answered Nayla. "Their pride cannot deal with a woman who is not in need of their brain or brawn."

"I beg to differ, Nayla," protested Arerys. "We are not all like that."

She studied Arerys' face, as though she was searching for a reason to doubt him before she continued.

"I fail to play the role of the damsel in distress. I prefer to take on the causes for those, weaker than I. And I do not believe in needing a man. To want is one thing, but to need? To be needful is not within my character. I myself would prefer to be wanted by a man, than needed by one," said Nayla with great conviction. Then she whispered: "I am more feared than loved by men."

"I do not fear you, Nayla," Arerys said as he took her small, dainty hands into his. Nayla's heart raced. She wanted to pull away, yet she could not. She watched as his fingers slowly entwined with hers.

She felt Arerys' powerful arms wrap around her small body as he drew her close. Nayla placed her hands on his chest, as if to shield her from his embrace, but his very essence was difficult to resist. Her head rested against his body, her ear pressed up against his chest; she could feel and hear Arerys' heart beating, steady and strong. As she closed her eyes, she felt as though her soul had found a safe sanctuary, a temporary reprieve from all the cruelties of the world.

With his right arm still holding her close, Arerys' left hand stroked Nayla's silky, crown of raven hair. He kissed her on the top of her head at which Nayla tightened her embrace around his waist.

Arerys' fingers carefully brushed the stray wisps of hair from Nayla's eyes, gently sweeping them behind her tiny, delicate ears. His fingers caressed her warm face as his fingertip traced the now thin, silvery scar on her right cheek - all which was left from her battle at Rock Ridge Pass.

Nayla pulled away from his touch. "Do not look upon this face, Arerys, it is made ugly by the ravages of war. Where such scars give way to character for men, it serves only as a reminder of my follies as a fool who chooses to wield a sword, than to do what is womanly."

Arerys gently drew Nayla's face to his. "Be not ashamed; this scar is a reminder of your duty to do what most men dare not even attempt. It should be worn proudly, as a badge of courage," whispered Arerys sweetly. "In mine own eyes Nayla, you are truly beautiful."

As though his words melted a heart that had been frozen in sorrow for a hundred years, silent tears fell from Nayla's eyes. Arerys' thumb gently swept her tears aside. His fingers traced the soft outline of her cheek, to her chin where upon he slowly lifted Nayla's face to meet his. The two silently gazed into each other's eyes. As if two lost souls had found each other, Arerys stared deeper. He now felt all the weight of sadness and loneliness she had bore for so long and it pained his heart so.

Arerys' eyes were of a gentle blue; a blue unlike any she had ever seen in a man. They seemed as deep as the ocean and shone like the stars in the heavens above. She studied the dark motes that randomly patterned his irises as she stared into his eyes.

Arerys lifted her chin, his fingertips softly caressed her full, sensuous lips, and then he drew her close and their mouths met. At first, Nayla seemed almost frozen in fear, but as Arerys' warm lips gently pressed against hers, her eyes closed. She felt as though she had stepped into a dream. As he drew his lips away, Nayla pressed her body tightly against his, but now all the tenseness in her muscles seemed to melt away. Her eyes slowly opened, Arerys still held her in a warm embrace. It was not a dream.

Nayla peered into his eyes as a shy smile appeared on his face. She placed both of her hands on Arerys' face, rising onto her toes, she reached up to kiss him, slowly and fully on his mouth, drawing in the sweetness of his breath as their lips met again.

Arerys' arms held her ever tighter, as though he feared he might somehow lose her now. He felt her body trembling against his. "Nayla, you are shivering with cold," said Arerys as he lovingly draped his cloak about her, wrapping her body closer to his.

Nayla was not trembling from the cold, but still, she welcomed the Elf's chivalrous gesture. For a moment, she reveled in the essence and warmth of his body still trapped in his cloak.

He continued to embrace Nayla as though she was a long lost love he had been reunited with, and dare not lose again.

"Nayla, my love for you is real. If only you could see beyond my fair complexion and blue eyes," whispered Arerys. "Strip away all that is earthly about us, you shall see that our two souls are one and the same."

She placed her fingers over Arerys' lips. "Hush... Do not speak to me of love. You do not see the blackness of my heart and the emptiness of my soul. And love? Love is fleeting."

Arerys gently placed both of Nayla's hands into his, and then he kissed them.

"You are wrong, Nayla. I do see the blackness and emptiness you speak of, but it is merely a heart that has been wounded by the treacheries of life's dealings. Inside you, there is goodness and light, but you choose to hide behind your sword to avoid your own dealings in these matters."

Nayla shrank away from Arerys' embrace. "You have no right to judge me, Arerys. You have not walked in my footsteps. You do not know or feel my pain or suffering."

"Then let me try, Nayla. I know what my heart tells me to be true, but if love is fleeting as you say, then let me embrace this time now should I meet an untimely death. I know I would rather have this one moment with you now, than my natural life without ever knowing your love."

Nayla was at a loss for words, her heart was buoyed by Arerys' gentleness and words of love. She felt safe in his arms; the beating of his heart against hers.

"Do you feel for me, as I do for you?" asked Arerys as he gently caressed her face with the back of his hand.

Nayla did not answer.

"Please Nayla! If you do, then do not deny me of your love. If I shall die tomorrow not knowing, then I am sure my soul shall never find peace!"

"I would deny my love for you, if but only to spare us both from grief, Arerys," said Nayla, touching the soft tresses of his flowing, blonde hair. "I am not like you. I am neither Elf, nor am I a true mortal. I may live well beyond the years of man, but I shall never live as long as you. I shall be a memory, long forgotten, before you have reached your twilight years."

"If you accept me as your husband, my father shall grant you eternal life. My father's love for me is such that he will not allow me to suffer alone without the love of my life. He will grant me this wish if you will take me as your husband."

"Arerys, look upon me. Look at what I am. The women of Wyndwood are tall and fair, with blue eyes and golden hair. They are gentle women who patiently wait by the warmth and safety of hearth and home while their men do battle for king and country. They sit and wait like obedient dogs, waiting for their master's return," said Nayla as she tried to calm the resentment growing inside her. "They choose to wield a broom; I choose to wield a sword. I am nothing like the women of Wyndwood."

"That is why I am in love with you, Nayla. Though I pray that harm may never find you on the front line of battle, you are a warrior maiden like none other I have ever known," Arerys acknowledged, his pride for her could not be contested. "To deny you of your sword is no different than to deny me of my bow. I would take great comfort if you were by my side to help me fight my fights, if but only to have you by my side, so I may die in your lovely arms and look upon your face one last time. It is true the women-folk of Wyndwood are fair and beautiful, but they are pre-disposed to running from the first sign of danger. You, my lady, you would stand your ground and fight the good fight to save friend or family," said Arerys with a reassuring smile. "That is why I love you so."

"I fear your father would never approve of such a union. He was the one to vanquish my father's people from Wyndwood. Surely his feelings have remained unchanged through the years."

"That was long ago, Nayla. Trust me, he has changed. If our love is true, I know my father will not stand in our way. He knows that my heart is for whomever I choose to give it to. It is not for him to decide."

Arerys gazed into her deep brown eyes, still waiting for an answer to his question. Nayla wrapped her arms around his neck and embraced him with a kiss.

"Listen to what is in your heart, Nayla. If it does not betray you, then I shall hear the words I long to hear," whispered Arerys.

Nayla placed Arerys' hand upon her heart, and then she softly answered; "I am in love with you, Arerys. I do not wish to be, but I am."

Arerys embraced Nayla with such joy, he swept her clear off the ground. He held her close, kissing her deeply as he gently laid her onto the soft, cool moss. As they kissed, his long blonde hair cascaded around her face like a sheer, golden curtain. She closed her eyes as his lips caressed her lips, her throat, and then the nape of her neck. His touch was so intoxicating, her head felt as though she had breathed in deeply the evening air, heavily scented with jasmine.

Her fingers felt the definition of Arerys' shoulders; his muscles were firm and yet, soft to her touch. Her fingers trembled as she worked to loosen the clasps on his vest. She felt the smooth, polished links of his protective mail against her hands as she slipped it off over his head, and then she worked to loosen the ties that bound Arerys' shirt.

As she placed her hands on the bare skin of his chest, she noticed it was smooth like that of a boy, yet his muscles were well-defined, like that of a man. They seemed as pale and hard as marble and yet, warm to her touch. She raised her head to softly plant a kiss upon his chest.

Arerys whispered into Nayla's ears, Elvish words of endearment that she had never heard spoken until this night. She looked into Arerys' eyes and smiled in understanding; they kissed with unbridled passion. Arerys drew his cloak over their bodies as they lay together under the moonless sky. At that moment, Nayla lost her heart to Arerys; stolen away by his soft kisses, gentle touch and loving words.

As Markus and the others readied for another night, the Prince turned to Lindras who sat in front of the fire, quietly puffing on his pipe. "Arerys and Nayla have been gone for a long while. I wonder what has become of them?" pondered Markus. "I pray they are safe."

Lindras' blue-gray eyes sparkled as they peered up from under his hood. He released a gentle puff of aromatic smoke. The Wizard smiled at the prince and winked. "Do not worry, Markus. They are both quite fine."

The men of the Order rose as the first light of morning crept into the sky. Markus woke to find Arerys and Nayla speaking softly under a large tree just out of his earshot. As he stretched and rotated his still stiff shoulder, he saw Lando and Faria returning from sentry duty.

The surviving members of the Order were still recovering from the loss of Darius. Each had thoughts of how his absence would affect them, and the final outcome of the quest. Their morning meal was eaten in silence.

Ewen was especially quiet and withdrawn. He ate and drank very little. Nayla knelt before him, begging him to keep his strength up. Ewen's mind was troubled; full of turmoil, fear and grief as he searched Nayla's eyes for possible answers.

"Why did this happen? Why was Darius taken away from us?"

"Who can say," answered Nayla softly. "Sometimes, life can be most unfair, Ewen. It often cheats those who are most deserving of life, while rewarding others who are not, with a long life that is only squandered away."

Ewen began to sob uncontrollably as he collapsed into Nayla's arms. The realization that Darius was truly gone had finally set in, he was overcome with sorrow as great tears tumbled from his eyes, rolling down his flushed cheeks.

Nayla held him close. She wished she was able to protect the boy from the cruelties of the world, but all she could do was to console him.

"Be brave, Ewen. Know that we all feel the loss of our friend," she whispered to him. "Darius would not want to see you shed tears for him."

As she said these words, Arerys saw her own silent tears spill from her eyes. He knelt down, gently sweeping them away with his fingertips as they slowly trickled down her cheeks. He knew Nayla would not want Ewen to see that she too wept. She looked into Arerys' kind eyes as she continued to console Ewen. She offered him a small smile, and then she whispered softly so only he could hear her words. "Thank you."

"Ewen, try to forget the manner in which Darius died, instead, remember how the man lived," said Nayla. Taking his face gently into her hands, she looked the boy in his eyes. "Do you believe in heroes, Ewen?"

"Yes," he whispered through his tears.

"Then take comfort in knowing that heroes live on forever. Darius lives on through all of us, and through the lives of all those he touched.

He was a great hero."

Markus placed a comforting hand on the boy's shoulder. "Ewen, do not remember Darius with tears, instead, honor him by finding the strength to carry on. He started on this quest because he believed in what we are striving for. We shall not let him down."

Ewen wiped the tears from his face with the sleeves of his shirt. Markus helped him to his feet. He took a deep breath and with a heavy sigh, he agreed, "His death shall not be in vain, Markus. We shall go on."

He thanked Nayla for her kindness before he turned to pack his bag. Nayla said nothing. She gave Ewen a smile of reassurance that he had made the right choice.

Arerys extended his hand to Nayla, helping her onto her feet. He could sense her sorrow as she watched Ewen put on a brave face. As she rose, he held her in a tight embrace to comfort her. She hugged him back as he gently planted a kiss her forehead.

As Markus gave the orders to move out, Nayla turned to join the others, but before she did, Arerys raised her right hand to his face and softly placed a kiss on the back of her hand. Nayla smiled sweetly at him before taking her leave to catch up to Ewen and Lando.

Arerys watched her as she strode along with Ewen. Lando retold tales of the adventures that Darius and he had shared in Cedona and Carcross. The Elf smiled, for it pleased him to see that both Ewen and Nayla took great comfort in Lando's memories of their dear, departed friend.

Markus walked along with Arerys. As they journeyed on, he noticed there was something different about the Elf. Markus could not place his finger on it, but he did sense the tenseness that existed between Arerys and Nayla seemed to have dissolved overnight. At least, he noticed that Arerys was more openly attentive to Nayla.

"So Arerys, you were absent with Nayla for quite some time last night. I was growing quite concerned for the two of you."

"I am sorry, Markus. I did not mean to cause you undue worry. We had much to discuss."

"So you have worked out your differences?" asked Markus, most intrigued by this news.

"So to speak."

"I knew there would be a meeting of the minds, if you both took the time to get to know each other," he smiled.

"She is the one, Markus," said Arerys in a whisper as Lindras and Faria were gaining ground on them.

"One? What 'one' do you speak of?"

"She is the one that Faria referred to as only existing in my dreams," answered Arerys into Markus' ear.

"Oh…" responded Markus, still looking momentarily baffled. "Oh! I understand."

"I told her of my feelings for her," confided Arerys in a hushed tone so all would not hear. "I declared my love for her, Markus."

"Ha! I knew something was afoot. I could see it in your eyes. So did you–" he asked with raised eyebrow.

"A gentleman does not talk of such things, Markus. Just know that I love her with all my heart, I wish for us to be trothed if we should return safely home."

"Did she accept?"

"I am still working on it," answered Arerys with a confident smile as he turned away to catch up with Nayla and Ewen.

The Elf's smile revealed all that his words did not. Markus was happy for him. Lindras strode along by the prince who turned to him; "You knew about Arerys and Nayla all along."

The Wizard gave him a knowing smile and simply replied, "It is a wonderful thing, Markus. When love can blossom like a beautiful rose in the midst of all this adversity, there is still hope for this world."

CHAPTER 12

THE DRAGON'S LAIR

For three days hence the fall of Darius Calsair, the Order continued their eastward trek along the shadows of the Aranaks, towards the towering pinnacles of the Iron Mountains looming ominously in the distance. Their peaks were shrouded by dark thunderclouds, heavy with rain.

Many leagues were covered as they traveled both day and night resting only long enough to eat and to escape the monotony of the grueling journey for a few hours of sleep.

What little time there was available for sleep, seemed to drain Ewen, rather than refresh him. His reoccurring nightmare continued to grow more intense and vivid as they drew nearer to Mount Hope. Each time Ewen dreamed; the voices, the unfamiliar faces, even the intensity of his fear became more palpable. It was only through Arerys' Elven touch that he was able to find some respite from his nightmares.

For the others, sleep was so fleeting, when dreams were afforded, they all dreamed of better days and happier times that seemed to elude them now. What little time that Arerys was able to steal away with Nayla, were spent together when both were assigned to sentry duty. Other than that, they would sleep briefly, resting in each other's arms, taking great comfort in each other's company.

As darkness swallowed up the land, the Order climbed to the top of a ridge overlooking a rolling, lush valley. Since the attack at the citadel, the lands had been strangely quiet. Arerys was haunted by the same uneasy feeling he had experienced then. It made him all the more cautious as they tread through the countryside.

When they reached the top of the ridge, Faria's heart was heavy with disappointment and anger as he peered into the small valley below.

A large encampment containing hundreds of Beyilzon's men could be seen milling about. It was now becoming obvious that all of his armies were withdrawing from Darross and beyond, to return north for the final battle on the Plains of Fire.

Faria looked up at the moon - that time was drawing ever closer. The moon that had remained hidden by cloud-cover for the past few nights, once revealed, was no longer a thin crescent of light. Instead, it now shone brightly as slightly less than a half moon. Lindras and Markus too, noted the movements of the constellations.

"We should move high into the slopes tonight. We should keep well away from that dark horde," advised Faria, looking to the valley below.

"I would not recommend that, Faria," stated Markus. "Beyilzon's men now know that somewhere between Heathrowen and Mount Hope, we still roam. I believe we should venture no further by the darkness of night lest we fall into their snares or traps on the outskirts of their encampment."

"I am afraid Markus is right," added Lindras. "As they await the others, they cannot be at all places, at all times. It would stand to reason that they might set traps to ambush us."

"Very well," said Faria. "At least from this vantage point we may keep a watchful eye on them."

"We shall wait until there is sufficient light for Arerys to escort us safely through the mountain forests," said Markus, preparing for another evening vigil.

As the stars flickered on, studding the deep blue night with their sparkling light, the group ate and spoke in hushed tones, so their voices would not be carried down into the valley.

Arerys took the first watch with Nayla by his side. The two took care to remain in the shadows of the trees so they would not be silhouetted against the night sky.

Below them, Beyilzon's Dark Army continued to grow in numbers, but nothing unusual occurred to alarm Arerys into waking the others. As Nayla peered down at the hive of activity below, she whispered, "I wonder if they have withdrawn from Orien?"

"I have no doubt they are on the move. Beyilzon would call on all hands to engage in this war. He will do whatever it will take to secure his victory."

"I fear I may have no home or people to return to when all is done," said Nayla sadly.

Arerys held her close, trying to reassure her. "Nayla, if the men of your army are half as skilled as you, I am confident you shall see them again."

Lando and Faria came to relieve Arerys and Nayla for a few hours before they were to move on. All was quiet in the valley below.

Arerys and Nayla returned to the others who still slept. As he lay next to Nayla, he drew his cloak to cover both their bodies. Nayla rested her head on Arerys' shoulder and soon fell asleep in his arms.

In the meantime, Faria was growing more distraught at the thought that the soldiers of the Dark Army were congregating in such numbers on his land. "How can we win against an army of this size, Lando?" Faria whispered bitterly, attempting to stifle his growing anger as he watched the soldiers below.

"That is not our job, Faria. Ours is to get Markus and Ewen safely to Mount Hope and that is what we shall do."

"We should have another plan," suggested Faria. "If we fail to bypass the hordes below, we may have to resort to other means to save ourselves and this quest."

Lando glared at Faria. "What do you suggest?"

Faria's eyes were glazed. "Markus and the boy… remember?"

"Now I know you have truly taken leave of your senses, Faria," growled Lando. "To consider your suggestion is to abandon all logic and reason. Where before I could account for such thoughts to the grief over the loss of your brother, it is now evident you still entertain this idea in your head."

"Consider it, Lando," whispered Faria, motioning him to lower his voice.

"I think not! Do not speak of this to me again. I know the odds of success may seem overwhelmingly against us when you look at what awaits us below, but to loose faith now shall only guarantee doom for all."

"But, Lando—"

"Do not have me tell Markus and the others that you are willing to betray us," said Lando. "You must put your trust in the prince."

Faria glared at him. To his disappointment, his words had fallen on deaf ears.

"I swear, if you make mention of this one more time, you shall give me no choice but to act accordingly," warned Lando, attempting to stifle his mounting anger.

The remainder of their watch was conducted in silence, the power of which was overwhelming. Words were no longer necessary.

With daybreak still another hour or so away, Markus gathered the Order in preparation for their trek through the mountain passage. Though the forest was still bathed in darkness, there was adequate light for Arerys to now safely lead the way.

As the group gathered their weapons and other possessions, Ewen stood out over the ridge, looking upon the many tents dotting the valley below. Other than the movement of the horses, all was quiet.

He turned away to join the others, but as he did so, the sound of frightened horses stirring below caught his attention. Arerys too, hearing their commotion, ran to Ewen's side. As he looked below into the still dark valley, his eyes made out the sinister forms of two dark riders on great, ebony horses, as they entered the encampment.

"Beyilzon's agents are here! We must leave now!" whispered Arerys as he grabbed Ewen, pulling him away from the edge of the ridge. Just as he did so, the Elf saw the dark emissaries suddenly cast their eyes in their direction.

They released an ear-piercing shriek that echoed from the depth of the valley, rattling them to their bones. Their horrific call caused the soldiers to come spilling forth in a panic from their tents.

"We shall never outfight them, Markus!" stated Lando.

"Then we shall outrun them." Markus turned to Arerys to lead the way.

"We shall take the passage that crosses before the Dragon's Lair and continue eastward," suggested Faria.

Lindras nodded in approval as Faria pointed the way to Arerys.

As the Order ventured into higher grounds, they could see the valley below come alive with the frenzied movements of the soldiers, like angry black ants disturbed from their nest. In the midst of this swarm of activity, the dark emissaries could be heard screaming their orders as they led the charge.

Although the army would have to emerge from the bowels of the valley and their pursuit would be uphill, Lindras knew it was only a matter of time before the dark horsemen and the other soldiers on horseback would intercept them on the pass.

The Order raced along, while the sounds of horses and the din of rattling armor and weapons drew closer with each passing minute. In front of them, their path crossed before the entrance to the Dragon's Lair; a labyrinth of deep and treacherous tunnels and caverns. Behind them, an army of several hundred foot soldiers followed those on horseback. Now in full view, they were quickly closing in on them.

"Lindras! We cannot keep this pace!" shouted Markus, helping Ewen to his feet as he stumbled from exhaustion.

"Into the cave!" ordered Lindras. "We must detour through the Dragon's Lair!"

"Is it safe to do so?" asked Markus.

"It is safer than facing that horde!" answered Lindras, waving them on to follow him into the darkness.

"Fear not, Markus. The dragon has not been seen in almost a thousand years," informed Faria.

"I shall seal the opening to the cave, and then we shall follow this tunnel to exit out through the other side of this mountain," said Lindras. "But first I must destroy the pass so they cannot intercept us on the other side."

As the Order entered the mouth of the cave, Lindras turned back to face the enemy. Taking his staff in both hands, he held it up high as he called upon the powers of the earth. He brought his staff down with a mighty crash as it struck the ground. The passage that detoured past the entrance of the cave disintegrated, collapsing with his power. *Now,* thought Lindras, *if the army wishes to seize us, they too shall be forced to enter the Dragon's Lair; if they could dig their way through.*

The Wizard darted back into the cave to join the others. He quickly breathed life into the crystal embedded into the top of his staff. As he did so, the crystal glowed, illuminating the interior of the large cavern. Huge stalactites and stalagmites hung from the ceiling and rose from the floor of the cave like the giant teeth of the dragon itself.

As they ventured deeper into the cave, they were almost overcome by a foul, powerful odor.

"What is that horrible stench?" asked Ewen as he drew his cloak over his mouth and nose.

"Bats - more precisely, bat droppings," answered Lindras.

The malodorous scent hung heavy in the air. Ammonia from the years of accumulated bat droppings burned their noses and lungs, stinging their eyes.

"Bats?" cried out a startled Ewen. His voice boomed and resonated against the walls of the cavern. His cry broke the solitude, launching thousands of frightened, roosting bats to take immediate flight. The Order ducked low to the ground to miss the churning, moving mass as the bats swirled through the air, all flying in the same direction in a broad, sweeping circle. The multitude of flapping, leathery wings created an almost deafening clamor as it echoed through the deep recesses and shadows of the cave.

Flying with greater speed as they gained their bearings, the surging, black whirlwind pulsated with life. The bats circled several times before exiting through the mouth of the cave into the still-dim, early morning sky. As the soldiers appeared at the entrance of the cave, they were forced to drop to the ground to avoid a collision with the bats as they streamed out in a frenetic flight. The horses reared and wheeled about, panicking at the approach of the black, living cloud that quickly overwhelmed and engulfed them.

Arerys readied his bow, while Nayla and the men drew their swords in anticipation of a battle. Markus grabbed Ewen by his arm, moving the boy behind to shield him from the next possible assault.

As the last of the bats vacated their roost in an erratic flight pattern, the army, led by the dark horsemen, advanced towards Lindras and the others. The Wizard raised his staff high over his head. The crystal's glow intensified as Lindras began to call upon the powers that were gifted to him. The ground began to tremble and quake.

"Quickly, Lindras!" ordered Markus. "Seal off the cave!"

The flustered Wizard turned to Markus as the ground continued to shake and shudder, as if a great giant had been awoken. "This is none of my doing!" called out Lindras, as large stalactites began to collapse from the roof of the cave with each reverberating quake.

An earth-rattling roar bellowed from the dank, dark depths of the Dragon's Lair. Beyilzon's soldiers froze in their tracks, as did Lindras and the others. Another roar, amplified by the great tunnels, sounded from deep within the cave. Whatever it was, it was now approaching in their direction… and with increasing speed!

"The dragon! It lives!" shouted one of the soldiers, turning to the source of the frightening sound. The army was now in full retreat, falling and stumbling over each other in a mad panic as they scrambled to exit the cave. Even the dark emissaries made a hasty retreat with the others.

Markus turned to face Faria. "You said the dragon no longer lived!"

"I said, he has not been seen in almost a thousand years!" snapped Faria. "There is a difference!"

"My efforts to destroy the mountain passage may have disturbed him from his slumber," said Lindras as he brought down the entrance of the cave. He succeeded in sealing out the soldiers of the Dark Army but now, he and the Order were trapped inside this dark and foul place, with a great beast that was obviously enraged by their presence. "Make haste, we must leave now! Go!" ordered Lindras.

As they fled through the dark corridor, dodging falling debris by the light of Lindras' staff, the tremors and roars were advancing in their direction, intensifying with each passing minute. The end of the tunnel lay yet another quarter mile away, the light at the narrow entrance was barely visible.

Suddenly, from the darkness emerged two huge, glowing, red orbs with black, slit-like pupils. It was the great dragon of the Anaraks. Lindras, Arerys and Nayla were the only ones to have ever encountered such creatures that, by all account, were now considered a beast of legend rather than reality. They continued to run, while the men of the Order all froze in terror.

Soon, the ancient reptile of monstrous proportions became fully visible in the glow of Lindras' crystal. Its massive, dull green scales - as big and as thick as the men's shields, rattled like a soldier's armor as the dragon moved forward. The huge, rectangular belly scales undulated with the creature's every movement, vibrating as it hissed its displeasure at the intruders.

Nayla and Arerys turned. Grabbing the others, they ran as fast as they could. Excited by their movement, the dragon pursued them with great relish. Although, this creature lacked any great speed, the length of each stride made up for its slow, heavy gait. It released another great roar; its forked tongue flickering in the air as it did so. The force of the colossal beast's call was so intense it sent them tumbling onto the cold, damp ground.

Markus and Lando scrambled to their feet, drawing their swords in a valiant attempt to ward off the dragon.

Lindras motioned for both to put away their weapons. "Your swords cannot pierce the scales of such a beast! I shall have to deal with him, myself!"

"Lindras! Do not be a fool! Run!" ordered Markus, seizing the Wizard by his arm.

Lindras defiantly shook off his grip. "Markus! Either I must stand alone to face the dragon or we shall all perish now!" shouted Lindras above the din. "At least I have a chance to *tame* the beast! So run, take them all with you!"

Lindras turned to face the towering creature. Taking the staff in his hand, he raised it high over his head. The steady glow of the crystal captivated the great dragon. The white light cast an eerie, crimson haze on the walls of the cave as it reflected off those menacing red eyes. Its cat-like pupils would dilate and contract with the changing glow of the crystal orb. Strangely drawn to this light, the beast turned to follow Lindras deeper into the cave, away from the others as they fled to safety.

The Wizard ran as quickly as his old legs could carry him; darting into an adjoining chamber. In the musty, cool darkness, a sudden sparkle of light caught his eyes. Lindras moved towards the object, steadying himself as the dragon's heavy movements shook the ground.

Lindras leaned over to closer inspect this unexpected source of light. *How can that be?* Before him lay the crystal and the shattered staff that once belonged to his old friend and ally, Tor Airshorn, the Wizard of the North. *He left for the Twilight long ago, but what is his staff doing here? He was never without it.* It was an unsettling mystery, but there was no time to lose, the dragon would soon be upon him. Lindras hastily picked up the crystal; it was still attached to the end of the broken staff.

The Wizard breathed life into the dirt and dust-encrusted orb; the faint light glowing within became more intense. *It still works*, marveled Lindras as his eyes glanced about the shadowy chamber. Before him, blocking the only way in or out of the cave, loomed the dragon. The creature stood before him, mesmerized by the light emanating from the crystal of the broken staff. Lindras was forced up against the cave wall. He slowly crept along, noticing how the fiery eyes of the monstrous beast traced his every move, following the steady glow of Tor's crystal.

Can it be? Lindras wondered as he fumbled along the dark walls, edging closer to the dragon. The beast seemed entranced by the crystal the Wizard held before him. All of the sudden, Lindras stumbled on the dark ground, almost dropping his staff and Tor's crystal.

The response from the dragon was immediate, the great beast reared up, towering well over twenty feet above Lindras. As its head recoiled in anger at the fading glow of Tor's crystal, its mouth full of jagged, yellow teeth opened wide. The dragon's head pitched forward towards the Wizard. As the terrible, yellow fangs came down upon him, Lindras forcefully rammed his staff into the gaping jaws, jamming its mouth wide open.

Unable to close its mouth, the creature roared in anger, shaking its great head to and fro, in a desperate attempt to remove the Wizard's staff. As it struggled, Lindras passed his hand over Tor's crystal; the light began to glow once again, growing in intensity. With unexpected swiftness, Lindras turned on the dragon. As the monstrous reptile's head recoiled, its body arched backwards, the vulnerable muscles between the great belly plates were exposed, but for only a brief instant.

Lindras moved quickly, driving the broken staff between the large ventral scales, impaling the great beast's heart. The dragon released a deafening bellow of pain as Lindras gave the stake a final, deliberate thrust, deep into the creature's large, convulsing body, until only the crystal was visible. An immediate burst of energy exploded from the wound, throwing Lindras violently to the ground and flooding the darkness of the cave with a brilliant, white light. An unexplained burst of wind swirled about the dragon and Lindras, accelerating rapidly as though they were caught in the eye of an angry hurricane.

As the others reached the mouth of the cave, Ewen screamed out Lindras' name as he heard the great dragon's final roar and saw the brilliant burst of light that temporarily blinded him. Markus and Lando grabbed Ewen's struggling body, attempting to drag him away through the entrance of the cave, but all three were caught in a sudden vacuum of air being drawn deep into the cave. Faria and Arerys struggled to maintain a hold onto Markus and Lando as they fought against the great force of wind funneling into the darkness. Suddenly, an explosive force of air howled through the narrow entrance, knocking all to the ground in its blind fury.

As the dust settled around them, Nayla helped the others onto their feet.

Arerys stood at the mouth of the cave. He stared inside; his eyes pierced through the thick dust that hung heavy in the air. The Elf's eyes quickly adjusted to the unnatural darkness. "Wait here, I shall go back for Lindras."

Before Markus could stop him, the Elf disappeared into the cave. He was immediately swallowed up in its deep shadows. The others waited, hoping for good news upon his return.

Eventually, Arerys reappeared from the depth of the Dragon's Lair - alone. "He is gone."

"Gone? We should have stayed with him," sighed Markus, in disappointment and sadness.

"I mean to say that he has disappeared! The dragon too!"

All were left in stunned silence upon hearing Arerys' news. They did not know, nor did they understand, the manner in which the Wizard met his demise; they only knew that Lindras had fallen in his bid to save them and the quest. Another member of the Order was lost.

Ewen fell to his knees, great sobs racked his body. Nayla tried to console him through her own tears. Faria trembled in fear - the Order was crumbling before his eyes. Lando was speechless; he was shaken as he imagined the terrible manner in which Lindras had sacrificed himself.

Markus, though his anguish was great, now knew that they must finish off what they had started. He was even more determined than ever to see the quest to its bitter end.

He walked over to Ewen, helping Nayla as she struggled to get the boy back onto his feet. "We must keep moving, Nayla. We cannot stay here," said Markus as he proceeded on his hike. "It shall only be a matter of time before this mountain shall be swarming with Beyilzon's men. We move now!"

The others did not question Markus' order. They were despondent, saying nothing as they turned away from the cave and looked at the long, meandering trail sprawling before them.

Markus gazed back at the others. "I know you think me callous, but there shall be time to grieve for Lindras later. This is not the time, nor the place."

Lando placed a heavy hand on Faria's shoulder. "Markus is right, my friends. We cannot afford to spend more time here than necessary. It shall only be a question of when, before the dark horsemen are back on our trail."

"We must honor Lindras," added Arerys. "He sacrificed his own life to spare us so we may complete this task. I, for one, shall not let him down."

"Our numbers grows thin…" lamented Faria, his heart burdened with worry. "How do we complete this quest when we are so greatly outnumbered… our ranks continue to dwindle?"

"Do not lose heart, Faria," said Lando, attempting to quell his growing despair. "If we remain strong and stand united, our combined efforts may still result in the greater good for the greatest number."

"I agree with Lando," said Nayla as she wiped the tears from her eyes. "We have come so far. Though our losses have been great, to give up now would be unthinkable. Our losses shall only pale in comparison if Beyilzon is not defeated."

As Markus stood before them, he witnessed the members of the Order call upon their inner strength to find the will to regroup and continue on with their mission. Although they were all deeply wounded by the loss of another dear friend, the desire and determination that drove this rag-tag band on filled Markus with great pride as he led them away from the Dragon's Lair.

Continuing on their long journey, the morning sun shone brightly over the Iron Mountains. Oblivious to the tragic events of the morning, it beckoned them on their eastward trek.

CHAPTER 13

A CRY IN THE NIGHT

The mountain path that led away from the Dragon's Lair was not steep, just long and meandering, as it wound down the sloping terrain. Low growing alpine flowers grew in scattered clusters amongst the rocks and boulders. They hugged the ground closely as their tiny, yellow, bell-shaped blossoms sweetly scented the morning air.

Arerys' senses were on high alert, he was ever vigilant as they forged on. His far-seeing eyes constantly scanned the horizon as he watched and listened for signs that may betray Beyilzon's men, but all was quiet.

As he walked along, he entertained the idea that the Dark Army was preoccupied with the task of exhuming their bodies from the cave. *Perhaps, they are still making their way around the mountain to search for us on the other side of the passage. Perhaps*, the Elf thought, *the soldiers believe we have met our demise in the jaws of the great dragon.*

Either way, Lindras had hampered their movements by bringing the passage down and by sealing the mouth of the cave. Arerys chose to believe that the soldiers thought they were all dead. If that was to be the case, they could now proceed without further disruptions or distractions.

A large, orange sun cast long shadows across the uneven landscape as dusk approached. Faria pointed out the village of Tyver that lay nestled on the hillside below. "Markus, this will be the last settlement that we shall see before we reach the Redwall Canyons. We may skirt the village; take to the fields and pastures."

"Think again, Faria," said Arerys, his blue eyes squinted as they surveyed the surrounding hilltops sheltering the little village in the diminishing light. "Soldiers are keeping watch and they do not wear the colors of Darross."

"They arrived before us?" asked Markus, his brows furrowed in disbelief. "How can that be?"

"I do not think it is possible, Markus. Not without us knowing of their movements," offered Lando. "I believe they may have already been here and I suspect that they do not even know about us, at least not yet."

"What tactical maneuver shall we employ, Lando?" asked Markus. "Should we attempt to dispatch the soldiers that keep watch before we go much further?"

"If they have been forewarned to watch for us, they will no doubt focus their attention on the fields and the outlying areas," advised Lando, studying the distant landscape, "not on the village itself."

"We shall wait for nightfall," decided Markus. "Then we shall pass through Tyver."

Once the countryside was embraced in darkness, the Order proceeded into the village. They divided into two groups of three, walking confidently on the main road passing through the center of the village, as though they too, were citizens of Tyver.

They strolled along basically unnoticed, even when a gray-haired woman rushed by, almost knocking Ewen over in her haste. She was accompanied by a harried farmer, whose son had fallen from a horse, breaking his arm in the process. Both she and the man were engrossed in worried conversation when she and Ewen collided. Noting the bag she was carrying, Markus assumed she must be the local healer on her way to tend to the injured boy.

The group quickly left Tyver behind, crossing a wooded field to continue on their eastward expedition. Eventually, they came across a stone quarry surrounded by the steep, rounded walls of a bluff.

"Where to now, Faria?" asked Markus, his dark eyes assessing their surroundings.

"We go up. If we climb this bluff, we shall have a good view of the lay of the land. If the Dark Army is in the area in numbers, they shall camp in the low lands," answered Faria. "Once we know what lies ahead, we may better determine our next course of action."

Ewen glanced up at the rock wall surrounding them. He was physically tired and emotionally drained by the disastrous events of the day. The idea of scaling this rock face did not appeal to him in the least. He slumped down on a small boulder, his weary head braced in his hands.

Aware of his condition, Markus approached Ewen. "Lando and Nayla shall stay here with you. We shall return shortly once we determine what path we shall take next."

Ewen nodded his head in appreciation as he slowly sank to the ground to rest. His legs felt as heavy as his heart, even more so than usual today. Nayla sat next to Ewen. He rested his head upon her small shoulder. His need for sleep far exceeded his need for food or drink.

After waiting for about fifteen minutes, Lando was growing restless. He knelt before Nayla and Ewen. "I shall be back shortly. I am going to scout out the area beyond this quarry in case we are forced to take this route instead."

"Be careful, Lando," cautioned Nayla.

"I shall," assured Lando, drawing his sword as he proceeded into the darkness. "I shall not be long."

Nayla quietly hummed to pass the time as Ewen slept. She listened for signs of Lando and the others, but all was quiet. Approximately twenty-five minutes had elapsed since Markus, Faria and Arerys climbed to the top of the bluff, forging on into the darkness. Lando was away for about ten minutes and Nayla was now becoming concerned by his absence, as he was on his own.

Suddenly, she sat upright, her ears straining to hear. Something, or someone, was running in her direction. Nayla shook Ewen awake and as she did so, she placed a hand over his mouth so he would not make a sound. She silently drew her sword from its scabbard, motioning Ewen to hide behind the large rock they were resting against.

Lando burst through the darkness, in a panicked whisper he said, "Nayla, we cannot stay! Just beyond this bluff is an army of at least two hundred soldiers!"

"How can that be?" asked Nayla, stunned by this news. "How could Markus and the others not notice?"

"There is a huge outcrop, like a massive land shelf that extends beyond this bluff. The army is set up within the shadows of this structure. Unless they walked to the very edge and looked directly below, the camp would certainly go unnoticed!"

Without another word, Nayla grabbed Ewen, leading him to the rock wall. "We must get to the others, Ewen. You must climb."

Lando and Nayla both sheathed their swords, turning to face the steep wall of stone.

"Lando, go ahead. You will be able pull Ewen up," coaxed Nayla, turning her head to listen to the sound that was now approaching the entrance of the quarry. "Did anyone see you?" she asked, her eyes scanning the dark perimeter.

"I do not believe so," whispered Lando, hoisting himself up.

"Make haste, Ewen. I do believe we may have company soon," said Nayla. She locked her fingers together, offering her hands to give Ewen a boost up against the rock face so he may reach Lando's outstretched hand. "Do not look down, Ewen! Take hold and keep climbing!" she urged him on.

Ewen clung to the rock face feeling for any gaps or irregularities on its otherwise smooth surface to place his fingers and toes to aid in his ascent. Up ahead, Lando was precariously balanced on a narrow ledge; his hand extended to Ewen. As the boy inched forward, feeling his way in the darkness, his left hand caught hold of a tree's root. He grabbed hold as he reached up to Lando with his right. As he strained desperately to grasp the knight's hand, the root suddenly gave way from the rock that Ewen thought it was securely anchored into. He let out a frightened scream as he began to plummet downward, but his fall was short-lived. Lando lunged down, grabbing hold of Ewen's hand.

Rocks and other debris that broke loose when Ewen bounced off the wall and scrambled for the safety of the ledge, fell upon Nayla. She leapt back to the ground to avoid being struck. As she stood up to resume her climb, Nayla felt the ground. It was alive with the reverberation of many heavy footfalls. She knew what was happening. She wasted no time to see how many, or how close, they were. She scrambled up the rock face as quickly as she could, but the falling debris seemed to erase all fissures and outcrops that had earlier provided finger and toeholds. Nayla frantically struggled to pull herself up in the darkness.

Lando reached the top of the bluff and lay on his stomach reaching for Ewen with both his hands. He looked up in time to see the massing of soldiers at the mouth of the quarry. "Hurry, Ewen!" he called out.

Ewen turned to see the cause of Lando's distress: the Dark Army! His heart pounded and his ears thundered with the approach of the incoming swarm that would soon descend upon them if they could not breach this huge wall of rock.

Nayla was quickly gaining on Ewen, pulling herself up with all her might. "Go Ewen! Faster! Take Lando's hands!"

To the boy's horror, he glanced down in time to see Nayla hanging by her fingertips as she desperately kicked out at the soldiers struggling to pull her down.

"Ewen, do not look back! Both of you, get away as fast as you can!" ordered Nayla, fighting to maintain her hold.

Seized by both her ankles and her cloak, she was forcibly yanked down. Ewen turned to see her falling backwards into the sea of black as a whirlpool of soldiers struggled to subdue her. Panic filled his heart. He turned to climb down, but as he did so, Nayla's voice cried out from the darkness. "Run! Do not look back!"

Ewen froze for a moment, then he clambered on and as he did so, he watched in fear and mounting resentment as Beyilzon's men overwhelmed Nayla with their sheer numbers. The surge of black soldiers moved on with their small prisoner in their clutches, as if she were a trophy.

"No, not Nayla," cried Ewen, forcing himself onward and up, anger welling inside him. "Lando, we must find Markus!" he said with determined resolve.

"We shall, Ewen. This way!" replied Lando, following the tracks that pointed in the direction Markus and the others had taken.

Nayla was dragged into the camp with great commotion and effort on the part of her captors. She fought fiercely. Unable to draw her sword, she lashed out kicking and punching as a multitude of hands fought to control and restrain her. Although the soldiers were many, some of her well-placed punches and kicks did manage to incapacitate some of them. Unfortunately for Nayla, each time she was able to drop one soldier; another was there to take his place.

Eventually, she was restrained and hauled into the middle of the encampment. Exhausted, her chest heaving as she fought to catch her breath, Nayla was cast down before a dark, imposing figure sitting high upon a horse.

"So you are the 'Little One' the Watchers spoke of!" mused the captain as he dismounted from his large black steed as Nayla stood up, struggling against the grasp of the soldiers attempting to remove her weapons. "My spies warned me that you are a fiery one!"

Little one? I have not been called that since Darius died, she thought as she recalled how he would fondly address her by this term of endearment.

With a rope tightly binding her wrists, swords pointing at her from all directions, Nayla ceased her struggle. One soldier quickly approached, seizing her by her hair. He forced her down onto her knees. "Show some respect! Bow before Captain Vorath!"

The captain sauntered up to her; his great black form cast a menacing shadow that engulfed her. "Yes, where are your manners?" he scoffed, looking down upon her.

Nayla spat at his feet.

The soldier who had forced down her to her knees abruptly grabbed Nayla by her braid. He yanked her head back hard so she was forced to face the captain, his sword poised - ready to slit her throat in an instant.

"Are you in a hurry to die, wench?" snarled the soldier. "You are as troublesome as the first time I saw you in Heathrowen.

Nayla gave him a cold stare as she struggled to recall his face from all those she studied on that frigid, rainy night at the inn.

"Have you searched her for the Stone?" asked Vorath. He glared down at Nayla as he forcibly seized her weapons.

"Yes, captain, it is not in her possession!" answered the soldier.

Vorath knelt down before Nayla. He studied her face for a moment, and then an lecherous smile crept across his face. "Perhaps your search was not thorough enough. Guldar, take her to my quarters!" Wrapping his large hand around Nayla's throat, he violently hoisted her onto her feet.

High on the bluff, Markus, Faria and Arerys came rushing down. Arerys had heard Ewen's scream when he had almost fallen. As they raced through the darkness Lando and Ewen met them.

"Where is Nayla?" asked Arerys, his eyes wild with fear.

"I am afraid she has been captured, Arerys!" said Lando, struggling to gain his breath.

Arerys bolted through the darkness, down to the edge of the bluff.

"Wait, Arerys!" pleaded Lando. "There are many of them, a good two hundred I would say!"

"I shall not leave her to those wolves!" shouted Arerys defiantly.

"Faria, stay here with Ewen, keep him safe until we return," instructed Markus, turning to join Arerys and Lando. "Remain here. Do not leave unless it is absolutely a matter of life or death. Wait for our return. Do you understand?"

"Yes! Just go! Save Nayla if you can!" answered Faria as he grabbed Ewen, retreating into the deep shadows of the forest.

The three disappeared over the edge of the bluff leaving Faria and Ewen alone in the blackness of the night.

With orders to deliver Nayla to the captain's tent, Guldar gave the rope binding her wrists a hard tug, causing her to stumble forward. Captain Vorath turned to instruct his soldiers to secure the perimeter of the camp, just in case there was an attempt to rescue their new prisoner.

As they neared the tent, Nayla no longer resisted the pull of her tether. Instead, she allowed the rope to go slack. Guldar turned around to see why there was no more tension, and as he did so, Nayla grabbed hold of the rope in her hands, whipping it in a tight, circular motion. The rope jumped to life, moving to Guldar in an arc. As it hit his hand, the rope wound around his own wrists.

Nayla jerked hard on the rope causing it to tighten around the soldier's hands. Quickly, she yanked Guldar towards her. Moving behind his body, she swiftly wrapped the length of rope around his neck and began choking the life out of him.

In her haste, consumed by her rage to do away with Guldar, Nayla did not sense Vorath closing in. He struck her between her shoulder blades with the butt of her own sword handle. She was hit with such force, it sent both she and Guldar crashing to the ground.

Vorath snatched the rope from the soldier. "What is wrong with you, that you cannot control such a tiny female!" shouted the captain, as he angrily whipped the humiliated Guldar with the end of the rope before handing it back to him.

The soldier struggled back onto his feet. Taking the coil of rope into his aching hands, he gave it an angry heave, forcefully yanking Nayla back onto her feet. She fought, resisting all the way to Vorath's tent where upon Guldar unceremoniously threw her to the ground.

Nayla was thrown down face first. Using her forearms to break her fall, she quickly rolled onto her back so she may face the soldier.

Guldar moved towards her to seize Nayla by her tether, but as he neared, she executed a well-timed kick, viciously striking the soldier in his groin. Guldar clutched himself with both hands as he slowly sank to his knees with a painful groan.

"You fool!" shouted Vorath, pushing Guldar over onto his side as he writhed in agony.

"You are a dangerous one!" Vorath angrily growled. Grabbing Nayla by the rope, he violently yanked her up onto her feet.

With one angry swipe of his arm, Vorath cleared all the maps that lay upon a heavy, wooden table that was situated in the middle of his tent. The Captain turned on Nayla. He glared down menacingly at her, but his hostility only grew when he realized that she was unmoved by his foul demeanor.

Suddenly, he lunged at her. His hand grasped and tightened around her throat as he picked her up off the ground. He forcefully slammed her small body down onto the table as though she were a slab of meat.

With both hands tied in front of her, she was unable to brace for the impact. Nayla's head struck the table with a hard *'thud'*; the force with which Vorath drove her into the unforgiving tabletop momentarily stunned her.

"I shall teach you! I shall break you, you insolent little wench!" shouted Vorath as he yanked the rope hard over Nayla's head, securing it to the other end of the table. "Guldar! Leave us!" ordered the Captain as he kicked the moaning soldier.

Guldar scrambled to his feet, ambling out of the tent still hunched over in excruciating pain.

Vorath turned his attention to Nayla as she lay in a daze. He approached the table and stared into her eyes. "Where is the Stone?"

"What makes you believe that I even possess it?" snapped Nayla.

"Do not insult my intelligence! The Watchers would never entrust the Stone of Salvation to a mere boy. They would only entrust it to one who is capable of protecting it from falling into the wrong hands. By all account, I have been warned about you, little warrior. Now, where is the Stone?"

"I shall never tell you."

A knife slammed down close to Nayla's head; the tip of the blade piercing deep into the table.

"You do not scare easily, do you?" growled Vorath. "Well, I shall show you what it means to be scared!"

Nayla said nothing, her head now throbbing from the initial impact when he violently slammed her into the table.

"Hmm, could it be that the Stone is on you, woman?" hissed Vorath, his face so close to hers that Nayla could feel his hot, putrid breath on hers.

"I am no fool, I would not carry it on my person. The Stone is safe!" Nayla answered defiantly.

"Let us see how safe it is," said Vorath, his hand reaching for the knife.

He leaned over Nayla's body, glaring coldly into her eyes. He sneered at her, but Nayla's face still showed no indication of fear, only immense loathing and contempt for her tormentor.

Vorath laid his hand high on Nayla's neck, forcing her chin up as he began to squeeze. Her mouth opened involuntarily as she released a desperate gasp for air. As she did so, Vorath forced his mouth down upon hers. He kissed her roughly, pressing down so hard his beard and moustache scraped and burned against Nayla's lips, as he thrust his tongue deep into her mouth.

Repulsed by his detestable action, Nayla gagged as she struggled for her breath. With her arms drawn tightly over her head, she fought against the ropes biting into her wrists, but to no avail; she was tethered down securely.

Vorath laughed, holding the sharp tip of the knife against her throat. "Still not scared?" he asked, as Nayla coughed and gasped, fighting for air.

The captain used the knife to trace the contour of Nayla's neck. He pulled back hard on her hair, causing her throat to be fully exposed, the cords of her neck, taut. His breath was hot on her flesh as he leaned in close, slowly running the cold tip of the blade against her skin. Blood slowly rose and trickled down from the long, thin cut.

Nayla closed her eyes, remaining frozen as she tried to leave this place and predicament for the safety of another. She tried desperately to escape in her mind, but all attempts to take her back to the sanctuary of her gardens in Nagana eluded her. Failing this, she tried to regain her focus, concentrating on the most opportune moment to execute a devastating kick to her tormentor. Timing and placement was absolutely critical – she would only have one chance.

Vorath laid his mouth on Nayla's neck; his hot, moist tongue felt as though it would burn through her skin and flesh, stinging the wound as he followed the trail of blood up to her chin. With the quickness of a wild animal, he sank his teeth into the side of her neck.

Immediately, her concentration was broken. Nayla flinched at the sudden sharpness of the pain he inflicted. She bit her lower lip in an attempt to stifle a scream.

"We shall see if this Stone is not about you," smirked Vorath as he rose up from Nayla's body. Taking her vest into his hands, he forcefully tore it open, causing the clasps to break and the cloth to tear. With the knife back in his hand, he held it against the tie that held her bodice closed. In one swift movement, the blade sliced through; the torn silk falling back down to expose the mounds of her breasts.

Vorath's leer quickly turned into a menacing smile. He reveled in his own cruelty as he held the tip of the knife against her pale skin. Nayla could feel the unadulterated hate emanating from his black, lifeless eyes as he watched her face. He continued his sadistic game, slowly drawing the blade from between her collarbone, down along the length of her torso. Blood slowly emerged where the blade broke through her skin. Nayla could feel it burning as the crimson droplets seeped forth.

In desperation, Nayla began frantically pulling and straining at the rope; it only served to bite deeper into her wrists, but still, it did not give. In a final bid to do away with her restraint, she grasped the rope into her small, outstretched hands. Taking hold, Nayla attempted to flip over the table to land onto her feet on the other side. As she threw her legs up to roll over, Vorath anticipated her movement. His large hands caught hold of her ankles, slamming her body back down onto the unforgiving surface of the table. The backs of her knees felt the shockwaves of pain as they smashed down against the hard, straight edge of the table as the Captain threw her legs down.

He laughed at her ill-fated attempt to escape before resuming his cruel game. To her disgust and shock, Vorath's tongue pressed hard again her body tasting the blood that began to pool between her breasts. Nayla wanted to cry out, but she could not allow him the satisfaction of knowing of her mounting panic. Her eyes were thrown wide open in horror when she felt Vorath's hand savagely groping between her thighs.

"Where is the Stone?"

"I would rather die now than tell you!" Nayla's eyes burned with hate and scorn.

"That can be arranged," growled Vorath with a smile.

Nayla flinched as she felt the cold, hard blade of his knife press up against her left thigh. With his left hand on Nayla's right knee, the captain angrily wrenched her legs apart. His hands were so calloused and rough, they bit into her soft flesh.

Nayla looked up at Vorath's dark figure. The candles that illuminated the space behind him sent forth an eerie, red glow that cast great shadows against the walls of the tent. As he rose up before her, he now seemed even larger and more terrifying than ever as his body loomed above her. Nayla began to tremble inside; she closed her eyes, wishing for her nightmare to end quickly.

Vorath released a sinister laugh as he laid the full weight of his body down upon hers. She felt as if her whole being would be smothered and crushed beneath him. She could feel him - a serpent insinuating itself between her thighs. With the brutality of a crazed beast, Vorath pressed down hard upon her small frame, she felt him begin to penetrate into her. A great pain tore through her body. In anguish and absolute desperation, Nayla cried out for Arerys.

With great urgency, they dashed from tent to tent. Markus, Lando and Arerys were looking and listening for any sign that may direct them to Nayla. They moved quickly and silently through the encampment, taking great care to remain in the shadows so they may go undetected.

"ARRRERYS!"

Instantly, the Elf's blood ran cold; somewhere in the night, he could hear Nayla's pained and frightened voice cry out his name.

"This way!" said Arerys, racing in the direction of Nayla's plea for help. Markus and Lando followed close behind.

Upon Nayla's terrified scream, Vorath violently slammed the back of his fist hard across her face. Pressing a hand forcefully over her mouth, he hissed like a snake into her ear: "The only name you shall call out tonight is mine!"

Nayla's world began to grow black. With that, Vorath groaned with pleasure as he savagely raised his body up against hers. He threw his hands behind her knees to draw her closer to the edge of the table so that he may thrust himself completely into her body.

As Vorath rose up to complete his assault, he was alerted to a strange sound.

Suddenly, three arrows, one following swiftly behind the other, tore through the wall of the tent. Each one struck its mark with deadly accuracy. Vorath reeled with the impact of each arrow, his cries of stolen pleasure turning to cries of excruciating pain, before falling backwards. Markus used his sword to cut through the canvas of the tent as Arerys leapt in with his bow already drawn.

Arerys' eyes gazed down upon Vorath; he lay dead on the ground. He waited for a reason to let another arrow fly.

"Oh no, Nayla..." whispered Lando, as he ran to her side.

The Elf looked up when he heard the sound of Lando's anguished cry. Arerys then began to tremble in fear when he cast his eyes on Nayla's still body upon the table. He dropped his bow as he dashed to her side. He looked upon her bruised and bloodied face, he then noticed the slow rising and falling of her bloodstained chest as she breathed.

"Please tell me she is alive, Arerys," said Markus, as he and Lando cut the rope that now bit deep into Nayla's raw wrists. They struggled to untie the bloodied tether.

"Yes, she is," Arerys whispered, removing his cloak and carefully wrapping Nayla's body inside. He gently lifted her into his arms, carrying her through the slashed wall of the tent. Markus grabbed Arerys' bow and Nayla's possessions that now laid scattered about on the ground. He swiftly followed behind.

Markus, Lando, and Arerys, with Nayla in his arms, slipped past the sentries posted along the perimeter of the camp. They could hear the noise of soldiers scuffling and arguing as to who was going to have the woman next. The four shadowy figures silently disappeared into the night.

Arerys tenderly cradled Nayla's body in his arms. "Markus, we must get Nayla to the healer in the village. I do not know the extent of her injuries, nor do I believe I possess the skills to help one who is half mortal."

"Do not worry, Arerys. We shall find her." Markus tried to reassure his friend as they turned back to Tyver.

As they entered the village, it seemed abandoned as they gazed at the darkened homes. Markus and Lando rushed from house to house, pounding on the doors.

Finally, one opened. The woman they had crossed paths with earlier in the night peered out.

"Yes, what is it?" a disgruntled voice called out. "What do you want at this late hour?"

"Please help us, I beg of you!" pleaded Arerys stepping forward with Nayla in his arms.

The woman threw open the door, inviting them in as she led Arerys into a room. She drew back the covers, instructing the Elf to lay Nayla upon the bed.

Shooing them out of the room, she proceeded to remove the cloak covering Nayla. She gasped in horror when she saw the bloodied and bruised body before her; the savage bite marks and the cruel wounds left by the blade of a knife against her neck, chest and thigh.

The woman returned to the main room where Lando and Markus patiently waited; Arerys frantically paced to and fro with worry.

"What level of beast committed such atrocities to her?" asked the woman as she fumbled through a basket in search of salves and dressings. She did not wait for an answer, quickly disappearing into the bedroom with her supplies and a bowl of tepid water.

The woman gently cleaned Nayla's wounds. Though they were not deep, there was always a chance they may become infected. She applied a salve and dressed the cuts on Nayla's chest, neck and her wrists. As she cleaned the abrasions and cuts to her thighs, she came to the terrible realization that this woman had also been raped.

She carefully tended to her wounds, gathered her torn and bloodied clothing, and then quietly slipped out to leave her to sleep.

As the woman stepped back into the main room, Arerys approached her. "Please healer, tell me. How is she?"

The woman collapsed into her chair, distraught by the nature of Nayla's injury. "She will live, the poor little thing."

The men could see she was greatly bothered.

"What is it? There is more. Speak, my good woman!" pleaded Arerys.

"I am sorry, sir, I know not the words to tell you this," answered the woman, searching the Elf's troubled eyes. "I am a healer and I also serve as the village mid-wife. This woman you bring to me; she has been terribly violated... in the worst way."

Arerys' greatest fear was now realized. What he thought in his mind was a possibility, he now knew in his heart was a reality. As though a knife had been thrust deep into his chest, he collapsed to his knees, weeping for Nayla.

Lando was silent. He stood motionless; he heart sank, both for Nayla and Arerys.

Markus embraced his friend and whispered, "Arerys, she is alive. She is still whole. That is the most important thing. Nayla is still alive."

"Yes, she lives and she is whole, but I am afraid her spirit may be shattered by her ordeal," added the healer. "Sir, if it is of any consolation, her assailant was not able to finish the deed, if you get my meaning."

Markus nodded in understanding. Arerys was numb; his soul was crushed by the news of the brutality of Nayla's assault.

"Arerys, she will need you now more than ever," said Markus.

The Elf wiped the tears from his eyes. "I have failed her, Markus," Arerys whispered with a heavy sigh. " I never should have left her side."

Markus placed his hands on Arerys' shoulders. "You cannot change what has happened, my friend." He searched for the words that may help to console him. "You have avenged her already by killing her tormentor, but what Nayla shall need now is your unconditional love. Do not fail her in this."

Arerys turned to the healer, "May I go see her now?"

"Yes, but she sleeps. It is wise to let her rest," said the woman as she placed Nayla's clothes and Arerys' bloodstained cloak into a large basin of water.

The Elf turned away from Markus and Lando. He crept into the room, shutting the door behind him. He sat on the edge of the bed, gazing down at Nayla's sleeping form as the moonlight poured through the window illuminating her face. *Strong Elven blood must course through her veins*, thought Arerys, noticing that the worst of the bruising on her face were already beginning to fade. He reached for her hand and gently kissed it, wishing to never let go.

He remained by Nayla's side and as the hours passed slowly, she lay in a troubled sleep. At one point, Markus stepped in, offering Arerys a reprieve so that he may sit with Nayla while the Elf rested. He politely declined, continuing his lonely vigil.

Arerys waited patiently, whispering words in his people's language, hoping his prayers would be answered. Finally, Nayla stirred from her sleep; her eyes slowly opened.

"Nayla," Arerys whispered, reaching out to touch her face.

Instantly, her eyes flashed open. They were dark and liquid, her pupils fully dilated - filled with fear when they saw Arerys' dark figure against the dimming moonlight. Like a frightened animal, Nayla recoiled from Arerys' touch. She quickly withdrew, huddling into a small, pathetic heap at the furthest corner of the bed. Trembling in fear, she clutched the bedding tightly around her body.

"Nayla, it is I, Arerys," he whispered, leaning out to reach for her.

Nayla sat in a tight ball, her knees drawn up to her chest, her arms clamped firmly around her legs. Her chin dropped to her chest as the tears finally began to spill from her eyes like a confused child, waking from a terrible dream.

Arerys moved across the bed to comfort Nayla, but she seemed to shrink further away.

"The nightmare is over, my love. You are safe now," said Arerys as he caressed Nayla's face with his hand.

Again, she withdrew from his touch. "Arerys, I feel tainted... poisoned," she whispered.

"Nayla, I am so grateful to have you whole, you will recover," Arerys promised her. "I am just glad that you are alive."

"Why do I feel that I am dead?" Her voice was trembling. "Why was I not able to escape this fate?"

"Nayla, you fought as best you could, there is a fate far worse than this. That madman was going to kill you!"

"It would be better had I ended my own life than to succumb to this," she lamented. "This does not happen to a warrior."

"Do not say that, Nayla. Do not speak these words," cried Arerys, his tears falling shamelessly. "For if this is a fate that you would embrace, then I shall surely perish without you. I would not be able to bear this earthly existence. I would wish to be struck down, here and now, if you had died."

Nayla was silent.

"Nayla, please forgive me," pleaded Arerys, "Had I been there, you would have never met with this terrible fate. Please find it in your heart to forgive me."

For the first time, Nayla raised her downcast eyes to look upon Arerys' face. It broke her heart to see his tears. She reached up with her fingertips to gently wipe them from his cheek. Arerys held her hand, pressing it to his face. His eyes closed in relief. Nayla now realized that Arerys too, was brutalized by her ordeal, but his agony was compounded by his own guilt and grief.

"I am sorry, Nayla. Please tell me that you forgive me."

"There is nothing to forgive."

Arerys gently kissed Nayla on her forehead. He enveloped her small body in his arms, holding her close.

Nayla closed her eyes as she rested her head against his chest. She felt safe in his gentle arms as she listened to the steady beat of his heart. She took great comfort in Arerys' presence, yet her tears seemed to flow endlessly.

Arerys felt her body finally melt against his as he gently whispered, "I love you, Nayla. No matter what, I will always love you."

Nayla heard the words she so desperately needed to hear from him. As a heavy sigh escaped her, exhausted by her ordeal, she slowly began to drift off. "I suppose I shall live to fight another day," she whispered wearily, sleep taking over her mind and body.

"Yes, you shall, my love. And I shall be there by your side," whispered Arerys. As she slept, Arerys proceeded to use his Elven touch in an attempt to speed the healing of Nayla's bruises and abrasions. He smiled inwardly, taking great comfort in knowing that somewhere in this small, healing body, the true spirit of the woman whom he loves was still very much alive.

Nayla had slept well into the morning. Arerys remained by her side, sleeping little, only wishing to be close at hand to watch her quietly breathing. Just knowing she was alive and safe, comforted him immensely.

In the other room, Arerys could hear Markus. He and Lando had only now returned with the others. Faria and Ewen were both safe after a lonely night on their own.

The healer knocked on the bedroom door before stepping in. "Forgive me, sir, but I thought you could use these," she said quietly, noticing that Nayla was beginning to stir. She placed Arerys' freshly cleaned cloak as well as Nayla clothes, now cleaned and newly mended, onto the bed.

"Thank you very much," whispered Arerys, drawing the blanket up around Nayla's shoulders.

The woman left the room, taking great care when shutting the door.

Arerys slowly stretched, and then he kissed Nayla on the nape of her neck as she stirred. He brushed back her dark hair to plant a gentle kiss on her shoulder, but as he did so, his eyes were drawn to something on her back. Arerys discreetly drew the covers down. To his surprise, a dark tattoo, a strange symbol – possibly words in the language of the mortals of Orien, was etched into her skin over her right shoulder blade. As he drew the cover down a little further, he was shocked by what his eyes saw: Nayla's back bore a number of long, silvery scars. Several were painfully obvious, but Arerys' eyes could make out a number of smaller ones. *How did this happen? Who would do such a thing to her?* The nature of these scars troubled the Elf. He shook his head sadly as he thought upon how much she must have endured in her life.

He quickly drew the covers back around her shoulders as Nayla stirred from a dreamless slumber. Her long sleep helped to heal her wounds much more quickly than if she were a mere mortal, but it troubled Arerys' heart to no end to see the worst of her injuries would not disappear soon enough. Vorath's handprint and vicious teeth marks around Nayla's throat and the thin scar of blood left by the blade of his knife were still visible.

Nayla's eyes slowly opened as she became aware of her strange surroundings and the unfamiliar softness of a bed. She slowly turned, painfully rolling over from her side, onto her back. A warm hand touched her shoulder to aid her as she lay back. It was Arerys.

He smiled at her, kissing her upon her forehead. "Good morning, Nayla," he said softly.

Nayla reached up to touch his face. The sight of the dressing that concealed the rope burns still raw on her wrist momentarily startled her. Arerys took her hand and kissed it.

"Rest, Nayla. I shall fetch some breakfast." Arerys gracefully rolled off the bed, throwing his cloak over his shoulders in one swift movement as he quickly disappeared out of the room.

Nayla slowly sat up, feeling terribly sore and stiff from head to toe. She touched her throat, tracing the lines of her wound. It was all still too fresh on her body and in her mind. She was filled with an overwhelming sense of anger and sadness as she recalled the events of the night. Her heart sank and she wished to cry, but she held back. In the other room, she could hear Arerys talking excitedly to Markus. She could sense his joy and gladness that she was back and safe again. She could not have Arerys and the others see her tears.

Nayla looked at her clothes that lay neatly folded on the edge of the bed. They appeared clean, as good as new, as though the reminders of the treacheries of last night had been washed away. Although her head still throbbed from the beating she had endured, she dressed as quickly as her battered, aching body allowed her to move as she heard other excited voices fill the main room.

Arerys soon returned with a tray of food and drink. He was surprised to see Nayla on her feet, already dressed – neatly braiding her tresses back into place.

"What are you doing, Nayla? Please rest, get back into bed."

Nayla fastened her belt; inspecting her sword before sheathing it back into its scabbard. "I am fine, Arerys," she reassured him. She walked past the Elf, kissing him lightly upon his cheek as she went.

As she stepped into the main room, the healer was the first to notice Nayla, startled to see that she was on her feet so soon. The men of the Order all turned to look upon her – a terrible silence filled the room. They were very relieved that she was alive, but the wounds Nayla now bore, crushed them. Even Faria, who was hardened by many years of battle, was moved and saddened by her now apparent fragility.

Nayla offered a weak smile; she pulled her cloak higher around her neck to better conceal the ravages of her attack. She did not want their pity.

Ewen looked at the bruises, horrified by the brutality of Nayla's assault. He ran to her, throwing his arms about her shoulders. He held her close and whispered in despair, "You saved my life yet again, my lady, but at what cost?"

"I would do it again Ewen; in a blink of an eye, I would do it again," she said with great conviction as she sought to ease his feelings of guilt. "This mission has been fraught with peril from the start. There is a price to pay to see it to its end, and I shall help to see it happen, no matter the cost."

Ewen held her tightly as Nayla looked upon the faces of the men in the room.

"We shall not speak of this again," warned Nayla. "Nothing happened. Do you understand?"

She searched the downcast faces for acknowledgement. None answered; they merely nodded their heads in understanding.

Nayla thanked the healer for her care and attention, and then without looking back, she stepped out into the bright morning sun. Though her body ached with each step, she swallowed her pain and tears as she walked on. She breathed in the cool morning air. "There is still many leagues to go, let us be on our way!"

Nayla walked away to the main road, her cloak fluttering in the brisk morning breeze, the others following behind her.

"I believe your woman is back," said Markus confidently, slapping Arerys on his shoulder.

"Yes, I believe she is," smiled Arerys, he watched proudly as Nayla led the way.

CHAPTER 14

TO THE CANYON LANDS

As the Order left behind the village of Tyver, Arerys and Markus became acutely aware of the absence of soldiers that were stationed on the surrounding hilltops the night before.

Faria led them into a thick stand of oak trees that grew in abundance on the lower slopes of the Aranak Mountains. There, they waited for darkness to fall before proceeding on.

Using only the driest wood, Faria built a small fire that burned without exuding a trail of gray smoke. Arerys had managed to hunt some grouse that Ewen prepared, removing all skin and traces of fat, so it would not flare up over the flames, sending smoke into the air.

For the men, it was a pleasant change from the dried meats and stale bread that had sustained them thus far. As they finished eating, Markus recommended that the rest of them get some sleep while he took the first watch. Before anyone else could respond, Nayla stood up from the fire, offering to join him.

Arerys was momentarily stunned. He thought she would be taking the next watch with him. Nayla did not even look back at Arerys as she walked away with Markus.

Lando could see that this troubled the Elf. "Arerys, Nayla has been through much. Permit her some time to recover from her ordeal," he said as he lit his pipe. "Give her some time to forget."

"How do you forget such a thing, Lando?" asked Arerys, feeling helpless as Nayla disappeared from his sight.

"She is strong; just be patient."

As Nayla glanced southward from their lookout, Markus could not help but to notice the wounds that the captain of the Dark Army had inflicted upon her. Though they were fading quickly, he could sense that Nayla was greatly affected by her ordeal. *How could she not be?* Markus thought, as he turned to see what she was staring at in the distance.

Nayla was quiet and withdrawn as her vacant eyes gazed ahead. Their time on the watch was painfully silent. She could sense his discomfort. "Markus, why do you not rest? I shall keep watch on my own."

"Why? Does my company bore you?" smiled Markus, attempting to lighten the air.

"No, Markus. I have much to resolve. I am afraid that I am the one who is unsuitable company at this time."

"What is it, Nayla? I will listen if you wish to confide in me. Or perhaps, you should talk to Arerys, I know he would want that."

"No, he would not," said Nayla, shaking her head. "He would not want to share in this."

"What troubles you so, Nayla?" Markus searched her dark, tormented eyes.

After a moment of silence, she reluctantly answered. "I fear that… I may be forced to carry a child that is not Arerys'," Nayla whispered, her voice breaking under the weight of her sorrow.

"Oh, Nayla," said Markus, now fully understanding the depth of her anguish. "If you are with child, it would not be by your captor. Arerys killed him before he could finish…" his voice trailed off unable to find a delicate way of telling her.

Nayla's head dropped as tears of relief welled in her eyes. Markus held her in his arms as she wept, her small form engulfed by his stature and flowing cloak.

Abruptly, Nayla pulled away from Markus. She recognized Faria's heavy, steady gait and Arerys' light footsteps as they approached. She hastily dried her tears, taking a deep breath as she composed herself. As Faria and Arerys came into view, Nayla turned away from Markus, rushing past them.

As she went by Arerys, she could not even look at him. He caught her by her hand as she passed. Nayla stopped for a moment, her eyes closing at the warmth of his touch. She gently squeezed his hand in hers, then slowly released her grip as she slipped away.

Arerys was at a loss. He looked at Markus for possible answers, but he knew none were forthcoming.

Markus rested a hand on Arerys' shoulder as he turned to follow her back to the others. "Nayla is only now realizing what had happened. I assure you, in time, she shall find her way back to you."

At mid-noon, Faria and Arerys returned to the camp when Lando came to relieve them of sentry duty. When they reached the camp, Ewen was still sleeping, as was Markus while Nayla sat alone, deep in meditation.

The thumb and index finger of each hand formed rings that were linked together, as the fingertips of each hand touched and pointed skyward. Each breath she inhaled and exhaled was long and deep. With each breath, Nayla felt her soul and energy sinking deeper into the ground, becoming one with the earth. She found some comfort, however the immoveable spirit she once associated with the earth element, now seemed somehow shaken to its very foundation.

The Elf watched her from a distance. He longed to reach out to Nayla, to provide her with whatever comfort she could not find in her solitude, but he resisted the urge to do so. He was torn by his own need to be with her, and yet, he desperately wanted to respect her need for privacy.

Arerys silently approached Nayla, quietly sitting beneath the tree where she sat. Leaning against the tree trunk, he closed his eyes and slept with Nayla within his reach. As he did so, Nayla could sense his presence. His life-force was like a warm energy that was very tangible to her; it seemed to envelope her in a comforting blanket, consoling her. Even with her eyes closed, Nayla could now distinguish his presence – this energy, from that of the others in the Order. Like a ship finding a safe harbor during a raging storm, she relaxed, taking great comfort in knowing that he was so close to her side.

Markus and Ewen woke with the dimming afternoon sky as Lando returned to report that nothing untoward could be seen on the lands. They ate a small meal before beginning another long trek.

Under the cover of darkness, Arerys escorted the group along a narrow trail that took them upwards. He wanted to bypass the rock quarry where the terrible incident of the night before had taken place. The route took them directly onto the bluff. The Elf silently moved out over the land shelf that had earlier concealed the presence of the Dark Army. To his surprise, they had pulled up stakes. All were gone.

Arerys darted back to the others. "The army has moved out. It would appear they have begun their march to the Plains of Fire. It would mean that we are now behind them, rather than being pursued by them."

"Interesting…" said Markus as he pondered the possibilities. "Faria, how far to the Redwall Canyons?"

"It shall be a two-day journey if we travel only by night."

"Let us be on our way," said Markus. "Now, we shall follow and watch the enemy."

As they turned to continue their journey, Ewen tugged at Arerys' cloak. The Elf looked down at the boy who said not a word, he merely pointed over to Nayla.

Arerys glanced up to see her standing at the very edge of the land, her small frame silhouetted against the night sky. She stared down below, her face strangely devoid of expression. He ran to her side, taking Nayla by her hand, he proceeded to lead her away.

"Look Arerys, it is as though they were never here," said Nayla in a whisper. "It is as though it was a bad dream and yet... I know what happened."

The Elf placed his arm around Nayla's shoulders, guiding her away.

Faria, with Arerys close at hand, moved swiftly through the darkness. Nayla stayed close to Ewen, with Lando and Markus taking up the rear, as they moved through the shadows.

As songbirds heralded the coming of the morning sun, the Order had covered much ground. They stopped to eat and rest until the skies grew dark again.

Arerys slung his bow over his shoulder, offering to take the first watch. Markus nodded in approval, and then turned to Nayla. "Why do you not take the watch with Arerys?"

"I am weary, Markus," answered Nayla in a small voice. "Perhaps, later."

Arerys heart sank as he turned away without a word.

Markus stood up, grabbing his cloak and sword. "Nayla, I understand the wounds you bear are still fresh, but it is unfair for you to wound Arerys in this manner," he said, turning to accompany the Elf.

"I do not want his pity."

"What he offers is not pity, Nayla. He offers his love." With that, Markus stormed off to catch up with his friend.

Markus found Arerys leaning against a large tree. There was no question that he was hurt by Nayla's indifference.

"She thinks you pity her," said Markus as he stood next to the Elf.

"I hate that this terrible thing happened to her. I hate the way she now seems to be slipping away from me," said Arerys, with great sadness. "But I love her, I know her too well. Pity is that last thing she is in want of."

After a moment of silence, Arerys lamented to his friend. "She will not even look at me, let alone speak to me, Markus. Why will she not talk to me?"

Markus was truly moved by the depth of Arerys' sorrow. "She is afraid to speak to you about what troubles her so."

"And yet, she speaks to you? I do not understand it."

Unable to hold back any longer, Markus confessed. "Arerys, Nayla was unwilling to speak to you, because the matter that troubles her would directly affect you."

"I love her, Markus. I wish to ease her burden if I can, but she is right, if it affects her, it shall affect me too. However, that does not mean that I am less willing to offer her love and support when it is needed."

"She was afraid that you would reject her if the worst of her fears had come true," said Markus, divulging this information with some reluctance.

"What is it, Markus?" asked Arerys, daring to pursue the truth.

"She was afraid that she might be forced to carry a child that was not fathered by you," said Markus with a heavy sigh.

"No…" gasped Arerys, the impact of this news hit him like a great wave smashing onto the shore, rearranging everything that was. He slumped to the ground. This revelation weighed heavily on him.

"I assured her that it was not possible, Arerys. I told her that you had killed the heathen bastard before he could complete his assault."

Arerys shook his head in regret. He now understood what was troubling Nayla so, but he also knew that other demons had now surfaced to torment her.

When they were relieved of sentry duty by Lando and Faria, Arerys returned to camp to find Nayla asleep. He quietly slipped next to her, drawing her small form against his body. She stirred, but her eyes did not open as he gently placed his cloak over her. Together, they slept for several hours until night returned to the land.

With the setting of the sun, the Order was ready to moved on. They traveled continuously, resting only once to eat and drink. The eastern range of the Aranaks was almost at the end, the Redwall Canyons would soon be visible. All were emotionally and physically drained by their journey, but they persevered, trudging eastward.

Arerys and Faria continued on as the others hung back. Suddenly, the Elf grabbed hold of Faria's shoulder, stopping him from advancing any further. He quickly motioned him for quiet.

"Nayla," whispered Arerys. "We have soldiers ahead. They are guarding the pass into the canyon lands. We are coming back."

Nayla warned Lando and Markus of what was ahead. They patiently waited for Arerys and Faria to return.

When the two regrouped with the others, Arerys reported that there were at least a dozen soldiers blocking their path.

"Five against twelve," said Lando, with a confident smile. "I like those odds! I believe we can take them on."

"You are sounding more like Darius with each passing day," replied Faria. He was not amused by Lando's cavalier attitude.

"Good odds or not, we have no choice," said Markus. "We must dispatch these soldiers as we have no other road to take us into Talibarr."

"Well, let us not waste any more time," suggested Nayla. "They are mortals; they are superstitious and fear the darkness. Let us take them by surprise while we are still hidden by the cover of night."

"What do you suggest?" asked Markus.

Nayla quickly arranged the men from the tallest to the shortest, with herself in the lead. She instructed them to follow directly behind her, to synchronize their footsteps so they were moving as one. When Nayla was satisfied, she instructed Ewen to stay back when the fighting began.

As the Order approached the soldiers' camp, the half moon shone down upon them from behind, making it impossible for those on sentry duty to make out the dark form advancing towards them.

"Who goes there?" called out one soldier, standing up from the fire.

The dark figure continued to press forward.

"Guldar? Is that you?" the voice called out again. The soldier's eyes squinted in their direction, trying to ascertain the identity of the encroaching shadow.

The single, dark apparition came to an abrupt halt. It immediately divided into five shadowy figures that were armed with weapons. This fearful apparition startled and frightened the soldiers. Before they could gather their arms, Arerys already dropped the three who had been sitting about the campfire with his bow, each arrow striking down a soldier with deadly accuracy.

Nayla's sword swiftly struck down the soldier that had called out. Leaping over his fallen body, she headed straight for the next one as he was stepping out from his tent, totally unaware of the fate about to befall him. The silver blade of her sword, now bathed in blood, glistened in the moonlight as it swept through the air, slicing through body and limb.

Faria, Markus and Lando followed suit, surprising their adversaries as they exited their tents to see what the commotion was about.

Nayla faced one soldier who had the good fortune of grabbing his sword. She squared off with him, skillfully deflecting each of his blows. Nayla held nothing back as she launched a vicious assault. She struck the soldier's sword so hard; it was knocked out of his hand, falling onto the ground before her.

The sword fell within her peripheral vision so Nayla was able to act without taking her eyes off the soldier. She quickly transferred her sword to her left hand. Using her right foot, she caught the fallen sword where the blade met the guard. Nayla deftly flicked up the soldier's sword, catching it in her right hand. She lunged at the unarmed soldier, slashing him across his chest with both swords. The last thing to be burned into his memory was Nayla hurling his own weapon, like a deadly spear, towards his chest.

Now armed with his sword, three soldiers encircled Arerys. He pivoted and dodged the incoming blades; his movements were swift and graceful as he countered with his weapon. Nayla came to his aid, slashing one soldier in his back then, ducking low to avoid the other soldier's blade. She swiftly lowered herself to the ground, sweeping her leg out to strike the soldier against the back of his knees. Caught off balance, the soldier was knocked forward to the ground. Nayla leapt onto her feet. Taking her sword in both hands, she drove it deep into the soldier's back. As she did so, she kicked her legs up, springing over the soldier's body. Flipping back onto her feet, she extracted her sword as she landed.

Arerys was in the midst of locking swords with his opponent when Nayla ended the contest quickly. She ran her sword straight through the soldier's back before turning her attention to Lando.

Lando held one soldier at bay with his sword as he used his shield to deflect the blows of the other. Nayla's approach was so silent the soldier did not hear her until she exhaled as she brought her blade down upon him. Lando was now able to focus all of his energy on one soldier as they locked swords. As they pushed against each other with all their might, Lando swiftly kicked out, striking the soldier in his stomach. As he fell backwards, Lando dispatched him with his fearsome weapon.

Hungry for redemption, Nayla glanced around to see who would be her next victim. As she turned to join Markus, she spun around just in time to pivot away from the downward stroke of a sword. Then Nayla ducked beneath the blade as a second sword sliced at her horizontally. As she rose up, a soldier swung out at her from behind, smashing her across her back with the flat edge of his shield. Nayla tumbled to the ground, dropping her sword as the soldiers pounced upon her.

The two soldiers immediately overpowered and subdued Nayla, restraining her by her arms. Markus and Arerys raced to aid her. They stopped in their tracks when a third soldier suddenly rose up from behind Nayla. He laughed as he grabbed her hair, holding the cold blade of his sword against her throat.

Although they were outnumbered by the men of the Order, Beyilzon's men now had the upper hand. The soldier pressed the blade closer to Nayla's throat, demanding the men to drop their weapons, lest they wanted to see her killed.

"So we meet again, little one," hissed the soldier into Nayla's ear.

Nayla attempted to control her rage upon recognizing the voice of Guldar.

"I said drop your swords or I shall kill her!" demanded Guldar, pressing the blade to Nayla's throat.

"Do not listen to him! It is a trick! He will kill me anyway!"

Arerys was the first to lower his sword. The others followed suit.

"No! Fight them!" ordered Nayla. "You can still defeat them!"

Suddenly, a familiar voice rang out from behind Guldar.

"Release her! Now!" shouted Ewen, thrusting the tip of his sword against Guldar's back. "Let her go or I shall run this sword through you!"

Panic rose in Markus. *Ewen cannot do this; he cannot kill, even if it is to protect another!*

"Ewen, make him back away," ordered Nayla.

She felt Guldar's sword slowly withdraw from her throat. Nayla abruptly seized the two soldiers holding her. Grabbing them by their shoulders, she kicked her legs over so she flipped behind them. As she came down, she landed with her heels sinking into the back of each soldier's knee. They howled out in pain as the impact drove their collapsing legs into the rocky ground, shattering their kneecaps. As they fell, Nayla dove for her sword, seizing it in her right hand as she rolled onto her feet.

As the men sprang on top of the soldiers, Ewen was caught off guard. Guldar wrestled the sword away from the boy. He clutched Ewen to his body as he held his sword to the boy's throat.

Nayla and the others turned to face the lone soldier. In a panic, Guldar held Ewen close, using him as a shield. His hand clutched the boy's chest as he struggled to maintain control and as he did so, Guldar felt an object hidden beneath his shirt. "What is this?" he asked as he pulled the velvet pouch into full view.

"Do not hurt the boy," pleaded Markus. "Inside the pouch is a rare and valuable stone! You may have it in exchange for the boy's life."

"What are you doing, Markus? He cannot have that!" shouted Faria.

The soldier, realizing he had stumbled upon unexpected fortune, examined the black pouch hanging from Ewen's neck. Holding himat sword point, he demanded the boy to reveal the content of the pouch.

Ewen looked to Markus, frightened; unsure what he should do.

"Go ahead, Ewen," encouraged Markus. "Show him the gem. In fact, *give* it to him."

Ewen nervously fumbled with the pouch as he emptied the Stone into his hand. He held it out for Guldar to see. The brilliant, red stone shone brightly, its many facets capturing and magnifying the pale morning light.

Guldar's eye widened with surprise as he gasped at the radiant beauty of the gem. He greedily snatched the Stone from Ewen's open hand. As he did so, the sound of skin being seared and the smell of burning flesh as he made contact with the Stone caused Guldar scream out in pain. The Stone abruptly dropped from his hand as he threw down his sword so he may clutch his wounded hand against his body as he collapsed to his knees in agony.

Nayla seized this opportunity to reach into her vest, extracting her poisoned darts. She took aim at Guldar's throat, but just as the deadly weapon left her hand, Ewen rose to his feet after retrieving the Stone from the ground. The dart struck the boy at the top of his left shoulder. Nayla quickly threw another one. This time, it hit its intended victim, piercing Guldar in his throat. Even before the soldier toppled over dead, Nayla and the others raced over to Ewen as he knelt on the ground.

"Ewen, I am sorry," said Nayla as she knelt before the boy, the dart still protruding from his shoulder. She threw back Ewen's cloak, pulling open his vest. The dart was caught in the fine mesh of his mail. To Nayla's horror the tip just penetrated through the protective links. It was just enough to break his skin. Ewen knelt on the ground in stunned silence; he could already feel the burning as the poison spread from the tiny puncture wound.

Ewen said nothing. He carefully placed the Stone back into the pouch, pulling the drawstring together before hanging it about his neck again. He stood up only to have his legs buckle beneath him. Markus scooped him up in his arms.

"Faria, get up onto the rise; keep watch for soldiers," ordered Markus. "Arerys! Lando! Collect and conceal these bodies in the canyon. Nayla, come with me!"

Nayla followed Markus into a now vacant tent. He lay Ewen down onto a bedroll. The boy was beginning to sweat as a fever began to creep over his body.

Markus grabbed Nayla by her arm, leading her to the entrance of the tent, away from Ewen. "Nayla, what is the nature of this poison?" asked Markus, speaking in a hushed tone.

"It is a derivative from the liver of a highly toxic fish. The poison paralyzes the muscles. It stops the heart," whispered Nayla. "In a powdered state, the poison is even more potent."

"Will he die?"

"I do not know," answered Nayla, glancing over at Ewen. "Even a little is highly toxic, but judging from his wound and how quickly he fell, it shall ultimately depend on how strong his will is to survive."

"Is there anything we can do to help him?"

"Yes, there is," replied Nayla, as she returned to the boy's side. "Stay with Ewen; talk to him. Try not to let him fall asleep. I shall return." She quickly disappeared from the tent.

Ewen gazed up at the prince. "It was not supposed to end this way, Markus," he said as his trembling hand touched the pouch that lay on his chest.

"This is not the end, Ewen," said Markus, wiping the perspiration that was beading upon the boy's forehead. "Nayla will help you."

"I cannot feel my arm. It grows numb... cold."

Arerys had just retrieved his spent arrows from the bodies. He and Lando worked together to discard the dead soldiers into the canyon when Nayla emerged from the tent.

"Lando, stoke the fire; boil some water," instructed Nayla. "Arerys, I need the bark of the willow tree."

None asked why. They proceeded to follow Nayla's instructions as she began to search the ground for a broad-leafed herb with dark green foliage and deep red stems that usually grew in close proximity to nettles and poison ivy.

As Markus waited for Nayla, Ewen was beginning to tremble with cold, even though he was burning with fever and sweating profusely.

"This is not the adventure I thought it would be," said Ewen, a look of woe etched across his young face.

"It is not over yet," stated Markus. "We are not done. You must hold on."

"Will you stay by my side?" he asked, his voice growing softer. "I am afraid to die alone."

"I will not let you die," answered Markus. "Not here. Not like this."

As the poison continued to spread from the wound, the color was draining from Ewen's face as his eyes slowly closed.

"I will be here, Ewen. I shall wait for you and watch over you until you are well again. I shall not forsake you," whispered Markus. As the fever took hold of his trembling body, the prince wrapped his young companion in his cloak.

Ewen stirred in his unnatural sleep. In this strange twilight, he saw images of Darius as he lay dying. He saw the great dragon that stole away deep into the cave in pursuit of Lindras, and he watched in horror as Nayla was dragged away by the Dark Army. Each had made a terrible sacrifice to protect him.

He screamed in terror, but none heard his cries for help. He was plunged into darkness. His eyes turned upwards to see a large, black figure looming over him, holding forth a man as he desperately fought to escape this deadly grip. This dark figure shouted at Ewen as he cowered on the ground: "Will you die for him?"

Ewen scrambled to his feet to escape his tormentor, but this time he was not surrounded by the soldiers of the Dark Army. Instead, he looked into the faces of Nayla and the men of the Order. They were overcome by great sadness.

Again, the resonating voice called out: "Will you die for him?"

Ewen turned to see that the man this menacing figure held forth by his throat was the Prince of Carcross: Markus. He dangled above the ground, struggling to free himself from this choking grip. Ewen turned to Arerys and the others for help, but they were fading away into a veil of darkness.

Ewen cried out and as he did so, his eyes chanced upon the Three Sisters: Elora, Enra and Eliya. Elora, the Watcher of the Past knelt before the boy.

"Try to remember, Ewen," she whispered.

"I do not understand!"

"You must try, Ewen. Life hangs in the balance."

"This is too much for me to bear!"

"Ewen, the Maker of All would never give you more than what you can bear," said Elora. "He would only give you what he knows you can handle."

As Ewen watched the sun grow black, he looked upon his hand. His tightly clenched fist slowly opened to reveal the Stone of Salvation as it sparkled brightly even in the dimming light.

"I cannot do this alone," whimpered Ewen.

"You are never alone, Ewen," replied Elora. "When you were too weary to carry on, it had been Markus and the others that carried you. You are dear to them, they shall never forsake you."

As the Three Sisters faded into the expanding darkness, Ewen heard a voice calling out to him. It was Markus.

"I have lost one son, Ewen, I shall not lose you too."

Upon hearing his words, a look of serenity came over Ewen's ashen face. Markus continued to cradle him as Nayla raised a cup of steaming water scented with chamomile and flavored with the scraping of the inner bark of the willow tree to Ewen's dry lips.

"Try to drink this, Ewen. Even a little will help," pleaded Nayla. "This shall ease your pain and fever."

Ewen scowled, sputtering as the bitter liquid passed over his tongue.

"Arerys, is the poultice ready?" asked Nayla as she set the cup down.

"Yes, here it is," answered the Elf, scraping the concoction of mud and crushed plant into a small heap into the center of the bowl.

Nayla worked quickly to undo the clasps that held the garment of mail in place. She pushed back his shirt to reveal the wound. There, at the top of his shoulder, the small puncture made by the poisoned dart was raised and hot. It looked almost purple against his pale, clammy skin.

"Hold him steady, Markus. This will hurt," she whispered. She quickly packed the poultice onto the wound. Ewen shrank away in pain as he cried out. The remedy Nayla had concocted penetrated into his inflamed flesh, biting deep into the entrance of the wound.

Nayla wiped her palms clean, and then drawing a deep breath, she blew into her cupped hands. Raising them over her head, she clapped her hands together once, then proceeded to rub them lightly, but briskly together, faster and faster. Her eyes were closed, as if she were in deep concentration. The palms of her hands quickly warmed so one could see steam rising into the cool, morning air. Taking her warmed hands, Nayla gently placed them over the area of Ewen's wound. The boy tried to pull away, groaning in pain as her hands felt as though they would burn right through his cold skin.

"This worked for my sore shoulder, Nayla, but will it work on this poison?" asked Markus.

"The heat from my hand will help to increase the circulation of blood to the wound. It shall help the poultice spread to the infected area faster. It will also allow the mud to dry quickly, thereby drawing out the poison," answered Nayla. She turned to Arerys. "Work your Elven magic. You know what to do now."

Arerys took his place next to Nayla as Markus continued to cradle Ewen's limp body. He quickly followed her instructions. As he placed his hand over Ewen's wound, he closed his eyes, focusing on the task at hand.

Nayla tore some cloth and packed some dried moss inside to dress the wound once Arerys was done.

"Will he survive, Nayla?" asked Markus as he lowered Ewen's resting body onto the bedroll.

"I cannot be certain of his fate, his body is weak, but I believe his will is strong," answered Nayla. "He must want to live."

As the darkness of the night retreated with the coming of the morning light, Markus remained by Ewen's side. He wiped the sweat from Ewen's face, continuing to cradle his head late into the morning.

Lando joined Faria on the rise overlooking the camp. So far there had been no sign of enemy soldiers heading their way.

Arerys resumed the grim business of concealing the last of the dead soldiers in the canyon. Nayla aided him with this task and as she did so, she came upon Guldar's now cold body.

She knelt down beside Guldar's lifeless form, removing her dart that was still lodged deep in his neck. Wiping it clean on the grass, she carefully hid it away in her pocket. As she slowly rose to her feet, she stared at his face; it was frozen in a contorted expression of utter pain.

"You did not deserve such an easy death," muttered Nayla, under her breath as her underlying rage and despair finally boiled to the surface.

Suddenly, Nayla leapt onto Guldar, straddling his dead body, she angrily beat and pound upon his chest with both her fists – her response totally visceral. Lando and Faria saw her from their watch and raced down as Arerys, alarmed by Nayla's fury, dropped the body he was in the midst of disposing.

Arerys dashed to her side as she repeatedly pounded on the corpse. "Nayla, stop it!" he shouted. "Nayla! Stop!"

She was so overwrought with anger; she could not even hear Arerys shouting at her as she continued her assault. Nor did she notice Lando and Faria standing over her as they tried to calm her with their words. It was as though the intensity of her rage blocked out everything else around her.

Arerys finally seized Nayla by her wrists at mid-strike. He could feel all of her anger balled up in her trembling fists as he tried to subdue her. "Nayla, stop it!" ordered Arerys. "He is dead! You have already killed him!"

His sharp words and sudden actions jolted Nayla back into reality. When her rage eventually subsided, she slowly raised her head to gaze up at Arerys' face. "He is the one who delivered me to Vorath," sobbed Nayla in a whisper, her small voice breaking as tears streamed down her face.

Arerys threw his arms around her as he lifted her off the cold body. He held her close, motioning Faria and Lando to remove Guldar from Nayla's sight. The men moved quickly, not wishing to cause her any more grief.

Arerys enveloped Nayla's trembling body in his arms, holding her close as she wept. He knew not the words to comfort her; he could only shelter her in his arms in hopes that her tears would absolve her of all her anger and sorrow.

As the morning became afternoon, Markus, exhausted by his long vigil, had fallen asleep with Ewen still in his arms. Nayla knelt by his side and gently woke Markus. His eyes opened with a start as he looked down upon the boy.

"He is still asleep, Markus. The fever has passed, but he is still weak."

Ewen's eyes slowly opened upon hearing Nayla's soft voice. He gazed up at Markus and smiled weakly.

"I was so afraid. I was lost in a dream that I thought would have no end," said Ewen in a soft voice. "Am I still dreaming, or am I dead?"

Nayla gently stroked his crown of soft, brown hair. "You are very much alive, Ewen. But here you shall remain until you regain your strength."

"I shall be well soon, Nayla," said Ewen confidently, as he struggled to sit up.

"Had I aimed slightly lower or had you raised yourself a little faster, you would not be alive right now," stated Nayla as she passed him some water. "There are spirits watching over you, my young friend."

Markus left Nayla to watch over Ewen as he went to inform the men of the Order to continue their watch for the remainder of the day and into the night. They should be ready to move out at the first light of morning.

CHAPTER 15

BREAKING VORATH'S HOLD

Ordered by Markus to conduct sentry duty together, Arerys and Nayla shared the watch from late afternoon, well into the night. Nayla was quiet and withdrawn, still struggling with the emotions that came to surface from her angry confrontation with Guldar's corpse.

Arerys too, struggled with his own feelings. He was not sure whether to continue to wait for Nayla to speak about the incident of that terrible night, or if he should just pretend nothing had happened, in hopes that she too would do the same.

Their time together passed slowly. Though no barbed words were exchanged to further strain their already fragile relationship, the time spent in silence did nothing to mend the growing rift between them.

When they did speak, Arerys took great care to keep their conversation benign, avoiding any subject matter that may only serve to upset her. When they did converse, it was to discuss the healing power and medicinal uses of various plants, or the manner in which Nayla had been trained in the traditions of the warriors of the east.

Arerys was fascinated by Nayla's skills and fighting prowess. He had never seen anybody do what she did - driving her sword into the body of a soldier, then taking hold of her weapon to spring over, extracting and drawing the blade to strike down the next soldier. It was also the economy of movement and the effortless way she redirected her opponent's energy, using his own momentum to manipulate him. Arerys found this most amazing.

Nayla was more than willing to share herbal remedies and to explain the finer points of how to employ simple moves, such as handsprings, rolls and body angling to avoid an attack, whether it be with or without weapons.

At least, Arerys thought gratefully, they were talking again, but he could sense that Nayla was still greatly troubled by her ordeal. He resolved to be patient - willing to wait and offer her a compassionate ear when she was ready to talk about it, if she wished to do so.

Later that night, Lando and Markus relieved them of sentry duty. Arerys and Nayla returned to the camp, where she settled near the fire to sleep. She refused to occupy the tents once used by the soldiers of the Dark Army. Arerys laid down next to her, wrapping his arms around her body as her head rested against his shoulder. He gently kissed her upon her forehead, hoping that she would find some solace in her dreams.

A short time later, Arerys woke from his sleep with a start - something was amiss. Nayla was gone. The Elf sat up, as he looked about. Sometime during the night, she had left his side. *How can that be? I was holding her in my arms,* Arerys wondered.

He stood for a moment, listening. Checking in the tent where Faria and Ewen slept, the two were embraced in a deep slumber. Nayla was not present. He stepped away from the tent to listen again; he knew to head into the wooded area overlooking the canyon.

As he glanced up at the rise overlooking the camp, Arerys could see Markus and Lando - they were quietly talking as they kept watch.

He moved silently through the stand of trees and it was not long before he came upon Nayla. She was a small, solitary figure hidden amongst the tall grasses. She sat beneath a large willow tree that grew next to a slow flowing stream that emptied into the depth of the canyon. It was clear she was wishing not to be found, but Arerys did not care.

He approached her and as always, by the lightness of his steps, Nayla knew it was he. Arerys stood before her, but her eyes seemed to look straight through him, as though he was not even there.

Arerys knelt before her and bent to kiss Nayla upon her lips, but his kiss went unanswered. She slowly pulled away from him.

"Nayla, what has happened to turn your heart so cold?" asked Arerys, his sadness he could no longer conceal. "Do you no longer love me?"

"It is not you, Arerys. The turmoil is within myself." There was a long pause before she finally confided to him. "I feel as though I am now tainted by Vorath's touch."

"Nayla, you are still you. Do not let Vorath take you away from me like this."

"Arerys, I am a warrior – the captain of my own battalion. This does not happen to a warrior. On that night I was prepared to die. Whether it was by Vorath's hands or by my own, I was ready to die. My greatest mistake was that I was not prepared for what hand fate had chosen to deal to me."

"Nayla, how can anybody be prepared for what you had endured?"

"I cannot help but to think that if I had only dressed as Faria said - as a real warrior, than flaunt the fact that I am a woman, I may have escaped Vorath's hands."

"Even if you had dressed in chain mail and armor, to hide the fact that you are a woman, Vorath would still see through your disguise," declared Arerys. "Please do not tell me that you blame yourself! The manner of your dress was not an invitation for Vorath's assault."

"And what if it was, Arerys?" asked Nayla in despair.

"Vorath's actions were not motivated by love, passion or even lust. He was driven by the blackness of his heart. His desire was to control and overpower you; to break your spirit! Now, it is as though Vorath has created a great chasm in your heart and I fear that I will not be able to bridge this gap."

Nayla's chin dropped to her chest as she began to weep.

"Please, Nayla, do not let this happen. Do not let your despair take over your life, for if you do, Vorath has surely won!" pleaded Arerys. He gently stroked Nayla's head and held it to his chest, "Please come back to me. Do not let Vorath claim you, even in his death. Though your spirit may be broken, let me be the one to help you mend it."

Nayla's tears fell, leaving a dark trail of sadness on Arerys' cloak.

"You did not ask for this to happen. You did not wish it upon yourself. And I… I shall bear the burden for the rest of my life that I was not there to prevent this from happening to you," Arerys cried with great sorrow. "Do not give in Nayla. In my darkness, you are the one light that guides me. Do not let this light go out."

Nayla did not speak; her head resting against Arerys' chest.

"Nayla, no matter what has happened, it does not change the fact that I still love you," whispered Arerys, holding her gently in his arms. He softly kissed her forehead, lifting her chin so their eyes met. He delicately kissed her tears away, gazing into her sad, brown eyes - searching for the woman he once knew and missed so. He could almost feel himself trembling inside as he placed his mouth upon her. His heart raced in fear that she would reject him again.

Nayla's eyes closed as Arerys' warm lips softly caressed hers. In that single touch, she felt all his sorrow, regret and loneliness. As though a heavy burden was lifted from her heart, she melted into Arerys' embrace, wishing to be one with his soul again.

She felt his unwavering love and his rising passion as his lips sought hers. She kissed him back - at first slowly and tenderly, then with great passion.

Arerys held her ever so gently as Nayla pulled him down on top of her body. She lay upon the soft, green grass as he gazed down upon her face. She smiled sweetly at him and it made his heart soar; it had been so long since he had last seen her smile. He held her tightly in his arms, kissing her deeply. He yearned for her as he had never yearned for another woman before, but he felt uncertain about Nayla's feelings. Maybe it was too soon after her treacherous ordeal.

Nayla stared into the calm of Arerys' blue eyes and for a moment, she was lost in the very depth of his soul. She touched his face. Drawing him close, she kissed his mouth deeply. She began to work at the ties that bound his clothes, slowly releasing the clasps of his vest.

The Elf's hands grasped her trembling fingers as he looked into her eyes. "Nayla, stop. You need not do this."

"Do you not want me, Arerys?" asked Nayla, looking somewhat forlorn.

Arerys gently stroked her face with his fingertips. "More than you will ever know Nayla, I just do not know if you are ready—"

Nayla placed her fingers gently over his lips so he could say no more as she pushed him onto his back. She continued to remove his clothing.

Her eyes closed as she reveled at the touch and warmth of the muscles on his shoulders. They felt smooth and hard against the palms of her hands. Her fingers followed the contours of the firm muscles of Arerys' chest down to his hard, flat stomach. Nayla gently planted feather-soft kisses upon his chest; he could feel the warmth of her breath as her lips ever so lightly brushed against his skin as she worked her way down his body. Her touch was so delicate, yet it was scintillating - arousing and tantalizing his senses. Every fiber of his being that had long laid dormant, was sparking with life and burning with intense desire for Nayla.

She slowly rose up against him, like a feline, seductively rising up to stretch. Then she leaned into his face, gently kissing his lips.

Arerys looked into her eyes as his fingers unfastened the tie that held her braid in place. He ran his fingers through Nayla's long, silky hair; it cascaded around her shoulders. He breathed in deeply, delighting in the light scent of her raven tresses.

He began to unhook the clasps of Nayla's vest, always searching her face for the first sign to stop, but she gave no such indication. He carefully untied her bodice, slipping her blouse down about her shoulders. Against her dark hair, Nayla's skin seemed to glow in the moonlight like delicate porcelain. Arerys' fingers lingered on the silky, warm skin of her shoulders before his hands moved slowly downward, softly caressing the curves of her breasts. Nayla sighed softly, her eyes closing at the gentleness of his touch.

Arerys slowly rolled over Nayla's body as he gently laid her upon her back. He gazed into her deep brown eyes for a moment before kissing her again. He felt as though her very touch – her every kiss, was life itself, replenishing his soul. He felt rejuvenated again; like a parched desert soaking up its first spring rain after a long period of drought. Arerys' hand gently caressed the length of her supine body. He felt the soft, warmth of her naked skin against his; he yearned for her as never before.

Nayla took his hand into hers as she placed it between her thighs. Arerys' eyes closed as he caressed her inviting, soft skin - it felt as though her flesh was on fire. She pulled his body down towards her and she felt Arerys' hips press up against hers. Her legs slowly parted as she drew him closer; a small gasp escaping her lips as Arerys entered her. He lifted himself up, slowly kissing Nayla as she raised her hips, wishing to connect deeply with him. His heart raced as his body merged with hers. Arerys' movements where gentle and unrushed until he was fully hilted, deep into Nayla; he felt absolute rapture as their bodies melted into one.

She took Arerys in fully, holding him tightly. He made love to her slowly and gently. His movements were steady and rhythmic as she raised her body to meet his.

Nayla wanted to feel Arerys deep inside her; she wanted him to cleanse away the past; to help her forget. His heart felt as though it was ready to burst as the sensation of her inner muscles clasped and tightened around him, enveloping him in complete and excruciating pleasure as she moved with him. A patina of sweat beaded on his skin, glistening in the pale moonlight.

Nayla held him close, clinging to him desperately - feeling Arerys' every movement deep inside her. Her heart was racing as her entire being felt as though it was being swept away on a great tide. Now this tide was rushing back as a powerful wave, crashing onto the shore, washing away everything in its path – purging her soul. With a final thrust, Arerys shuddered powerfully as he collapsed into her arms, his body completely spent.

At that moment, it was as though Nayla's body and soul were whole once more. It felt like the first time they had made love, but this time all of Nayla's fears, sorrow and pain that had haunted her up until now, were finally vanquished. They were replaced by an exhilarating sense of intense pleasure. Her head felt light as her heart beat rapidly; she was overcome with a dizzying feeling of complete ecstasy as she lay in Arerys' arms. Eventually, this feeling gave way to an overwhelming sense of peace and calm. Vorath no longer had a hold on her; his spell was broken.

Beneath the soft glow of an opal moon, the two lovers lay in the warm embrace of each other's arms. Arerys gently kissed the nape of Nayla's neck and the soft skin of her shoulder. His cloak covered their bodies, protecting them against the chill in the night air. They lingered in the glade, in no hurry to join the others.

CHAPTER 16

AN ORDER DIVIDED

As the darkness of night gave way in a calm surrender to the first light of morning, the last stars faded from the sky. The Order made their way down the steep canyon wall. As the group peered into the depth of the divide that separated the Aranaks from the Iron Mountains, it was easy for them to envision the giants that gave rise to these great mountains. They must have created this canyon with the intention of using it as a moat - to help further define and secure their territories.

Ewen, after a full day and night to recuperate from his injury, was fit and in good spirits after eating breakfast. Despite all he had endured, he seemed to be driven by some unseen force that buoyed him, allowing him to forge on.

It was a long, arduous trek into the floor of the steep canyon. As they gazed upwards, it was as though the earth had split into two; the Aranak and Iron Mountains themselves would swallow them up. The walls of the canyon were deep, rust red from the iron that had oxidized from years of exposure to the elements. Even the moist, morning air was heavy; strong with the smell of iron. They could taste it in the back of their throats.

The floor of the canyon slowly ascended as they traveled northward. The journey was not a difficult uphill climb, just time consuming as they picked their way around rocks and boulders that seemed to block and hamper their every move. In some areas, they were forced to make their way from the protective shadows of the west wall of this great divide to cross rough terrain.

The group stopped briefly to rest and drink some water. "We shall reach the mouth of the canyon by late morning," said Faria, pointing to the distant trees that concealed the entrance from Talibarr into the Redwall Canyons.

"In all likelihood, the army we saw on the Plains of Fire as we crossed back into Darross has grown," warned Nayla. "They shall continue to congregate in greater numbers in preparation for war."

The prince nodded in agreement. "We shall travel as far as we can safely do so before we rest again," said Markus. "Then we shall proceed in the darkness of night.

All agreed as they ventured forth. Arerys was attentively watching and listening for signs of danger as they trudged on, out of the depth of the red walls.

When they eventually emerged into Talibarr; Nayla, Ewen, Faria and Lando were sequestered into a secluded thicket while Arerys and Markus scouted ahead to determine what lay in wait for them.

After three hours had elapsed, Arerys and Markus returned with confirmation that the Dark Army now gathered in greater numbers than they had anticipated. Skirting the southwestern edge of the Valley of Shadows, westward into the Plains of Fire, then north along the Shadow Mountains, a vast army gathered, waiting for the war to begin.

"We shall move north to the border of this forest, then we must wait for the cover of night," instructed Markus. "We shall have no choice but to cross a stretch of open land to enter the Valley of Shadows."

Markus and Arerys led the way through the trees until they came to the edge of the forest. They waited for night to blanket the land in darkness once more.

As a bright moon, now slightly more than three-quarters full, illuminated the land below, the Order moved forward from the protective cover of the forest. In the distance, they could see many small, dark figures scurrying in and about the base camp.

Using great stealth, the group moved cautiously across the open land as Markus led the way. The trek was painstakingly slow. They took great care to remain motionless when they felt the slightest inclination that eyes were cast in their direction. As they neared the border of the Valley of Shadows, a strange silence hung heavily in the air.

Arerys' eyes turned towards the camp; the blood in his veins felt an icy chill. "Make haste! They are coming!" shouted the Elf, just as an ear-piercing shriek rang from the camp, breaking the unnatural solitude. "The dark horsemen are here!"

The Order raced towards the cover of the primeval forest, its towering, dense stands of coniferous trees seemed to shroud the Valley of Shadows in a constant gloom. Arerys turned to face the fast approaching incursion; a large infantry led by the two dark emissaries.

Luck was with Arerys as he took aim, releasing his arrow. It struck one of the dark horseman square on. He tumbled to the ground, quickly vaporizing into a swirling heap of black ashes. As Arerys let go a second arrow, the last of Beyilzon's dark agents abruptly wheeled his black steed about, narrowly missing the Elf's projectile. He screamed in anger, charging straight towards Arerys.

Seeing that the infantry was quickly gaining ground, Arerys retreated into the forest after the others. There was no other choice but to call for help. In the luminous glow of the moon, he raised his sword up high above his head. Arerys closed his eyes, using an ancient incantation known only to the elders and those born to the House of Wingfield.

A mysterious white fog seeped in, rolling across the dark forest floor. The mist quickly rose, taking on many ghostly forms. Standing before Arerys was an army; the shadowy figures of Elves lost in battles fought on the Plains of Fire. Their spirits, unable to enter the Twilight, and now condemned to this earthly realm, awaited Arerys' instructions. The Elf turned them in the direction of the encroaching Dark Army before running to catch up with the others.

The soldiers reluctantly followed Beyilzon's dark agent into the haunted forest of the Valley of Shadows. It was only by the threatening gestures of the dark horseman as he urged them on, that they entered the deep shadows with great trepidation - their swords held cautiously before them.

The soldiers slowly crept through the forest. Their frightened eyes scanned the dark, sinister surroundings as they moved, searching for any ominous signs that would give them reason to flee this forsaken place. As they advanced in the direction of the Order, they were engulfed by an eerie chill, so cold they could see their breath suspended in the air. High above, tree boughs began to stir and rattle, but the air was still. There was no wind, or even a light breeze, to speak of.

The soldiers nervously glanced about for the unseen evil advancing towards them, as the dark horseman's steed became increasingly agitated. As his rider wrestled for control, the great black horse reared and fought against its reins. The dark beast finally bolted with the dark emissary still on board when, from the depth of the dark forest, a ghostly army mysteriously emerged with weapons drawn.

Arerys turned once upon hearing the frightened screams and gasps of horror as the soldiers encountered the apparitions the Elf had called upon. Although he knew these spirits were not capable of fighting against those who were alive, Arerys took advantage of the fact that mortals were easily frightened by things they did not understand. If anything, he hoped the phantom army would detain Beyilzon's men long enough to allow the Order to gain some ground.

Most of the soldiers automatically turned, fleeing in fear upon coming face to face with the souls of the departed warriors. The only ones that persevered were the soldiers who were more frightened of Beyilzon, than of their ghostly adversaries. They faced the frightening specters and after some hesitation, gathered sufficient courage to confront the apparitions; desperately thrashing and slicing at them with their swords. The spirits quietly dissipated into the cool night air from whence they came.

As he caught up, the Elf warned the others to keep running; he could hear the fast approaching sounds of a horse at full gallop as well as the pounding of many footsteps following closely behind.

"Arerys, there shall be too many of them to fight off! We must separate," cried Markus. "Brannon's sword is useless, its power can only be unleashed if both Ewen and I are present. One is useless without the other; the sword will need the Stone!"

"I understand," stated Arerys.

"We shall meet again," said Markus, "on the summit of Mount Hope."

"Nayla and I shall deliver Ewen safely," promised Arerys.

"Faria, Lando and I shall advance along the western slope of Mount Hope; you shall approach from the south," ordered the prince.

Arerys nodded in understanding. Nayla took Ewen by his hand and they began to run. With the Order divided, now heading in different directions, even if they failed to defeat Beyilzon, if Markus and Ewen should both die in their attempt to reach Mount Hope, the Dark Lord shall not possess the same degree of power if he were to claim King Brannon's sword as his own. Even if he had any success at removing the sword from the ground, without the Stone, its true powers shall never be realized.

As the army neared, Nayla could sense that Ewen was tiring. With only she and Arerys to protect the boy, she knew they could not outfight the approaching soldiers. The warrior maiden turned to them with an idea.

"We must conceal ourselves, but to hide is not good enough. We shall take to the trees and remain motionless," instructed Nayla. "Ewen, listen to me carefully. When you are safely hidden, close your eyes: think of home; or friends; or flowers. Think of anything, but do not show your fear. They shall feel your intention and will know of your whereabouts as surely as if you called out to them. Do you understand, Ewen?"

Ewen nodded to Nayla in acknowledgment as Arerys boosted him into a large tree.

"Just trust me," said Nayla. "Do as I say and no harm shall come to you."

She turned to the Elf. "Arerys, when the army nears, use your arrow to create a diversion. Direct their attention well away from us."

Once Ewen was well concealed, Arerys and Nayla's selected two neighboring trees, with great agility, they climbed effortlessly into the high branches. There, they waited.

The army, led by the dark horseman, converged on the area where the Order had divided, going on their separate ways. The shadows cast by the trees were dark, making it impossible to detect with any certainty the direction the Order was now moving in.

Ewen glanced down to see the dark horseman directly below. His great, black steed paced and stomped about impatiently beneath his tree. Ewen's heart began to race; his breathing became short and panicked. The horseman dismounted, searching for signs of his quarry's presence.

Think happy thoughts. Think happy thoughts, Ewen repeated to himself as he tried to conjure up images of his carefree days back in Carcross, safe within the walls of Prince Markus' castle. As pleasant memories began to calm his worried mind, the dark horseman turned away. Suddenly, Arerys released an arrow that he sent deliberately crashing through a dense growth of shrubs in the distance.

The dark horseman released a blood-curdling shriek as his head turned abruptly in the direction of the sound. He raised his sword high over his head, commanding the army westward; pointing in the direction he wanted them to resume the search.

When the enemy disappeared into the darkness, Nayla, Arerys, and Ewen swiftly climbed down from the trees, proceeding to the south face of Mount Hope. If luck stayed with them, they would reach the foot of the mountain by tomorrow night or perhaps by the following morning.

Nayla and Arerys slowed their pace as they darted through the shadows of the forest. Ewen was exhausted. It had been some time since they had last eaten or drank. They would rest briefly, then continue on through the night.

When the sun finally peered over the jagged teeth of the Iron Mountains, Arerys recommended that they all get some rest; just enough to provide them with the strength needed to complete the final leg of their trek. He knew that once they reached the south face of Mount Hope they would have no choice but to charge to the summit with all their might. They would no longer have the luxury of resting, the anticipated full moon would rise with the coming of the night.

Markus, Lando and Faria had covered a great distance on foot in the darkness. Their pace slowed when the morning sun cast a warm glow over the Valley of Shadows, but the light of day could not penetrate the thick stand of trees, leaving the forest floor shrouded in a constant shadow. The three men finally came to a rest by a small stream.

"Markus, you and Lando should rest. I shall watch over you," suggested Faria.

Lando slumped wearily to the ground. "Give me an hour or two to rest, then I shall take over sentry duty," said Lando as he closed his eyes.

"Very well, Faria. Thank you," responded Markus, resting his back against a tree. He too, closed his eyes. As sleep quickly laid claim to his mind and body, Markus thought about Ewen, Arerys and Nayla. He was confident that they had escaped from the Dark Army. Between their determination, ingenuity and skill, he was sure they had outwitted and eluded Beyilzon's soldiers. Even now, they were probably well on their way to Mount Hope. Markus had no doubt that Ewen was in good hands.

Completely exhausted, a deep sleep soon took hold, over both Markus and Lando. It was late into the afternoon when the snapping of a dried branch caused Markus to bolt up from his sleep. His sudden movement alerted Lando. He also stirred from his slumber. It was much more sleep than they had wanted although it was badly needed.

Markus looked about. "Where is Faria?"

Lando stood next to Markus, he noticed that the sun had traveled far to the west. Surveying their surroundings, Faria was nowhere to be seen.

"This is not good, Markus."

Just as he spoke these words, Faria appeared from the shadows.

"Where were you, Faria? Why did you let us sleep so long? You know we are running out of time," stated Markus, with a scowl of disapproval.

"Prince Markus, I have taken it upon myself to bring you help from the most unexpected source," Faria proudly announced.

Markus was ill at ease; it was long ago since Faria had last addressed him by his proper title. "What are you speaking of?"

"You shall turn the tide against the Dark Lord by turning the men of his army against him."

"I do not understand," said Markus, with growing suspicion.

"Beyilzon's men now know that you hold the key and the power to slay the Dark Lord," declared Faria. "They knew not, what powers you possess as the direct heir to King Brannon. Now that they do know, there shall be a new leader who shall rule over Imago. They want to ensure that they align themselves with the victor."

"Faria! Do not tell me you have betrayed Markus!" cried Lando.

"I have not betrayed Markus, I have secured him some badly needed allies," Faria responded defiantly.

As if on cue, the soldiers of the Dark Army emerged from the shadows of the forest. With swords and bows drawn, they surrounded Markus and Lando.

Faria turned to the captain of the battalion. "There is no need for this. You heard him answer to Prince Markus."

"Faria, how dare you!" shouted Lando, lunging at him. All weapons turned on Lando. He froze.

"If you require further proof, he bears the insignia of the House of Whycliffe on his brooch," added Faria.

As soldiers confiscated Markus' sword, the captain approached him. He stared coldly into the prince's eyes before throwing open his cloak. To his delight, there was the blue stone bearing the stars and the white cross: the brooch worn by those born under the House of Whycliffe. Markus was indeed a direct heir to King Brannon.

"Seize him!"

"What are you doing?" asked Faria, startled by the captain's order. "He is Prince Markus of Carcross. I told you, he is the scion of King Brannon!"

"Yes, you did, fool!" laughed the captain. "Thank you for delivering the enemy!"

"You lied to me!" shouted Faria angrily. "You have betrayed my trust!"

"No, I believe it is you, who has betrayed the prince," answered the captain, shoving Faria out of his way.

"Faria! You bastard! You have forsaken us!" cried out Lando as he turned on the bewildered knight, knocking him to the ground.

"I believe they shall take care of themselves," scoffed the captain, watching with mild amusement. His men proceeded to gag Markus, binding his hands behind his back.

The soldiers seized the prince by his shoulders as they forcefully led him away, leaving the two men on the ground struggling against each other. An enraged Lando straddled Faria's body as he frantically beat upon him.

"Damn you, Faria! How dare you betray Markus and jeopardize this mission!" He repeatedly struck Faria hard with his clenched fists.

"Lando, I beg of you, forgive me!" pleaded Faria as he covered his head with his arms to protect him from the onslaught of Lando's fury. "I never meant for this to happen. You know what we are up against. You saw the Dark Army awaiting battle on the Plains of Fire! We are destined to lose. Where were the knights and soldiers of the Alliance? I saw none!"

"Faria, what happened to your faith?" cried Lando in anguish. "They are coming! They will be here! Now, because of your misguided actions, we shall all go down in defeat!"

"What have I done?" groaned Faria, trembling in fear. He turned away to retch as the realization of his deed finally sank in. It made him sick to his stomach. "What have I done, Lando?"

"There is still hope," said Lando as he stood up. "If they are smart, they shall hold Markus until Beyilzon is unleashed from his prison. We must rescue him. If he is still alive, Faria, we must save him."

"I swear on my life, I shall do whatever it takes to make things right," promised Faria, struggling onto his feet.

"I shall tell you this now, *my friend*," growled Lando. "You have no choice but to help me."

Faria nodded in understanding. "Follow me, I know the way to their camp."

Lando disappeared into the deepening shadows of the forest as he followed the distraught Faria.

By the time they reached the encampment, darkness had swallowed up the land. Lando determined the number of soldiers assigned to this camp was decidedly small - perhaps two dozen. They must have separated from the others last night in their search for the Order.

At the far edge of the camp, a large bonfire crackled and roared. Its yellow and orange flames danced and licked high into the night sky. Beyond this fire was Markus. He was gagged and bound to a large post. His head hung down, his chin resting on his chest. He did not move as soldiers took turns taunting and beating upon him.

Faria was overcome with guilt. He never expected this to happen, and now, the last hope for mankind was tied to this wooden post. The Prince was tormented and tortured as though he were but a common criminal awaiting justice to be served on him.

"I shall distract the soldiers and lead them away from the camp," whispered Faria.

"How do you intend to do that?"

"I shall tell them I have the Stone of Salvation."

"What are you speaking of? You do not possess the Stone."

"They do not know that," said Faria as he left Lando's side. "Concern yourself with Markus. Get him away from here."

Lando watched Faria skirt the perimeter of the camp, and then proceed up the hill.

Suddenly, Faria called out: "Gentlemen, you have been deceived! I know where the Stone is that you seek! If you want it, then take it from me, if you can!"

The captain ordered his soldiers to pursue Faria, for it was already evident that Markus did not have the Stone of Salvation in his possession. As the soldiers quickly dispersed from the camp, the captain turned his attention back to Markus.

"So, your man had the Stone all along," he growled as he struck Markus across his face with the back of his fist. Grabbing him by his hair, he forced the prince to look into his eyes. "It shall only be a matter of time before he is hunted down like an animal - his carcass dragged back to camp."

With none of his men present to witness his sadistic streak, the captain turned to the bonfire, extracting a long, thin piece of wood that was burning in the flames. As he withdrew it from the fire, he blew upon it, causing the end that was buried in the amber flames to glow red-hot. He slowly approached Markus, holding the burning poker before him.

"Let us have some fun! Shall we?" taunted the captain, yanking back on his prisoner's head. He slowly raised the burning branch to his left eye, smiling cruelly as he contemplated the level of pain he should dispense. The prince did not flinch, nor did he turn away. He stared directly into the eyes of his tormentor.

The captain moved to plunge the burning ember into Markus' eye when Lando suddenly leapt from the darkness, lunging at the prince's cruel foe. His sword sliced the burning tip of the wood away, just as he was about to inflict Markus with unthinkable pain.

Dropping the piece of wood from his hand, the captain drew his sword on the knight. He lunged straight for him as Lando angled out of the way to avoid the tip of his blade. Lando swung his sword downward, striking the incoming weapon. As his adversary raised his blade to slash out horizontally, the knight seized him by his own sword handle, jamming his movement. The captain struggled against his hold as Lando kicked him over. As he went crashing down backwards, Lando's sword swung about in his hand as it came down in a deliberate arc upon his sadistic foe. Death was delivered swiftly, the lethal blade piercing him through his chest.

Lando extracted his sword from the captain's body. He quickly flicked the blood off of blade before using it to cut the ties that secured Markus to the post. As the ropes loosened, he caught the prince as he collapsed to the ground.

"Quickly, Markus! On your feet!" ordered Lando, gazing upon his bruised face. He removed the gag from Markus' mouth. It was heavily stained with his blood from the cut to his lower lip.

Lando left him for a moment, gathering two horses that were tethered to a nearby tree. "I think we deserve to ride for a while, Markus," stated Lando, helping the prince into the saddle.

"Where is Faria?" asked Markus, taking the reins into his hands.

"The army is in pursuit... he led them up that hill. Frankly, as far as I am concerned, they are free to do with him what they please."

"Lando, we cannot leave him like that."

"He betrayed you, Markus!"

"He made a mistake, Lando. Faria is frightened – confused. He erred in his judgment."

Taking a third horse and releasing the rest in a frightened stampede, Lando and Markus headed up the slope. In the distance, they could see the soldiers still pursuing Faria as he raced along the crest of the hill.

"This way, Lando," shouted Markus, leading the way to intercept Faria. The men rode their horses hard as they charged up the hill.

The soldiers were quickly closing in on the knight. Faria turned to see Markus and Lando racing towards him.

"Go, Markus!" shouted Faria, drawing his sword as he turned to face the enemy.

"No Faria!" ordered Markus. "Come with us now!"

"Markus, forgive me for my transgressions!" shouted Faria as he held his sword high over his head, turning his shield to the advancing soldiers. "Say you forgive me!"

"I do! Now come!" demanded Markus as he rode towards him.

Faria stood his ground as the soldiers began to encircle him. He looked upon Markus and Lando; his eyes were like those of a wild animal - cornered with no chance of escape.

Like hungry wolves circling their prey, the soldiers moved in for the kill as the knight stood his ground.

"I am Faria Targott, protector of the House of Northcott, knight to King Sebastian of Darross! I do this for my king and my country!" declared Faria; his voice rang with pride and defiance. With a final glance at Markus, he bowed in respect and farewell; "I do this for you, my prince. Now go!"

Markus and Lando watched in horror as Faria charged directly into the soldiers. His sword, swinging wildly as he lashed out at the men who now came at him from all directions. They swarmed Faria, who soon fell to a torrent of anger and revenge.

Markus and Lando knew there was nothing they could do to help save Faria. Outnumbered, and now, quickly running out of time, they rode away with heavy hearts as another member of the Order met a violent end. Faria's final selfless act not only allowed Lando to rescue Markus, it also bought them some time. It will now take the soldiers twice as long to find them, as all the horses were gone, at least from this one camp.

The two rode long into the night. Markus glanced up into the dark, cloudless sky.

"It is happening, Lando," announced the prince, pointing towards the now full moon and the brightest star that shone in the heavens. "The stars have aligned themselves with earth. It has begun."

As Arerys, Nayla and Ewen finally emerged from the forest of the Valley of Shadows, they stood before a small lake. The placid body of water was as dark as the night sky. Barely a ripple broke its still surface as the reflection of the stars shone down from high above.

"We shall rest now," said Arerys. "Tomorrow we shall make our final run."

"Do you think Markus and the others will be there?" asked Ewen hopefully.

Arerys did not know how to answer his question. He slowly turned away from the boy.

"Of course, Ewen. They shall meet us on the summit," assured Nayla. "You will see. They shall be there, waiting for us."

"Look!" said Ewen as he pointed skyward. "The full moon is turning red!"

Nayla and Arerys gazed up into the clear night sky. The moon that had provided them with light through the dark forest was indeed turning to an eerie shade of red. To the right of the moon, a star shone, brighter than all the other heavenly lights that dotted the ebony sky. It was a sign of things to come. Soon, Beyilzon would be released from his underworld prison.

As the blood-red moon bathed the land in an unsettling crimson haze, under the cover of an ancient tree, Nayla and an exhausted Ewen huddled against Arerys.

"Sleep now," said the Elf as his arms wrapped around their shoulders. "We have a task to finish tomorrow. It shall require all of our strength and will to see it done."

CHAPTER 17

THE RACE TO THE SUMMIT

The calm of the early morning belie the true urgency of the task that awaited them. Arerys led Nayla and Ewen to the edge of the small, but deep lake. There was nothing pristine about this dark body of water. Iron sediment from the surrounding mountains, the accumulation of pine and fir needles as well as decaying peat moss that brewed in the depth of the lake infused the water so it was as black as day-old tea.

Ewen sighed wearily as he looked towards the north where the Shadow Mountains butted up against the Iron Mountain Range. "Arerys, we shall never make it," he lamented, clutching the Stone tightly against his chest. "Even if we arrive at that great mountain, we shall never reach the summit in time, it will take at least two days." His eyes glazed over as he took in the vastness of the largest peak of the range.

"Take heart, my young friend, that is not Mount Hope," stated Arerys as he turned Ewen's head away from the towering spires that lay before them. "There is our final destination."

Ewen's heart was surprised and his spirit lifted by what he saw. Rising from the opposite end of the lake, the water lapped at the foot of a gently, sloping mountain that had been worn down by the ages. Strangely, it was the smallest, erect land formation that rested between the bosom of the Shadow and Iron Mountains.

"How can that be?" asked Ewen, astonished by this news. "I had always pictured Mount Hope as a great peak of monumental proportions. This is nothing more than an oversized hill!"

"Be grateful that it is, what it is," answered Arerys as he assessed what direction they should advance.

"Besides, Ewen, have you not yet learned that size is not a determining factor of greatness?" asked Nayla.

Ewen smiled at her sheepishly.

"We shall go at an easy pace around the lake, but once we reach the base of Mount Hope, beyond the shelter of those trees, be prepared to run," warned Arerys. "There shall be no place to hide. Beyilzon's men will know where we are."

The last of the evening stars reflecting off the calm, black surface of the lake faded into the dim morning light as Arerys led Ewen and Nayla through the forest growing along the western edge of the lake.

Ewen stopped for a moment; his gaze turning to the east. The low-hanging clouds that snagged onto the jagged pinnacles of the Iron Mountains glowed red as the morning sun began to rise and burn through. The boy felt a terrible sense of foreboding. In the pale blue morning sky, he saw the moon. Sitting low on the southeastern horizon, it was a ghostly form; no longer glowing in the light of day, but it was still strangely visible. Ewen drew in a long, deep breath as if it would somehow help to steel his nerves before turning away to keep up with Arerys.

The sun finally burst through the clouds, bathing the land in light and long shadows as the trio reached the north end of the lake to begin their ascent.

Arerys' head abruptly turned to the south as an ear-piercing shriek echoed from across the lake. It was Beyilzon's agent, and behind him followed an army at least five hundred strong!

"Make haste, Ewen!" ordered Arerys. "Do not look back! Just keep running!"

As the trio began their race to the summit of Mount Hope, Ewen realized the slope was much greater and steeper than he originally thought from a distance. His heart pounded and his legs ached, feeling as heavy as lead, as he struggled to keep up with Arerys and Nayla. He stumbled forward, only to have the Elf catch him by his shoulder. As he righted himself to continue on, he looked behind to see the dark horseman, with sword raised high, quickly closing the distance.

"Arerys!" cried out Ewen, as the dark emissary proceeded up the slope after them.

The Elf turned swiftly, arming his bow as Nayla grabbed Ewen's hand to lead him upwards.

Arerys took aim, and as he did so, he could see the soldiers swarming behind the dark horseman. As he prepared to release his arrow, he was suddenly pitched forward. The mountain was shaking violently as though it were the epicenter of an earthquake. Ewen and Nayla tumbled to the ground as the tortured land buckled and heaved before them.

Amid the sound of crashing rocks, tearing earth, and boulder grinding against boulder, the tremors that rocked the mountain gave rise to a massive form that emerged from the slope at the edge of the lake. As it grew in size; earth, rocks, trees fringing the shore of the lake – even several soldiers of the Dark Army, too slow to retreat, screamed in terror as they too, were sucked up in the wake of the creature as it erected itself to its full height.

With their bodies protruding from the creature's expansive chest, the soldiers screamed and struggled in vain to free themselves. The colossal being, annoyed by their terrified ranting, quickly stifled them. Its large stony hand swatting them as though they were merely annoying flies, smearing the squashed bodies against its massive form.

The horse reared and spun as the dark horseman fought to control his frightened steed. Behind him, the soldiers froze in terror. None had ever seen the likes of this behemoth; a giant, made of earth and rocks, towering well over forty feet above the Elf!

Although the giant loomed over him, Arerys quickly let his arrow fly, but the panicking horse moved just enough to save the dark horseman. He was spared the arrow as his horse retreated, galloping down the slope.

Regaining control of his steed, the dark horseman waved the faltering soldiers on to pursue the trio. They hesitated as the ground shook - the giant taking a deliberate, heavy step towards them. The captain of the army shouted at his soldiers to let their arrows fly, but as the giant was showered with the tiny projectiles, it only served to agitate it all the more. The arrows merely ricocheted off its massive stone body, exploding into shards of wood or becoming embedded into the trees and earth that made up its huge form.

The ground trembled violently as the great giant took another slow, deliberate step forward. Another hail of arrows was launched in the giant's direction. In response, the colossal form hoisted a massive boulder above its head.

It quickly became obvious that the weapons of mortal man could not fell this massive creature. None of the soldiers dared to approach to attempt an attack with their swords.

The men of the Dark Army began to retreat, but for the soldiers at the front line; escape could not come soon enough. In retaliation, the giant hurled the boulder down towards them, crushing those who could not move from its path and bowling others over as they tried to escape.

The giant picked up another boulder, hurling it towards the Dark Army. As the monster stepped forward, rocks and earth tumbled and fell into the lake. The water's surface rippled and splashed with the reverberation of its heavy, lumbering footfall.

The soldiers that felt compelled to follow the orders of the dark horseman surged forward, only to be met by the oncoming boulder. The massive projectile thrown by the giant swiftly stifled their screams.

The remaining soldiers proceeded to retreat into the shadows of the forest with the dark horseman following close behind. Beyilzon's agent violently waved his sword, shrieking in disgust and anger as the soldiers fled in fear.

With the army dispersing into the forest, the giant stood at the edge of the lake. It turned towards the trio, pondering what to do next as Arerys ran towards Ewen and Nayla.

"We cannot outrun it!" shouted the Elf. "Nor can we hope to fight it!"

"Distract it, Arerys," said Nayla, grabbing the coil of rope from her pouch. "I have an idea!"

Arerys quickly drew his bow, aiming an arrow directly at the colossal earthen form. His arrow struck the giant, lodging itself between the cracks of rock on its chest.

"Keep it by the lake, Arerys," called Nayla, as she darted down between the giant's huge feet.

Arerys and Nayla both knew that although this giant was massive, its movements were also very slow, labored and cumbersome. Its colossal size and sheer bulk worked against it as the creature struggled to maintain its balance each time it reached out to grab Arerys.

The Elf easily darted out of the giant's way as its large, stony hands slowly passed over him. As he kept the behemoth occupied, Nayla wove in and out between its feet. As she did so, she wrapped the thin, strong silken rope around the ankles, effectively hobbling it. When she reached the end of the rope, she gave it a final yank to secure it as best she could.

Nayla stood at the edge of the lake. She began taunting the giant, hurling rocks at it to make the moving monolith turn to face her. The giant struggled to turn and as it did so, she held her ground. It stooped forward so its great hands could grasp Nayla, but as it reached out to grab her, she darted between its legs. She proceeded to run up the slope.

The giant leaned down to peer between its legs, but in doing so, the incline it stood on was far too steep, causing it to begin teetering forward towards the lake. With its feet tangled together by Nayla's rope, the giant was unable to maintain its balance. Compounding its predicament, its immense weight was causing the shore of the lake to crumble away.

"It will fall," shouted Nayla. "Just give it time."

"Let us move," instructed Arerys, pulling Ewen back onto his feet to continue their ascent.

"Suppose it gets out, Nayla?" asked Ewen, as he watched the stone giant struggling to regain its balance.

"Believe me, Ewen, it shall sink like a rock!"

As the trio charged up the slope, they turned only briefly to see the giant finally topple forward, as if in slow motion. The living wall of stone and earth fell into the water with an resounding splash! It hit the surface with such force, it would seem that the lake would be half emptied of its contents. The water exploded in all directions as the giant disappeared into the depth of the black lake, its earthen body quickly disintegrating as the water's touch eroded its great form.

"That is incredible, Nayla," marveled Ewen. "The Watchers were right - the creature that could not be destroyed by the hands of man was downed by a woman."

"That is all very interesting, Ewen," said Nayla, pulling him away to move on. "Right now, we have other pressing matters to be concerned with. Run!"

Ewen's glance went beyond the lake to the edge of the forest. He saw the dark emissary screaming orders at the remaining soldiers that did not scatter and flee. He was angrily demanding them to resume their pursuit.

"To the ridge!" shouted Arerys as he pulled at Ewen to keep moving.

Ewen struggled to catch his breath. His legs ached with each step as they charged up the slope to the ridge that lay ahead. As he looked back, he could see that the Dark Army was gaining… surging ahead, up the slope like a terrible black tide that would soon swallow them up.

As they struggled to reach the ridge, Arerys happened to glance west-ward; something caught the corner of his eye as he turned to help Ewen along. The Elf strained to identify the riders that were quickly advancing up the slope. When they came into focus, Arerys shouted to Nayla. "It is

Markus and Lando!"

Ewen and Nayla tried to focus their eyes on the swift moving objects in the distance. She noted that there were three horses, but only two riders.

"Where is Faria?" asked Nayla.

"I suppose we shall find out soon enough!" answered Arerys.

"Arerys!" shouted Ewen, turning the Elf to face the east. "We are being surrounded!"

As Arerys faced the eastern slope, to his surprise an army consisting of approximately three hundred warriors surged forward. Unlike the frenzied, disorderly rush of the soldiers of the Dark Army approaching from the south, these soldiers were quickly advancing in a steady, orderly march.

"This is not good, Nayla," said Arerys, his eyes squinting into the golden sun.

Nayla's eyes widened as a smile spread across her face. "This is very good, Arerys! Look! The banner of my people! My men have come!"

"That is your army?" asked Ewen.

"What is left of it," answered Nayla, in relief as she drew her sword from its scabbard.

She held the sword horizontally over her head as she faced the bright morning sun. She signaled to the approaching army by angling the flat edge of the blade to reflect the sun's light down towards her soldiers who were advancing rapidly up the slope.

The entire battalion came to a halt upon receiving Nayla's signal. The captain proceeded on horseback, moving swiftly up the slope to meet her.

In the meantime, Arerys watched as Lando and Markus changed direction; they were now charging along the slope to intercept them. Arerys noticed too, that the Dark Army had become aware of Markus and Lando. They had momentarily stalled in their movement. It was as though they were unsure of their next course of action; waiting for instructions from the dark horseman.

Nayla sheathed her sword as the warrior from the east approached at a gallop. As he dismounted, he knelt before Nayla with his head bowed.

"Rise, Joval. There is no need for this," said Nayla. The Elf rose before her and they greeted in an embrace. Arerys looked on as the Elf beamed at her, his long, dark hair fluttering in the breeze as his blue eyes flashed when he caught a glimpse of the fair Elf.

"So, Captain Treeborn lives," smiled Joval. "Dahlon will be pleased, as will the men of your company."

"Joval, continue to act on my behalf. Direct the men to delay the Dark Army," instructed Nayla, pointing to the encroaching soldiers. "Use your archers to take them down. You know what to do. I have some unfinished business to tend to. Time is of the essence."

"Very well, my lady," answered the dark Elf as he raised his banner. Upon his signal, the army advanced quickly up the slope, positioning themselves along the top of the ridge.

Arerys, Nayla and Ewen raced on upwards following the slope, finally meeting up with Markus and Lando.

"Where is Faria?" asked Arerys.

"That fool! He—" said Lando, but his words were cut short.

"He sacrificed himself so Lando and I may escape," finished Markus, giving Lando a stern look. "We shall grieve for our fallen friend when time allows it, but right now we must hurry. We must stop Beyilzon before it is too late!"

The ground began to shake violently as a dark shadow began to creep over the land; the moon slipped across the great yellow orb in the sky. All five stopped to gaze skyward; the solar eclipse that was foretold by the Three Sisters was now taking place. In less than an hour's time, the entire sun would grow black and the world would be bathed in darkness.

With the quaking of the earth, Ewen looked to Arerys. "Is it another giant?"

"Worse… it is Beyilzon! He has been turned loose," answered Arerys.

Markus lifted Ewen behind him, as Arerys and Nayla took the spare horse that was intended for Faria. As his gaze turned to the ridge, Markus was surprised to see an unfamiliar army comprised of both mortals and Elves assembling under an unknown banner. "Are they from Orien?" he asked.

"Yes, they are mine," replied Nayla. "They shall keep the Dark Army preoccupied."

Nayla turned to see Joval orchestrating their attack. The first row of archers, kneeling with their bows and arrows at the ready. The second and third rows of archers, standing close behind with arrows poised, ready to launch on command.

Joval waited for the right moment to begin their assault. Timing would be critical for they could not afford to allow the Dark Army to deploy a counterattack. As Beyilzon's soldiers, led by the dark horseman, raced forward to face their adversaries, Joval raised his sword high above his head. When they were within striking distance, his sword came down swiftly with the order for the second and third rows of archers to aim high.

As a hail of arrows cascaded down upon the Dark Army, the soldiers were forced to raise their shields overhead to avoid the shower of deadly projectiles.

When Joval saw the shields being hoisted over the soldiers' heads, he immediately ordered the first row of archers to take aim with their arrows horizontally. With their shields still held over their heads to deflect the arrows that rained down upon them, the marksmen of Orien swiftly struck down the soldiers of the Dark Army.

Nayla was satisfied with what she saw as she rode off with Arerys up to the summit. Joval Stonecroft had the situation well under control.

Down below on the Plains of Fire, Markus could see a legion of soldiers of the Alliance preparing to engage in battle. The banners of Cedona, Carcross, Wyndwood and Darross were now unfurled, blowing in the wind. The war was about to begin.

CHAPTER 18

MOUNT HOPE

Markus and the others charged to the summit as a pale, phantom moon continued its journey between the earth and the sun. The ground trembled and quaked as the eclipse advanced with a steady determination. Already, it concealed half the face of the sun in darkness.

As they neared the top of Mount Hope, the horses refused to budge any farther. They spun and reared, squealing and whinnying in protest when urged to venture on. Even under Arerys' persuasive tone, they refused. Markus ordered all to dismount and run.

The members of the Order stopped briefly to look upon the Plains of Fire as the horns of Cedona trumpeted to muster the soldiers of the Alliance to face the enemy. Arerys' sharp eyes could make out his father and brother leading the Elven warriors of Wyndwood onto the front line of battle as they marched forward in an orderly procession.

Sitting high and proud on their gray dappled steeds, Kal-lel and Artel charged along the length of the battle line to deliver final instructions to the army. Row upon row of Wyndwood's legendary warriors patiently waited for their orders to attack.

From the north, the dark soldiers poured forth from the forbidden places of the Shadow Mountains, joining those that had already congregated on the outskirts of the battlefield for the great war. Their advance was unorganized and frenzied as they charged onto the Plains of Fire.

Kal-lel turned to face the dark encroaching hordes. He silently observed their harried movements. He noted that nothing had changed since their last deadly encounter one thousand years ago: these soldiers were untrained, undisciplined and lacked leadership. In typical human fashion, there was much infighting amongst them as they vied for positions of power. Internal strife between captains left little, if any time for soldiers to be trained in combat, or for strategy to be incorporated into their battle plans. Their fighting style was a non-descript, unskilled, random style of 'slash and dash'.

The Elf King concluded that there would be even more chaos and pandemonium for the Dark Army as this time, Beyilzon was not on the front line to lead the attack. Without his unearthly powers to shield them, Kal-lel dared to hope that the Alliance had another chance for victory.

Artel brought his steed about so he too faced the enemy. "Shall we give the orders to charge into battle?" he asked, his blue eyes flashed in anticipation.

Kal-lel calmly looked on; his face showed no sign of fear or anxiety as war loomed before him. "No. We shall wait for the enemy to come to us. Even now as they race onto the Plains of Fire to do battle, they tire. There is no need for our men to waste valuable energy, just be patient."

With the soldiers and knights of Darross, Cedona and Carcross already in position behind the great marksmen of Wyndwood, all braced for war.

The Dark Army surged forward like a ragged, black wave. Driven by sheer adrenaline and hate, they were building up in speed and numbers as they advanced.

Kal-lel signaled for his marksmen to arm their bows. The rows of archers, weapons at the ready, waited. With the dark soldiers advancing within striking distance, Kal-lel raised his sword high over his head. In response, the first row of soldiers drew their bows.

"Now!" shouted Kal-lel, bringing his sword down to signal the first wave of assault.

The first row of archers released their arrows, immediately dropping to their knees. Subsequent rows let their arrows fly, each dropping down, below the line of fire so the archers behind them would have a clear aim at the advancing enemy.

Like an undulating wave, the archers released a relentless torrent of arrows with devastating results. As the last row of archers discharged their arrows, Kal-lel signaled the first row of marksmen to begin the barrage all over again. The dark soldiers, caught in a steady hail of deadly projectiles, fell before they could even engage in combat against the Alliance.

As the marksmen of Wyndwood depleted their supply of arrows, they took up their shields in preparation for the soldiers of the Dark Army to retaliate. Just as Kal-lel predicted, the enemy armed their bows, letting their arrows fly.

He motioned for the soldiers of the Alliance to raise their shields. As the arrows rained down, those on the front line were held forward at the ready. The subsequent lines directed their great shields overhead to shelter them. Like the overlapping shingles of a roof, the shields created an effective barrier, deflecting the incoming barrage.

In a matter of time, both sides had used up their arrows. Kal-lel motioned for King Augustyn to sound the horns as he and Artel lead the charge into battle. With swords and halberds raised up high, the warriors of Darross, Cedona and Carcross joined forces with those of Wyndwood.

The tremors that signaled the release of Beyilzon from the underworld now reverberated with the thunder of thousands of footsteps as the two armies collided headlong into battle. Soon, the Plains of Fire was engulfed in war as the deafening crash of swords and halberds, and the painful screams of those cut down in battle, filled the air.

With the war now well under way, the Order raced to the sacred ground where King Brannon faced his adversary, one thousand years ago to the very day. Lando, Arerys and Nayla drew their swords as they rushed ahead with Markus and Ewen. They were prepared to fight the enemy to the death in order to aid the prince in this final bid for peace, but instead, they were astounded by who awaited their presence.

"Well, it is about time you arrived, and not a moment too soon!"

"Lindras! You are alive!" shouted Ewen, running to embrace the Wizard.

"Of course I am, my boy," answered Lindras, with a smile. "I may look old and feeble, but I assure you, I am more difficult to do away with than most people would imagine. It would take more than an old dragon to do me in!"

Markus and the others were surprised and pleased by this unexpected turn of events. They noticed Lindras now donned a silver belt around his waist and a second band of gold around his silver beard. He had evolved to a higher level of being.

"We have lost Faria," said Markus, to the Wizard.

"I know," responded Lindras with sadness. "We shall mourn him once our ordeal is done."

Having said those words, the Order watched as the ground made a horrific tearing sound as it split open. From its depth rose a hideous laugh that was not of this world.

"Beyilzon! He is coming!" shouted Lindras to the others. "The eclipse is the key that unlocks the Dark Lord from his underworld prison. Brace yourself, my friends!"

Lindras led Markus to the sword that had been embedded into the ground for one thousand years. "Ewen must mount the Stone of Salvation into the handle of the sword," instructed Lindras, pointing to the vacant, oval ornament clasp that decorated the pommel of the sword handle.

"Once the Stone is set into place, you shall be able to extract the sword to slay Beyilzon."

Ewen was frozen in fear as the ground continued to shake; Beyilzon could be heard from the depth of the earth. Nayla grasped Ewen by his hand, pulling the boy to where the sword protruded from the ground. Markus looked skyward, only a quarter of the sun remained; the rest concealed as the moon continued to journey across the ever-darkening sky.

"Quickly, Ewen!" ordered Markus. "The Stone!"

They gathered around Ewen as he fumbled to remove the blood-red gem from the black velvet pouch. It wore heavily on him as though he had carried the weight of the world for what seemed like an eternity. As he struggled to position the Stone with his nervously trembling fingers, a deep, resonating voice rattled his body.

"Scion of King Brannon, your time is at hand!" bellowed a sinister voice. It was Beyilzon - he rose from the dark depths of his underworld dungeon on a great, black plume of smoke.

Markus' eyes were cast upwards as Beyilzon's towering frame loomed threateningly before him. The Dark Lord's eyes burned a fiery red, his ancient black armor smoldering as though he had stepped out from burning bowels of Hell itself. The imposing horns that extended from his helmet made him look much taller and even more menacing.

Without hesitation, Markus drew his sword, standing between Beyilzon and the others.

With a mighty swipe, Markus' sword was knocked clear from his hands. Although the Dark Lord did not physically touch his weapon, a burst of energy emanating from his hand sent the prince's sword flying out of his grip.

"Do not waste my time," roared Beyilzon with a maniacal laugh as the others turned their weapons upon him.

Beyilzon swept his great hand before them. "My destiny is with Brannon's heir and the boy!" An invisible burst of energy sent Nayla, Lando, Arerys and Lindras flying backwards, hitting the ground hard. There they remained, struggling, but immobilized, unable to come to the aid of Markus or Ewen.

"Ewen, quickly!" ordered Markus. "Get the Stone in place now!"

The boy rushed to place the Stone into the handle, but sheer anxiety and fear caused him to fumble, dropping the Stone onto the ground. In a panic, he struggled to pick it up.

Beyilzon stepped forward, seizing Markus by his throat with his massive hand. The black metal of the smoldering gauntlet worn by the Dark Lord burned into his neck as he tightly clenched his hand around Markus' throat, squeezing hard. He slowly raised the prince off the ground so he was struggling in mid-air, dangling in the midst of Beyilzon's grip.

Ewen's eyes were opened wide in horror as he witnessed Markus struggling for his life. He glanced up to see the world slowly being swallowed up in darkness as the sun was now almost totally eclipsed by the moon.

"Will you die for him?" Beyilzon's voice bellowed at Ewen, as he held out Markus' struggling form before the boy.

Beyilzon was confident that mankind was about to fail again. The one the Maker of All so cherished, and believed held so much promise, would let him down once more. It gave the Dark Lord great pleasure to flaunt this weakness.

Suddenly, Ewen was overwhelmed by images of the nightmare that had been haunting him. It was now playing out before him, but this time he was not dreaming, his nightmare had now become reality. He looked over to Arerys who lay struggling on the ground with the others. Ewen knew that the Elf could no longer help him find respite from this terrifying nightmare.

Ewen attempted to steel his nerves - steady his trembling fingers as he desperately scrambled to place the Stone into the handle. Many dark images replayed in his mind: Darius risking his own life to save him in canyon; the men of the Order as they fought against Beyilzon's soldiers to keep him safe; Arerys diving into the River of Souls to spare him a death by drowning; Nayla as she was carried off by the Dark Army in a bid to allow him to escape to safety with Lando; and Lindras facing the great beast in the Dragon's Lair.

Beyilzon's sinister laugh broke Ewen's train of thought; the perils he shared with those in the Order abruptly disappeared.

Again, the Dark Lord mocked the boy as he continued to squeeze the life from Markus' struggling body, shaking him about as though he were a rag doll. "Will you die for him?" Beyilzon's voice boomed as he shook his helpless victim before the boy.

The oval stone miraculously snapped into place on the sword handle. At that very moment, Elora's words came back to him, Ewen did remember - he knew exactly what he had to do. The boy looked up at the Dark Lord, without any hesitation, his voice rang out true and clear: "Yes, I will die for him!"

In defiance, Ewen snatched the sword in both his hands, heaving it from the ground. He held it up high. The last rays of the dying sun shone down on Ewen. Its light amplified as it kissed the blood-red jewel. A magnificent burst of white light exploded through the Stone. The light was so brilliant, its radiance projected an energy so intense, all were thrown to the ground, as if hit by an invisible tidal wave.

Ewen's own life-force fueled the power of the Stone of Salvation, intensifying the brilliance of its light. This radiance now emanated from the boy's body as the last of the sun's diminishing glow shone through the Stone. His energy bathed the land in a dazzling, white light. Beyilzon released his deadly grip on Markus, abruptly dropping him to the ground. Falling upon his knees, the Dark Lord shielded his eyes from the divine light that radiated and grew from the boy.

Suddenly, Ewen collapsed upon his hands and knees, tossing the sword to Markus with the little strength he had left in his body.

Markus scrambled to his feet. Before the sword could touch the ground, he dove to catch it by its handle.

Just as the moon's dark form swallowed up the entire sun, Markus rose defiantly to his feet. Taking King Brannon's sword into both his hands, he charged towards Beyilzon. He rammed the sword to its hilt as he drove it straight through the Dark Lord's black heart. With a final, angry thrust, he gave the blade a vengeful twist.

Beyilzon roared in rage, not because he had been mortally wounded, but because he now realized that this time, the boy did not falter. Where Markus resolved that his fate was sealed; Ewen had the same choice presented to him as he did one thousand years ago. However, this time, Ewen's love and compassion for his friends overrode any reservations he may have had in the past. His doubts and fears gave way to a courage and humanity that shone through during mankind's darkest hour.

By coming to the prince's aid, Ewen made the ultimate sacrifice for mankind. Daring to wield the sword that was to be handled by none other than the heir of King Brannon, his determination to change the coarse of destiny was paid for with his life. He chose to die so Markus may be permitted to do as Lando had once said, 'accomplish a greater good for the greatest number'. Ewen's act proved to both Beyilzon, and the Maker of All, that mankind was truly worthy of salvation.

In a world filled with cruelties and inhumane acts carried out in Beyilzon's name and perpetuated in the darkest reaches of the heart, Ewen proved that good and justice shall prevail. The Dark Lord was shocked by this turn of events; it was an outcome that he did not even consider. To his dismay, evil was driven back once again.

As the Dark Lord slumped to the ground in agony, Markus hastily withdrew his sword from Beyilzon's body. Holding the ancient weapon on high, he pivoted as he swept the sword over him, coming down horizontally to swiftly separate Beyilzon's head from his shoulders.

A disembodied voice screamed out in pain as the Dark Lord's head tumbled to the ground, disappearing into the dark abyss. An eerie red glow pulsated, and then began to radiate brightly from Beyilzon's wounds. Markus stumbled back from the intense show of light. The Dark Lord's body began to tremble and convulse as smoke seeped out from the joints and chinks of his black armor.

With the passing of the solar eclipse, the moon finally revealed a new sun, its first light shone down illuminating the landscape. Beyilzon's body was bathed in the sun's golden glow and with a sudden burst of energy, the Dark Lord's body abruptly imploded. His remains were sucked back into the depth from whence he came. He was quickly followed by the screams and shrieks of all the dark souls that were killed in battle on the Plains of Fire, below.

A whirling funnel of wind, comprised of the many howling apparitions of the soldiers in the Dark Lord's service, was drawn into the depth along with their master. When it finally stopped, an unsettling quiet befell the land.

Across the Valley of Shadows, Arerys could see the surviving soldiers of the Dark Army, who had engaged in battle on the Plains of Fire, were now in full retreat. They fled deep into the dark forests of the formidable Shadow Mountains with the combined forces of Elves and mortals of the Alliance in full pursuit.

After Beyilzon and all the dark souls he controlled had disappeared into the bowels of the earth, Lindras held his staff high over his head. His eyes closed as he drove his staff to the ground with a mighty *'crack'*! The earth groaned and began to quake once more. The Wizard pointed the crystal mounted to his staff at the gaping wounds torn into the mountain, sealing them so the earth looked whole again.

Arerys helped Nayla and Lando onto their feet. They rushed to Ewen's side.

Markus finally stood up, turning to Ewen, whose still body lay only a few feet away. Nayla knelt by the boy as Markus helped her gently turn him onto his back. His face was ashen and cold.

"Ewen," Markus called, as Nayla cradled his head on her lap. He called his name again, "Ewen, can you hear me, son?"

The boy's eyes slowly opened. He smiled up at his friends who had gathered around him.

Arerys looked down upon Ewen. "Lindras, my father said you had once helped King Brannon. Surely you can do the same for Ewen."

Lindras recalled how Brannon was forced to insert the Stone into the sword himself. The king's body was drained of its life-force, as was Ewen's, when he handled the sword.

"Though I am now endowed with greater powers, I am afraid, as with King Brannon, I can only prolong his life for a short while," answered Lindras, with great regret. "I am the mover of mountains, I am not the Maker of All. I do not possess the power to give life."

Ewen looked into the Wizard's mournful, blue-gray eyes. "No, Lindras... I was given a second chance," said the boy in a weak voice. "I have done what I was meant to do. My time here is now complete."

He reached up with his hand, gently touching the tears that spilled from Nayla's eyes and softly fell upon his own cheek.

"Why do you cry, Nayla?" asked Ewen in a whisper. "Be happy that I have been blessed with this chance."

Nayla looked into Ewen's young face. He smiled weakly at her. She noticed that Ewen did not shed a single tear for his impending demise, for at last he found the peace that had eluded his soul for so long.

"I remembered, Markus," said Ewen with great relief. "I made things right, did I not?"

"Yes, you did," said Markus. "Because of you, our people and lands are safe from the Dark Lord."

Ewen sighed heavily, his eyes closed for a moment: "I regret that I had not the strength, nor the conviction, to have aided King Brannon. Had I done so, it would have spared the lives of many, including Darius and Faria."

"Do not despair for there are many things in life that we cannot control, try as we may," said Markus. "We have lost our dear friends, but know that both Darius and Faria were valiant knights who willingly gave their lives to protect the innocent. That is what they were born to do; to deny them of their purpose in life, is to deny them of life itself."

"Yes, they are great heroes, Ewen," added Lindras. "This quest could not have been completed without the sacrifices they had made."

The boy smiled in acknowledgement, as the lids of his eyes grew heavy.

"Do you still believe in heroes, Ewen?" asked Nayla softly.

"Yes…"

"Good. You shall live on forever."

With those last gentle words that Nayla spoke, his eyes closed and a small smile crept across his face. Ewen finally found the peace he had longed for. As his body went limp, a final breath escaped from his lips as his heart beat for the last time. He no longer looked pale and sickly; instead he looked in good health - his face was graced with a serenity gifted to only those who have truly found peace.

Markus lifted Ewen's body into his arms as Nayla wept. Arerys raised her to her feet, holding her close as he shared in her sorrow. Though he understood that Ewen had fulfilled a prophecy, he too would still miss the boy.

As he held the lifeless body before him, Markus faced the surviving members of the Order. Ewen looked as though he was merely sleeping in his arms. Then to his surprise, Ewen's body became as light as a feather - like air. Markus and the others watched in amazement as Ewen simply faded away like the early morning dew that evaporates with the warming rays of the sun.

"Where did he go?" asked Nayla, in surprise.

"Look!" said Lindras as he held his staff before them. The Wizard smiled as the crystal orb revealed Ewen in the company of the Three Sisters. Elora, Enra and Eliya greeted Ewen as he entered their temple on Mount Isa.

He was smiling broadly as he ran to meet the sisters. Markus and the others found great comfort in knowing that Ewen was truly at peace. For all these long years, he wished for his soul to be set free; now he was.

Elora, the Watcher of the Past embraced him first, for indeed, Ewen did remember his own past - conquering his fears and doubts. The Three Sisters turned Ewen to face a brilliant white light that shone down before him. He slowly walked towards it, and as he turned for one last time, he seemed to smile as though he knew his friends were still watching over him.

Ewen turned away from the Sisters; he confidently walked towards the light until he was completely enveloped in its radiant beam. The Sisters had released his soul. He was no longer bound to the earth.

The members of the Order breathed an audible sigh of relief. Ewen was safe, and so was Imago. As the horns of Cedona trumpeted the defeat of Beyilzon and his Dark Army, Markus and the others looked down upon the Plains of Fire. Both the Plains and the Valley of Shadows rang with many voices that cheered as the triumphant soldiers waved the banners of the Alliance on high against a new, blue sky.

Nayla looked down at the southern slope of Mount Hope, many bodies lay strewn on the ground, but to her relief, as far as she could tell, they were those of the Dark Army. She smiled as she saw Joval sitting high on his steed. Her men awaited her instructions.

As the Order prepared to leave the summit, Markus took up the sword of King Brannon. Taking the handle into both his hands, Markus plunged the blade deep into the ground. The earth seemed to shudder in protest. Lindras used his staff to remove the Stone of Salvation, thereby locking King Brannon's sword back into the earth. He carefully wrapped the Stone into a piece of cloth and tucked it into his belt. The ground trembled once more as the blade became one with the earth again.

These final tremors gave way to the distant sound of hoof beats racing down the slope of Mount Hope. Arerys turned in the direction of the sound.

"Look!" said the Elf as he pointed to the east. "It is the dark horseman! But who does he ride with?"

Lindras turned with a start. "That cannot be!"

"What is it, Lindras?" asked Markus, straining to identify the two riders.

"It is the Sorcerer of Orien," answered Nayla, startled by his presence.

"Also known as Eldred Firestaff, formerly the Wizard of the East," added Lindras as he pondered the long forgotten Wizard and his part in all of this.

"So it is true then, Eldred of the East lives," replied Markus, watching as the two figures charged away.

"Apparently so," answered Lindras, his troubled eyes following the two dark figures riding off towards the Iron Mountains.

"Shall we pursue them?" asked Lando.

"Let us not concern ourselves with the Sorcerer at this moment. The people of Imago await word from their savior," smiled Lindras. "We shall not keep them waiting, Prince Markus!"

CHAPTER 19

THE WARRIORS OF ORIEN

With a sharp whistle, Arerys beckoned their horses from the lower slopes of Mount Hope. The three steeds returned to the Elf at full gallop. He lifted Nayla onto his mount, his arms around her body as he took the reins into his hands. Lindras rode with Lando as Markus led the way down the southern ridge where Nayla's army waited patiently for her return.

The warriors of Orien had regrouped after the last surviving soldiers of the Dark Army had retreated into the Valley of Shadows. No doubt, they were seeking refuge in the deep forests before escaping northward into the treacherous terrain of the Shadow Mountains.

As the Order approached, Joval dismounted from his stallion to greet Nayla. Arerys hopped off his steed, lifting her down.

"Very well executed, Captain Stonecroft," Nayla complimented Joval. "How do we stand?"

"All the men are accounted for," answered Joval as he watched Markus and Lando dismount and approach. "There are no casualties, but there are some who are injured, some more grievous than others. Fortunately, we were able to make the first strike. Once we began our assault, it was impossible for the Dark Army to counter until our supply of arrows was depleted."

"I shall help tend to the wounded," assured Nayla, glancing at the injured warriors that had been moved to the back of the line, out of harm's way.

Lindras stepped forward. He smiled as he extended his hand in greeting. "Joval Stonecroft! It has been too many years since our last meeting."

The dark Elf smiled back, his broad hand encircled Lindras' own wrist in greeting. "Yes, Lindras Weatherstone! Here, I thought you had long entered the Twilight to seek refuge from the woes of the world."

Taking Joval by his arm, Lindras took great pleasure in introducing his old friend to the men of the Order.

"This is Joval Stonecroft…" Lindras paused as he turned to the dark Elf; "By what title do you go by now, my friend?"

"In her absence, I was appointed the captain of Lady Treeborn's battalion, but as she is alive and well, I suppose I now resume my role as the Steward of Nagana and advisor to Lord Dahlon Treeborn."

"Joval, this is Prince Markus of the House of Whycliffe, from the fair land of Carcross," announced Lindras.

"You are of King Brannon's bloodline?" asked Joval.

"Yes, I am. Thank you for answering our call to arms. Your presence was timely and most appreciated."

"Captain Treeborn's men are loyal to her," said Joval, bowing deeply in respect before the Prince. "If she summoned them from the furthest corner of the earth, her soldiers would come."

"How many days have you and your men traveled?" asked Markus.

"It has been twelve days now. We had marched at a relentless pace after receiving a message from Captain Treeborn. We were in the midst of pursuing the enemy back towards the Iron Mountains when I had intercepted the message she had sent to Nagana by way of her falcon."

"Nayla, mentioned that when she left the fortress city of Nagana, it was under siege," said Markus. "Does your city still stand?"

"Yes, fortunately the elders of Orien were wise to send only three messengers, otherwise the walls of the fortress would have collapsed. Beyilzon's men would have overrun us. Unfortunately, we could not spare a larger contingent for this trek. Many of our men were killed or were wounded with the last invasion."

"So you had difficulty traveling to Mount Hope?" asked Markus.

"To the contrary. We were unimpeded. After our last battle, Beyilzon's men were withdrawing from our lands quickly; we merely followed them westward after receiving word from Captain Treeborn."

"Take your men down to the Plains of Fire. We shall take care of your wounded," offered Markus.

Joval nodded, thanking the prince for his generosity.

Nayla left their side to greet and thank her warriors. She instructed them to fall out of line so they may help her with the wounded. Those who were able-bodied assisted the injured, helping to deliver them to where care could be administered. The wounded with more serious injuries, too hurt or weak to walk, were placed on horseback to be carried down the mountain slope.

Lindras turned to Lando to continue with his introductions. "This is Lando Bayliss, loyal knight to King Augustyn of Cedona."

Lando and Joval grasped wrists. They exchanged no words, but they bowed in mutual respect.

"And this is Prince Arerys of Wyndwood, son of Lord Kal-lel Wingfield," said Lindras.

Joval approached the fair-haired Elf who was slightly taller and perhaps eighty or ninety years his junior. "I am at your service, my lord," said Joval as he knelt, bowing low before Arerys.

"The kings of the Alliance await us on the Plains of Fire," said Arerys. "I urge you to join us, I know my father shall wish to speak to you and Lady Treeborn."

Joval studied Arerys' face for a moment, and then he tersely responded, "I shall consult with Captain Treeborn first." The dark Elf's long, brown hair fluttered in the breeze as he took a step backwards, bowing once more before turning to join Nayla.

Accompanied by the warriors of Orien, the Order proceeded slowly down the slope of Mount Hope. Markus, Lando and Arerys offered their horses to carry down those too incapacitated by their injuries.

There was an obvious tension that hung in the air, even though the war was over. A sense of apprehension was apparent - the men and Elves of Nayla's battalion silently considering the members of the Order, in particular, the Prince of Wyndwood and the Wizard.

Most of Dahlon's people that still remained in Orien had never seen the likes of Arerys, a fair Elf. He was basically regarded as a being that only exists in legends of old, much in the way the *fair* Elves of Arerys' generation have no recollection interacting with Joval's kind.

To the mortals of Orien, they could hardly discern any glaring differences between the Elves that had lived amongst their people, and the likes of Arerys. Aside from superficial differences, such as his fair complexion and hair, they could not understand why there was a need for segregation between the races of Elves. To these mortals, all the Elves look alike!

The mortals and Elves of Nayla's army both shared a common concern for Lindras. Their dealings with Wizards were limited to that of their encounters and battles with Eldred, the Sorcerer of Orien. They tried to take comfort in knowing that Joval Stonecroft and Nayla Treeborn were both acquainted with Lindras, appearing to be on good terms with this mysterious, silver-haired Wizard from the West.

Lando, Markus and Arerys also made note of the dark Elves, most of whom were as tall as Arerys, or taller. They had dark brown or blue eyes and all had medium to dark brown hair. Most were armed with a bow and a sword, similar to what Nayla carried, but with a blade that was about six inches longer than hers.

The mortals in their company were all shorter than the shortest Elf, but what they lacked in stature, they made up for in their sturdy, muscular physique. Their hair, black as the darkest night, was worn long and straight, drawn up into a topknot. Their eyes were dark brown like Nayla's.

Like their captain, they carried a single-edged sword of forged steel at their side and a short sword worn at their front. They were also armed with a weapon similar to a halberd, but much lighter. This six-foot staff was equipped with a single-edged blade that was slightly curved.

These mortals spoke in a language that was foreign to the men in the Order, but these same soldiers seemed to understand all that Nayla said, whether she spoke in Elvish or in the common speech.

"Thank you for keeping Lady Treeborn safe," said Joval, in appreciation to Arerys, as he watched Nayla walking amongst her wounded men.

"I can hardly say that we kept her safe… Nayla is a very capable warrior. In fact, it was she who came to our aid on a few occasions."

Joval smiled proudly, "Then, I am glad she did not forget my teachings."

Arerys noticed that his eyes showed genuine relief in knowing that Nayla was safe after her long absence.

"She is very precious to me," Joval said as a weary sigh escaped him.

Arerys could not help but to look at the dark Elf as they walked side by side. *What does he mean; she is precious to him?* He thought upon Joval's words. He noticed Nayla struggling to keep a wounded warrior on his feet; he politely excused himself as he turned to assist her.

"Let me help, Nayla," said Arerys as he placed the warrior's arm over his shoulder. Though the wounded Elf was much lighter than a human of the same size, Nayla struggled with the height difference as he leaned heavily onto her small frame.

"Thank you, Arerys," said Nayla, smiling in appreciation of his kindness.

"My father shall want to meet with you, Nayla. He shall be awaiting my arrival on the Plains of Fire."

Nayla did not answer. She walked silently along with Arerys and the wounded soldier.

"My brother, Artel, should be by my father's side too." Arerys was troubled by Nayla's silence. She looked pensive as she listened to his words.

After a moment, she responded to him. "Arerys, my men are in need of attention as I am sure there are soldiers of the Alliance also requiring care. Their need is greater right now. Do you understand?"

"Yes, of course, Nayla," replied Arerys, quietly stunned by her reply. "If you allow it, my father's people shall aid your injured."

"It would be both selfish and foolish of me to refuse such help," said Nayla. "Thank you."

Arerys stopped for a moment, looking at her intently. She seemed withdrawn – lost deep in her thoughts. "Nayla, please tell me that you do not intend to disappear as suddenly as you had appeared in my life."

"No, I would not do that to you, Arerys," assured Nayla.

"I shall hold you to your words, my lady. We have some unfinished business to discuss before we tell my father that you are my betrothed."

Nayla stopped in her tracks as Arerys kept walking on. He turned once to glance back, seeing the bewildered and surprised look on her face. He smiled before continuing on his way.

CHAPTER 20

A GREAT CELEBRATION

The members of the Order and the warriors of Orien were met with much jubilation and great fanfare as they approached the huge encampment comprised of the knights and soldiers of the Alliance.

Amidst the exuberant cheers from the soldiers of Carcross, King Bromwell greeted Markus with a great embrace, kissing his son on his cheeks.

Nayla watched as King Kal-lel, with his usual reserved composure, embraced Arerys, as Artel, his younger brother was obviously elated with being reunited with his sibling.

Nayla turned to Joval. "Do me the honor of speaking on Dahlon's behalf, Joval. I now appoint you as the Ambassador of Orien."

"As an envoy, yes... but an ambassador? Nayla, you are Lord Treeborn's daughter. It should be you meeting with the kings of the Alliance."

"Joval, I trust you. My father trusts you," continued Nayla as she slipped away from his side into the crowd. "I feel a need to be with my people at this time."

"As you wish, my lady," responded Joval, turning to greet the approaching members of royalty.

Lando knelt and bowed before his king. After his long absence, King Augustyn was grateful to see that one of his most trusted knights had returned to his service. Lando rose to his feet, then he turned, bowing before offering his condolences to King Sebastian for the loss of his knight, Faria Targott. He recounted Faria's final, valiant moment in a bid to save the quest, for he knew it was what Markus would want him to say.

Markus turned to introduce his father and the other Kings to Nayla, but she was nowhere to be seen. Joval stepped forward, kneeling before them with head bowed.

"It is with great regret that Lady Treeborn had to take her leave," said Joval. "She asked that I speak on Lord Dahlon Treeborn's behalf."

"Very well," said Markus, with a broad smile as he introduced Joval to those who had gathered around the dark Elf.

Arerys, in his joy and excitement at being reunited with his father and brother, did not even notice Nayla had departed his company. It was only when he turned to introduce them to her, that he was startled by her sudden absence.

"Stonecroft! Where is Lady Treeborn?" demanded Arerys, seizing Joval by his arm.

"She is with her people." He indignantly yanked his arm from Arerys' grasp.

Without excusing himself, Arerys abruptly left his brother and father to search for Nayla. His eyes scanned the multitude of people gathering around them.

Inside, he felt a growing void and mounting panic; his heart beating wildly as the thought crossed his mind that Nayla had left. He listened in earnest, amid the noise and confusion, for her voice.

He moved quickly through the throngs of soldiers to where the wounded had gathered beneath the shade of a massive canopy. There she was, moving through the crowd of wounded soldiers of both Orien and the Alliance. She looked weary, her energy quickly dissipating as she tended to one wounded soldier after another.

Arerys knelt next to her. "Nayla, come now. Your men shall be well taken care of," assured the Elf as he placed his arm around her shoulders.

She stood up and Arerys proceeded to lead her away from the wounded. As they wove through the crowd, the Elves of Wyndwood that had marched into battle with Arerys' brother and father greeted him. Nayla could not help but notice the frowns and puzzled looks she received from them as Arerys took her by her hand, searching for his father's quarters, in need of some privacy.

As he rushed through the throng, he led Nayla through the entrance of his father's tent. Alone at last, he quickly turned, drawing Nayla close to his body. He kissed her deeply.

Nayla did not resist as she raised herself up on her toes to meet Arerys' lips. It had been so long since they last had a moment of intimacy. They both sighed with relief as they held each other tightly; with the quest now over, the heavy burden it had placed on them had all but melted away.

"You scared me, Nayla," confessed Arerys as he stroked the stray wisps of hair from her eyes. "I turned away for a moment and you were gone."

"Did you think I had left?" asked Nayla, staring into his troubled eyes. She noticed how Arerys' eyes turned a deeper shade of blue whenever he was extremely happy or deeply disturbed.

"I did not know what to think. I was about to introduce you to my father and instead, I find Stonecroft standing in your place."

"Tell me, Arerys," said Nayla, her eyes dark with genuine concern. "How do you plan to introduce me? Father, this is Dahlon Treeborn's daughter. We plan to wed. Oh, and by the way, she is of mixed blood, half of which is mortal."

Arerys' smiled at Nayla as he watched the spark in her eyes ignite. "That is not a bad idea!"

"Seriously, Arerys," smiled Nayla, gently shoving him away at his teasing. "King Kal-lel will not take this news lightly."

He reached out, pulling Nayla towards him. "You worry more than you should," responded Arerys as he kissed her again.

"Well, you do not worry enough. Besides, what will become of all the fair maidens of Wyndwood?"

"What of them?"

"How do you think they shall respond to this news? No doubt they all have grand dreams of being chosen to become your wife."

"I believe they are more interested in becoming a princess, not so much with becoming my wife. Besides, none can hold a candle to you. Plus, I am doing this as much for Artel," answered Arerys with a smile.

"Artel? What do you mean?"

"Well, he shall have one more maiden to choose from when he decides to marry," answered Arerys with a laugh.

"This is not amusing, Arerys!" scolded Nayla as she tried to conceal her smile. Her expression slowly changed as a look of sadness passed over her face. "Do you not understand? It is over now; the quest is done. It is time for us to go our separate ways."

"The quest may be over, but it is not over for us, Nayla," responded Arerys defiantly. "You said you were in love with me, if that remains unchanged then accept my hand, say that you will be my wife."

"Then what, Arerys? Are you willing to leave Wyndwood to live your life in exile in the east with me, if your father should reject our union?"

"If it comes to that, then yes. I shall gladly renounce my title as heir to the throne. I am prepared to leave my father and his people to be with you."

"Arerys, I cannot have you do this," Nayla whispered sadly. "You have a duty to fulfill as the Crown Prince of Wyndwood."

"My duty in life is to be true to myself; something I have learned from you by the way. My life would be meaningless without you by my side. Besides, Artel is a more suitable heir to the throne than I; his heart belongs in Wyndwood. Mine belongs with you, wherever it shall take me."

"I am serious, Arerys. You cannot shirk your responsibilities like this."

"Nayla, would you not be prepared to leave Nagana if it is your father who forbids our union?"

"Of course I would."

"Then why do you feel that my sacrifice would be greater than yours? As far as I am concerned, we both stand to loose, or gain, as much as the other."

"Arerys, I have not even accepted your betrothal," reminded Nayla with a frown.

"Then I shall follow you to the ends of the earth and I shall persist... for I know in my heart there is no one else for me. You shall say 'yes' just to spare yourself the embarrassment of this love-sick Elf following you about."

Nayla's hands touched Arerys' face. He took her small hands into his, gently planting a kiss on them.

She said nothing, quietly studying the dark motes that patterned the blue irises of his eyes.

"Nayla, why do you hesitate, so?" asked Arerys, searching her deep brown eyes for a possible answer. "Is there another who is waiting for you in Orien? Or is he already here?"

Her eyes dropped away from his as she slowly turned away.

"Nayla, is it Joval Stonecroft? Have you already promised yourself to him?"

"No, Arerys. Joval is a loyal and trusted friend. If we were to wed, I would seek his blessing before that of my father's."

"Well, speak to him then, Nayla. He is here now. Or do you wish for me to speak to Joval on your behalf?"

"No, it is not your place to do so. I wish to speak to Joval myself."

"Then you will take me as your husband?" asked Arerys, full of hope.

She let out a sigh and gave him a gentle smile. "Only because it may stop you from hounding me."

Arerys' embrace swept Nayla clear off the ground. As he lowered her back down to earth, they kissed.

"I love you, Nayla," whispered Arerys.

In the midst of a very passionate kiss, the entrance of the tent suddenly flew open, there stood King Kal-lel and Prince Artel.

Arerys and Nayla were so engrossed in each other; neither heard their approach. They were equally as startled as Kal-lel and Artel were upon seeing each other.

"Forgive me, my lord," said Nayla, quickly bowing as she exited the tent. "I must go now, my warriors await my presence."

Arerys had a broad smile on his face; the sparkle in his eyes was something he could not extinguish as his father and brother walked into the tent.

"I assume that was Nayla Treeborn," said Kal-lel in a rather flat tone, unimpressed by what he had just witnessed.

"Yes, that was she," answered Arerys, quite proudly.

"Prince Markus and Lando Bayliss have been telling us about this mysterious warrior from the east," said Artel. "Somehow, I had pictured someone much taller. She is... she is very small."

"Do not let her size fool you, brother. She is much more than what appears before your eyes."

"Well, it is interesting to know that you have kept yourself preoccupied with matters of the heart and still managed to see this quest to a happy end," said Kal-lel with raised eyebrows.

"If you can spare some time, father, I shall be pleased to tell you all about the quest, and about Lady Treeborn," said Arerys, settling into a chair after pouring a goblet of wine for each of them.

"I would love to hear of your adventures, Arerys!" said Artel excitedly, settling into the chair next to his father's.

As Nayla left King Kal-lel's tent, she came upon Lando and Markus preparing to leave camp.

"Surely, Beyilzon has not chosen to return so soon?" she asked, approaching the two men as they mounted their steeds.

"No, Nayla," answered Markus. "I am in need of closure. Lando and I shall return to the Valley of Shadows in hopes of retrieving Faria's body. I cannot leave this place until I know that he rests in peace."

"Do you wish for my company?"

"No. It is not necessary. Tend to your men, Lando and I shall return before nightfall."

With those words said, he and Lando led the way, accompanied by the soldiers of Darross in search of their fallen captain.

The horses galloped northward into the heart of the Valley of Shadows. It was only a matter of time before Lando was able to retrace their steps to where Faria met his demise on the hillside.

All about them, there were areas of trampled grass, broken tree branches, and other telltale signs that a battle had ensued. It soon became obvious Faria had put up an incredible struggle. In scattered places, the ground was stained with dried blood, but nowhere could they find their companion's body.

Lando turned the horses back down the hill, leading the men to where the Dark Army had set up camp the night before. As they entered, all was quiet. The enemy soldiers had fled some time ago, leaving behind their tents, some weapons and a supply of food by the now cold pit of a large bonfire.

Markus dismounted from his steed, surveying the abandoned camp. He walked around the fire pit, quietly contemplating the wooden post that still stood nearby. It was a terrible reminder of his ordeal when he was taken captive; tormented and beaten before Lando came to his rescue.

The prince was about to climb back into his saddle when something in the fire pit caught his attention. He slowly knelt down before the heap of cold ashes and much to his sadness; he found the burnt skeletal remains of a human body.

Lando dismounted from his steed. Kneeling next to his side, he examined the charred remains. "Markus, it may well be the body of the captain I had slain that night."

"No," replied Markus in a hushed voice, his fingers sifting through the ashes. "Here is Faria's brooch."

Markus held before him the soot-covered pin that Faria once proudly wore over his left breast. He carefully wiped the ash and soot away with his fingertip to reveal the dragon emblem.

Lando acknowledged that it did indeed bear the insignia of the House of Northcott. He bowed his head in regret and sadness as he reflected on Faria's terrible demise. "I pray he met a quick death, that he was not made to suffer."

"Lando, let us never forget that Faria always worked with the best intentions - to do what he believed in his heart what was right for his people," reminded Markus as he polished Faria's brooch before carefully placing it into his pocket. "Let us be off. We shall deliver this reminder of Faria Targott to his king."

It was late in the afternoon when Nayla finally wandered into the camp set up by her soldiers. Joval waited for her outside the tent. His servant finished moving Nayla's belongings into her quarters. He had taken the liberty of packing a few things for her in anticipation that she had survived her dangerous journey.

Joval held the entrance to her tent open as she passed through. He followed her inside.

"Nayla, I am so relieved to see that you are safe," said Joval, embracing her small frame. "I believed something evil had happened, for there was one night that I felt your soul cry out in anguish. I feared for your life."

"I am fine now, Joval," Nayla smiled, looking upon his familiar, friendly face. "I am fine."

"I know something troubles you as we speak, Nayla. I have known you all of your life and I know when things are not right."

After a moment of silence Nayla finally spoke. "What do you think of Arerys Wingfield?"

"The Prince of Wyndwood?" questioned Joval, with a frown. "I do not know him well enough to pass judgment on his character. Why do you ask?"

"I need your blessing, Joval. We wish to wed, but I need to know that you will be fine with this."

Joval looked as if he had been dealt a hard, physical blow. He slowly sank down into a chair; his head was bowed low.

"Joval, say something. Say anything," pleaded Nayla.

"You know how I feel about you, Nayla. Though we are no longer lovers, my feelings for you have never wavered. I know I cannot make you feel something for me that you do not, but by now, you know that above all else, I want you to be happy."

Nayla knelt before Joval; it broke her heart to see the tears that slowly rolled down his cheeks. It was no easier than the first time they had parted company. Nayla had no idea that men did indeed cry until that sad day, many long years ago.

"Joval, you have been the one thing that has been constant in my life," said Nayla as she touched his face. "You shall always be my trusted friend and you shall always have a special place in my heart. I owe my life to you."

"You owe me nothing, my lady," said Joval sadly. "Just know that I shall always be available to you in every sense of the word."

He took Nayla's hands into his. "The Prince of Wyndwood should be warned though, if he does anything to hurt you, if he proves to be an unworthy husband, he shall have to deal with me." He gently squeezed Nayla's hands in his.

"Spoken like a true friend, Joval," said Nayla, as the two hugged.

"I have said this to you before, Nayla," said Joval, kissing her forehead; "I shall wait an eternity for you. I love you enough to let you go in hopes that one day, you shall return to me."

Nayla was touched by his devotion and love, for she knew Joval was a man of honor, sincere in both his words and actions.

Joval's servant cleared his throat to gain their attention as he stood at the entrance to Nayla's tent. Next to him stood Arerys, he appeared momentarily startled upon seeing Nayla and Joval together.

Joval immediately released his embrace, quickly stepping out, passing Arerys without a word.

"Nayla, what is wrong?" asked Arerys as he stepped towards her.

She turned away to hide her tears.

"Did you speak to Joval? Is that what it is? Did he disapprove?"

"No, in fact, he gave his blessings. I only wished that my decision did not hurt him, that is all."

Arerys, having heard some of their conversation as he neared the tent, knew what Joval had said to her and how deep his feelings for Nayla truly ran. He now needed to hear from Nayla herself, that she was positive about her own feelings for him before he was about to announce their betrothal.

"Tell me that you love me, Nayla," whispered Arerys. "Tell me that you truly want to spend your life with me."

Nayla smiled sweetly at Arerys. "I do love you, Arerys. To the very depth of my heart, I do love you." She sealed her words with a kiss upon his lips.

Outside Nayla's tent, Joval stood alone. He watched as the sun cast long shadows across the land as it slowly sank into the west. He sighed heavily upon hearing the words Arerys whispered to her. It broke his heart to know that Nayla was now with another. His only solace was in knowing that Arerys was sincere in his love for Nayla and that perhaps, she had finally found the happiness she deserved, although it was no longer with him.

A great show of light and color filled the night sky over the Aranak Mountains. The explosions of fireworks sent a shower of brilliant, sparkling lights high into the heavens; a sign to the citizens of Imago of the Alliance's victory.

The start of the Third Age of Peace was to be celebrated with a magnificent banquet under a brilliant, full moon, with many blazing torches lighting up the row upon row of tent canopies. Royalty and commoners were about to partake in this great feast to mark a new beginning.

Joval was waiting outside of Nayla's tent as she readied for the great celebration when Arerys returned.

"Good evening," said Arerys politely. "I am here to escort Lady Treeborn."

"She will be ready momentarily, my lord."

Upon hearing Arerys' voice, Nayla quickly stepped out of her tent. The fair Elf was stunned; he was left momentarily breathless as he beheld her in the soft glow of the moonlight.

Nayla wore a long, silk gown of red with silver and gold threads embroidered into an exquisite pattern of flower blossoms. The long sleeves flowed down from her wrist, almost to her knees and the wide belt that cinched her waist made her look very delicate and dainty. Her dark tresses were no longer tied into a braid. Her hair was worn up in a very feminine manner, secured with tiny floral hair ornaments traditionally worn by her mother's people. These delicate little blossoms were woven carefully into her hair.

Nayla looked at Arerys as he stood before her speechless.

"Do you not like this?" asked Nayla, stepping back towards the tent ready to change into another attire. She studied his face, and then sighed with great disappointment, "I look like a child's oversize doll."

Arerys caught her by her hand, smiling kindly upon her, "You look absolutely beautiful, Nayla. I never dreamed -"

"That I would look so different without my weapons by my side?" asked Nayla with a smile.

"I never dreamed that you could be any lovelier than when I first set my eyes upon you. You are an absolute vision."

"Well, you look very handsome yourself, my lord," said Nayla as she admired Arerys' formal dress: a high-collared shirt worn beneath a long tunic with matching trousers, all in sylvan colors. A heavily embroidered cape worn almost to the ankle of his dark boots made him appear taller than his six-foot frame.

Arerys looked over at Joval who remained, patiently waiting in silence. "Nayla, may we have a moment alone?" asked Arerys.

"Of course," replied Nayla. "Joval, I shall meet you there, please secure a seat next to mine."

Joval nodded, bowing to them both before parting company.

"What is it, Arerys. Do you wish for me to wear something more Elven?"

"No, absolutely not! However, I do have something for you, I wish for you to wear tonight."

Arerys reached for the silver chain that he wore around his neck, hidden beneath his shirt. Looped through this chain was a beautiful, silver ring. The polished band was carved with a delicate design of tiny leaves woven together. The intricate leaf pattern gave the ring an appearance of fine filigree.

He carefully removed the ring from the chain, presenting it to Nayla. "This was my mother's. She gave it to me before she departed into the Twilight. I know she would have loved you, had you met. She would want me to give this ring to the one I chose to be my wife."

Nayla smiled at Arerys. She was touched by his gift. She knew not the words to express her feelings, but the single teardrop that fell from her eye and slowly trickled down her cheek, spoke volumes to the Elf.

"Please tell me that you shall wear this with the intention to be my wife, Nayla," said Arerys, looking hopefully into her brown eyes.

"I will," whispered Nayla as she stared at the exquisite ring he presented to her.

Arerys lovingly slipped the ring onto the finger of her left hand. "Let this be an eternal symbol of my undying love for you, Nayla."

He dried the tear that rolled down her cheek, kissing her gently upon her lips. He held out his arm for Nayla to take into hers as he proudly escorted her to the celebration.

As the night wore on, all listened to Lindras as he regaled them with the tale of their great adventure. They listened intently as the Wizard conjured up images of the Temple of the Watchers, where the Three Sisters awaited their arrival through a wall of fire.

They marveled at Arerys' bravery and marksmanship when they first encountered the four dark emissaries, learning how he had single-handedly turned on them when they were forced to flee to King Augustyn's great white castle at Land's End.

As Lindras went on with his tale, they stared in disbelief at Nayla as he recounted how she first came to their aid when Ewen was taken from them. He explained how she had come to their assistance once again when they were trapped in the gully, creating a human ladder to escape.

Artel, seated next to his father, looked across to Arerys. He smiled at his brother. "I can understand why you are so impressed with Lady Treeborn. Not only is she beautiful, she is indeed a skilled warrior. It is truly a rare combination!"

"Yes, I did tell you there was much more to her than meets the eyes," smiled Arerys. Nayla gazed down, her cheeks blushed as Arerys' kind words both embarrassed and flattered her.

Lindras continued with their adventure at the abandoned citadel, where Nayla and Darius faced an army alone to protect Ewen. He told his captivated audience how the valiant Darius Calsair met his tragic end. Markus could see how this saddened his father as King Bromwell lowered his head in remembrance of his friend and loyal knight.

Nayla too, was overcome with sadness as she recalled the tragedy that befell Darius. Arerys reached for her hand under the table, giving it a gentle squeeze.

As the evening wore on, all were enthralled by Lindras' tale of his encounter with the great beast at the Dragon's Lair. Even the members of the Order listened with great interest for they too had thought Lindras had perished in the cave.

The Wizard wove a wonderful tale of how he came upon the shattered staff that once belonged to his brother, Tor Airshorn, the Wizard of the North. When he realized the dragon was strangely drawn to the glow of Tor's crystal, nearly going berserk when Lindras almost smashed the orb when he fell, the Wizard came to the realization that the dragon was not what it really appeared to be.

Taking Tor's staff, he had impaled the great beast; the dragon's blood, in combination with the still potent magic of the Wizard's old crystal, broke the terrible spell. The deep chamber of the Dragon's Lair was filled with the energy of Tor's element - the air.

Lando leaned over to Markus. "That explains that sudden gust of wind that billowed through the cave, almost taking us with it!"

Markus nodded in agreement.

Through Lindras' actions, the Wizard of the North had been miraculously resurrected into his original form. Lindras explained how Tor Airshorn, with every intention of leaving this earthly realm for the Twilight, had the misfortune of encountering Eldred Firestaff, the Wizard of the East. Eldred had called upon unnatural powers – powers that were not of his own, to place a terrible spell on Tor. He turned him into a dragon in hopes that he would be persecuted and killed by man; the very ones Tor and the other Wizards sought to preserve when they had combined forces to bring Eldred to justice.

Because Lindras had no intention of doing harm to the great dragon, even before he discovered that the beast was actually his old ally, he was rewarded for his good deed. By showing compassion, rather than acting in fear and haste - for the great dragon wanted nothing more than to be left alone, Lindras was granted greater powers within his own element of earth.

Lindras went on to explain how he was previously limited to breaking apart or moving the earth. Now, vested with greater powers, he was also able to call upon such fantastic creatures as the Keeper of the Gate, the guardian of Mount Hope.

Arerys laughed out loud. "So that behemoth of earth and stone was a manifestation of your powers?"

"Yes, indeed it was!" answered the Wizard, quite proudly. "It appeared that you were in need of some assistance when the dark horseman arrived at Mount Hope with Beyilzon's army."

"I recommend before you conjure up such monstrosities, you learn to better control your creations," said Arerys with a broad smile. "Your giant turned on us after he frightened away the Dark Army."

His comment was met with a round of laughter. Nayla watched Arerys as he smiled. He usually looked quite pensive and serious, or somehow sad, but she noticed how his face softened when he smiled. *Perhaps, now that our ordeal is over, he shall smile more often,* she thought.

Lindras waved off Arerys' comment with a chuckle, threatening to allow the ground to open and swallow up the Elf.

Eventually, the laughter turned to sadness as Lindras finished their tale of great adventure with the fall of Faria Targott and the selfless act of compassion Ewen had committed himself to, allowing Markus to defeat Beyilzon, driving him back to an eternity in Hell.

Markus rose to his feet. Holding his goblet high, he made a toast to his fallen comrades.

"To the memory of Darius Calsair, Faria Targott, Ewen Vatel and all those brave souls of Imago who gave their lives to preserve ours and to keep our lands safe," said Markus. "We shall never forget the sacrifices they made. May their souls be at peace."

Everyone raised their goblets in memory of their fallen comrades. A profound silence prevailed as they took a moment to honor and remember them.

Kal-lel eventually broke the silence. "As we enter a new era of peace, I would like to welcome Lady Nayla Treeborn, daughter of Lord Dahlon Treeborn and Joval Stonecroft, the Ambassador of Orien, to our table. The success of this quest was not possible without their involvement and that of the great warriors from the east," acknowledged Kal-lel. "Though there has been a great rift between Dahlon Treeborn's people and mine, I hope we can mend this relationship in due time."

The crowd cheered in agreement and to welcome the strangers from the faraway land beyond the Iron Mountains.

Arerys rose from his chair to make his own announcement. "I wish to take the first step to rebuild this relationship," declared the Elf. "Nayla Treeborn is my betrothed. We plan to wed."

Arerys' announcement was met with stunned silence.

Nayla glanced about at the faces of those seated across from her. Artel stared at her, obviously shocked by the news, while Kal-lel looked at her with little expression. His face showed nothing to reveal whether he was angry or pleased with Arerys' decision.

Nayla slowly rose from her chair to leave, as did Joval.

"Father, I told you that I love Nayla," stated Arerys as he stepped away from the table, taking Nayla by her hand. "This is not a passing fancy. I mean no disrespect to you father, but whether you approve of this union or not, I shall take Nayla as my wife."

Kal-lel slowly rose up from his chair, his icy blue eyes felt as though they would pierce straight through his son's heart. "Well, my bold and insolent son... through your brash actions and your total disregard for your own family and people, you have done something that I could not. After almost one thousand years of segregation brought about by two old, bull-headed, stubborn fools, by joining in wedlock, you and Lady Treeborn shall finally unite our people as one. It is long overdue." He finally smiled his approval to Arerys.

Artel rose, lifting his goblet. "Here is to my brother, Arerys and his betrothed, Nayla Treeborn. He has finally found the woman of his dreams. Nayla, I am glad that you are real; you shall spare my brother a lifetime of pining. I wish you both an eternity of happiness."

Arerys took Nayla by her hand, escorting her back to the table. As she faced Arerys' father, his usual cool demeanor thawed as he smiled kindly at her.

"Welcome to our family, Nayla. If anyone can keep my son in line, I am sure it shall be you."

Nayla smiled back at Kal-lel, bowing in respect. Arerys' father reached across the table to take Nayla's right hand into his. He reciprocated with a bow, and then he kissed her upon her hand.

Arerys sighed with relief as he looked upon Nayla. He could see and feel her joy.

"What are you waiting for Arerys?" called out Markus. "Go on! Kiss the woman!"

Arerys smiled down at Nayla, taking her into his arms. He kissed her with great passion amidst the clapping and cheers of all who were present to share in their joy. For that one moment, no one else seemed to exist except Nayla.

Lindras approached, hugging the happy couple as he congratulated them.

"I am so pleased!" said Lindras. "But there is one matter that must still be addressed."

"What is that?" asked Arerys.

Lindras pulled a piece of cloth from his belt, holding it forth, the Wizard carefully opened it up to reveal a small, bright object. It was the Stone of Salvation.

"It must be returned to the Temple of the Watchers, Arerys," said the Wizard.

"My father shall accompany you and Markus," said Arerys, his smile slowly dissolved from his face.

"I am sorry, Arerys," said Lindras. "This responsibility must be taken on by you now."

"I am afraid Lindras is right, my son," confirmed Kal-lel. "It must be you. Just as I accompanied King Brannon, now you must do so with Prince Markus and Lindras."

Arerys' heart dropped. He peered down at Nayla's face. Her distress was apparent.

"Then we wish to marry now," said Arerys.

Joval turned on the fair Elf. "You cannot do this," he interjected, shocked by Arerys' impromptu decision. "Lord Dahlon Treeborn has a right to know of this union before it takes place."

"Joval is right, Arerys. As a matter of respect and diplomacy, you cannot rush ahead with this," warned Kal-lel.

Markus came to Arerys' side. "My friend, we can leave as early as tomorrow, by horseback perhaps we can complete the trek and be back here in two weeks." He attempted to buoy the couple's sagging spirits.

"Arerys, if your love for Nayla is as strong as you claim, then your time apart shall be a mere blink of an eye if you are meant to spend an eternity together," said Kal-lel.

Finally, Nayla spoke up. "Arerys, Joval is right. At the very least, for diplomatic reasons we must follow protocol. And King Kal-lel is correct. If our love is true, it shall withstand this separation."

"Will you travel with my father to Wyndwood to await for my return there?" asked Arerys.

"No, I shall journey back to Orien with my army," answered Nayla, her mind already set. "I have some unfinished business with the Sorcerer, Eldred. His presence today leads me to believe he is up to *mischief* again. I intend to end his reign of terror in Orien."

"Eldred Firestaff lives?" asked Kal-lel, momentarily stunned by this news.

"Indeed, he does," answered Lindras. "In fact, he has a long overdue meeting with the Maker of All, so I shall be arranging this appointment for him. After I journey to Mount Isa, I shall be joining Lady Treeborn in hunting down that disreputable character."

"Then I shall journey eastward with Lindras. We shall be reunited in Orien and I too shall see the Sorcerer brought to justice," stated Arerys.

Lando stood up from his chair as he spoke: "If my King allows it, I shall venture into Orien with Lady Treeborn to assist her until your arrival, Arerys."

King Augustyn nodded his approval to his knight.

Nayla smiled at Lando, thanking him, as did Arerys.

"Well, I believe Lindras and Arerys shall need my help to keep them safe for the long journey to Orien," said Markus, with a broad smile. "Carcross is safe once more, and in the care of King Bromwell. I am not urgently required back home."

King Sebastian offered the use of his horses. Word would be sent forth for fresh steeds to be kept at the ready throughout Darross. Their journey shall be much faster if they are able to ride hard.

"Well, I do believe the Order shall be united for one last mission," said Lindras in approval.

King Bromwell rose up from the table with his goblet in hand: "Here is to the Order. May you meet with success and return home safely!"

Nayla and the men smiled at each other, knowing they would ride together one last time.

As the night wore on, the last of the late-night revelers went their own way to find sleep. Arery wished Markus and the others a good night before escorting Nayla back to her tent.

When they arrived at her quarters, Arerys hesitated. "It is dark inside, Nayla," said the Elf, holding open the tent flap to allow her to enter. "Perhaps I should go in first to light some candles for you... it may not be safe."

"Is that your way of asking if you may spend the night with me?" asked Nayla with raised eyebrows.

"What do you think?" replied Arerys, drawing Nayla close. He kissed the nape of her neck. "It will be some time before we shall be together again."

Arerys kissed her passionately as he lowered her onto the soft blanket. He struggled with the broad belt that held Nayla's silk gown closed as she removed Arerys' cape.

Suddenly, a voice at the entrance to their tent interrupted their romantic interlude.

"Lady Treeborn, are you in need—" Joval's valet stopped in mid-sentence when he realized it was the Prince of Wyndwood lying next to Nayla.

"I am sorry, my lady," apologized the servant as he averted his gaze away from them. "Master Stonecroft asked that I check in on you, to see if you required anything before you retired for the night."

"Yes, I bet he did," Nayla responded tersely. "I am quite fine, you may go now."

The servant remained at the entrance of the tent, not saying anything.

Arerys picked up his cape. "I was just leaving."

"Very good, my lord," replied the servant.

"I said, you may leave now," ordered Nayla to the servant.

"As you wish, my lady," said the servant as he slipped away from the tent.

"Arerys, do not go," pleaded Nayla.

"I am sure your friend, Joval shall be sending his personal valet over to your tent throughout the night. In fact, I am surprised he has not posted a guard at your tent."

"Do not be concerned with Joval," insisted Nayla, her arms slipping around Arerys' waist.

"No, Nayla," the Elf said with a mischievous grin. "Desire can be a powerful emotion. I shall make you wait for me."

"Arerys, you are not being fair," groaned Nayla with disappointment.

"Believe me," Arerys smiled confidently; "I shall make it worth your while."

"Is that a promise?"

"Oh, most definitely." He embraced Nayla, placing his mouth upon hers as he kissed her passionately. Arerys gave her a disarming smile as he silently slipped away from her tent, disappearing into the darkness of the night.

CHAPTER 21

PARTING OF WAYS

A glorious morning sun was already high in a pale blue, cloudless sky when Markus and Lando rose from the first restful night of sleep they had experienced in a long while.

Across the Plains of Fire, they could see soldiers collecting the last of their dead comrades for burial. As Markus surveyed the landscape, he was relieved to see that most of the casualties belonged to the Dark Army. It would appear that he and Ewen were able to put an end to the battle before it became a full-blown war. The death toll could have been much higher.

Nayla, Arerys, Artel and other Elves that possessed the power to heal were up before dawn already at work, tending to the injured.

Under the great canopy where last night's celebration took place, Lindras was holding counsel with the Kings of the Alliance and Joval Stonecroft. Plans were being made for their departure; messengers were already dispatched to their respective kingdoms to spread the word of Beyilzon's defeat.

Markus and Lando greeted and bowed before the men, prior to joining them at the table. Bromwell smiled proudly at his son as he made room for him by his side. "Did you sleep well, Markus?"

"Yes, father, it has been a long time since I had slept and actually awoke feeling rested," answered Markus, taking his place by the king's side.

Lando took his place next to King Augustyn as Lindras continued with his discussion.

"Talibarr is basically an uninhabited wasteland, even more so, now" said the Wizard. "We may encounter a few supporters of Beyilzon, stragglers of the Dark Army who either deserted or survived the war and fled in fear, but I do not anticipate any great resistance. If anything, those fools will most likely take to hiding in the caves and tunnels of the Shadow Mountains. There, they may lick their wounds in relative safety."

"If you take Rock Ridge Pass back into Darross, my people shall welcome you. You shall share in our great hospitality," said King Sebastian. "Plus, if your horses tire, we shall replace them with fresh steeds that will carry you far. In fact, I have already sent word for horses to be kept at the ready throughout my kingdom."

"Your offer is generous, my lord," replied Markus. "It is certainly worth consideration."

"I insist," said King Sebastian. "If it were not for you and the Order, Darross, and all of Imago for that matter, would be crushed under the weight of Beyilzon's fist."

As they began to plot out a course for the journey to Mount Isa, Arerys and Nayla joined them. Nayla looked twice at the stranger seated next to King Bromwell, not recognizing his face. It was not until she heard his voice and gazed into his eyes that she realized it was indeed a clean-shaven Markus. He looked much younger than his years after he removed the thick growth of beard that appeared during his long absence from Carcross.

Arerys reported that the men who were mortally wounded would pass on by day's end, if not sooner. Any Elves in such condition, wishing to enter the Twilight would be prepared to do so at dusk. Here, they would be relieved of their pain and suffering. Their souls would not be bound to this earthly realm. They would be free to join friends and family who had already departed for this haven.

Arerys also mentioned that some of the less seriously wounded soldiers were sufficiently healed, ready to move on with their battalions. The remainder would be well enough to travel within the next week or so.

Kal-lel gave instructions for some of his men to remain with the recovering soldiers to continue to provide care. He ordered that there be sufficient provisions left for them to last the duration. His men would also provide protection against the marauding bands of deserters of the Dark Army, if any dared to show their faces.

With these details tended to, the men returned to the subject of the journey to the west; returning the Stone of Salvation to the Temple of the Watchers.

"We shall enter Darross through the Aranaks via Rock Ridge Pass," recommended Markus. "Then, we shall travel southwest through the hills of Crow's Nest Pass, to Wyndwood, due west through the Fields of

Shelon onward to Mount Isa. Or perhaps, we shall travel directly eastward - passed Castle Hill."

Lindras nodded in approval. "That would certainly be the most direct route and the least time consuming," said the Wizard, smiling at Arerys and Nayla.

"How long will it take to complete this journey?" asked Nayla. "I have no idea how far away Wyndwood or Mount Isa is."

"Hmm, it should take a week, give or take a day or two, if we ride hard to Mount Isa," answered Markus. "I do not anticipate any problems that may impede us as we travel through friendly territories."

"Nayla, from here to Nagana, how long is the journey?" asked Arerys.

"I can say that it shall easily take at least one month, perhaps longer."

"Nayla, I anticipate three weeks on horseback if they ride hard" said Joval. "I do not believe they shall run into the same degree of resistance you had experienced when you traveled to the west. Plus, the passage through the Iron Mountains that divide Imago is not as treacherous as it was when you passed through a month ago."

Nayla agreed with Joval's assessment.

"That is six weeks or more before we are reunited, Nayla," said Arerys, his disappointment he could no longer conceal. He hugged her and as he did so, he whispered, "Come with me, Nayla. Return with me, please come to Wyndwood."

"Arerys, you know that is not possible, not at this time." She too was saddened by the prospect of being separated from him. "I am the captain of my own battalion. Though Joval had stepped in during my absence and he fulfilled his duties to the best of his ability, I cannot ask any more from him. These men are ultimately my responsibility. It is now my duty, as their captain, to see them home safely."

Arerys understood. He appreciated what Nayla was saying. He could also tell that her words and actions impressed his father; this type of dedication and loyalty was rare these days.

"I shall be leaving immediately," said Nayla. "The Sorcerer of Orien shall not wait for our return before he begins to wreak havoc of unknown magnitude on the citizens of Orien."

"As I said before, Nayla, as soon as the Stone of Salvation is delivered safely to the Temple of the Watchers, we shall make haste," promised Lindras. "I shall return with Markus and Arerys. We shall meet again in Nagana."

"Lindras, it has been at least two centuries since you last ventured into our lands," said Joval, with great concern. "Much has changed, it is too easy to lose your way."

"You are right, my friend," nodded Lindras in agreement.

"I shall send one of my most trusted men to accompany you on your journey so you may have a guide once you cross over the Iron Mountains."

"Thank you for your generous offer, Joval," responded Markus. "That would certainly make our trek more expedient."

"Then, we shall make ready!" stated Lindras, rising up from the table. "Arerys! Markus! Prepare to leave, we shall be on our way soon!"

As the noon hour approached, the Order shared their last meal together as squires gathered and readied the horses. Joval's servant, Valtar Briarwood, silently approached Joval, whispering into his ear. He nodded in acknowledgement, instructing Valtar to make the proper arrangements – Nayla and he would be available in a moment.

Joval turned to Nayla, explaining that they were required to attend to two warriors wishing to surrender their lives.

"Let us get this over with now," said Nayla, speaking to the Elf in a whisper. She and Joval rose from the table, excusing themselves.

"Where are you going?" asked Arerys, watching as Nayla turned to follow Joval.

"You would not understand, Arerys," she answered. "It is best that you remain here with the others."

As Nayla caught up to Joval at the edge of the encampment, Valtar was waiting amongst a growing crowd of soldiers. The warriors of Orien had formed a circle, holding those of the Alliance at bay as two of their mortal brothers knelt on the ground, their short sword placed before them. The blade edge was turned towards them as the handle was positioned to their right side.

Nayla and Joval pushed though the crowd. She knelt before the two warriors, speaking to them in Taijina, the language of the mortals of Orien. She nodded in understanding as the thumb and last finger of each hand linked together forming rings, joining her two hands together. Her remaining fingertips met, pointing to the heavens. Nayla's eyes closed as she tried to block out the growing noise that engulfed them. She breathed in quickly through her nose, exhaling slowly through her mouth as she called upon the energy of the wind to embrace the two warriors - to accept and deliver their spirits, far to the east.

Once the din and commotion surrounding her was reduced to a mere, distant drone, and she could feel the gentle caress of a light breeze, Nayla gave her blessing to each warrior before silently rising to her feet. She nodded to Joval upon which, they both unsheathed their swords, gently touching the blade on the back of each warrior's neck. They both raised their swords as the warriors took up their short swords into their hands. Suddenly, Kal-lel invaded the circle, calling out in protest.

"What is going on here? What is the meaning of this?"

A sea of soldiers parted to allow Kal-lel access. By his side were Arerys, Lando, Markus and Lindras.

The warriors who knelt on the ground looked up disapprovingly at Kal-lel for interrupting their rite of passage.

"They wish to be relinquished of their lives," answered Nayla. "It is their right."

"This is murder!"

"No. In their culture, ritualized suicide is considered to be an honorable method to die."

"This is barbaric! It is a shameful waste of life," declared Kal-lel.

"There is no shame in what they are attempting, in their eyes, a warrior's destiny is to live and die by the sword. This is what they know and understand," countered Nayla.

"But, by their own sword? I fail to understand this logic," responded Kal-lel.

"There is more honor in embracing death and choosing one's own destiny than to expire when fate decides to make its claim. Besides, just because you do not understand their logic, it does not mean that it is not logical to them."

Kal-lel shook his head. "This is an absurd notion…"

"My lord, please understand, in your world this may seem like a brutal, callous act, but for the mortals of Orien, life and death is one in the same, to all things there is a balance – a beginning and an end. These people view death as another level of being, another chapter in the story of life itself. What I have been asked to do, I do not do lightly. These men, my warriors, they are my family. This is their dying wish, I intend to honor them."

"Is there not a better way?"

"These two warriors are mortally wounded. They are dying as we speak. They shall never return to Nagana. They do not wish to die alone in this strange land. They wish for me to release their souls so it may be carried back to Orien."

"You have no right to do this."

"With all due respect, sire, you have no right to stop me. Nor do you have the right to force your own beliefs on these warriors. They chose this path, not I. They wish to control their own destiny. Do not deny their souls of eternal peace."

"If they are to die, then let it happen – on its own, in its own time."

"Unlike your kind, they do not have the option of entering the Twilight. Can you not see they suffer?"

Kal-lel looked down upon the two warriors. They were both trembling - so weak, they were barely able to sit upright. The two men were sweating profusely as their bodies fought a losing battle against a raging infection. For the first time, he noticed their blood-soaked dressings, realizing that the nature of their wounds were even beyond his own capability to heal. He studied their clouded and pained eyes. He could sense they were pleading to him.

"Please, sire, I beg of you, allow my men to die with dignity, do not extend their suffering needlessly," Nayla pleaded, her stance softening. She knelt before Kal-lel, her head bowed low, praying for some degree of compassion and understanding.

"Father, Nayla is right. This is what these mortals believe. I can understand their fear to die alone, in a strange land. Nayla spared my soul once; what she does for these warriors is really no different," Arerys stated, placing a hand on his father's shoulder.

"Very well, do what you must," said Kal-lel, turning away from Nayla. "I shall not bear witness to this."

Nayla thanked Arerys for speaking up on her behalf as she and Joval took their places again. "You may not wish to witness this Arerys. If it is possible, can you ask the soldiers of the Alliance to show my warriors some respect by giving us this moment alone?"

"Of course, Nayla," answered Arerys, as he and Markus motioned for their men to stand down and move away.

As they watched from a distance, the Elven warriors took their place next to their mortal brothers, forming a circle around the mortally wounded men. With their fingers woven together, they joined Nayla in summoning the energy of the wind to accept the two spirits, to deliver them home.

Within this circle, the two warriors picked up their swords in both their hands. Turning the tip of the blade towards their trembling body, they carefully placed it just below the base of their breastbone. As a cool wind embraced the men, Nayla opened her eyes and offered her blessing. As she spoke the final words, each warrior deliberately rammed the blade upwards into his chest – piercing his heart. At the very same moment, Nayla and Joval brought their swords down swiftly, ensuring that the two warriors met an instantaneous death. After a moment of silent prayer, the remaining warriors carefully tended to the bodies, preparing them for burial as Nayla turned away.

As she walked past Lindras and the men of the Order, Arerys could see the tears staining her cheeks. "Nayla…"

She raised her hand, motioning him not to follow her. "They were my family, Arerys."

He watched helplessly as she disappeared into the crowd as Joval approached him.

"A captain's duties can be most difficult, even at the best of times. This is never easy for her," said Joval, sheathing his sword. "But it must be done."

"It is a terrible responsibility to bear. I can understand why her men are loyal to her," answered Arerys. "I am sure her loss is great."

"Oh, yes, she will miss them, but there is more. Nayla fears she will never see them in the afterlife. Being neither Elf, nor mortal, she believes her soul will diminish, trapped somewhere between the Twilight and this earthly realm – alone."

Arerys thought upon Joval's words as he and the others returned to the business of preparing for their departure. As he followed behind Markus, Joval caught him by his arm, turning Arerys to face him.

"My lord, I know it is not my place to make such a request, but this I must do. For Nayla's sake, if you truly love her, I beg of you, ask your father to grant her the eternal life of our people."

Arerys stared into Joval's blue eyes, he could see his love for Nayla was still very apparent. "Of course, Joval. This I will do, but whether Nayla accepts..."

"Then you must make her accept." Joval searched Arerys' face, searching for his understanding.

Arerys nodded in acknowledgement as he left Joval to join Markus and Lindras.

Nayla entered her tent. She wiped the tears from her eyes as she proceeded to pack her belongings for the long journey back to Orien. Joval stepped inside, without a word, he proceeded to gather Nayla's bedroll and blanket. He knew better than to engage her in any kind of conversation. He quietly helped her with final preparations.

Arerys arrived to find her in her tent, Joval by her side, helping with the last minute details before moving out. As he entered, the dark Elf bowed, exiting to allow them some privacy.

Nayla rose from her chair and as she and Arerys embraced, tears began to well in her eyes. He held her tightly in his arms; she could hear the steady beating of his heart as she rested her head against his chest.

"We shall be together again, Nayla. I promise you."

"I know, but it still does not make this parting any easier, Arerys."

The Elf kissed her lightly atop her crown of hair. "Do not despair, for as long as I know you shall wait for me, I shall do everything in my power to return to your arms. We shall wed and I will show you all the glories of Wyndwood and western Imago."

Arerys' hand gently lifted Nayla's chin to his face. He kissed her upon her full, soft lips. She threw her arms about his neck, returning his kiss. It was very long and slow as she savored his touch. Arerys smiled down at her, drying her tears with his fingertips.

"It is time to go, Nayla. You are a captain; dry your tears, put on a brave face."

"Yes," answered Nayla in a small voice, securing the scabbard of her sword to her belt before forcing the short sword through the knot of her belt at the front of her body. Together, Nayla and Arerys walked out into the bright afternoon sun to face the throngs waiting to see them off.

Joval was already sitting high on his steed as the warriors of Orien, standing in formation, waited for their captain.

It was then Nayla realized that Joval's close friend and personal servant, Valtar Briarwood, had been assigned the task of accompanying Markus, Arerys and Lindras. She slipped away from Arerys' side as she swiftly walked up to the Elf; seizing him by his arm. Nayla quickly led him away from the group.

"Valtar, I should have realized that Joval would appoint you to this task," whispered Nayla angrily.

"Is there a problem, my lady?" asked the Elf, quite innocently.

"There certainly will be if you do not watch your tongue," hissed Nayla. "I understand you are loyal to Joval Stonecroft, but if you should breathe one word to Arerys about my relationship with Joval, you shall have no tongue to concern yourself with when I am done with you. Do you understand?"

"I understand, my lady," answered Joval's servant ratherly tersely. "Discretion is part of my job."

Nayla released his arm, returning to join the others.

The kings of the Alliance bid farewell to the Order once again. King Bromwell embraced Markus in a hug, wishing him a safe journey. Augustyn made Lando promise that he would return to his post in Cedona when he was done in Orien. Kal-lel and Artel embraced Arerys, wishing him well as Nayla looked on.

Kal-lel turned to her. "For Arerys' sake, I wish I may convince you to return to Wyndwood with us, but I know it is not possible for now. Keep safe, I wish to become better acquainted with my headstrong, outspoken, daughter-in-law. I shall see you again when you wed my son." Kal-lel smiled. Taking Nayla's small hand into his, he kissed it.

Lindras, Markus and Arerys turned to Lando and Nayla to wish them a safe journey. As they embraced, she lingered in Arerys' arms just a little longer. He gently kissed Nayla upon her forehead before turning away to claim his steed.

Nayla took the reins of her horse from Joval, lifting herself into the saddle.

With Arerys and Lindras ready to depart, Markus turned to Lando and Nayla for the last time. With his right fist over his chest, his voice ranged out, "For the Alliance!" He raised his hand high and proud above his head.

The surviving members of the Order did the same amidst the cheers of the warriors who were now preparing for the long journey home.

Arerys, Lindras, and Markus mounted their steeds, charging westward to Rock Ridge Pass as Nayla, Lando and Joval proceeded eastward
with her army.

Suddenly, the sound of thundering hoof beats caused Nayla to turn
about. It was Arerys, his horse at full gallop, racing towards her. As he
brought his steed about to hers, Arerys reached over for Nayla's face,
drawing her close. He kissed her passionately in full view of Lando, Joval
and her entire army.

"I love you, Nayla. Nothing shall keep me away from you," promised
Arerys. "Only death itself will prevent us from being reunited."

"Lando, keep her safe," instructed Arerys, turning to his friend.

Lando nodded in understanding. "Of course, Arerys."

"Try to keep out of trouble, Nayla," smiled Arerys, kissing his ring
that Nayla now worn on her left hand. "If the fates should conspire and
luck is on our side, I shall be back sooner than you think."

Nayla gently touched his face with her small hand. "I love you,
Arerys, I shall always keep a part of you in my heart," she whispered,
leaning over to steal away with one final kiss. "Remember, I am always
near to you – in the warm touch of the sun, the gentle caress of the wind,
even the soft kiss of the spring rain. Remember me…"

He searched her deep brown eyes and through the incipient tears, he
could see into her soul and the very depth of her sadness.

"No tears, Nayla, this is not farewell," he whispered back to her, placing a tiny wooden figurine of a winged fairy into the palm of her small
hand. "I made this for you shortly after our first meeting."

Nayla smiled at the tiny fairy Arerys had so carefully crafted. She
nodded in understanding.

"I swear, before the coming of the summer solstice, I shall be by your
side again," pledged the Elf, offering her a reassuring smile.

She watched as Arerys turned his steed about, galloping off to join
Markus and Lindras. As he did so, he shouted to her, "I am a man of my
word, Nayla! You shall see! We will be together soon!"

Arerys, Markus and Lindras would now follow the sun, to the west.
With the Stone of Salvation safely in their possession, they were about to
embark on the final step in completing their mission.

In her heart, she wished them a safe journey; free of peril. She also wished for their speedy return so that she and Arerys may be reunited.

With Lando and Joval by her side, Nayla headed east with her army, back through the Iron Mountains, onward to Orien. Though it weighed heavily in her heart to be separated from Arerys, she continued to justify her decision by reminding herself there would be no peace for her people as long as the Sorcerer was allowed to roam free.

As the members of the Order traveled in opposite directions, they soon became small specks on the horizon. Nayla glanced back across the Plains of Fire one last time before she and her men disappeared over the ridge on Mount Hope. Her eyes strained to search out Arerys in the distance, but he was too far-gone for her to see.

At the same time, something inside his heart told Arerys to stop. He turned his horse about, scanning the slopes of Mount Hope. He drew in a heavy breath as he watched Nayla disappear eastward. He longed to be with her, but he knew for now, until the day they were to be reunited, they were about to embark on their own separate adventures. The Elf turned his stallion about, galloping off to catch up to Markus and the others.

In his haste, Arerys failed to notice that north to the Shadow Mountains, two dark, ominous figures sitting high on ebony horses silently waited and watched; observing this parting of ways.

Suddenly, the great, black steeds reared up, charging off in separate directions, one dark rider galloping to the east, the other thundering off to the west.

It was far from over...

ISBN 155369656-5

9 781553 696568